THE
SNOW
STORM

TRÍONA WALSH

Published by Bookouture in 2023

An imprint of Storyfire Ltd.
Carmelite House
50 Victoria Embankment
London EC4Y 0DZ

www.bookouture.com

ISBN: 978-1-80314-850-2
eBook ISBN: 978-1-80314-806-9

For Dan, who never once asked when was I getting a real job.

THE
SNOW
STORM

PROLOGUE

'Don't blame this on me,' she spat, stepping backwards. It was freezing in here now. The frigid air crept in through the open door.

She threw a quick glance over her shoulder, trying to navigate the obstacles of her living room. One step back. A second. A dangerous dance. Still the space between them narrowed. There was nowhere for her to go.

The crack of the fist took her by surprise. She tumbled.

Her head smacked against the coffee table as she fell.

She lay there dazed. The pain all-consuming.

She shouldn't have come back here. That had been stupid. It was too isolated. Too far away from the village. She should have stayed where there were people.

Where someone could have heard her scream.

She tried to get up. To get away. But she was cornered.

How had it come to this? She never thought such betrayal was possible.

'This could all be over. You know what you need to do.'

The words fell on her from above. Icy. Stinging. This face

looking down on her that should be so familiar. But now it seemed unrecognisable, wearing this mask of rage.

'No,' she said, shaking her head. Understanding what defiance would mean.

She braced herself, praying it would at least be quick.

ONE

INIS MÓR, ARAN ISLANDS

In the summer, the cliff divers come.

They line up to leap, fearless, from the temporary diving board. They twist and spin, tumble like inverted fireworks that head not heavenward but earthbound instead. They launch themselves from a platform extended from the cliff edge. The brave – or foolish, depending on who you talk to – men and women glide through the air one by one, falling with grace and trust into the mouth of the Serpent's Lair. This cliffside pool is carved from the island's limestone rock by nature, not man. A millennia of waves and fierce storms have formed this perfect rectangular pool, a witchcraft explained away in former times by stories of a sleeping beast, a serpent resident, resting within. Wide and deep, the pool is filled by seawater that crashes through underground channels to feed the swell. Eager now to receive the divers.

With the best seats in the house, the cliff-dwelling seabirds – the cormorants, the guillemots, the jealous diving gannets – watch these strange featherless birds fall into the serpent's hungry maw.

Cheers rise from islanders and tourists, who gather to watch the spectacle, feeling the sea breeze on their necks, the summer sun on their faces. A glorious way to spend a summer's day on their island, on the edge of the world. An island that has no neighbour on its western coast, only the vast, lonely Atlantic. The very edge of Europe, the gateway to the New World. There are picnics, and smartphones held aloft to capture the dramatic jumps. A day out for all the family.

All watchers feel the thrill of adrenaline as each competitor steps up to the platform, toes curled on the edge. Spectators hold their breath as the diver throws themself off the board just like the guillemot chick, a leap of faith and fear, falling through the air, hoping for the magic of flight and the welcome of the waves below.

Waves that are less welcoming now, in the darkness of a winter's dawn. Daylight is hibernating like the frigid serpent below, sleepy and starved. Frozen gulls, the only spectators left, bored and huddled together for warmth, mutual protection from the snow that is falling again. A few scatter at the noise. The grunts of effort, the muttered oaths from the shadows. And the sound of something heavy being dragged. But most of the birds remain, disinterested, more concerned with surviving the gales and blizzards of the storm, with not being blown away into the vast ocean. They pay no attention until a different kind of diver is flung, thrown off the cliff edge. As winds that threatened to rage pick up, as the dark morning hours linger, this diver of a different kind falls, arms not outstretched like an arrow to split the waves. These wrists are bound. Their eyes closed not out of nerves or tension or concentration – but by death. They plummet, a graceless, tumbling descent into the Serpent's Lair. A neck most likely broken on impact, an injury that at this point is a mere insult to the corpse. With the crash and crack of the body hitting the water, the surprised birds scatter, prisoners caught between fright and the terrorising weather. A shadow on the cliff edge looks down, willing the current to take the body out to sea, through those underground channels, far away from here. Leaving no trace. With one last look, they turn and make their way back, fighting the blizzard like the frightened birds.

TWO

'Bloody hell,' Cara exhaled, out of breath, as she pulled the door shut behind her. She shook herself like a wet dog. It was wild out there. Jostled by the wind like an unpopular kid in a school corridor, Cara had been pushed and shoved from the station door to her car. She looked through the windscreen out over the dusk-cloaked harbour. It was only 5 p.m. but the sun was already mostly set. The glittering Christmas lights strung between the coastal lamp posts jumped and shook in the wind as if being electrocuted. She watched huge waves crash against the pier, the fishing boats in the bay tossed like children's toys during a rowdy bath time. The storm had descended with a personal grudge. Enveloping the island. From early afternoon Cara had lost sight of the mainland. It was as if the wind had blown their little island further out into the Atlantic. Further away from the world.

And, they said, snow was coming next.

Cara really hoped not.

She started the car and pulled out, following the main road through the village, making her way to Derrane's, Daithí's pub. The streets were empty. Islanders heeding the warnings and staying safely inside, at home. Home, where Cara would like to be too. But she was the island's only Garda. She had responsibilities. Compared to her colleagues on the mainland, she usually had a quiet life, corralling an island of 800 mostly law-abiding citizens. But when a storm cut them off, that's when she earned her crust. She'd spent her day helping the island's more vulnerable residents get storm-ready.

Cara pulled in outside the pub. Taking a deep breath, she braced herself for another battle with the gales. She launched herself out of the car, racing up the path. Through the tinsel-framed windows, she could see the soft light of the crackling fire. The space seemed to shrink around the handful of hardy islanders who'd risked going out for a pint. She pushed the door and fell inside.

Everyone in the pub stopped.

Drinks midway to lips, conversations paused. Silence fell on the inhabitants. She felt like the new sheriff in town. All that was missing were the swinging saloon doors. Only she'd been here ten years. And she didn't know why they bothered going silent. They could have kept chatting and it would have done as much to exclude her as the silence. The first language of the islanders was Irish, a language they knew she didn't speak. Like the majority of Irish people, it was a language Cara had a tentative relationship with. A fact that had done nothing to endear her to the locals.

'Sergeant,' muttered one or two of the drinkers as she passed, accompanied by a barely there nod and even less eye contact.

She headed for the bar. She could see Daithí chatting to a regular there, an old man in a flat cap. Cara passed an unfamiliar gang in the corner, chatting happily to themselves. Tourists, even at this time of year. The island and its mystical past, its ruins, and its place at the edge of the world drew people here relentlessly.

She stopped at the counter and leaned in, resting her elbows on the polished oak bar. She didn't interrupt Daithí and the man. As much as the language was a bone of contention between her and the people she served, just listening to it flow from Daithí's lips, its lyricism was music to the ear. She stole a quick glance over her shoulder to see if the drinkers were ignoring her yet. More than one head snapped away. She knew their aversion to her wasn't just down to the language. She was also an outsider. Sure, her father had been a native, and she had lived here for a decade with her *mamó* – her grandmother, an island woman, one of their own. But her newborn lungs had first taken in tainted city air, not the icy pureness of the Atlantic breeze. And no one let her forget that.

Sometimes, lying in bed, when her kids and Mamó were asleep, as she listened to the waves crash against the shore, Cara wondered if maybe the problem actually had nothing to do with the language. Had nothing to do with her not being born on the island. Perhaps the truth was they resented her because of the accident. Maybe they blamed her for what had happened to Cillian.

'Hey there, you okay? You're looking very serious.'

Daithí's voice cut through her thoughts. She looked up and smiled.

'I was just miles away, that's all. Long day.'

'Everyone is dying to see you tonight.'

Cara's smile ramped up another notch.

'I can't wait to see them too.'

Tall and strong as a fisherman, Daithí had no need to keep a bouncer on his door. On the rare occasions there was trouble he never had to raise his voice. A look was enough. He was a quiet and thoughtful man. And one of her best friends. Together with Maura Conneely, the local primary school teacher, they formed a tight-knit trio. Friends since they'd met as eight-year-olds on the white sandy Kilmurvey Beach. Visiting city girl Cara had met wild islander child Maura and sensible Daithí. Three glorious months of summer together each year had laid a foundation that lasted until today.

'Guests of yours?' Cara inclined her head in the direction of the group in the corner.

'Yep, they've booked out the B&B.'

'Nice little earner for you this time of year.'

'Definitely welcome. Anyway,' Daithí continued, 'I'm relieved to see you. The gang was afraid the storm would stop you getting back from Galway this morning.'

'I know, me too. Imagine, everyone finally all back home, after all this time, and me stranded on the mainland.'

Daithí shook his head.

'It was the last boat too. I was very lucky.' The boat ride back from the mainland that morning had been hairy, at any moment it felt like the wind would tip the boat over. The captain had ushered queasy passengers off in double-quick time. Turned the boat around and headed back to the mainland before the storm left him stranded here for New Year's.

'That's us cut off now till the storm passes.'

'As usual.' Cara hated that feeling when the boats were stopped and the small ten-seater plane couldn't do its ten-minute journey over. So near yet so far. The reality was that despite this being the 21st century, they were as cut off as the monks who had lived and prayed here half a millennium ago, whose cold stone monastery ruins still littered the island. Cara didn't think she would ever get used to that. The vulnerability. That if anything bad happened, they were on their own. Maybe that was the real difference with the islanders. They knew this isolation in their bones. It was part of them. Outsiders like Cara would never really get it.

'How is everyone? Maura sent me a video of you all last night. Everyone looked like they were just about managing to have a great time without me.'

'We did actually miss you, don't worry.' Daithí smiled. 'It was strange to start off with. Seamus has a bit of an American accent. Ferdia and Sorcha, well they haven't changed that much but they've gone all London sophisticated, you know?'

Seamus, Ferdia and Sorcha. The rest of the gang from those glorious summers. The ones who hadn't stayed on the island when they'd all grown up. After the accident.

'I'm surprised you don't have a terrible hangover,' she said.

'I was behind the bar for most of it. It wasn't that wild, despite what the video looked like.'

'You should have had a lock-in. Seeing as the only Garda on the island was elsewhere?'

'Ha, no... I knew your spidey sense would be tingling all the way across the water!'

'I wouldn't have minded.' Cara raised an eyebrow, a small smile playing on her lips.

'Ah, it didn't actually come up. Maura flagged at around eleven thirty and decided she needed to head home.'

'Really? That's not like her.' The eyebrow stayed raised but the smile slipped away.

'I know, I walked her home. She said she was fine, but I wanted to be sure.'

'Maybe even the wild and crazy Maura Conneely is getting old.'

'Thirty-four isn't that old, Cara.'

'True, it just feels like it sometimes.' Cara rubbed her face with her palms.

'So,' Daithí wiped down the bar around them, 'have you seen them since you got back this morning?'

'No. I stopped by the house after I got off the boat, but no one answered when I rang the bell.'

'Sleeping off the hangovers probably.'

'Hangovers from a night that ended at eleven thirty? Perhaps we *are* getting old.'

'I suspect they had a few nightcaps when they got back. Seamus told me the heating isn't working at the house so if they needed any encouragement for a nip of Jameson before bed, they had it.'

'Yeah, that sounds quite likely.' Cara looked at the time on the clock above the bar. 'How soon are you free?'

'Courtney's on her way for her shift now, so once she's here I can leave.'

'Great. Okay, I'll go wait in the car for you. Come out when you're done.'

'Don't go to the car. Grab a table over there, I'll bring you something.'

Cara looked over her shoulder at the pub inhabitants.

'Ignore them, Cara.'

'It's hard.'

The older man at the bar turned and looked down the counter at them, his eyes a little unfocused. He pointed at Cara.

'Féach ar do chuid gruaige rua,' he said. 'Ní maith liom an phiseog sin i láthair na huaire!'

'In English for the sergeant, Liam,' said Daithí.

Understanding took a moment, then he smiled and cleared his throat.

'Sorry, my dear,' he coughed again, 'I said that I don't like the look of your red hair, considering the *piseog*... the ah, *superstition*... at this time of year,' he said.

Cara said nothing in reply.

With an oblivious smile he teetered off his stool and wandered toward the gents.

'Oh that bloody *piseog*, stupid stupid superstition,' said Cara, turning back to Daithí. 'It always struck me as weird that in a land supposedly full of red-headed people, there's a superstition that if the first person you saw on New Year's Day was a red-headed woman, then you'd have bad luck for the rest of the year. Surely no one would dare leave the house for the day!'

'Probably invented by someone sick of people after Christmas,' said Daithí. '"Sorry, I can't leave the house today, I might run into a red-headed woman. Pass the Quality Street and the remote control."'

'Ha, you might be onto something there,' laughed Cara. Then she sighed. 'I can't wait for the extra-wide berth they give me over the next few days.'

Daithí looked at Cara.

'I know I've said it before, but why don't you give learning the language another go? People might appreciate it?' he said, kindly. 'It might help with these things.'

'I try the couple of words I have and that never seems to impress them.'

Daithí frowned but said no more.

'Right,' said Cara, 'I'm off out to the car. See you when Courtney gets here.'

'Shouldn't be more than ten minutes, okay?'

The pub door opened and a weather-dishevelled regular blew in. The gust followed through and rattled picture frames on the wall. One in particular swung back and forth. It then clattered to the ground, the glass shattering all over the wooden floor. Shattering the quiet chatter of conversation. Silence descended on the pub for a second time. All eyes turned to where the picture had been.

'Oh, now, that's not a good *piseog*,' said the old man wandering back from the gents, sucking in his breath. 'Not a good one at all.' He tutted and shook his head.

Daithí ducked into the back to fetch a sweeping brush.

'What does it mean?' asked Cara, annoyed at her curiosity.

'A picture falling off the wall? It means someone is going to die.'

THREE

Cara pushed open the door and left the pub. She couldn't get out of there quick enough. She wanted nothing to do with their superstitions and harbingers of death. She'd had enough of the real thing in her life without having to listen to that nonsense.

Catching her off-guard, a gust snatched her cap and tossed it through the air to an accomplice squall which ran with it, lodging it in one of the trees that lined the road.

'Give it back!' yelled Cara to the evening sky. This spot was the only place on the island with enough shelter for trees to grow. Everywhere else, fighting against the winds that came in relentlessly off the ocean, only a few stunted trees survived. Ninety-nine per cent of the island was just a messy patchwork of limestone-riddled fields. Flat and featureless. This was the only place where she wouldn't be able to get her cap back.

Cara stared up at it, trapped now in the branches. She could just about make it out against the dark, cloudy sky. With a sigh she abandoned it. If it came loose in the storm it would find its way back to her. Everyone knew precisely where to return it.

She sat in her car and checked her reflection in the rear-view mirror. The brief moments without her cap had wreaked havoc with her tidy bun. Flames of her rich auburn hair had escaped and now, medusa-like, snaked off at every which angle. She ran her hands over her head, trying to smooth them down, and looked more closely at herself in the mirror. Ran a hand down her cheek, her fingers touching her chin. Did she still look like the Cara the gang had known ten years ago?

She fished out her phone, and called up the video message Maura had WhatsApped her last night. Sitting in a cheap, and not entirely cheerful, hotel room in Galway – a reluctant trip for work purposes – Cara had been lifted by it. And, if she was honest with herself, been a bit jealous too. She clicked the play button again. The noises of chatter and traditional Irish musicians filled the car. The cacophony of a good night out.

'We misssss you, Sergeant Cara-ra-ra-ra!' Maura's voice yelled as her face bobbed and dipped. Her long, dark brown hair was tucked behind her ears, large hoop earrings partly entangled in stray strands. She fixed a strap on her black and white striped top, momentarily distracted by her image on screen. Maura's blue eyes were dilated and unfocused, her cheeks blushed pink. All testament to a fun night being had. She grinned ear to ear. Then the video shook violently, the view momentarily of the ceiling, then back to Maura's face, now with a drink in her hand. 'Whoops, sorry, what was I saying? Ah yes, we miss you, *cailín*! We wish you weren't in stinkin' Galway but here in Derrane's, with... drum roll... the gang!' and the video swung around, making Cara's tummy lurch, and four more faces joined Maura's on-screen. Each of them as hot and happy-looking as her. Ferdia, Sorcha, Seamus and Daithí.

Ferdia had visited last summer, he'd come back to the island to scatter his mother's ashes. But before that it had been nine years since she'd seen him. And now it was just short of ten since she'd seen the other two. Ten years since the accident. When the group had crumbled. Bonds they'd all thought were unbreakable turned out to be as fragile as butterfly's wings.

She'd seen them last all dressed in black. And then they'd scattered, driven apart by grief.

But as Cillian's tenth anniversary had approached, so had the contact. First the email from Sorcha saying she and Ferdia had been talking and wanted to come home, to mark it. A phone call from Seamus, the first in a very long time, and the beginnings of a conversation with him about coming back too. Gradually it had come together. And now here were their sweaty, happy faces – older, not quite the fresh-faced friends of her youth but proper grown-ups.

'*A Chara! Tar ar ais anois!*' Sorcha blabbered at the screen, drunkenly slipping into her native tongue. Cara! Come back, now! She beamed unfocused into the camera. Despite Daithí's description of her as a London sophisticate, her hair was still dyed dirty-blonde with her dark roots showing, a look she loved so much. Her obsession with early eighties Madonna obviously hadn't gone away.

'*Airímid uainn thú, a stór!*' We miss you, darling!

'English, Sorcha, English!' From behind her, Ferdia's clipped posh voice admonished his wife. She looked up at him, eyes wide, her hair falling back over her shoulders, her comprehension slowed by alcohol. Ferdia shook his head. Seamus then chimed in.

'See you tomorrow, Cara! Missed you tonight!' The s's of 'missed' were slurred, but that was the only giveaway that he had had as much to drink as the others. He looked great. The Californian sun and lifestyle clearly agreed with him. His light-brown hair was swept back, cropped close at the sides, his blue eyes sparkling – so many blue eyes among them – and those freckles. Just like his brother. Seamus was nearly *too* like his brother, it was hard to look at him. And then Maura swung the camera around, Daithí coming into full focus. He waved and smiled. Maura filled the frame again. Glistening eyes and rosy cheeks. Little tendrils of loose hair at her hairline stuck to her forehead in the heat of the rowdy pub.

'See you tomorrow, Cara!' she chirruped. Maura stretched out her arm, and caught the whole gang on screen again, arms around each other, the fiddle and bodhrán and tin whistle playing in the background, the chatter of happy people, the twinkle of gaudy fairy lights that Daithí liked to string around his pub at Christmas time, sparkling behind them like technicolour halos.

'See you tomorrow, Cara!' they all yelled in unison, even Daithí in the background joining in. Maura blew her a giant kiss, the video ending with Maura mouthing, 'Love you, chick,' before her giant fingers loomed in and stopped the recording.

The tell-tale slap of sleet on the windscreen made Cara look up from her phone. It was beginning. She sighed and clicked off her phone. Put it down beside the gearstick. More sleet. Heavier now. Cara looked out the car window and spotted Courtney, Daithí's barmaid. Huddled into an oversized puffer jacket, she was battling the wind walking up the street. Cara rolled down the window.

'Hi, Courtney!' she called out. Sleet landed inside the car. Melted on Cara's navy uniform trousers, leaving dark damp stains.

The dark-haired girl looked up and smiled.

'Officer Cara!' she called back in her thick New York accent. She approached the car. 'I'm heading in for my shift. I'm sure Daithí will be out to you in a minute.' Cara listened to how she pronounced Daithí's name. *Daaaay-hee*. It wasn't bad. Especially considering how it was one of those Irish names that confounded all foreigners. It was just softer, Dawh-hee. Soft and gentle like the man himself.

'Thanks, Courtney. And thanks for letting him get away tonight.'

'No problem. I'll be fine on my own. This weather,' she

looked up at the sky, 'I think it'll keep people away. It'll be quiet tonight. I'll manage!'

'We'll just be over in Seamus Flaherty's if you need us anyway. Look, go on, get out of this horrible weather.'

'Thanks. Have a great night tonight. Bye!'

The girl smiled and waved as she hurried off. Cara rolled the window back up. Five minutes later, wrapped up and heading towards her was the man himself. He hopped in.

'Hey,' she said.

'Hey,' he said, 'love the hair.'

'Ah, stoppit.' Cara looked at herself in the rear-view mirror and ran her hands over her hair again. 'The bloody wind. If you could see it, my hat is in your tree up there.'

'Oh dear.'

'I'll email the superintendent for another one. So, are we picking Maura up or are we meeting her there?'

'I don't know. She said she'd ring me, but I haven't heard from her.' Daithí pulled out his mobile and checked it. 'No, nothing still. That said, I believe her Wi-Fi is on the fritz.' Mobile signal was practically non-existent around the island. It was Wi-Fi or nothing.

'Seriously, no Wi-Fi?'

'Yeah, Ferdia and Sorcha dropped over to her house yesterday morning to say hi after they arrived and she told them it was down.'

'She's not getting that repaired this side of the new year.'

'Nope, not a hope. The joys of island life.'

Cara smiled. 'Okay, that means she'll have a problem contacting us. Let's swing by her house on the way to Seamus's then.'

Cara started the car. She checked her mirrors and hit the indicator. A habit she couldn't kick despite the grand total of three hundred cars on the island and the near non-existent traffic. She put on her lights and wipers, and pulled out onto the road. Just outside the village she spotted a brave pedestrian on the road. She slowed to a stop and wound down her window.

'Be careful out here, Tomás. The weather is wild.'

The man stopped and looked at Cara.

'I've lived through more storms than you've had hot dinners, Sergeant. Don't you worry about me, I'll be fine.'

Cara grimaced a smile back at him.

'Just trying to be helpful, Tomás. Enjoy your night.' Cara began closing the window. '*Slán.*'

'Goodbye,' he replied and walked on into the wind and sleet. Cara turned and looked at Daithí with a tight smile.

'You see, Daithí. I say goodbye in Irish and all I get back is goodbye in English.'

'You can't judge everyone by grumpy Tomás.'

'I dunno. Anyway, I suspect what I really need, instead of a crash language course, is a time machine. One that would take my mother back here about,' Cara consulted an imaginary watch on her wrist, 'thirty-four years, five months and erm, two days ago. That might do it.'

'We'll agree to disagree, Cara.'

'We will,' she replied.

They pulled up outside Maura's house two minutes later. A small cottage, it was immediately apparent no one was home. It was in complete darkness.

'I'll knock, just in case,' said Daithí, getting out.

Cara watched him hop from one foot to the other as he waited. He then hurried back, alone. He jumped in and slammed the car door behind him. Slapped his hands together to warm them up.

'Okay, she's not here,' said Daithí, 'she must have gone direct.'

'Alright. On to Seamus's then. To the Flaherty house.' Cara

reversed out of the drive and pointed the car west, winding around the island until she found herself on the coast road. Conversation went quiet, driving taking all of her concentration. More exposed out here, gusts from the sea rammed the side of the car like charging rhinos. Cara had to hold the steering wheel with a grip of iron to stay on the road. All around her, the island cowered from the storm. The unrelenting grey of the island – the carpet of limestone rock that broke through the surface of the island's soil, the maze of stone walls and the scattered prehistoric ruins – usually found relief in the wide open expanse of the blue sky and sea. But not today. Today Cara had watched the grey stretch seamlessly from the earth to the heavens. There'd been no horizon, no respite. She felt like she was surrounded on all sides.

Cara drove on, following the line of the sea. Ravenous waves attacked the coastline as if intent on devouring the island. The sleet that had begun falling outside Derrane's was lightening and proper snow was emerging from its shadow.

Quickly, the Flaherty house came into view. Quicker than Cara would have liked. Looking much like every other home on the island. Nothing special about it.

It had been ten years since Cara had set foot inside the Flaherty house. Until this morning it'd been ten years since she'd even stood in its driveway. Over the years she'd looked doggedly straight ahead anytime she'd been forced to drive by it. Ten years had been a long time to avoid a house on an island this small.

FOUR

Cara pulled into the drive of this ordinary little house. A brick-built bungalow, with a pitched slate roof, it was whitewashed like most of the other homes on the island.

She looked over at Daithí, who was staring straight ahead, unmoving. Even sheltered by the house, the storm still rocked the car as they sat there.

'You okay?' asked Cara.

'I am. Don't worry... Look, I picked them up from the boat... dropped them home.'

'That was good of you.'

'I think perhaps you might need to be prepared...'

'Prepared for what?'

'The house... it's....' He sighed, then took a deep breath. 'You know how quickly somewhere around here goes into decline if people don't take care of it? What with the harsh weather and everything? The house is cold, damp, the heating isn't working. It all feels really run-down.'

'It'll be fine, Daithí, don't worry. They have that massive fireplace, we'll all just gather around it.'

'It's not just that.' Daithí took a moment. Cara watched him as he gathered his thoughts. 'I think Seamus just locked up and walked away after the funeral. I don't think he's touched the house since. It's all a bit... a bit Miss Havisham-like, Cara. That's the real problem. He didn't pack anything up, he didn't throw anything away. I presume he found it too hard. It looks exactly as it did ten years ago. Pictures on the walls, the books on the shelves. And all the rest.'

'Oh.'

Cara's head dipped.

'Will you be okay? We don't have to go in there. We can just go back to the pub. I can rope off a corner for us.'

Cara looked up.

'No. I can manage it.'

'You sure?'

'I've avoided this place too long. Seamus isn't the only one not facing up to things.'

Daithí stared at her.

'Honestly, Daithí. It'll be okay. And if not, sure we can leg it back to the pub. Deal?'

'Deal.'

Cara pulled up her hood and opened the car door. Stepped into the storm. A flurry of snow flew at her, stinging her eyes. The temperature had dropped further, the bite of cold now baring its teeth. Despite the forecast, Cara hoped the snow wouldn't get too bad. They ran up to the door. She raised her hand to knock, but it flew open before her hand touched it.

'CARA!' a giddy choir of voices cried in unison. This three-headed creature crowded and jostled the doorway, arms outstretched, so many arms, grabbing her. A long-forgotten green flock wallpaper just visible over shoulders in the background. Overjoyed, Seamus, Ferdia and Sorcha dragged her into the house.

'You're here!' Sorcha cried, pulling her in for a full embrace.

Daithí, ignored, crossed the threshold and shut the door behind him.

'Oh, it's so good to see you, Cara,' Sorcha gasped, holding her back out at arm's length, taking her all in. 'I'm sorry it's been so long, it's just been so... hard. Hard leaving here but harder to return, you know?'

Cara drank in the sight of her old friend, who looked so much the same. Her blonde hair was pulled up into a messy bun. She looked tired, but she'd been out late last night, no one looked their best after a session. She was as petite and pretty as she'd ever been.

'I understand,' said Cara. Sorcha drew her back into a hug.

'Give her some space to breathe, Sorcha.' Ferdia stepped forward. As tall as Daithí, Ferdia was otherwise an entirely different creature. Slender, sallow and louche, his dark brown hair was practically black. Officially hazel, the pupil and iris of his eyes merged into each other, forming dark unreadable pools. He placed his hands on Cara's shoulders and looked down at her. Cara noticed he still wore the leather wristbands that he'd adopted during his rocker phase as a teen, the frayed edges of the knot just visible inside his shirt cuff.

'You haven't aged as well as me,' he said, grinning. 'But sure, I noticed that last summer. I just didn't want to say.' He smiled, those dark eyes sparkling.

'Thanks!' laughed Cara.

'I have to say though, that Garda uniform is really doing it for me. Smokin'!' He laughed and gathered Cara in as she smacked his chest in mock annoyance.

'Careful or I'll arrest you,' she said, laughing into his chest. She grabbed him close, giving him a bear hug.

'Steady now, Sergeant!'

Cara felt her fingers being unlinked and her arm being pulled, dragging her away from Ferdia. Seamus was demanding her attention. They stopped and looked at each other, saying nothing. She hadn't seen him since he'd left for America. And here he was, in all his glowing Hollywood glory. They just smiled and then grabbed each other, hugging. Cara felt the warmth of him against her, as if he'd brought that golden Californian sunshine back with him. She leant back.

'Not so long next time, kid,' she said.

'I'm sorry. I... I...'

'No. Say nothing. You don't have to say a thing.'

Seamus nodded. Cara could see the tears she was holding back reflected in Seamus's eyes. She touched his cheek. He smiled and his blue eyes glistened.

'Come on now, let's get out of this freezing hallway!' Ferdia yelled. 'To the kitchen and the heat!' Cara agreed. It was frigid here, not much better than outside. The reunion could continue by the fire.

'Is Maura here yet?' she asked Seamus as they headed for the kitchen door.

'No.' He shook his head. 'We thought she might be with you.'

'No, not with us.' Cara felt the pressure of her phone in her trouser pocket. Her fingers found its outline and she considered taking it out.

'She'll be along soon, I'm sure,' Seamus said. 'It's good to see that ten years hasn't changed her at all!' he laughed. Cara grinned, took her hand away from her phone. There probably wasn't signal anyway.

They all piled into the large kitchen. Lining the wall by the back door was a bank of 1970s kitchen cupboards. No two mustard and silver trim doors hung at quite the same angle. Opposite them, as you came into the room, was a laminate counter-topped row of cupboards which extended out, separating the kitchen from the rest of the space. A damp smell hung in the air. Cara stared at the place. That horrible kitchen was already twenty years out of date when she first stepped in here as a shy fourteen-year-old.

The rest of the room was a little better. Cara ran her hand over the rough surface of the old oak farmhouse table, battered and scarred with history. She looked up at the fireplace that dominated the centre of the far wall. In the style of the island's old cottages, where this sort of room would once have been the entirety of the family dwelling, it was large and wide, big enough to cook on and heat the whole space. Cara was feeling a little dizzy on her feet, the whirring of the years spinning backwards, shaking her. She didn't know whether to laugh or cry when she saw the old sofa and armchairs arranged around the fire. Brown and mustard, they were upholstered in a fabric which Cara reckoned had only a casual relationship with natural fibres. Its pattern was one that no one with a hangover should be forced to look at. It was so awful and out of date that Cara felt it was probably fashionable again. A simple veneered coffee table with black angled legs completed the picture. There were a lot of homes like this on the island. The expense of shipping in anything larger than you could carry meant people held on to things. If they worked, they stayed.

Cara touched the sofa, expecting a static electric shock from it. A similar jolt to the one she was getting from being back here. Daithí had been right to warn her.

She looked up at the walls, searching out the framed photo she knew would be there. Cillian...

Cara felt an arm around her.

'You okay?' Daithí's soft voice was in her ear.

Cara nodded.

'You weren't wrong,' she said. 'Nothing has changed. It's a time capsule.' She leant into Daithí.

'It gets too much, let me know.'

'Thanks.'

Seamus rounded the sofa, lugging a basket full of turf. He grinned at the pair of them.

'Ten-year-old turf I found in the shed. Think it'll burn?' He tossed a brick of the fuel into the fireplace. The flames licked around this newcomer, testing its flammability. With a bang as loud as a firework, the damp turf spat out a shower of sparks.

'Jaysus!' said Ferdia, the word odd in his mouth. His private school tones sounded wrong paired with the working-class oath. A singed smell alerted them to a stray spark that was smouldering on the carpet. The aroma of dust and damp and burning was a nauseous mix.

'Feck!' Seamus yelled as he stamped it out. 'It's okay, it's okay, I got it. Don't worry, folks. I've saved us all.'

'Thank you, Seamus,' sang Sorcha from the kitchen.

'Our hero,' agreed Cara.

'Will I risk another?' he asked, holding a second large slab of turf in his hand.

'Go on, live dangerously.'

Seamus lobbed it in, and similar sparks erupted. Dancing, Seamus stamped them all out.

'Anyone want to help me chop the veg?' Sorcha called.

'Sure thing,' said Daithí. He squeezed Cara's arm and went to join Sorcha. Cara looked over her shoulder, watched the pair of them. Daithí picked up a bunch of carrots and a knife. She then saw Mrs Flaherty beside them, her memory splicing in frames from the past. Cillian and Seamus's mother, standing there, reeled through her mind's eye. By the cooker. Taking plates out of the mustard-coloured cupboards, the doors back then not quite so askew.

'You know when Maura is getting here?' Ferdia sat down on an armchair and looked up at Cara, pulling her out of her memories.

'Maura? No, I don't. She's gone a bit AWOL.'

Seamus approached, two wine glasses criss-crossed in his left hand, a bottle of red in the right.

'Here, grab one.' He proffered the glass-laden hand at them. Ignoring wine etiquette, he filled Ferdia's large glass to the brim. He turned to Cara.

'Wine first or do you want to go get changed? I presume you've brought some things with you? You will stay tonight?'

Cara looked down at her uniform. It didn't quite scream party. She could have gone home first and changed, but she'd already missed a whole evening with the gang, she hadn't wanted to miss another minute.

'Wine,' she said, unzipping her jacket and placing it on the back of an oak chair. She held out her hand for the glass. 'And yeah, I'll be staying. Mamó is minding the kids. I've already missed enough of the craic.'

'Great.' Seamus beamed and filled her glass. 'So, sit, sit. We missed you last night! We have a lot of catching up to do.'

'We certainly do,' said Cara. She picked the nearest armchair, a musty smell releasing from the fabric as she sat. She stuck her nose in her wine glass, inhaling instead its fragrant aroma.

'How's your mamó?' asked Seamus. 'And the kids, how are my niece and nephew? I'm such a terrible uncle. You've been great, emailing me pictures and updates and I've been so bad at replying.'

'Don't worry about it. We're all fine. Ticking along, as you do. Mamó is my rock, seventy-eight and still going strong. Saoirse and Cathal, they're doing great. Sure, you'll see them while you're here.'

'I can't wait, they must be so big now.'

'You'd be shocked, they're half reared.' Cara smiled. 'And how are you? How is Hollywood?'

'Living the dream, Cara!' Seamus laughed, eyes sparkling.

'It's great, actually. I love the screenwriting. Guess how much my last movie took?'

'Tell me.'

'A hundred and fifty million dollars! Can you get your head around that?'

'No, I don't think I can.' Cara shook her head, eyes wide.

'Show-off,' barked Ferdia.

'Feck off,' said Seamus with a smile.

'I thought it was a gang of writers anyway, who wrote these movies?' said Ferdia. 'So, it's not actually "your movie", is it?'

Seamus shook his head. 'You're thinking of TV shows, that's a gang of people around a table. My movies, it's just me. Well, occasionally they get someone in to tweak my scripts... apparently I'm rubbish at endings! But, it's always ninety per cent me anyway.'

'That's so cool,' said Cara.

'It's not *that* cool,' said Ferdia. 'Everyone knows writers are the bottom of the food chain in Hollywood.'

'Don't be jealous,' said Cara, smiling. 'Sure, aren't you living the high life in London?'

'High life, I'm not sure about that. But we're surviving. Keeping the wolf from the door.'

'What are you doing there?' asked Cara.

'Oh, you know... this and that.'

'Illuminating.'

'I've a big deal about to happen for me, after a good long while, so, I'm happy. It's no hundred and fifty million, but we can't all be as lucky as Seamus, can we?' Ferdia stuck his tongue out at Seamus.

Seamus frowned and opened his mouth to say something, but stopped. He looked back at Cara.

'So what about you and island life? How's that treating you?' he asked.

'Well...' she began. It wasn't a day for whinging. But it was a hard question to answer. Ferdia saved her by interrupting.

'Have they started that thing yet?' he said, sitting forward, gathering enthusiasm.

'Has who started what yet?'

'The locals and the red hair, New Year's superstition thing?'

'I can't believe you've remembered,' said Cara.

'How could I forget? It was the highlight of my new year watching people running scared from you!'

'I'm glad you found it funny.'

'Remember how we used to lock you and Cillian into his room at five to midnight so he could absorb all the bad luck!' laughed Ferdia. Seamus's smile vanished.

'Jesus, Ferdy. Engage your brain,' hissed Sorcha from the kitchen.

'Oh, guys,' he said, understanding his gaffe. 'I'm really sorry.'

Cara looked at her feet. She said nothing for a moment, then glanced over at Ferdia.

'Yeah, I remember alright. I think, unfortunately, he absorbed it all.'

FIVE

'And then I said, "I think you'll find that's my seat, Mr DiCaprio!"'

'Oh you never did!' said Sorcha, spoon stalled midway to her mouth.

'Bullshit!' said Ferdia. Sorcha gave him an elbow in the side.

'What's that for?' he snapped.

'Stop it, Ferdia. I just didn't think the vulgarity was necessary.' Sorcha lowered her voice despite the fact that all five of them gathered round the table could hear what she was saying.

'Sorcha, this tiramisu is gorgeous. You'll have to give me the recipe for the pub,' Daithí said, scraping his spoon around the plate, gathering up every last morsel.

'Ah, thanks, hon,' she replied, grateful for the distraction. 'Are you doing food there now?'

'We'll do anything that makes a few bob.'

'Yeah, there's strippers there on a Monday night,' laughed Ferdia.

'That would probably give a lot of the clientele a heart attack.' Daithí smiled, thinking of the old lads who propped up his bar seven days a week, rain or shine.

Seamus hopped up and grabbed another bottle of wine from the kitchen counter. He filled everyone's glass.

'Don't leave yourself out,' said Cara, noticing his glass wasn't full.

'Ah, I'm a bit of a lightweight these days, I'm afraid.'

'Never!' exclaimed Ferdia. 'Not seventeen-pints-Seamie, surely! What have those Americans done to you?'

'It's more specifically the Californians. It's not like here – you go for a jog, not for a bellyfull.'

'Sounds like a sad life to me,' said Ferdia, taking a giant slug of his wine.

'And everyone goes to AA.'

'Have you?' asked Sorcha, eyes wide.

'Just for the contacts you make!'

'Ha!' said Daithí.

Cara got up from the table and crossed over to the fireplace. Gingerly placed another piece of turf on the fire. She stopped at the bookcase on the way back to the table, her gaze lingering on one book with a black spine. She picked it out, turning it in her hands. She could see and smell the mildewed spots on its edges. Seamus came over and joined her, his wine glass in his hand.

'Will you ever write another?' Cara looked over at Seamus.

He shrugged.

'I don't know. It was the story I needed to tell. I don't know if I've another one in me.'

Cara looked down at the book. She read the title to herself – *I Am The Island: A Memoir. Seamus Flaherty.* The memoir that had started as Seamus's diary. It had been so successful, been such a hit. A hit that had surprised everyone, including his publisher who had hastily printed another run. And another. And another. Until it felt like there wasn't a home on the planet that didn't have Seamus's story of growing up on a tiny island, on the edge of the Atlantic, with a father who drank, a mother who fought for them, and a brother he loved, who died. She flicked it open and read the dedication. *For Cillian. For Every-thing.* She knew she shouldn't but instinctively she thumbed through to the end of it. To the pages that recounted that night on the fishing trawler, New Year's Eve ten years ago. The two of them, brothers, Seamus and Cillian. A squall, a vicious wave, Cillian going over and lost to the sea.

Cillian, her husband.

Lost to her. To their children. Forever. Cara had read the entire memoir. Its prose, exquisite, had brought Cillian back to life. But it had been too hard. Because in reality, nothing could really bring him back to her. She'd read it once and put it away. Now, she closed it without reading a word, and put it back on the shelf.

'It's a beautiful work. Even in translation. I suppose it helped that you translated it from the Irish yourself.'

'Thank you. And yes, I think that made a difference. *Is Mise An tOileán* will always be the authentic telling of it. That's the one I'd want people to read, if they could. But if I'd stuck to that it would have had very few readers.'

They sat down on the sofa. Seamus leaned in to Cara.

'Look,' he said quietly. 'Sorry about the state of the place. I should have had someone come in, do something with it before we got here.'

'I think,' called Ferdia from the table, Seamus's voice not quite quiet enough to avoid being overheard, 'that unless you set fire to the place there is nothing you could have done to save this kip.'

'Ferdia!' Sorcha cried. 'Don't call the place a kip!'

Seamus shrugged and looked over at them. 'No, don't worry, it is!'

'You don't need to apologise,' said Cara, 'and the place isn't that bad, honestly.'

Seamus surveyed the room and lowered his voice again. 'I'm sorry about the *things*. I should have come a few days earlier.

Done something... I don't know, just made it ever so slightly less of a... what was the name of that mysterious abandoned ship?'

'The *Mary Celeste*?'

'Yes, that's the one. Made it less of a living, breathing ghost. I know how it's been for me to see this all again, just like... just like, *back then*... so you must be feeling the same.'

'It's strange, I won't lie. But you don't have to apologise at all. This morning, when I swung by to see if anyone was awake, I had to force myself to come up the drive. I can't blame you for being similarly reluctant to come back.'

'You came by this morning?'

'Yes, once I got in off the boat. I missed you all last night.'

'So you've been here already?'

'Just outside, no one answered when I knocked. I presumed – after that video I witnessed,' Cara laughed and shook her head, 'that you were all so hung-over that you didn't hear. Sleeping it off.'

'Absolutely. Sorry about that, I didn't realise. That was very rude of all of us.'

Seamus looked over at the table.

'Guys, Cara called by this morning, and none of us were awake to let her in! We're the worst!'

'Ah, Cara, sorry, hon!' said Sorcha.

'Sorry, Cars,' said Ferdia. The couple and Daithí got up from the table and came over to sit with Cara and Seamus on the sofa. Cara looked at her friends with a smile.

'Stop it, all of you, it's no problem, really, don't be worrying. I wouldn't have been able to stay long anyway.'

There was a knock at the back door.

Conversation stopped and, like meerkats, everyone turned and looked over the back of the sofa at the back door. A figure was indistinct behind the frosted glass. The light above the back door outside cast an eerie glow around the arrival.

'That'll be Maura now,' said Ferdia, making to get up.

Sorcha placed her hand on his leg and stopped him. He rolled his eyes. Daithí got up instead.

He crossed the floor. Unlocking the door he muttered, 'Glad you could make it.'

But instead of Maura, bright and buzzing energy like a Duracell bunny, full of explanations for her late arrival, full of stories, bounding in – there was a short, bearded man, in a baseball cap and swamped in a coat the kind Arctic explorers wore.

He looked at Daithí and beamed up at him.

'Hello again, Mr Derrane!' the man said in a strong American accent.

'Mr Jackson?' Daithí frowned, but ushered him in. Cara recognised him from earlier in the pub. The tourists in the corner.

'Is there a problem with your accommodation?' Daithí asked, puzzlement still in his voice.

'No, no, not at all. It's A1. No, I'm here to see Seamie.'

The American looked across the room at Seamus, who had already stood, and was making his way over.

'Noah!' said Seamus, extending his hand and meeting the man halfway with a hearty handshake and a weighty back slap. 'Delighted you're finding the B&B at Derrane's to your liking, he's a fine host.' Daithí looked from his friend back to the American he'd checked in that morning.

'You know each other?' asked Daithí. '*Cad atá ar súil*, Seamus?' What is going on, Seamus? asked Daithí, slipping deliberately into Irish.

Seamus ignored him.

'Noah, come over and meet Cara, Ferdia and Sorcha. I'm afraid Maura isn't here yet. And, obviously you've met Daithí already.'

Cara looked at Sorcha and Ferdia and they both shrugged back at her.

The new arrival strode over to the sofa, hand outstretched.

'Cara, Ferdia and Sorcha! *The* Cara, Ferdia and Sorcha? Wow!' he exclaimed. Cara shot a look over the crazy American's shoulder at Seamus who was masking some nerves with a megawatt smile. Cara had known Seamus since he was seven years old, she knew when he was looking for forgiveness instead of permission.

'Seamus? Who's your friend?'

'Cara.' Seamus placed a hand on Noah's back. 'Everyone. This is the acclaimed arthouse film director, Noah Jackson.'

Noah Jackson looked at the sitting trio.

'It's a real pleasure to meet you guys, finally.'

'Finally?' said Ferdia, bristling. 'What are you going on about?'

'Noah and I, we're going to produce a movie version of my memoir! Isn't that exciting?' said Seamus. 'It's going to be a classy, authentic vision of it. A bit experimental, it won't be a linear retelling, there will be some fantasy parts...'

'We're still discussing that bit, Seamie,' said Noah.

'Yeah, yeah.' Seamus waved away the director's words. 'Sure, it's still a work in progress, somewhat. But I'm producing it, which is amazing, and the guys have come all the way over here to begin filming, and it's all very exciting...'

'You're filming a movie, of your memoir, here on the island? Now?' said Cara.

'Yeah, that's it... yeah.' His eyes were wide with a desire for approval.

'I don't know what to say,' said Cara.

'Say you're happy for me?'

Cara managed a small smile, his eager eyes hard to resist.

'And, em, I guess I should mention the guys – the actors and crew – will be about a bit, over the week.'

'Here?' asked Daithí.

'Yeah. But not much. It won't interfere with our time together, I promise.'

No one looked impressed.

'Can I get you a glass of wine, Mr Jackson?' asked Daithí.

'Thank you, but no. I have the van outside. Best not drink and drive.'

'No, agreed.'

'In fact, I'm not staying. Seamus suggested I pop over and introduce myself. So I just wanted to say hi. I know you're having a special few days and I don't want to intrude.'

'Thanks, Noah,' said Seamus.

'Great to meet you guys. I look forward to seeing more of you all over the next few days.' The director saluted them and then turned, walking with Seamus to the back door. He was gone as quickly as he'd arrived.

Seamus returned to his friends by the fire.

'Sorry to spring that on you all. I meant to say something, but the moment never seemed right.'

'Chancer,' muttered Ferdia.

'I think it sounds really exciting, Seamus!' said Sorcha. 'Is there someone playing me?'

'There is,' beamed Seamus, happy that one of them seemed okay with the surprise. He sat down on the sofa. 'Her name is Ari, and she's lovely. You'll like her. Not as pretty as you, of course.'

'Oh, stop it,' she said, smiling.

'Is there a Maura actress?' asked Ferdia. 'You might get her down here tonight seeing as it looks like we've been stood up by the real one.'

Seamus craned his neck round to the clock in the kitchen which was miraculously still working.

'She might still make it,' he said. 'Perhaps she got confused and didn't realise we were meeting up tonight? We did have a lot to drink last night.'

'Anything is possible with Miss Conneely,' said Ferdia. 'Maybe she got a better offer!'

Cara caught Daithí's eye at this comment. Sorcha noticed.

'What was that?'

'What was what?' said Cara.

'You two. What was that look?'

Cara looked at Daithí. He shrugged.

'Hmm. Well, I'm not sure I'm allowed say this. But. Well, Maura has a secret boyfriend. We don't know who he is, where he's from, we know nothing at all about him. She just disappears occasionally and comes back looking happy and doesn't tell us a thing about him. It's all very mysterious. Maybe he's in town and she did indeed get a better offer.'

'Oh,' said Sorcha. Her happy expression melted away. 'Ditched us, has she? For a mysterious guy. Great.'

SIX

Cara gathered up plates. 'You guys cooked, I'll do the wash up.'

'I'll help you,' said Ferdia, standing up.

'Really?' said Cara. 'Wonders will never cease.'

They carried all the dishes over, and Cara filled the kettle and set it to boil for hot water. Ferdia leant back on the counter. He took out his phone and looked at the screen.

'Bloody reception here. This is something I don't miss from these islands. My friends in London would be horrified. Have you any signal?'

'I never have any signal, Ferdia. No one has.'

'Why don't you have Wi-Fi, Seamus?' called Ferdia over to the sofa.

'I don't live here any more, Ferdia, I'm not getting Wi-Fi in for one weekend.'

'Some host you are.'

'Maybe you would enjoy unplugging for a few days?' said Seamus with a smile.

'Maybe you'd enjoy shutting up, eh?'

Cara scraped off a few more dishes. The kettle clicked off and she filled the sink. She plunged the dishes in.

'Grab that tea towel, will you?' she said. Ferdia looked up from his phone.

'No, don't worry. I think you're doing a grand job there yourself.' He wandered back around the counter, back to the sofa.

'Gee, thanks,' muttered Cara.

'Cara,' called Sorcha, 'what do you want to do on Sunday? When we go over to the cemetery?'

Cara paused over the sink, suds on her hands. She thought about the question. It had been on her mind for the last few weeks. She looked down and watched a few of the bubbles, rainbows sliding across them, burst.

'I want it to be something nice, you know?' she started, looking up. 'There's been enough sadness, I want a celebration instead.' Daithí got up from the sofa and came over, grabbing the tea towel as he went. He waited for the first clean dish as Cara plunged her hands back into the warm water. 'I think maybe we could play some of his favourite songs, someone could read something – from the memoir perhaps, Seamus, some of the happy bits.'

'There aren't many of those,' muttered Ferdia.

'Sure thing,' said Seamus, ignoring him. 'I like that idea.'

'And perhaps, Sorcha, you might sing? Would you do that?'

'Of course, hon, I'd be honoured. What would you like me to sing?'

'Do you know "My Love Returns"?'

'Aw, yeah, that's a beauty. Will you accompany me? On the fiddle?' Sorcha asked Cara.

'Are you still at that awful cat strangling?' asked Ferdia.

'A bit,' Cara replied.

'Hang on a moment.' Seamus stood up suddenly and left the room. Everyone around the table looked at the space he had left behind. And then over at Cara.

'I don't know...' she answered the unasked question.

Seamus reappeared a few moments later, a violin case in his hands.

'Here, I forgot we had this. Mam had some notion when I was ten that I should take it up. Dadó had been a great fiddler in his time or something... I don't know if it's in a decent condition or anything, but would you play for us if it is?'

'Oh, Cara, yes, do,' said Sorcha.

Ferdia leant forward and refilled his wine glass.

'Alright.' Daithí handed Cara the tea towel and she dried her hands. She came out from the kitchen, took the proffered violin case and sat on one of the armchairs. Opening the case, she took out a beautiful, nearly pristine, violin.

'One good thing from you not blitzing this place,' she said, smiling at Seamus. Daithí came over and sat down. Sorcha grabbed the open wine bottle from the table and placed it to the side of the hearth. She sat down on the rug in front of the fire. Sitting forward in the chair, Cara leant the fiddle to her shoulder, the way fiddlers did, not under the chin like the classical violinists. She tested the strings, played some notes and tightened the pegs at the end of the violin neck, tuning the old instrument. Then she positioned the bow across the strings. Pushing it gently, the first notes began to form. Sorcha sat up straight, her legs crossed, and began to sing sweet, sad words. Beautiful, plaintive notes filled the air. The clear pure wisps of Sorcha's words rose heavenward, intertwined with Cara's keening strings, soaring sweet grief, a lament so familiar to the generations who had gathered in sorrow on these islands. Cara felt treacherous tears slip and roll down her cheeks.

As the last notes were played, Cara let the fiddle and bow rest on her lap. No one in the group said a thing. Cara drew her hand across her face, rubbed her eyes. She heard the sniffles from the sofa, and looked over. Seamus was red-eyed, Daithí staring out the window into the black snow-speckled night, meeting nobody's eye.

'Christ,' said Ferdia from the opposite armchair. 'That wasn't actually awful.'

Sorcha, also swept up in the emotion of the moment, turned and looked at her husband. Cara watched as her eyes narrowed and her lower lip trembled.

'Just... just be serious for once, Ferdia. Can't you.'

Ferdia ignored her.

Seamus leant forward. Stretched an arm out to Sorcha and squeezed her upper arm.

'Beautiful. Just beautiful.' He smiled, then looked over at Cara. 'Wow, Cara, you were always good at the fiddle, but, that now... that was really special.'

Cara beamed back at him. She could feel a little redness come to her cheeks.

'I've been practising. A lot. I've quite a lot of time on my hands these days. The locals aren't exactly queuing up to fill my dance card, let's say.'

'Well, their loss is our gain.'

'Thank you, Seamie.'

Ferdia hopped up and leaned over Sorcha to grab the wine from the hearth. He filled his glass and sat back down, leaving the bottle at his feet.

'No, I'm fine, thanks,' said Seamus, irritated.

Ferdia grinned at him, but didn't bother to refill Seamus's glass.

'Give us another tune, Car,' commanded Ferdia. 'A happy one this time.'

Cara looked at Sorcha.

'Follow my lead,' she said.

Cara began to tap her foot and lifted the fiddle to her shoulder. Sorcha smiled after the first few notes and began to sing. And then everyone joined in. Ferdia even cracked a smile and gave it some welly at the chorus. Seamus jumped up and took Sorcha's hands, getting her to her feet. He swung her around, the pair of them dancing and singing, Sorcha's face lighting up with laughter. Skipping over wine glasses, they circled the room, still giggling and singing.

'More!' yelled Seamus as Cara played the last notes. Obliging, Cara struck up another tune, and five minutes later a shy Daithí produced a tin whistle from somewhere and joined in with her. Ferdia fetched another bottle of wine from the kitchen, sidestepping the still dancing Sorcha and Seamus – Seamus swinging Sorcha round, hands grasping her elbows, traditional ceilí style, the pair flying around at a dizzying speed. This time Ferdia filled everyone's glass, and chuckled as Sorcha and Seamus, red-faced and laughing, bounced off the table. They nearly ended up knocking the framed photos off the wall as they ricocheted around the place, gasping and laughing, almost hyperventilating from the amusement of it all. Cara watched the frames sway, then slow and settle. Relieved, despite herself, when they didn't fall.

Seamus threw another lump of ancient turf on the dying fire, giving it a little boost. The one working lamp in the room was casting a warm glow, the only other light source after the fire. They'd left the curtains open all evening. With no near neighbours to hide from, they'd decided instead to leave the falling snow as a backdrop. Daithí collected an armful of empty wine bottles and took them over to the kitchen.

'Oh, hold on to one,' cried Sorcha, sitting on the ground, her head resting against Ferdia's knees. Ferdia absent-mindedly stroked the top of her head. He stopped occasionally to wind loose tendrils around his fingers. Lost in thought, he stared out the window.

Daithí came back, one of the bottles in his hands. He handed it to Sorcha.

'What do you want it for?' he asked.

'Remember, when we were kids, all those games we played? Truth or Dare, Never Have I Ever... and everyone's favourite – Spin the Bottle!'

With a tipsy smile, she placed the bottle on the carpet, on its side. 'Oh, I don't know,' said Daithí, sitting back down on the sofa beside Seamus.

'Cara, Seamus, come on, it'll be a laugh.'

Seamus, the most sober of them all, smiled at her. 'Aren't we a bit old for that?'

Sorcha spun the bottle, propelling some remnant drops of wine across the carpet.

'Oops.' She giggled and spun it again. 'Come on, everyone, it'll be a bit of a laugh.'

The bottle stopped. Pointed in Daithí's direction. Unsteady, Sorcha moved from her kneeling position to all fours. She crawled across the carpet, stopping in front of Daithí. Seamus laughed nervously. Ferdia, as if woken from a dream, looked over at his wife. Sorcha placed her hands on Daithí's knees, kneeling in front of him.

'Heya, Daithí,' she said, and winked.

Cara watched Daithí place a hand on Sorcha's, and look gently down at her.

'Perhaps Truth or Dare was a better idea.'

'Jesus, Sorcha,' Ferdia glared at his wife, 'what are you at, you drunken fool? Stop humiliating yourself.'

Sorcha twisted around and looked back at him.

'Humiliating myself? I wonder where I learnt to do that?' she spat. She looked back at Daithí. 'Sorry, Daithí, I don't think we can play Truth or Dare because someone here doesn't understand the meaning of truth.'

'Oh funny. You're hilarious,' said Ferdia. 'Get off your knees, hey? Have some self-respect.'

Sorcha hauled herself up onto unsteady feet.

She pointed at Ferdia. Her face screwed up into a ball of fury.

'You... You are a dickhead!' She swallowed a giant sob, and rushed from the room, knocking against the table and counter as she went.

Ferdia sat up, rubbed his face with his hands and sighed. He looked up at Seamus, Daithí and Cara.

'Sorry. We've had too much to drink.' He stood up, his balance not so great either. 'I'll go talk to her. Goodnight, guys.'

He left the room and Cara looked at Seamus and Daithí.

'Oh dear. That wasn't great.'

Daithí and Seamus shook their heads.

'They've been bickering since they got here,' said Seamus. 'It's sad.'

'And awkward,' said Daithí.

'Hopefully they'll work through it,' said Cara. 'I wonder how long things have been rocky? Seamus, do you and Ferdia talk much any more?'

Seamus shook his head, his eyes melancholic.

'No, very little.'

'Ah, that's a real shame. So much has changed. Which shouldn't be a surprise, I guess. But those two used to be so happy. And you and Ferdia, you used to be so close.'

'I know. But look, we're not kids any more. Things change.'

'They do,' Cara sighed. She was quiet for a moment, remembering. Remembering a young Ferdia and Sorcha. The young Ferdia and Seamus. The closest of close friends.

'You two were so obsessed with that myth,' said Daithí. Cara looked from Daithí to Seamus, a smile back on her face.

'Oh God, you were!' she cried. '"Setanta and Ferdia".' The legend of two warrior brothers. Ferdia named by his hippy mother for one half of the mythical duo.

'I don't know why we were so obsessed though,' said

Seamus, laughing. 'Like, did we just ignore the bit of the legend where those two ended up fighting to the death?'

'That got in the way of how cool it was!' laughed Cara.

'I used to really wish my mam had named me Setanta.' Seamus shook his head.

'You made us call you Setanta all one summer, do you remember?' said Daithí.

Seamus groaned.

'Oh God, how cringe,' he laughed. 'Yeah, unfortunately I do remember that!'

'It seems so long ago,' said Cara.

'That's because it was. Twenty years since we were kids, Cara.'

'I guess so. Doesn't mean you can't still be friends though. Look at me and Daithí and Maura. What happened with you and Ferdia?'

Seamus shrugged.

'Distance? Growing up? I dunno. Just after Cillian... I think I wanted to put everything that reminded me of that night behind me. And that included Ferdia, I guess. Anyway, he had his whole new life with Sorcha in London. I think he was much the same, wanted a new life.'

'What does he do there, do you have any clue? He's been a bit vague,' asked Daithí.

'I think Sorcha said something about gigs and bands?' said Seamus.

'That sounds fun,' replied Cara.

'I got the impression,' said Daithí, 'from some tense words between him and Sorcha, that it mightn't be as glamorous or as well-paid as it sounds.'

'Oh dear,' said Cara.

'Maybe that's part of the tension,' said Seamus.

'Perhaps,' replied Cara. She slumped back into the sofa and gave in to a large yawn. She shook her head, rubbed her eyes.

'Guys, it's been great – well, except that last bit. I think I need to sleep.'

'Of course,' said Seamus.

Cara stood and stretched. She then bent down and retrieved the wine glasses Sorcha and Ferdia had left behind. She walked a line to the kitchen that was generous with its definition of straightness. She placed the empty glasses on the counter with exaggerated care.

'Seamus, where have you put me?'

Seamus stood.

'If it's not too weird, I thought Cillian's old room made the most sense.'

Cara nodded. It would indeed have been wrong to have someone else in his room.

'Seamus. It's been so good to see you.'

Seamus walked over to her. He opened his arms and gathered her into a hug.

'It's been wonderful to see you too. I've stayed away too long, I see that now.'

Cara touched his cheek.

'It's been difficult, for all of us. Don't be hard on yourself.'

'Thanks, darling.'

'Night, Daithí,' Cara called over to Daithí on the sofa.

'Sleep well.'

Cara walked over to the kitchen door.

'You know where you're going anyway,' said Seamus.

Cara smiled.

'Yep, I won't get lost.'

SEVEN

Seamus was right, there was no fear of her getting lost. Down the oh-so-familiar corridor, feet sinking into the dark green hall carpet, past the front door. Cillian's room was the first room on the left. It still had little wooden letters on the door that spelt out his name. Cara traced her fingers over them, a bittersweet smile playing on her lips as she felt the smooth surface and rough edges of the letters. At home, Cathal had similar on his door. Directly across the hall was Seamus's childhood bedroom. A 'Keep Out' sign, with a circle with a red line through it, still hung there. Cara understood, now she had children of her own, why Cillian and Seamus's mother had been slow to take them off the doors, even long after they were adults and had left home. It was hard to have your babies grow up and fly the nest. Cara got it. And they both had extra reasons to dread that time, hold on to the past. Awaiting Cara, when the time came, was a lonely widowhood. Facing Mrs Flaherty had been an even more unpleasant future, alone with a violent husband. Cillian had tried to get her to leave, many times, but she'd never quite been able. In the end, the bodily destruction caused by her husband's drinking, a personal, karmic version of the destruction he wrought on those around him, meant he died not too long after Cillian and Cara got married. It had been a relief for everyone.

After Seamus's room was the bathroom. And behind the last door at the end of the corridor was his parents' room where Ferdia and Sorcha were staying. Cara could hear a soft snore vibrating from the room, one of them at least was asleep already. She felt relief that she wasn't confronted by the muffled sounds of an argument.

Cara turned the handle on Cillian's bedroom door and stepped back twenty years. Hugging her arms to her, fighting the cold, she turned on the spot, revolving, taking it all in. It was just as she remembered it. Nirvana and Eminem posters on the wall, hiding an older historical layer of dinosaur wallpaper. The single bed (which thankfully Seamus had made up freshly – she had begun to get worried) in against the wall. The desk under the window, his books, from Ladybird books right up to school-books from his final year in school, all sharing space on the slightly sagging white shelves. And the louvred doors of the built-in wardrobe. Cara took hold of the small brass handle and pulled it open. It wasn't full, but there were clothes hanging there. Clothes Cara remembered Cillian wearing. She reached out a hand and ran it gently down an army surplus jacket that he'd loved when he was sixteen. There was also the hideous knitted jumper his mamó had made for him and he'd dutifully worn. Cara touched that too, itchy under her fingers, and she smiled at the memory of Cillian telling her how he'd endured it just to make her happy. Cara's fingers found moth-eaten holes, a few of the startled creatures flew out of the wardrobe. Seamus really needed to tackle this place. And she should have offered to help years ago. There was a pair of them in it when it came to letting this place go.

Shutting the wardrobe, she walked over to the desk, pulled one half of the curtains over. She was shocked at the height of the snow already. She could see the driveway from here and her car was slowly being consumed by the snow. The blizzard seemed to stretch all the way from space, the Milky Way falling on them. Cara couldn't remember the last time they'd had snow like this on the island. It could have been as long ago as when teenaged Cillian had put those posters up on his wall.

She pulled the other curtain and turned to the bed. Daithí had put her overnight bag there. She zipped it open and pulled out fleece pyjamas. Cara reckoned she'd still be cold. After a speedy visit to the bathroom, Cara climbed under the blankets in this childhood room of her dead husband. Lying in a bed they'd often hurriedly made out on as teens. Where they'd sat and listened to music. Held hands and chatted. She switched off the bedside light and shivered as she waited for her eyes to become accustomed to the dark and the memories to recede. But the dark lent the room a grotesque feel. The dinosaurs on the wallpaper seemed blood-thirsty, the slats on the wardrobe door peepholes with unseen eyes behind, peering in at her. The bookshelves seemed too heavy, the bed too small. Cara closed her eyes and hoped she would sleep soon enough, that the fine wine and tiredness would be her friend.

Cara opened one bleary eye. Confused. Her feet were blocks of ice and she wasn't sure where she was. A leering T-Rex jogged her memory. The remnants of a dream slipped away. Cara wasn't sorry about that. Disappearing half-remembered images of Cillian, the boat, and the sea receded. Cara reaching out and screaming. She wished, like she had many times before, that when Cillian came to her in a dream that it could be in a happier form, from some of the good times they'd had. Not those last, awful moments.

Cara sat up. Her head was thumping and her mouth was furry and sticky. She felt awful. Why so much wine? Like Seamus she was a lightweight these days, she only had a drink when out with Daithí and Maura, otherwise the creep of drinking on your own, during those long evenings, could cause a problem.

It was still dark but at this time of year that could mean it was anywhere between two and nine a.m. There was a slight glow coming from the window though, but the brightness peeped out from under the curtains, from the ground, not the sky. With a gasp at the cold, Cara got out of bed and went to the window. She pushed back the edge of the curtains and looked out. It was still dark outside. It was the snow that was the source of the hint of brightness. It was everywhere. Up against the walls the drifts looked a couple of feet deep. It was snowing gently now, but there was no hint of sky, the clouds still an endless blanket covering all.

What time was it? How long had she been asleep? Long enough to develop a hangover anyway. Cara went back to the bed and picked up her phone: 6.15 a.m. She crawled back into the bed for warmth, lay back and closed her eyes, but sleep was firmly gone. Her head was pounding and she was thirsty. Was there ten-year-old paracetamol knocking around this house? She'd be happy to take it. Cara got out of bed again and grabbed her jumper from earlier as an extra layer.

She opened the bedroom door. Gentle snores still came from Ferdia and Sorcha's room. The door to Seamus's room was closed. She tiptoed as quietly as she could down the corridor, opened the kitchen door, every creak and squeak sounding as loud as a rock concert in the silence.

The fire still had a few embers glowing, and Cara could hear the sleeping Daithí. His soft breaths in and out. She could just make out his toes sticking out beyond the end of the sofa. Searching the cupboards as quietly as she could, she found a blister pack of tablets only twelve years out of date. She filled a glass with water, which had the roar of Niagara Falls in the stillness. She threw an eye over to the sofa but didn't see any movement.

She rounded the counter and headed for the fire, intending to put some turf on it. Daithí would be grateful and she might just put herself in one of the armchairs and warm up a bit.

There was a movement. Cara spun around.

So still she hadn't noticed him.

Seamus, in one of the armchairs.

'Jesus,' Cara hissed, her heart pounding in her ears, louder than any of the sounds she'd made since leaving the bedroom. She'd barely held on to the glass. Dropping that would have definitely woken everyone up.

'Cara, sorry, I saw you come in,' Seamus whispered, 'but I didn't want to startle you.'

'Bad job!' Cara whispered back. 'Christ.'

'Sorry,' Seamus repeated quietly.

Cara looked at the outline of Daithí whom she could see a bit better now, but in the dark she could still barely make out his features. There were no street lights outside, no light pollution on this island to throw some illumination back into the dark room. Only the faintest glow of the snow providing any break in the gloom. Daithí was deeply asleep. She put her glass down, and carefully placed a piece of turf on the fire. A few sparks spat, but an encouraging glow suggested it would take.

'Good idea,' whispered Seamus.

'It's so cold,' said Cara, matching his quiet tone. She took an ancient throw off the back of the armchair and stepped closer to the sleeping Daithí, taking slow careful steps to avoid bashing into anything. She laid it over him, giving him an extra layer. She sat down on the ground next to the fire and pulled her jumper closer around her. Small flames were beginning to lick into life. The ever so slight glow began to throw a little light into the room. She could just about make out Seamus's face now.

'You okay?' she asked. His eyes were sad, and the perfect smile from the previous evening was gone.

He shrugged. 'Not really.'

'Memories?'

'Yes. So many of them. I had a dream about... that night. It woke me up.'

'Me too,' said Cara.

'It's being back here. I think we were right to avoid it. It's... it's just filled me with all the feelings again, the sadness, the loss, the guilt...'

'You have nothing to be guilty about, Seamus.'

'Don't I?' he asked, his voice rising from the whispering. He shook his head. And even in this darkness, Cara could see the tears at the edge of his clear blue eyes. 'I was the one there, Cara. On the boat. If I hadn't gone back into the cabin, I'd have seen him go over, I'd have been able to call the coastguard sooner, gone in after him, thrown him a life ring... something... Not just turn the boat around and hope I spot him... oh, Cara...' His voice cracked.

Cara crawled across the hearthrug and knelt in front of Seamus. Leant in and hugged him. He was an ice block, much colder than even she was. How long had he been sitting there?

'Not your fault, Seamie, it wasn't your fault. It was no one's fault. There's no one we can rage against.'

'There must have been something I could have done better... He protected me all those years. When Dad was rampaging around here, his belly full of drink and rage in his fists, not caring who he hurt, Cillian hid me in the wardrobe, or under his bed, took the blows for me,' Seamus's voice collapsed, Cara could feel his chest heave as he cried silently, big, wracking sobs, 'and I couldn't save him when he needed me.'

* * *

A banging on the back door woke Cara up.

It was brighter now so it must be morning proper. She was still in the kitchen, legs curled up in one of the armchairs, a blanket around her – Seamus must have put it over her. She stretched her legs and looked around, trying to make sense of what was happening. She dimly remembered him heading back to bed after crying his eyes out. It had been awful. Cara knew the pain he carried, she had her own version of it. But he'd been there that night, when Cillian had gone overboard, hit his head on the way down and drowned. And despite the happy face Seamus showed to the world, it obviously haunted him.

The banging came again. Louder this time.

Cara, properly awake now, turned towards the back door where she could see the outline of a figure in the glass. Daithí was stirring on the sofa, bleary eyes and hung-over head confused.

'What's that?' he mumbled, rubbing his eyes as he sat up.

'Someone is at the door.'

Cara got up, pulled the blanket around her and went to the door.

She opened it and was instantly blinded by the glare from the ice-white snow and the chill of the sub-zero wind that rushed the kitchen. Standing there, wrapped up in a coat, scarf and hat, was a freezing-looking Courtney, Daithí's barmaid. She looked anxious.

'Courtney, are you okay? Come in,' said Cara, standing back to let the girl in.

'Thanks, Cara,' she said, coming in.

'Is everything alright?' asked a croaky Daithí, leaning over the back of the sofa from the other end of the room. 'Is the pub okay?'

'Yes, don't worry, the pub is fine. It's Cara I need,' she said. Cara frowned – whatever could Courtney need with her?

Seamus and Sorcha appeared in the kitchen at that moment, making a quartet of hung-over, bleary-eyed residents.

'What's happening? What was that banging?' said Sorcha, hair askew, rubbing sleep from her eyes.

'Courtney's here,' said Daithí.

'What is it?' asked Cara of the worried-looking girl.

'I have a message for you. They've been trying to reach you but couldn't get you on your mobile.'

'Yes, the signal's awful here.'

'And when they couldn't get you on the mobile, they tried you at home. Your mamó said you were here, she rang the pub hoping to get Daithí, but he's here too, obviously...'

'Thank you for coming all this way. What's the message, who was trying to reach me?'

Courtney took a deep breath.

'It was the police, your guys in Galway. They got an anonymous phone call... someone says there's a body in the Serpent's Lair.'

EIGHT

'It's too dangerous,' Daithí cried, the words barely out of his mouth before they were whipped away by the wind. The blizzards had started again. Lashing the pair of them on the cliff edge. Rocking them and reducing visibility to what felt like mere inches. But there was one thing they could see despite everything. The body in the Serpent's Lair. Whomever had made that call had been right.

'We can't go down there,' Daithí yelled again. He'd insisted on coming with her and she hadn't tried hard to stop him. A trained volunteer for the island's RNLI, a role he'd taken up after Cillian's death, he understood the risks.

Cara could hardly hear what he was saying though. Odd syllables got caught like shrapnel in her ears. But she knew what he was trying to communicate. It was written clearly across his face. She dragged a shaking, sodden arm across her forehead to move hair that was plastered there and getting in her eyes. She had to maintain at least one of her senses.

Cara braced her feet in indents in the snow as solidly as she could, fearful she'd follow Daithí's words off the cliff. She looked down. Down the sheer cliff face into the Serpent's Lair.

The water in the straight-edged pool at the base of the cliff, formed by a millennia of storms just like today's, crashed through its underground channels, flooding it. Kinetic energy thrashing the waves against its sides. Hurling and tossing the body caught within.

'If we don't get down there,' Cara yelled back, cupping her hands around her mouth, 'the body could be pulled out to sea by the undercurrents!'

Daithí shook his head. She could see him mouth, 'No.'

Cara looked around, ignoring Daithí's reluctance. She looked to the path along the cliffs that led down to the pool. She knew the way. They used to go down to the Serpent's Lair as teenagers, to swim during those glorious summer days that seem to only exist in the past. Days that didn't seem possible at times like this. In recent years they'd come here to watch the cliff divers compete. But this was no summer's day.

She began walking.

Cara looked over her shoulder. Daithí was following her through the snow, using the holes left by her footprints as a path. She felt a momentary pang, leading her friend into the path of danger. But it had to be done. There was no one else to do it. Even the volunteer lifeboat team whom she might have called upon to help were stranded elsewhere, having gone to the aid of a stricken trawler in the night. It was just her, and Daithí.

Cara began the descent. It was slow and tentative, her feet unsure as often as they were solid. She grabbed hold of rocky outcrops to steady herself, Daithí following her lead, doing the same. She looked back again, saw him caught by an extra strong gust, slammed against the rock edge. The snow and wind was like a late commuter, pushing and hustling from behind, threatening to send them toppling in its haste.

It took a frustrating half an hour to get down to the level of the pool. With each step Cara thought of Seamus, Ferdia and Sorcha back at home, eating breakfast, the kitchen warmed by the fire. She longed to be back there. To get out of this horrendous weather and enjoy the lazy morning as planned with her friends. But this was what she'd signed up for when she'd taken the job. She couldn't complain. And as much as she wished she was back at Flaherty's, part of her came alive, doing this job, knowing she was making a difference.

Conditions were even worse at the bottom of the cliff. The ground was pockmarked with mini craters – the entire landscape felt more like a distant planet than a West of Ireland coastline. At least the salty seawater from crashing waves had kept it clear of snow. That was something. But the driving blizzard meant each low-visibility step was a chance to break an ankle. Cara was only thankful that the wet rock wasn't frozen, the salt doing them a favour there too.

Down here the raging ocean was so much closer. Louder. Cara feared a large wave could engulf them at any moment, dash their heads against the rocks, and then pull them out to sea. Daithí had been right, this was far too dangerous. And whoever was in the pool was long gone, no one's life was going to be saved here. But she wanted to at least try to retrieve the remains. So many islanders had been lost to the Atlantic, mortal remains without a memorial to them. At any moment an underground current could suck the body out or a wave could whip it from above. She had to try. What if she hadn't been able to bring Cillian home? She couldn't let that be the fate for some family if she could do something about it.

Daithí grabbed Cara's arm and drew her close. He yelled right next to her ear. His hot breath on her skin the only warmth Cara had felt since they'd set off from Seamus's.

'There's no way in hell we can get the body out!' he roared. 'Not without being killed!' Cara stared into his fear-fuelled eyes. Dragged her arm across her face again. She looked over at the raging pool. They were so close. Foamy spray erupted with the rhythm of the crashing waves.

'We'll work something out!' she yelled back.

'We need a plan now! I don't want to drown!'

'I don't either!'

A massive wave rose up from the sea and crashed against them, slamming them against the wall of limestone cliff behind. Vertically submerged, then released from the curtain of water, Cara gulped and gasped, the air forced out of her. Daithí shook beside her, winded too. Any remaining part of them that hadn't been soaked to the skin was now completely saturated. Cara admitted defeat. Daithí was right. This was foolhardy in the extreme. She had a responsibility to the community, but her children had already lost one parent to the capricious sea. Her responsibility to them was more important. Whoever was in the pool would have to take their chances with fate.

She shook her head. Opened her mouth and shouted.

'You're right! It's too dangerous! Let's go!'

And wham. They were walloped by another massive wave. This one with added venom in its bite. It grasped Cara's ankles, pulling her with it. Daithí lunged. Grabbed her arm. Narrowly keeping her on land.

Cara shook, half-crumpled beside Daithí as the water retreated. Her heart pounding. Her shoulder smarting, wrenched by Daithí's saving grab. She coughed and gasped, spat out salty sea water. Her mouth burned. She looked up at Daithí and saw, rather than heard him say, 'That was close.' She nodded, exhausted. Daithí's head turned. She followed his gaze.

A spat out husk, a spent shell sat metres from them.

The waves had left them a gift.

The body from the Serpent's Lair had been tossed, expelled bitter from the beast's mouth.

Cara, still low to the ground, dropped fully to all fours. She felt the rock surface scrape the palms of her hands. The knees of her trousers soaked in more water. She lifted her arm as a shield above her eyes, straining for a clearer view of the ocean in the battering sleet. Checking for incoming danger. She didn't want to risk being pulled out to sea again. She inched forward, crawling towards the body. It was a woman, Cara reckoned, though the body was curled away from her and she couldn't be sure yet. Long, dark, water-logged hair was clumped and splayed, some sections stuck to the shoulders, others fanned out on the rocks.

With one more snatched glance out at the Atlantic, Cara sped up and crossed the last few cratered inches. She reached out, grabbed the body's shoulder and pulled. Two arms, bound at the wrist, followed through with the momentum and rolled the body all the way over to face her. From behind her, a sudden, shocked sob.

'Oh, God, no...' Daithí's voice, robbed so much by the wind, was now achingly clear, as if the gales heard his pain and fell silent in respect.

Cara stared, struck dumb, at the body.

She squinted at it. As if looking at it differently would somehow change what she was seeing. She leant in, closer, examining each and every feature on this lifeless face. Did it really add up to what it seemed?

Those eyes, though closed. The nose, mouth, ears. The hooped earrings still in place.

Maura.

Her Maura. Maura Conneely with the wildness in her blood, and the joy of the unsullied way of life in her heart. Lying here lifeless.

Unbelievably.

Inconceivably...

...dead.

Her wrists were bound, and Cara could see a bulge to her cheek, the end of cloth just visible through a closed jaw. She had a gag stuffed in her mouth.

'No,' whispered Cara.

She sank back on her heels and stared. Flakes of snow settled on Maura's grey, sleeping face, but no warmth from her skin melted them. They stayed, cold as she was.

Daithí came and dropped to his knees beside her, the two of them like penitents at prayer. Cara looked Maura up and down. She could see under her denim jacket the black and white top Maura'd been wearing at Derrane's. Her hooped earrings. The blue jeans, Maura's favourite pair.

'But I just saw her, yesterday morning...' Daithí whispered. He reached a hand out to the body.

'No. Don't.'

They shouldn't touch her. Cara couldn't think straight. She had to work out what Sergeant Cara Folan should do. Right now, she was only Cara, disbelieving, confused, horrified friend. Daithí took his arm in.

She understood his instinct, and desperately wanted to do the same. Wanted to reach out to her friend, gather Maura to her. Hold her. Cara balled up her hands into tight fists, squeezed her fingernails into her palms. Tried using the pain to cut through her shock.

Daithí was trying to say something to her. She leaned in close to him. 'Cara, what's happened? Her hands... look at her face...' He grasped around for the words. 'I only saw her yesterday morning,' he repeated.

Cara shook her head. Squeezed Daithí's arm. An effort to comfort him. But also an action to see if this was all real. He put his arm around her and Cara leaned in, welcoming his reciprocal comfort. The storm made sense now. The earth had lost one of its own and was rightfully enraged.

Cara looked up at the darkening sky. Not feeling the snow sting her eyes and face. The sky looked like an early winter's evening even though it was only 9 a.m. It was a sky that seemed to get ever closer the darker it got. She thought she could nearly reach out and touch it.

Cara felt tears threaten. Even in her confusion, she knew tears wouldn't help them now. She couldn't fall to pieces. There would be time for that later. Now, Cara had to do something. Get them all out of here. She moved forward. Began crawling around Maura, trying to detach herself and pretend this was someone else. Taking in every bruise and cut. Thinking of her training at Templemore. And though there was no let-up in the tempest, Cara felt like time had slowed down around her. That the snow that had lashed against her like a medieval torture tool only moments before, now moved to different laws of physics. Moving around her, not touching her. There was only Cara, on her hands and knees, looking at what remained of her friend.

Slowly, as she detached and focused, Cara could see there were two stories being told. Damage done when the body was left defenceless against nature. Long, brutal cuts. Cara could see one particularly deep, jagged rip on her side, where her top was pulled up. But there were other, smaller, lighter touches. The tidy cut lip, the black eye that had no graze around it. Injuries too delicate for the might and fury of limestone rock and thrashing waves.

She turned and looked back at the distressed Daithí, to make sure he was okay. Behind him, on the cliff above, a flash of movement caught her eye. Dark against the all pervasive white. She scrambled to her feet. Slipped, bashing her knee. She gasped and grimaced but got up again. She dashed towards the sea then turned to look back – running further out to gain a greater panoramic view of the clifftop. What was that?

She squinted through storm-obscured eyes.

'Cara!' bellowed Daithí.

She turned, a wave was coming. She dashed back towards Daithí, narrowly missing being swept out again. It retreated and she followed it out once more, desperate to catch sight of what-ever – whoever? – she had seen above. But there was nothing. If it hadn't been a trick of the storm, it was gone now.

She looked across the cratered landscape. And then on out to sea at the storm's fury. They needed to get out of here. She and Daithí would have to carry Maura out. As awful as that thought was. And in these conditions, how hard it would be.

And then what? They were cut off completely. She'd been on the last ferry yesterday. And the plane certainly wasn't running. Even the RNLI lifeboat was stuck elsewhere. For a moment, the wind died down. A tantruming child who needed a moment's pause to catch their breath. Cara tried to think of her next move. She looked down at Maura.

This storm was forecast to break in three days.

Until then, nobody was coming to help them.

No one was riding to their rescue.

NINE

Cara ended the call. She rested her elbows on the steering wheel and stared at the phone screen. A picture of Cathal and Saoirse smiled back at her from the lock screen. She disconnected from *Powell House Wi-Fi*. Not that she thought Mrs Powell, who lived in the cottage near where they were parked, would mind. It just seemed polite and Cara was on autopilot.

'What did they say?' asked Daithí from the passenger seat.

'I spoke with my superintendent. As we expected, it's too dangerous. The cavalry aren't coming... the cavalry *can't* come. Even the coastguard helicopter won't risk it.' Cara took a deep breath. 'They said I should secure what I can until they can get here.'

'What does that mean?'

'Who knows. I don't think I can tape off the Serpent's Lair, do you?'

Daithí shook his head.

'They don't even want me to investigate. Not for me to do, a lowly sergeant – I might mess something up, it seems.'

'I'm sure they just want to do it by the book. It's not a slight on you.'

'So I'm to just sit back and do nothing until the storm breaks while some monster, some animal, did that to... to...' Cara's voice cracked. She gulped down a sob and walloped the car with her fist.

Daithí flinched at the violence.

'Cara, don't...'

They sat in silence for a moment. Then Cara opened the car door, holding hard to the armrest to stop the wind whipping it off its hinges.

'What are you doing?' said Daithí in alarm.

'I need a moment.'

Cara got out. She walked to the back of the car, letting the wind and snow rock and batter her. She looked out at the impossible horizon. Then turned her back to the Serpent's Lair path, and looked instead towards Kilmurvey Beach. Where'd she'd first met Maura. So long ago and on a day so unlike today. Both eight years old, the sun bouncing off the white sandy beach. Maura, dark-haired and blue-eyed, so full of mischief. And Cara, with her wild auburn hair, pale skin and blue eyes too, a girl born ready to pose for the Irish tourist board, her father always said. A girl who really wasn't sure of her place in the world, but who came alive around her new friend, Maura. At the end of every summer, when Cara was heading back to Dublin, back to the other place she didn't fit in, they cried in each other's arms, making promises for next year, which always seemed so very far away.

It was Maura who had introduced her to the others. Included her as if she wasn't the blow-in. Given her the gift of belonging, of a gang who accepted her for who she was, even if it was just for those three months each summer. When June came, and with it the boat across from Galway – sometimes with Ferdia aboard as well – she'd be welcomed as if she'd never been away. And it was Maura who had first whispered, giggling in her ear at fourteen, that Seamus had told her that Cillian had told him that he thought Cara was cute.

The others. She would have to tell them. Cara's heart sank. Her superintendent said they would look after contacting the family – Maura's parents were in Australia for Christmas visiting her brother and his family. At least Cara would be spared that horror. She felt cowardly at her relief. But how would Seamus, Sorcha and Ferdia react? Especially poor Seamus. Sure it had been a long time ago, but Seamus and Maura had seemed destined to be together forever, like her and Cillian. Even if that relationship turned out to have a symbiosis with her and Cillian's, and hadn't been able to survive after his death, Cara couldn't imagine this news would be easy for Seamus.

The blizzard of snow swirled round Cara as an even more awful feeling took hold of her. She didn't know what had happened to her friend. Other than something truly awful. But what she did know was that last night, as the gang had hung out, they should have been worried. They should have gotten up from the dinner table and gone looking for Maura. Not just assume she'd not bothered showing up. Not just put it down to her being a flake. And getting a better offer. Those words burned in Cara's mind. A better offer. This had been that 'better offer'. Something deep inside Cara cracked. Splintered. She leaned against the car to help her stay standing, the storm inside her the culprit this time.

Cara wiped snow off the car's rear window. Looked in. To the back seat where she and Daithí had gently laid Maura. Looking for all the world as if she'd just fallen asleep in the back of a taxi after one of their mad nights out in Galway.

Cara got back into the driver's seat, rubbing her eyes with the heel of her palm.

'Are you okay?' asked Daithí.

'No, and I doubt you are either.'

'No, not at all,' he agreed.

Cara shivered. Her clothes were sticking to her. Melted snow dripped down her face. She started the car and turned towards Kilronan. They drove in silence.

'Someone did that to her,' said Daithí, his voice quiet.

'It appears so,' Cara said through gritted teeth. The car shook in the wind and the wipers were barely coping with the volume of snow. Cara reached out and tried to force the heater dial higher. A chill was colonising her bones. Daithí must be just as frozen. Sitting here in sodden clothes, the water soaking into the car seats. Condensation was forming on all the windows faster than the car heater could get rid of it. Cara leant further forward, risking keeping a hand off the steering wheel a moment longer, she rubbed across the interior windscreen, desperate for even the smallest bit of a clear view ahead of them.

'What are you going to do?' asked Daithí.

'Not sit on my hands anyway.'

'Cara, you were told not to do anything.'

'We did nothing last night when she needed us. There's no way I'm doing nothing now.'

'Don't think like that.'

'How can I think any other way?'

They drove on in silence again.

'So, do you have something in mind?' Daithí asked after a while.

Cara shrugged.

'I dunno. Collect what forensic evidence I can? I don't have any facilities but maybe Dr De Barra can help me.' She sighed. 'But again, I don't know, it's not like I'm preserving her body without contamination – I had the bloody O'Reilly brothers and their dog in the back there last week and I certainly didn't bleach the car afterwards.'

'Dr De Barra is a good idea, I think.'

'Is she?' Cara snatched a glance at Daithí.

'Yeah, she is.'

'I'm not trained for this, Daithí. I'm not a detective. I'm a stupid sergeant on a stupid island in the middle of the ocean.'

'Don't underestimate yourself...'

Cara took a long, deep breath.

'Okay,' she said. 'We'll head to the clinic and call her once we hit signal in Kilronan.'

Cara knew she could just sit around, wait for the detectives and the machinery of murder investigation to arrive. But she also knew enough to know that this weather would destroy so much evidence, and time was always of the essence. Even three days' wait till the storm ran its course would make a difference. Let a killer off the hook. She'd not mess with anything that could make the situation worse, but she'd do what she could. For Maura.

They drove through the island, finding themselves on the coast road on the way to Kilronan. The road that would take them past Seamus's. Cara's long habit of averting her eyes as she passed the Flaherty house kicked in, but not before she saw a bleary-eyed, unshaven Seamus, mug of coffee in his hand, staring blankly out the window. They were too far from the house for him to have seen their tragic passenger, even if he'd realised it was the squad car that was passing the house. His sleep-deprived attention didn't seem to even react to them.

'That's going to be a tough conversation,' said Daithí, joining Cara in averting his eyes, and staring straight ahead.

'Yes,' she sighed.

Within a couple of minutes, they were on the outskirts of the village. Cara wound their way through the streets and pulled up outside the doctor's clinic. She parked the car.

'Daithí, I'll do this bit, alone, with Dr De Barra. I'll need you to help me carry her in, but then you get home, okay? Get into dry clothes.'

'No, let me stay, let me help.'

'You've already done more than anyone could ever ask.'

Daithí looked at her; Cara could tell he was sizing up how far he could push it.

'Okay,' he conceded defeat. 'Can I at least get you a change of clothes?'

'No, it's okay, I'll manage. Just look after yourself.'

'If you're sure, but I'll meet you back here, once I'm changed and you're done with the doctor. I'm going to ask Courtney to come in again and do some hours in the pub tonight. I can't face it now, and we've got bad news to share.' Daithí's face was grey, his eyes clouded with emotion. 'We'll tell them together.'

'Alright. I'll message you when I'm done,' said Cara.

'Thanks.'

Daithí reached out to open the passenger side door. He stood out into the squally street.

Cara got out her side of the car.

'Daithí,' she said, pausing – a thought had come to her. 'Something you said earlier...'

'Yeah?'

'What you said at the Serpent's Lair... that you saw Maura yesterday morning?'

'Yes. I was cleaning tables in the pub, putting out beer mats, the usual. She cycled by. She didn't wave to me as she usually would, though.'

'What time was this, can you remember?'

'It was about ten thirty. I glanced up at the clock after she passed.'

Cara nodded thoughtfully.

'What is it?'

'There've been no ferries or planes since then. The planes

stopped on Tuesday night and I stepped off the last boat at 9 a.m. yesterday.'

'I know. So?'

'That means she was killed after the ferries and planes stopped.'

Daithí frowned.

'Whoever did this to her is still on the island, Daithí. No one has been able to leave since yesterday morning. And they're stuck here until the storm breaks. There's no way to escape.'

TEN

'Here, drink this, it'll help warm you up.' The doctor handed Cara a Styrofoam cup of steaming tea.

'Thank you,' Cara replied, her grateful hands grasping the drink. The doctor then opened a press and rooted inside. She withdrew a towel and placed it around Cara's shoulders.

'You should really get out of those drenched clothes.'

'There'll be time for that later,' said Cara. 'First things first.'

'Okay, if you're sure.' Cara nodded. Dr De Barra turned and circled the examination table, a slight limp from an arthritic hip noticeable as she went.

The lights flickered. Cara and the doctor looked up at them and then out the window at the storm. Frosted for privacy, the turmoil outside was still obvious. The outline of distorted trees twisted to unnatural angles. The howl of the gale was audible even through triple glazing.

'I hope the electricity holds out,' the doctor said.

Cara didn't reply. She didn't even want to think about that.

De Barra sat down on her swivel chair. Turned it around so she was facing away from her desk, with its stethoscope and prescription pads and leaflets covering flu shots and cholesterol tests. And a miniature Christmas tree which twinkled obliviously.

She was on an eye level with Maura's body.

'This is certainly a tragedy, I can sadly diagnose that.'

Cara sighed.

'Yes, it is.'

'She was a lovely girl. My grandkids had her as a teacher. They loved her.'

'She was great.' The past tense stuck in Cara's throat.

'So someone has done this to her, I see. This is no accident.'

'Nope.'

'Do you know who?'

'I'm afraid not. Not yet anyway.'

The island was twelve kilometres in length, and three kilometres in width. Eight hundred people lived here. These numbers contained the secret of who had done this and why.

'That's why I'm here. I don't want you to just certify the death, I want you to have a look at her, see if there's anything you can tell me that might help. If you can.'

'I'll have a look. I can't promise you anything. I'm no forensic pathologist. Very far from it.' She bent in close and peered at the body through thick glasses. 'I'm an island GP. Coughs and colds, blood pressure and antenatal checks.'

'I understand that's your usual practice, Doctor. But we both know you're far more than that. Forty years as the only doctor here, with support an emergency helicopter ride away. You aren't the average GP.'

'True, true.'

'And you're all I've got, anyway.'

'Ha!' the doctor barked. 'True again.'

'If you can have a look and tell me anything you notice.'

The doctor took a pair of latex gloves from a box on her desk and pulled them on with a snap. She stood and again walked around the examining table, this time gently lifting and looking and examining the body. A thumb raised each eyelid and she shone a light into Maura's staring eyes. She examined the long gashes on her back, and the cuts and bruises to her face.

She pointed at the ropes that bound Maura's wrists together.

'Can we untie these?'

Cara pondered what her bosses would say. They probably wouldn't be happy.

'Can I ask why?'

'It'll help me make a stab at the time of death. Which should help you, I believe.'

'If you were to wait three days to try and work that out, would that make a difference?'

'In three days, the evidence I'm looking for will be gone.'

That was all Cara needed to hear.

'Okay, you can do it. Let me just take some pictures first though.' Cara put the tea down and took out her phone. She documented every angle of the bindings. She then took a pair of gloves, pulled them on and picked up one of the sterile bags on the desk.

'Okay, let's put it in here, and label it.'

The doctor undid the knot. It came loose with an ease that Cara could see surprised the doctor as much as her. De Barra dropped the rope into the bag. Cara placed it back on the table. Wrote a note on it with a Sharpie marker.

'Interesting,' De Barra muttered. Cara resisted the urge to ask the doctor to explain.

She looked over at Cara.

'I'd like to look at her legs. Is it okay to take off her jeans?' Is it okay? Cara had a feeling, probably not. That the Galway detectives would be horrified. They'd probably all yell no. But they weren't here right now.

'Is this still to do with time of death?'

'Yes.'

'Okay. Let me just take some more photographs again.' Cara took photos from every angle she could think of. The doctor offered her a plastic bag.

'I can't guarantee how sterile it is, but I've done what I can and it's the best I have for something the size of her trousers.'

'No worries, thank you.'

'I think you're going to have to help me, too.'

'Sure, of course.' She joined the doctor at the table, took a deep breath, and unbuttoned Maura's jeans. Cara was reminded of the old traditions of the islands. Where the women came together to prepare the dead bodies for burial. They had learned to be self-sufficient, to do everything themselves. Cara's mamó spoke of helping as a young girl. If Cara felt cut off now from the mainland and civilisation, what must it have been like a hundred years ago? Ferries? Planes? They had small, animal-hide-covered boats to get them from the island to the mainland. It must have been impossible.

Cara helped pull the jeans down over Maura's unmoving hips, the soaked denim unyielding. She felt cold bare legs, colder than anything she'd ever felt before. As freezing as she was herself still in the clothes she had retrieved Maura in, it didn't come close to the cold of Maura's naked flesh. She spotted the small blue dolphin tattoo on her left hip. Slightly faded at the edges. Cara's hand dropped and touched her own hip. Thinking of the dot there which had been the beginnings of a matching dolphin, but which she'd chickened out of after the first dip of the needle. Cara remembered how annoyed Maura had been for a moment, then how she'd laughed and laughed, stuck forever with a lone, stupid tattoo.

'Are you okay?' De Barra looked at Cara over the top of her glasses and the body. Cara wanted to answer truthfully that no, she wasn't, this was truly, truly awful.

'I'll have to be,' she said instead. She took the jeans and carefully folded them. Before she put them in the plastic bag, she looked at the pockets. Should she check them? She turned the jeans over and back. She slid her hand into the back pockets. Pulled out Maura's phone. Cara pressed the home button but nothing happened. It had been destroyed by the seawater. She placed it in its own separate bag. Then she checked the front left pocket and found Maura's house key. Cara put it with the phone. She slipped her hand into the last pocket, the front right. Something was in here. She pulled out the contents. A crumple of white petals, leaves, stems emerged.

'Oh, Maura...' Cara whispered, looking down at the little white flowers and heart-shaped seedpods resting in her latex-covered palm. Shepherd's purse. It was called a wildflower, but was really just a weed. As teenagers she and Maura had loved the seedpods, nipped them off and collected the tiny hearts, all giggles and silliness.

'Are you okay?' the doctor asked her again. Cara looked over her shoulder at the doctor. Nodded, not trusting herself to speak. She took a small ziplock bag and put the flowers inside. Checked the jeans again in case she'd missed something – she hadn't – then put them in the large plastic bag. Put them on the desk beside the rope and flower.

Her gaze lingered on the flower. Why had Maura a clump of weeds in her pocket? And nothing else either? No old tissue, or crumpled receipt, nothing else in any of the other pockets. Just this clump of weeds with the dirt still on the roots.

'Sergeant?'

Cara turned around.

'Yes?'

'Do you want to hear my thoughts?'

'Please.'

The doctor sat down on her swivel chair. She picked up a pencil from her desk and turned back to the body.

'Firstly, I do have to reiterate that I'm not an expert. So

much of this is me remembering from university. And that wasn't today nor yesterday.'

'I understand. I appreciate anything you can tell me.'

'Well, as long as we're both clear on that... okay, I'll start with some general observations.'

Cara unlocked her phone, ready to take notes.

'To begin, estimating a time of death isn't easy. Even for experienced pathologists it's a tricky task.'

'Someone saw her alive yesterday morning, around 10.30 a.m. That's the last sighting I have so far.'

'I see. Well, I probably can't give you much more to work with. From the state of rigor mortis, I think the window for when she died is from about 3 p.m. to 10 p.m. yesterday. But it could possibly have happened even earlier, 12 noon. maybe, as cold slows down the progression of rigor mortis.'

'So, sometime in that ten-hour window she was killed. Possibly not too long after my sighting even.'

'Yes, that's my best guess.'

'You don't think any later than 10 p.m. last night?'

'I'm sure there is some margin of error there, perhaps even midnight, but I don't think any later, not from the condition she's in now.'

Cara made some notes on her phone and tried not to think about what she'd been doing during that time. Tried not to think of the fun she'd been having with the others.

'Is there anything else you can tell me from examining her?'

'Yes, a few things. Let me talk to you about her wounds.' The doctor looked up at Cara. 'I've sadly seen enough fistfights in my time to recognise the injuries to her face as an assault.'

As Cara had suspected.

The doctor moved the chair forward, closer to the body. 'The rest of the damage looks pretty much like damage from the environment she was found in.'

'Yes, I agree,' said Cara.

'But look at this.' De Barra gently rolled Maura's body to one side, pointed with the pencil to her exposed lower back. And then to the back of her neck. They were dark, as if entirely bruised. 'You see these two areas? This is where it gets strange.'

Cara looked at where the doctor had pointed.

'I can see signs of fixed lividity.' She let Maura lie flat again and looked up at Cara. 'I'm going to presume you're unfamiliar with what lividity is?'

Cara nodded her head.

'It's when the heart stops beating,' the doctor explained, 'and gravity causes the blood to pool in the lowest part of the body.' She pointed again to Maura's discoloured neck and lower back. 'Wherever it pools, the skin looks darker. The lividity I'm seeing here – all along her underside – tells me she was laid on her back for some time after she died.'

'Really?' said Cara. 'That makes it sound like she didn't drown?'

'I can't say how she died without a post-mortem. But for lividity to show like this – on the underside of her body – it means she has to have lain on her back for some hours after her death. In the one position, against a hard surface – like a floor, for example.'

'So she was thrown into the Serpent's Lair after she died?'

'It's the only explanation.'

'I suppose they could have been trying to get rid of the body? That makes sense.'

'Perhaps, but there's more going on that doesn't.'

'No?'

'Look here...' The doctor indicated to Maura's upper thighs. They were pale, no dark signs of pooled blood. 'Wherever there is pressure on the body, where it's directly in contact with the ground, or clothes are tight perhaps,' she pointed to where the waistband of the jeans would have been, 'there is no dark lividity. The pressure keeps the blood away. It's areas like the back of the neck, the small of the back, those parts without direct contact with the ground, that's where the blood pools. And we get that look of bruising.'

'Okay...' said Cara.

The pencil was now pointing at Maura's arms.

'I wanted you to untie her arms so that I could check the degree of rigor mortis that had set in. But look at this – her wrists are dark.'

Cara looked, saw what the doctor meant and nodded.

'Yes, I see it.'

'If her hands had been bound like that before she died, then the pressure of the ropes would have meant we wouldn't see lividity there. But because we can, it is consistent with her arms being free and lying flat beside her wherever she lay, after she died.' The doctor turned in her chair and rested her own arm on her desk. 'Miss Conneely's arms are quite stiff now. But look... see how my wrist is raised off the desk? No pressure. That's how her arms would have rested. And that's the only way we could see the lividity that we see here now.'

'They tied her up *after* she died?'

'It's the only explanation.'

'Why on earth...' Cara frowned. She looked down at her friend, her confusion detaching her momentarily from the horror before her. The doctor shrugged.

'That, I cannot answer.' She turned back in her chair.

'Maybe it was done to make carrying her to the cliff easier?' ventured Cara.

'I'd have said that was a good theory. Except for the other strangeness.'

'There's more...?'

The doctor moved up to Maura's head. Pointed at the jaw. With one gloved finger she gently opened and closed Maura's mouth. Cara could see the gag stuffed within. She looked away.

'When we die rigor mortis starts setting in after a few hours.

But it doesn't develop uniformly – it starts in the smallest muscles of the body, moving gradually to the largest.' The doctor swept her arm over the body. 'So her arms, with their larger muscles, would have been easy to manipulate for a good while after she died. They'd have had no problems binding the hands as they did, for some hours after she died. But, rigor fixes in the face quickly. All those small muscles. That means for me to be able to open and close her mouth like I just did – someone must have forced her mouth open after death, broken the rigor. It seems likely to put the gag in. Why, God only knows.'

'Christ,' said Cara.

'It's gruesome, I agree.'

Cara stared at her poor friend. Half-naked, bruised and broken on the doctor's bench. What had they done to her? Bound and gagged *after* she was killed? Tossed already dead into the Serpent's Lair. Why on earth?

ELEVEN

Finished here.

Cara hit send on the text and looked up as De Barra closed the door of the clinic behind her.

'Thanks again, Doctor.'

'That's no problem, it had to be done.' She nodded solemnly. 'Maura will be safe in the therapy room behind the surgery for the next few days. I expect with the storm, the temperature out there will be very low. Not ideal, not very dignified, but it's the best I can do right now.'

'And I appreciate it.'

'Keep in touch, Sergeant.'

'I will,' said Cara. 'And if you see anything suspicious in your practice, can you let me know?'

'Of course.'

'If you can be discreet as well...'

'That goes without saying, Sergeant.'

'Thank you.' The doctor waved as she walked away, hair whipped up by the gusts, her shoulders hunched in defence against the snow. Cara watched her walk all the way to her nearby front door. Saw her battle briefly with the wind to open it. Another wave and she was safely inside. Cara looked up and down the street. People were still being sensible and staying inside. She could hear the excited screams of stupid teenagers somewhere in the distance. They'd go home once they got cold, and that would be soon.

She opened the door of her car. Inside was dank with moisture and cold. Cara bent over and felt the fabric of the seats. Wet. She retrieved a few plastic bags from the boot and lined the front passenger seat with them. She was still wet so didn't care, she didn't really care about anything other than Maura right now, but Daithí would appreciate the effort. She sat in and closed the door behind her. The snow was easing off, but everywhere was blanketed. Another time she'd have thought the island beautiful. Magical. But not today. Right now it was like a bandage, a gauze, covering up a wound. Cara sat there without turning the key in the ignition. She looked out over the harbour. The clouds, pregnant with more snow, assembled bulging over the sea, waiting, holding the line until they decided to unleash a second assault. This storm wasn't going anywhere anytime soon. The siege would continue.

Cara's phone beeped. A text message from Daithí.

On my way.

A few minutes later she saw Daithí approach. He looked warmer in a fresh set of clothes, but his expression was as bleak as it had been earlier.

'Hey,' he said as he sat in.

'Hey.'

Cara leant over and hugged him, the contortion in the front of the car awkward. She heard his jagged breathing in her ear. The same lava of emotion punching at the crust, inches from the surface and eruption, that she was struggling to contain too.

'Cara, you're freezing,' he said as he sat back. 'We need to get you home and changed, you'll get sick.'

'No, I want to go back to Seamus's, I want to tell them. They need to know.'

'Cara, it can wait. It's not as if anyone is going to tell them in the meantime. It's like in an aeroplane: look after your own mask first. Come on.'

'What will I say to Mamó?' Cara's voice teetering on the brink, thinking of sharing the news with her sweet, kind grandmother. A woman who'd loved Maura as much as she had.

'I know.' Daithí sighed. 'This isn't going to be easy.'

Cara shook her head and started the car. She headed for the high road and the way home. She'd do as Daithí said, and look after herself first. He was right, she needed to be strong, she needed to be in the best condition to do this for Maura.

'How'd it go with De Barra?' Daithí asked as the low stone walls passed them, the wipers running, swiping the lighter fall of snow off left, then right.

'It was very strange.' She told Daithí what she'd learnt from the doctor. About the rigor and the lividity. How it didn't make sense. Silence settled as they both digested the information. Both of them lost in their thoughts. So many thoughts Cara felt she could be lost for a long time and not find her way out. Daithí eventually spoke.

'Everybody loved Maura. I keep coming back to that. There's no reason why anyone would want to hurt her. Even the most disliked person on this island doesn't have to worry about something so awful.'

The light was already starting to fade even though it was only noon. That second offensive of snow looked increasingly trigger happy. Cara was cold, exhausted and emotionally spent. She had no idea either who would have done this to Maura. But someone had.

. . .

The home Cara shared with her children and Mamó was towards the north of the island where the land was higher. The views were stunning but they were even more exposed to the elements. The mighty Dun Aengus, the prehistoric fort ruins that sat cliffside looking out over the Atlantic, looked down also on Cara's home.

The wind helped usher Cara and Daithí in, nearly lifting them off their feet as she tried to open the front door. Inside, Cara put her shoulder to the door to force it shut. The kitchen door, across the hall, was opened by the gusts that had barged their way past Cara. She looked through and could see her grandmother moving around the kitchen, pots on the cooker, lids rattling, the smell of stew in the oven and the earthy aroma of a turf fire coming from the sitting room beyond. If there was a scented candle that could convey all this, Cara would buy up every last one.

'Mammy, heya, you're back. Is Uncle Seamus with you?' Cathal, her eleven-year-old son, appeared from down the corridor, iPad in his hand, sidestepping Christmas cards the wind had dislodged from the hall table. 'Dia duit, Daithí.' Hello, Daithí, he said, beaming at his favourite honorary uncle.

'Dia duit, Cathal,' replied Daithí with a wink.

Cara smiled at the lad. Fair-haired and freckled, he was a miniature of his late father. Cara ruffled the boy's hair, much to his good-humoured annoyance. The horror of the last few hours receded a moment.

'No, Uncle Seamus isn't with me, but you'll meet him soon. And I see you're having some extra screen time – here, hand it over.'

'Ah, Mammy.' Cara put her hand out and with reluctance Cathal gave her the tablet. He shot Daithí a pleading look, but Daithí just shrugged.

'I hope you were good for Mamó last night.'

'We had popcorn and watched a movie. Mamo let us watch the *Avengers* movie, it was cool.'

'That sounds fun.'

'It was.' Cathal paused for breath. 'You look really wet, Mammy. You look a mess.'

'Charming. But yeah, I'm soaked. If you looked up from that screen occasionally you'd see there was a storm raging out there.'

'Ha, ha. I did notice actually. What have you been doing?'

'Garda stuff.'

'Wow, never!'

'I know, right!'

'Oh cringe, Mam, don't try to be cool.'

'God forbid, Cathal.'

The boy rolled his eyes and headed for the kitchen door. Cara and Daithí followed him.

'Oh, hello there, dear, I didn't know when to expect you.' Mamó looked up from her baking and over her shoulder at the pair. 'And Mr Derrane, always a pleasure. How was last night? I hope you had a lot of fun. Any news from London or California? I hope that Ferdia Hennessy isn't still too much of a yahoo...'

Mamó – actual name Áine – wiped her floury hands down her apron and turned to face them properly. She shared Cara's blue eyes and heart-shaped face. Her hair had been the same shade of deep, rich auburn before it had gone white.

She looked at Cara more closely. 'Oh, look at you, you're drenched! What's been going on? I know it's bad out there but you look like you went for a swim! You'll catch your death of cold so you will.'

'That's why I'm here, to get myself sorted out.'

'You look shattered. Are you okay?'

Cara exhaled a weary sigh and nodded.

She looked at Daithí and then back to her grandmother.

Looked further into the room at Cathal who was now eating a mince pie at the kitchen table as he pored over a Beano annual.

'Hey, Cathal, what you reading there?' asked Daithí, as he squeezed Cara's arm and joined the boy at the table.

Cara could hear the TV on low in the next room. Her daughter Saoirse, twelve, appeared in the doorway. Red-headed and blue-eyed, she was the smallest Russian doll of the trio. She had her black and white cat, Madra – the Irish word for dog – in her arms.

'*Dia duit, a mhamaí,*' she said. Raised on the island since she was two years old, like her brother she was fluent in Irish. Mamó spoke it to them instead of English. There were times when Cara felt like an outsider in her own home too. But those were thoughts she had to shake off. If the child wanted to say 'hello, Mam' to her in the language she used ninety-nine per cent of her day, then the child was allowed.

'*Dia duit, a stór,*' Cara replied. Hello, darling. Words of love, she knew. With a wave, Saoirse went back into the TV.

She looked back at Mamó. This wasn't the time nor place to discuss what had happened today. It could wait.

'I'll tell you later, Mamó,' said Cara, turning to leave the room. 'I'm going to go have that shower.'

'Off you go.' Áine returned to her breadmaking, and Cara left the room and headed down the corridor to the bathroom.

'Oh, Cara.' Mamó's head appeared around the kitchen door.

'Yes?' Cara stopped midway down the hall.

'I just remembered. Maura called here for you yesterday morning. Quite anxious to talk to you. Did she find you?'

TWELVE

Cara stopped. Her heart paused with her. She turned back to her grandmother.

'Maura?'

'Yes.' Áine stepped out into the hall. 'It was early, maybe about elevenish? She knew you'd have been back on the 9 a.m. boat. I told her you were somewhere on the island helping with storm preparations.'

'Hold on, Mamó. Let me be sure I'm hearing you right. Maura came looking for me? At eleven or so yesterday morning?'

'Yes, that's it. She was anxious to talk to you. Worried-looking, even. Did she find you?'

That must have been not long after Daithí spotted her through the pub window. She must have been on her way here.

'No, she didn't.' Cara walked back down the corridor, closer to Mamó. 'She didn't make it to Seamus's either.'

'Oh, really?'

Cara waved away Mamó's curious expression.

'Did she say why she wanted to see me?'

'No, I'm afraid she didn't. That girl usually has such a smile on her face. But not yesterday morning. Maybe things with Seamus haven't worked out.'

'Seamus? That was over a decade ago, Mamó.'

'Was it now? Why, then, was that the second time I'd seen her yesterday? When I went for an early walk yesterday morning, didn't I see her coming out of Flaherty's? Seamus on the doorstep.' Cara was about to tell her that Maura had probably stayed over after the pub. But hadn't Daithí said he'd walked her home?

'Mamó, this isn't the time for gossip. It really isn't.'

'Fair enough, darling. Anyway, she had a package in her hands. She was fiddling and fussing with it. I asked her if she needed to give it to you. I told her she could leave it for you here. She thought about it, but decided no, that she'd go find you.'

'A package? Any idea what it was?'

'It was wrapped up in old tatty brown paper so it wasn't a Christmas present, nothing like that. She kept turning it over, looking down at it, as if checking she still had it.'

'What sort of size are we talking?'

'Hmm, maybe about this big?' Áine held her hands apart about a foot. 'It wasn't very thick, whatever it was. Just a couple of inches maybe.' She demonstrated the width with her fingers.

'And she didn't tell you what it was?'

'No, I'm afraid not.'

Cara was silent as she tried to take this in.

'What is it, Cara? What's going on?' Cara looked up at her grandmother's worried face. She would have to tell her. She'd hoped to wait, but it was probably better now.

'Close the door behind you there, Mamó. I don't want the kids to hear. Not yet.'

The older woman pulled the door shut, her expression tense.

'Hear what, Cara?'

Cara took a deep breath. This was a preview of what was to come. Of telling people, breaking this awful news.

'Mamó, something really bad has happened.'

Cara watched as the old woman's face shifted. Braced itself. Life on the island was hard. And it had been harder still when Áine was growing up. You learnt to deal with tragedy. You learnt to expect it as the norm.

'What is it? Is it to do with Maura?'

'Yes.' Cara floundered for a moment, selecting then rejecting different words.

'Is she... alright?' Mamó asked, knowing the answer already.

Cara shook her head and the tears she'd been keeping in for hours began to flow. Áine went to her granddaughter and gathered her into a tight embrace.

'*Oh mo stór, mo croí*, shssh, shssh.' The old woman rocked her gently, hugging her and whispering comforting words into her ear. Oh my darling, my heart, she whispered over and over as Cara let out all the grief she had forced into hiding.

'What happened? Did the storm cause an accident?' Áine asked.

Cara stood out of the embrace, and dried her tears. She should plug this dam, before it cracked wide open and she couldn't stop it. She'd put her grief away for another time. She'd had lots of practice with that. When small faces needed comforting after cries for Daddy went unanswered. Bearing the awfulness of telling a mother she'd be burying a son in the prime of his life. She'd make room for it alongside the grief she woke with each morning, the space beside her in the bed as cold as the ocean bed where her dearest love had died. She'd put it there and lock another door of her heart shut.

'We found Maura's body a few hours ago. In the Serpent's Lair.'

'Oh sweet Lord,' Áine blessed herself. 'How did she let that happen? Why was she out in the storm, always a wild one, that girl!'

'She didn't let it happen, Mamó. Someone hurt her. Put her in there.'

Áine looked horrified.

'No... surely not?'

Cara nodded.

'I'm afraid so. I know it's so hard to believe. Someone on the island, someone did that to her.'

Áine shook her head.

'I don't want to believe that.'

'I don't either.'

'What are you going to do?'

Cara threw her arms up.

'I don't know. No one can come from Galway until the storm breaks. I'm going to have to do the best I can until then. I'm not sure where to even start.'

'Are we safe?'

'To be honest with you, Mamó, I don't know. I don't know why this happened to Maura and without that knowledge I can't work out how at risk the rest of us are. Keep the doors locked. And maybe you could ask Maurice and Conor to stay over for a few nights, so it's not just you and the kids on your own. I suspect I'll be coming and going a lot and I'd be happier if I knew they were here.' Maurice and Conor were friends, and while the aged Maurice wouldn't be up to much protecting, his son Conor would.

'Also, don't tell the kids anything. I want to see if I can work out what on earth is happening first.'

'What are you going to do now?'

'Get changed. Then I have to go over to the Flaherty's and break the news there.'

'This is so tragic, my dear.' Mamó shook her head, tears

gathering in the old woman's eyes. 'The old gang back together to honour Cillian, and now you've lost another, my poor love.'

Cara smiled sadly at Mamó and turned and headed to the shower. She stepped into the bathroom and locked the door then turned the shower on to let it heat up. She started to strip. Taking off her saturated socks. Peeling off the trousers that were stuck to her. She pulled her jumper, arms crossed over her body, up and over her head. As she tossed it aside onto the pile of wet clothes, she watched a tiny heart-shaped seedpod from the shepherd's purse, a stowaway from the doctor's surgery, fall from a concealed cloth fold and land silently on the cold tile floor by her feet. As the room filled with steam, as the mirror fogged up, Cara let the door of her heart open a crack. And the tears came again.

THIRTEEN

'You okay?' Daithí asked as Cara opened the car door. She threw a towel onto the driver's seat and sat in. She put the key in the ignition, started the car.

'I had to tell Mamó,' she replied, turning on the lights and the wipers.

'Was it bad?'

'She was stoic.'

Daithí nodded.

Cara started down the drive. Snow that had accumulated on the roof and windscreens fell off the car as large sheets, landing with muffled thumps as she moved off. She stopped at the gate, her foot on the brake. She turned to Daithí.

'Mamó told me something curious though.'

'What was that?'

'Maura stopped by yesterday – probably after you saw her. She wanted to see me, was anxious about something, and very curiously, she had a package with her. Something she wanted to show me.'

'A package?' Daithí's eyes narrowed.

'Yeah, Mamó had no idea what it was. Does that mean anything to you?'

'No, afraid not.'

'I was thinking that maybe we should stop by Maura's place now, secure it if necessary, and maybe just look and see if there's anything amiss. See if we can find this mystery package. We should do it now. Breaking the bad news can wait a bit longer.'

'Yeah, no problem. That sounds wise.'

Cara took her foot off the brake and turned left out of the gate. Took the road to Maura's. Like Cara's and the Flaherty's house, Maura's home was a little outside one of the island villages. She'd inherited her grandmother's cottage, on the same land as her parents' place. The second wave of snow hadn't started yet, but the wind was still as strong. Cara needed to hold firm to the steering wheel to make sure she wasn't pushed off the road.

'What if we find something there?' asked Daithí.

'We'll deal with it. In fact, I hope we do find something, Daithí, I'd love to know what the hell is going on. Don't you?'

She risked a half glance at Daithí.

'STOP!' he roared. Cara whipped her attention back, to front and centre. A figure was in the middle of the road. She slammed on the brakes. The car skidded and spun on a river of snow and ice and loose gravel, careering towards whoever it was. Inches from the unflinching spectre, the car stopped.

Cara jumped out, slamming the door behind her.

'YOU ALMIGHTY FOOL!' she roared, rounding the car to confront the figure on the road.

A young man, as drenched as she had been until recently, stared back at her, eyes wide with alarm, as if only just aware now of the car that had been speeding towards him. Stopping only inches from him. Cara knew him, like everyone knew everyone on this island. Patrick Kelly. He was a difficult, withdrawn young man. Cara had cautioned him in the past over drug use, but not for a few years now. Maura, his teacher at one point – like she had been to most of the kids under a certain age – had said he had a good heart under it all. Though she would have said that. Maura had believed everyone had a good heart under it all. How wrong she'd been.

'Patrick! What the hell are you doing? You can't be out here in this weather. Nearly getting us all killed!'

The young man was silent.

'Patrick, are you listening to me?'

He remained mute.

'Are you okay? Can I take you home?'

'It hisses, but only I can hear it,' he mumbled, looking through her.

'What's that, Patrick?'

'It hisses, if you listen.' He looked at Cara, then started to take some steps back.

'What hisses?' asked Cara. She could see his pupils were dilated. It looked like he might be having trouble with drugs again.

A voice in the back of her exhausted, distraught mind whispered to Cara – *You know what hisses? A serpent.*

'Patrick. Were you up at the Serpent's Lair this morning?' Cara remembered the flash of movement she'd seen this morning, up on the cliffside. 'Was that you? Do you know something?'

He looked at her, eyes more focused for a moment.

'Stay away from me.' Patrick turned and ran, skidding and slipping on stones. He threw himself over a low stone wall and ran faster than he looked capable of.

Cara took off after him.

'Come back! Come back!' Cara skidded on the same stones, and fell, the efforts of the last few hours taking their toll. She scrambled up and kept going, stopping at the wall. Frantically scanned the fields, the white expanse. But he was nowhere to be seen.

She heard the car door slam and the rapid approach of footsteps. Daithí appeared beside her.

'What's happening?'

'Patrick Kelly. He was high, I think, acting really weird. And he was going on about something that hisses – I asked him if he was at the Serpent's Lair this morning. And he just took off.'

'He is pretty out of it most of the time, Cara.'

'I know, but I thought I saw someone. On the cliff at the Serpent's Lair, Daithí...'

'Where is he now? Where'd he go?'

'He legged it that way, over the wall. But he's disappeared – I can't see him! There's not a feature on this barren bloody island for miles yet he's completely disappeared.' Cara threw her hands up. Which only let darting icicles of snow slip down her cuff onto bare skin. She shivered.

She surveyed the fields. Put her hands on top of the low wall. Tested its stability.

'Don't go after him, Cara. Like the rest of us, he isn't going anywhere. He lives in that caravan near Seamus's, you can track him down there, when you get a chance.'

'But—'

'Cara, you've only just got warm and dry. Let's keep going to Maura's. Anyway, he's a strange kid, but I can't see him being capable of killing someone. He was probably raving and you're, understandably, reading things into it.'

'I saw someone up there this morning, Daithí.'

'I believe you, but running after him through the fields – look at the bloody drifts over there – it's a fool's errand. You need to be smart about this. Pick your battles. C'mon, let's get back in the car. We're getting hypothermia out here.'

Cara took one last look out over the fields. Daithí was right.

Running after the boy through the snow wasn't the smart choice.

'Alright. Let's go.'

Cara pulled up outside Maura's house.

She and Daithí got out of the car and walked up the drive.

'Don't touch anything if you can help it,' she said to Daithí, as he pulled up his hood.

'Sure.'

'Maybe you can walk around the property and I'll check the house itself?'

'Okay, will do.'

A noise grabbed their attention. Cara whipped her head around.

A rustle by the garden wall.

'What the—' gasped Cara.

From under a snow-capped gorse bush a brown rabbit dashed across the garden, disappearing into the undergrowth.

'Jesus,' she hissed.

Daithí placed a hand on her back.

'Breathe.'

Cara nodded her head.

'Bloody rabbit. My heart... it's thumping.'

'Mine too.'

Cara looked at the bush the rabbit had darted from. Took a deep breath. She had a feeling there would be bigger surprises in store for them.

'Okay, let's do this.'

Daithí headed left, and began a search of the garden. Cara walked around the entirety of the house. It was a small old cottage, Maura's grandmother's originally. In the summer, an unruly abundance of pink fuchsia and flame orange montbretia surrounded it. But now nothing could be seen under the snowdrifts. The only colour at all were dashes of red from the painted window sills. The snow, which had been threatening, had started to fall. Cara was thankful for the relative shelter from it at the back of the house. She'd checked the front door and all the windows before coming back here. There had been no signs of damage or forced entry. Now she was at the back door. No signs here either. Any footsteps in the snow had been hidden by fresh snow. The only thing amiss was Maura's bike. It was propped against the wall by the back door. Maura would have put it away, in the shed, especially if there was a storm coming. It was her main mode of transport about the island and she looked after it. To Cara, this looked like Maura'd been in a hurry or interrupted.

Cara stared in the window of the back door. Everything looked as it should from this angle. She took out a pair of latex gloves from her inner jacket pocket, spares she'd picked up at the doctor's surgery, and tried the handle. It didn't budge. She looked at the ground, to the left of the back door. Locating the bulge of a submerged plant pot under the snow, Cara's hand sank into the snow and found it. She tipped it up, revealing the spare key hidden underneath.

Cara's heart rate, which had leapt at the fright caused by the bunny, hadn't settled. And now, with the key in hand, she could feel its accelerated pulse vibrate throughout her entire body. Her hands were shaking. Her fingertips tingled.

'Heya,' Daithí trotted around from the front of the house, 'nothing strange that I can see about the place.'

'Okay, thanks,' Cara replied.

'We going in?' he asked, nodding at the key in her hand.

'No, not really. I'm just going to open the door and step in. But I won't go any further. It could well be a crime scene. If this is where...' Cara paused, she couldn't bring herself to say the words. *If this is where she was killed.*

With a shaking hand she inserted the key and opened the

door. She stepped into the house, stopping just inside the door. Cara looked around the open-plan room. A beautiful light and airy space, with an unexpectedly modern look, so at odds with the cottagey exterior. It looked the same. Cara felt it should look different. Somehow altered now that Maura was no longer with them, that it couldn't possibly look and feel the same without her. But treacherously, it felt just as it always had.

'Can you see anything strange?' asked Daithí, standing at the kitchen window, peering in.

Cara surveyed the entire space from the doorway, where she stayed rooted. She turned 180 degrees. But nothing screamed out at her. Nothing was upturned, nothing out of place, it looked just as it always did. The Wi-Fi router in the corner wasn't blinking, but hadn't Maura told Ferdia and Sorcha that it wasn't working? Without it, Maura had been cut off. No cellular signal and no Wi-Fi made her phone useless. Made her vulnerable. Cara felt a chill. Her poor friend. If this was where it'd happened, she'd have been unable to call anyone for help. Had that been deliberate?

'No, nothing out of place,' she replied to Daithí.

Cara looked to her left, at the window sill beside her. Sitting atop a pile of letters and newspapers was a snow globe. Her shoulders sagged and her tummy lurched at the sight of it. She had given it to Maura, years ago, as kids. Maura usually kept it on the shelf in her bathroom. Cara picked it up in her gloved hand and shook it. A cloud of glittery snow swirled and swam, two figures caught within it. A snowstorm encased in a glass globe, contained, unlike the one that raged for real outside. Gradually the flakes settled, and the two figures, hugging friends – the reason Cara had given the cheap holiday memento to Maura – were revealed once again. Cara wished it was that simple. That when the storm moved on, her friend would be revealed again, together once more.

She placed it back down on the folded newspaper. But she

continued to stare at it. Why was it here and not in the bathroom? It sort of felt like a message. Did Maura want to tell her something? But what? Something about the storm? Cara couldn't think what the message might be.

'Oh hi, guys. What you doing here?'

A voice from behind them made Cara jump.

'Bloody hell,' she gasped, turning around.

Ferdia. Wrapped up in a weird mishmash of layers, all looking like they'd come from the charity box of a farmer. From a couple of decades ago. His feet in green, ancient wellies. The normally stylish Ferdia looked so ridiculous that despite everything Cara laughed.

'Gee thanks, Cara. Kick a guy while he's down.'

'You look so...'

'Ridiculous. I know. But Sorcha and I didn't pack for snowmageddon. I found this lot in a bag at the back of the wardrobe. Old man Flaherty's, I imagine.'

'I think so,' said Daithí.

'Why are you here?' asked Cara. 'It's so horrible out.'

'I thought I'd come find Maura, the lazy heifer. See why she's been giving us the cold shoulder.'

At the mention of Maura, the spark of good humour that had surfaced at Ferdia's ridiculous get-up vanished. Cara pulled the back door shut, and locked it. Popped the key in her pocket. She looked at Daithí, and then back to Ferdia.

'Question for you, Ferdia. When you and Sorcha dropped by here, the first day you were back in town, and the Wi-Fi wasn't working, did Maura say anything about that to you? Like, why it wasn't working?'

Ferdia laughed.

'Yeah, that's a funny one. Apparently the neighbour's cat wandered in and peed on it. Maura said there were sparks and everything.'

'Goodness,' said Cara. Well, that answered that. Not

sinister then. Cara had more questions, though. 'How did you find her then? She seem okay?'

Ferdia looked at her, puzzled.

'Why do you ask?'

'I'll explain in a minute.'

'Okay.' Ferdia eyed her suspiciously. 'She was the same old Maura. Like, we didn't stay long. It was just a flying visit. It would have been even quicker if we hadn't stayed for the cat sabotage story.' A smile played on his lips at the memory.

'Okay, thanks.'

Cara took a few steps away from the house.

'Is she not there?' asked Ferdia.

'No,' said Daithí.

'And why all the questions?'

'Hmm,' said Cara. 'Why don't you come join us in the car? We're heading back to Flaherty's now anyway.'

'Cara, where's Maura?' he asked, not moving.

'Come on,' she said, leading the way around the house. 'I'll explain on the way.' She'd tell him in the car, on the way back to the house. It would mean she'd have to do it all again when she saw Seamus and Sorcha, but Ferdia deserved more than misdirecting small talk.

'Fine,' said Ferdia, following them. 'So what happened this morning then? It was a prank, right? I've a fiver riding on it with Seamus.'

FOURTEEN

With the return of the blizzards, Cara needed every ounce of concentration to stay steady on the roads. But hard as it was, she preferred the idea of driving. Of staying on the roads, going round and round the island. Battling with the storm was forcing out all other thoughts from her head. The ones she didn't want there. If she kept driving then maybe by the time the storm broke in two days it wouldn't hurt quite so awfully as it did now.

Heading along the coast road, she knew they'd pass Patrick Kelly's battered little caravan before getting to the Flaherty house. She slowed as they got near and turned her head to look up at the small dwelling, but she didn't stop. With a shocked and silent Ferdia in the back of the car, she wanted to get the telling to the others over with. She'd head to Patrick's later, when she had a chance.

She pulled into the Flahertys' drive and parked. But not at the front door. Already there was an unfamiliar navy van.

'Who does that belong to?' Cara asked.

'I think that's Noah Jackson's rental,' said Daithí.

'Oh, great, that's all we need right now.'

Cara and Daithí got out of the car. They looked in at the

grey-faced Ferdia still in the back seat. Cara opened the rear passenger door.

'Come on, Ferdia. We need to go inside.'

Without a word, he got out and followed them as they headed towards the back of the house, and the back door.

As they passed the living room window, they stopped.

In the window stood Seamus. And a second, identical Seamus. Cara looked at an equally confused Daithí and then back in the window. One of the Seamuses smiled and waved at them. The double frowned and turned to look at him.

'What on earth?' said Cara.

They headed to the back of the house. Pushed open the back door. American accents greeted them. The room was loud and full. Among them Cara spotted a face she recognised, Noah Jackson, the director, over by the fire. He looked up as they came into the kitchen.

'Oh, hi!' he said, a smile lighting up his face as he spotted Cara. 'Sergeant. It's good to see you again.'

Seamus... and his double... turned around from the window.

'Cara,' said Seamus. 'You're back.'

Cara stared at the man beside him.

'I don't think you've met Aiden yet.' The two of them walked over. Closer up, it was easier to see differences. This guy was a good decade younger than Seamus. But it was still startling.

'What do you think? My twin, no? Aiden's playing me in the movie.'

'It's... unnerving,' said Cara.

Daithí put out a hand. 'It's good to meet you, Aiden.'

'Thanks,' the young man said. 'It's great to meet you all as well. An honour to be involved in this project.'

'No one else is quite as identical,' said Seamus, 'but let me introduce you to everyone.' Seamus turned to the film crowd.

'Lexi, Ari, Kyle, Will, want to come over and meet the gang?'
Four of the group broke away and came over to the kitchen.

'Cara, this is Lexi, she's playing you.' Cara looked at the
actress. She had red hair, but that's where any similarity ended.
Her sallow skin and hazel eyes were entirely Mediterranean.
And as pretty as Cara was, Lexi was a different league. Cara
noticed her slip her hand into Aiden's.

'And this is Will and Kyle. Ferdia and Daithí
respectively.'

'Is it not pronounced Die-tee?' asked Kyle, looking at
Seamus with a frown.

'*Daaawh-he*, Kyle, *Daaawh-he*... come on, I've told you this a
few times already.'

'And finally, this is Ari, she's playing Sorcha.'

'Hi!' The petite blonde actress smiled at them.

'Where is Sorcha?' asked Cara.

'She just went down to her room, to get away from the
chaos,' said Seamus.

'Right,' said Cara. She looked around the room. This wasn't
the set-up she'd expected to find when she got back here. She
needed some quiet.

'No Maura?' asked Ferdia quietly. The first thing he'd said
since Cara and Daithí had broken the news to him. Cara turned
and looked at him.

'We haven't cast her yet, and the scenes we're hoping to film
this week won't require her character...'

Ferdia nodded.

Noah trotted over.

'We were just about to rehearse a scene. Would you like to
watch?' He tapped Will and Aiden's arms and beckoned them
back to the fireplace.

'No, actually...' began Cara, but Noah wasn't listening.
Muttering directions to the two actors, he placed them in position, stood back and barked, 'And, action!'

The kitchen door opened and the two actors paused. All eyes turned and looked at Sorcha as she came in.

'Oh, sorry,' she said.

'No worries,' said Noah with a strained smile. 'Let's try that again.' Everyone resumed positions. 'And... action!'

Aiden – Seamus of ten years ago – started his lines.

'Look, Ferdia, I'm sorry, I'm asking Maura out on a date and you can't stop me. She likes me, not you.' Aiden stepped forward, pointed a finger at Will. He put his hands up and backed off.

'Sorry, Seamus. I didn't mean to step on your toes. Forgive me.' Will turned away, his face a picture of anguish.

'Oh God,' muttered Daithí under his breath. Cara stepped forward. Opened her mouth to speak, to stop this. But Ferdia got there first.

'That never happened,' he said. Everyone stopped and looked at him. Noah looked very irritated at this second interruption.

'It's artistic licence, Ferdia,' said Seamus, from across the room.

'It's not artistic licence to make me look like a fool. Change that.'

'Is this really important right now, Ferdia?' asked Cara. 'Seriously?'

Ferdia glowered at her.

'Ah, well,' stammered Noah. 'We can't really be tampering with the script just because people don't like certain bits.'

'I'll tamper with you,' said Ferdia, taking a step towards the director.

'Ferdia, stop,' said Sorcha, crossing the room and grabbing his arm. He shook her off.

'Get off,' he snarled at his wife.

'Stop it, everyone,' bellowed Daithí. The room fell silent, Daithí's uncharacteristic outburst grabbing all attention.

'Sorcha, Seamus, we've something we need to tell you.' Cara looked at her friends. She eyed up the film crew. She didn't really want to do this in front of them.

'Is there any way you guys could clear out for a bit, please?'

Noah looked confused.

'Leave?'

'Please,' said Cara.

'Cara, no, they're not going anywhere – look at it out there,' said Seamus, pointing at the heavy snow falling outside. He turned to the crew. 'Look, stay, don't worry.'

He looked back at Cara.

'Whatever needs saying, the crew here are documenting my authentic life, they can stay and hear it.'

'Seamus, you don't want that, honestly.'

'Really, it's okay, don't worry.'

Cara sighed. She'd no more energy for this. She took a deep breath.

'It's about the call that came in this morning.'

'About the body in the Serpent's Lair?' asked Sorcha, her tone not quite as blasé as Seamus.

'Don't worry, Sorcha, that was a prank phone call, right, Cara?'

'I'm afraid it was no prank,' said Cara, quietly.

'What?' asked Seamus.

'Really?' said Sorcha, eyes wide, incredulous.

Cara nodded. She looked at Daithí. I hate this, she thought. This is where it all changes. For everyone. There is a before, and an after. You slip between alternate universes. You move to a less kind one. Where someone you love is gone and the reality you thought you had is forever lost. She herself had been unwillingly pulled from one universe to the next once before. She hated doing this to her friends. But it had to be done. Even with those stupid actors in the background, the stakes non-existent for them. They'd probably feed off it like emotional vampires, saving it up for their next performance.

'There was a body,' she said. 'And now I've the hardest message ever to deliver.'

Cara paused. Looked around at the expectant faces.

'She's gone.' Cara took a deep breath. 'The body... It was Maura.'

There was silence. All faces staring at her. On Seamus and Sorcha's faces comprehension came slowly, like a creeping glacier. Changing everyone's landscape forever in its wake.

'Which one was she...?' began Aiden by the fire, a swift nudge from Will shutting him up.

Seamus pulled out a kitchen chair and fell rather than sat into it. Sorcha looked from them to Cara and back again. Ferdia headed for one of the armchairs, slumped into it, ignoring the actors standing awkwardly around him.

'What?' Sorcha said, the first to speak.

'Maura is dead,' said Daithí. 'There's no easier way to put it.'

Seamus's sob took everyone by surprise. A jagged, gulping, shattering sob. His face collapsed into his hands.

'How?' Sorcha whispered.

'We don't know yet.' Her friends needed to know that Maura was dead, but they didn't need to know any more details. It wasn't just because of police procedure, but it might help them preserve her memory better. She didn't want to share with them the shattered body, beaten and bruised, frozen, that would be her last memory of Maura. That was a burden she would share only with Daithí, and she was sorry that he had to be part of it. He hadn't signed up for that.

Sorcha pulled out a chair and sat down.

'Wow.'

'Wow? What kind of reaction is that?' said Ferdia from the armchair, still blanched pale. '*Wow.*'

'I'm shocked!' Sorcha retorted, turning to look at him.

'Shocked? You barely look like you care.'

'Of course I care! Not as much as you, obviously,' she spat.

'It doesn't look like it.'

'I saw her for the first time in ten years a couple of days ago, it's not as if we were close any more. But I'm sorry she's dead, okay? Is that okay with you?'

'What on earth?' Ferdia sat forward, his eyes blasting from paralysed to blazing. 'She was one of our best friends! How can you be so cold?'

'I'm not being cold!' Sorcha threw her hands up. 'And you're wrong, she wasn't one of our best friends! Best friends are people you see all the time. People you hang out with. People who actually care about you. Stace and Lucy from work are my best friends. Maura Conneely was someone from a long time ago, who wasn't that nice to me then, and did nothing since to make me feel any better. Quite the opposite, in fact.'

'Jesus, Sorcha,' said Cara, as if the wind had been knocked out of her. 'We just found her body a few hours ago.'

'Ah, there you go, the Maura groupie! Maura and Cara, Cara and Maura. You thought the sun shone out of her ass! She didn't give a damn about me!'

'Maura cares... cared about everyone,' said Cara, straining to keep her tone even. 'It's not true that she didn't give a damn about you, Sorcha. Not true at all.'

'Listen to you! Of course you're defending her. St Maura of Inis Mór could do no wrong in your eyes... You'd be surprised, Cara. Very surprised. The things I know about her. The secrets – the truth I could tell you about Maura Conneely.'

FIFTEEN

Seamus passed a glass with a finger of whiskey over to Cara. She took a grateful sip from it. Daithí appeared from the hallway and sat down on the sofa beside them.

'The crew gone?' he asked.

A dour Seamus nodded. 'I asked them to pack up.'

'Okay, thanks. Sorcha says she's going to stay down there, for the moment. She's going to lie down. She took something she said her doctor had prescribed for her?' Daithí looked at Ferdia, who nodded. He then turned to Cara. 'It's the shock, Cara. Don't mind what she said. I know she didn't mean a word of it.'

'I agree with Daithí,' said Seamus. 'It's the shock. Like... I mean...' He just shook his head. The writer among them, even he had no words enough to express the horror they were all feeling. He handed Daithí a glass and topped it up with whiskey.

'Is she okay, generally?' asked Daithí, looking at Ferdia. 'Why has she a prescription? You two haven't seemed that happy the last few days.'

'She's fine,' said Ferdia. 'We're fine.' *End of discussion* was left hanging in the air.

Cara stood up and went over to the fridge. She grabbed some leftovers, a loaf of bread, some cheese, and carried them back to the fireplace, with plates and knives and forks. She knelt down on the fireside rug and started organising a simple meal. The sun was already setting and the room was getting dark. The smell of damp turf burning in the fire filled the room. The ceiling light flickered. Everyone looked up.

'Not the electricity too,' said Seamus.

'I'm surprised it's held out this long,' said Daithí. 'Do you have any torches, candles, just in case?'

'I'm sure there are candles at least.'

'What happened to her?' Ferdia's empty voice cut through the practical chatter. 'You haven't said.'

'It was an accident,' said Seamus quietly, looking at Cara with heartbroken eyes. 'Right?'

'Well. Maybe not.'

'What?' asked Ferdia, the words molasses-slow from his mouth. 'Of course it was an accident, Cara, because... because otherwise...' The sentence was left. No one wanted to hear the rest of the words said out loud.

'Cara? What on earth?' said Seamus, glass paused halfway to his mouth. Frozen mid-air.

'Guys, I can't give you details. You have to understand that,' Cara pleaded.

'You can't just dump something like that on us and then say no more.' Ferdia stood up. Stared at Cara with a frightening intensity.

'Calm down,' said Daithí. 'This isn't Cara's fault. She has a job to do.'

Ferdia glowered and sat. Slipped back into a morose silence. Cara offered him a plate of food, a peace offering, which he took without looking and just left on his lap. He sipped his whiskey.

'Seamus? Something to eat?'

'Sure, thanks, you're a treasure.' She handed over a plate.

Daithí was next and gratefully accepted the food. The noise of quiet eating filled the room. No one knew what to say. Cara was jealous of Sorcha, slipping into a chemical sleep, away from the harsh reality of what had happened.

'Is there anything we could do? Can we help?' Seamus said eventually. Cara sat back on her heels, placed a slice of bread down on the plate beside her.

'I don't suppose she said anything to any of you at the pub, the other night?' Cara looked around the room at Daithí, Ferdia and Seamus. 'And how was her form?'

'She was fine, normal,' said Seamus. 'But we hadn't seen her in so long, we mightn't be able to tell if she was "off" somehow.'

Cara turned to Daithí.

'How did you find her?'

Daithí thought about the question.

'She was fine. Her normal self. Maybe she was a little quiet on the way home, but she was tired, so it didn't strike me as odd, or worrying in any way.'

'What about yesterday, Seamus? How was she?'

'Yesterday?' Seamus frowned. 'We didn't see her yesterday.'

'Mamó said she saw her here. In the morning, at the door talking to you.'

'Really?' Seamus raised his eyebrows. He shook his head. 'No, she didn't call by. Last I saw Maura was at Daithí's, the night before. With everyone else.'

'Really? Okay, I'll have to ask Mamó about that again.' Mamó wasn't as young as she used to be, and had a habit of not wearing her glasses.

'There's something else I want to ask you,' said Cara. 'Maura came looking for me yesterday morning. Daithí, you saw her cycle by the pub around then too and you said she seemed distracted and didn't wave at you like you normally would? Well, Mamó said she seemed worried. She had a package with her. Something wrapped up in old tatty paper. She wanted to show this to me for some reason. Does that mean anything to you? Have you any idea what that package might have been or why she was worried? She never found me so I'm clueless.'

Seamus shook his head.

'Sorry, no idea.'

'Ferdia?' Cara looked at him. He stared into the fire. Then turned to look at her, saying nothing.

'Ferdia, does this mean anything to you?' Cara repeated herself, in case he hadn't taken it in. 'Can you help?'

Ferdia lifted the untouched plate of food off his lap, placing it on the coffee table. He then stood, and walked past Seamus, knocking against his legs, sending food slipping off the plate onto Seamus's lap and the sofa cushion.

'Watch it,' snapped Seamus, but Ferdia walked out of the room without a word.

A minute later, they heard a car starting.

'Is that my car? The squad car?' asked Cara, jumping to her feet. There weren't any other cars at the property. She got to the window just in time to see Ferdia leaving the driveway in her car. 'It is!'

The other two joined her at the window.

'What is he doing?' said Seamus.

'God knows,' said Daithí.

The crunch of tyres on the snow alerted them to Ferdia's return. Daithí and Cara, on their knees searching the back of the low cupboards for candles, got up. Seamus came back into the kitchen.

'Was that a car? Is he back?' he said.

'Sounds like it,' said Cara, coming round the counter. She glanced back at the clock. He'd been gone nearly an hour.

They heard the front door open then slam, and Ferdia's footsteps stomp down the corridor toward his room. After a moment, Ferdia's raised voice could be heard, though the words weren't clear.

'What's he at?' said Daithí. 'Is he yelling at Sorcha? That's not on.' He headed for the kitchen door.

'No, don't, Daithí. I'll go,' said Cara, her hand on his arm. Daithí paused reluctantly. Cara shook her head.

She walked down the hall and stopped at the closed door to their room. Raised a hand to knock, but paused. Ferdia's angry voice was clearer here. Cara could make out a lot of what he was saying. 'Did you tell her? I don't know who else it could have been, do you? You've no idea what you're messing around with.' What was that about? Cara leaned her ear closer to the door. Inside, a sleepy and confused-sounding Sorcha wailed, 'I don't know what you're talking about.' Ferdia, slightly quieter now, replied, 'Sure you don't. Maura was murdered, did you know that? It wasn't an accident.' Cara couldn't make out what was said next. But then she heard footsteps. Approaching fast. She jumped back. The door flew open. A furious and surprised Ferdia stopped in his tracks, then sidestepped Cara and stormed off down the hall. A teary Sorcha was sitting up in the bed, rubbing her eyes.

'Are you okay?' asked Cara.

Sorcha looked at her miserably.

'Can I come in?' Cara asked and Sorcha nodded. Cara walked over to the bed and sat down on the end.

Sorcha sniffled.

'I'm okay.'

'Ferdia was out of control there. Would you like me to ask him to leave? Do you feel safe with him here?'

Sorcha shook her head.

'No, no. It's fine. He's just upset. He'll calm down.'

'Are you sure?'

She nodded.

'I couldn't help but overhear some of what he said,' Cara

said, keeping her tone casual. 'What was he asking you? He seemed pretty cross.'

'I wish I knew. I don't know what he was on about.' Sorcha shook her head. 'He's just upset,' she repeated.

'We're all upset,' said Cara. Sorcha looked genuinely puzzled. She pulled her legs under her and ran a hand through her hair. She looked directly at Cara.

'Was she really murdered? Maura?'

Cara nodded. 'I'm afraid so.'

'Do you know who did it?'

'No. I haven't a clue what's going on, if I'm honest.'

'Are we in danger, Cara?' Sorcha snatched a quick look out the window, the dark early evening was already setting in. 'I'm not sure I like this. At all. We're sitting ducks.'

'Sorcha, there's no evidence that we need to be worried. These kinds of crimes, they tend to be personal, not random.'

'If it's personal, Cara, then we might be at risk. We're her friends!' Sorcha's eyes darted from the door back to the window.

'I think you made the point earlier that you guys weren't quite so close. You won't need to worry.'

Sorcha looked away. Twisted and pulled at a strand of her messy hair.

'Look, Cara,' she said without meeting Cara's eyes. 'I'm sorry about what I said earlier. I shouldn't have...' Sorcha took a deep breath and looked up. 'I was always jealous of you two. And jealous of how happy the pair of you were with Cillian and Seamus. And even though Maura and Seamus were always breaking up and all that, it was so very Heathcliff and Cathy. It just seemed so romantic. Not like me and Ferdia. I sometimes wonder if we just paired up because we were the last two on our own. Ferdia always fancied Maura more than me, you know?'

'Did he?' asked Cara, surprised. 'I don't think so, I never saw that.'

Sorcha looked at Cara long and hard.

'There were lots of things you didn't see.'

'Let's not go there again.'

'I'm sorry, Cara. She wasn't perfect.'

'I never claimed she was.' Cara stood. 'As long as you're okay, I'll let you get back to sleep.'

The bedside lamp and ceiling light flickered. A strong gust of wind rattled the windows. The lights flickered once again and then, with one last blink, they went out. Plunging the room into complete darkness.

'Shit,' said Sorcha, jumping off the bed. 'Someone's cut the lights! Where are you?'

Cara reached out and grasped for her hand, felt Sorcha jump in fright at the touch in the pitch black. Sorcha screamed.

'Sorcha! Sorcha, it's okay, it's just me. Take a few breaths. And it's just the storm, that's all. No one's cut the lights. You lived here long enough to remember all the power cuts. This is normal.'

'You don't know that! You said it was personal, someone might be here, coming for us!'

'Come here.' Cara drew Sorcha towards her, turned her in the dark to face where the window should be, not that either of them could see anything. 'Look, there's no lights out there either. The whole island has gone dark. It's the storm, that's all. Don't worry.'

'Well... maybe, but God, Cara,' Sorcha began to cry, 'we're stuck on this island and there's, there's some psycho out there and he killed, k-k-killed Maura.' The rest of her words were lost to gasps and sobs. Her breathing erratic and shallow.

The sound of the kitchen door being opened and rushed footsteps came from the hall.

'Are you okay in there? We thought we heard a scream.' Seamus, Daithí and Ferdia appeared at the bedroom door. Candles in hand, illuminating their faces like ghouls.

'Are you okay?' Daithí handed Cara a candle. Seamus put his arm around the quivering Sorcha.

'I think it's just a bit of a panic attack, which is understandable,' said Cara.

'Come on, Sorcha, come to the kitchen,' said Seamus. 'Daithí just made a pot of tea before the power went, we'll get you a mug.'

'Or perhaps just pop another pill, hey,' said Ferdia, sneering at his wife.

'Ferdia, please,' said Cara.

'She needs to calm the hell down.'

'I think everyone needs to calm down.' Daithí stared at Ferdia in the gloom, challenging him. Ferdia turned and walked out of the room. Like a procession at midnight mass, the others followed, back down to the kitchen.

The kitchen was suffused in the soft comforting glow of candlelight. Clusters of candles by the fire, on the kitchen table and dotted about the room continued the ambience of church, and a solemnness that felt appropriate. Soft elongated shadows stretched into the room. Cara sat on the sofa, next to Daithí. Seamus sat down in an armchair. Cara kept an eye as Sorcha approached Ferdia who was lingering in the kitchen area. Their body language was tense, but an unspoken truce seemed to be agreed. The pair of them came over.

'Where'd you go in my car, Ferdia?' asked Cara, looking at him in the gloom.

'Out.'

'Right.'

'You took her car, dude, a bit of respect, no?' said Seamus. 'And you left us here, defenceless against whatever psycho did this.'

'The car wouldn't have been much use to you,' Ferdia sniped back.

'Would have been nice to have the option to get away quickly.'

'Cut it out. Let's drop it. We're all upset, we don't need to all be fighting,' said Cara.

'Because we've got bigger things to worry about?' asked Sorcha. 'You said we didn't need to worry about him coming for us.'

'No, Sorcha, we don't... whoever it was, probably isn't going to trouble us.'

'Probably?' snapped Ferdia. 'Probably? That'll be good to know when I've a knife in my effing back!'

'Calm down. Please, guys. This is helping no one. Keep the doors locked, keep an eye on each other, mind each other. Once I know anything I'll share it, don't worry, I'll keep you safe. But right now we need to pull ourselves together.'

'Who did it, Cara?' asked Seamus, tearing up again. 'Who hurt her?'

'I don't know, Seamus, but I'm going to find out. And they'll be sorry, don't you worry.'

Sniffling, Seamus stood and retrieved the bottle of whiskey, and seven glasses. He brought them over to the fire and handed everyone a glass. He placed two down by the fireside, filling them first, then went round to each of the friends and poured a few fingers of whiskey into each of their glasses. Standing in the centre of the circle around the fire formed by the sofa and armchairs, he raised his glass.

'To Maura, and to Cillian.' His voice cracked. He then turned and gently clinked his glass against the two set by the hearth.

'To Maura, to Cillian,' the gang joined in.

Sorcha quietly began to sing.

> *'Tis the last rose of summer,*
> *Left blooming alone;*

All her lovely companions,
Are faded and gone;
No flower of her kindred,
No rosebud is nigh,
To reflect back her blushes,
Or give sigh for sigh!

I'll not leave thee, thou lone one,
To pine on the stem;
Since the lovely are sleeping,
Go, sleep thou with them;
Thus kindly I scatter,
Thy leaves o'er the bed,
Where thy mates of the garden,
Lie scentless and dead.

So soon may I follow,
When friendships decay,
And from love's shining circle,
The gems drop away!
When true hearts lie withered,
And fond ones are flown,
Oh! who would inhabit,
This bleak world alone?

The words of the last verse stuck in Cara's ears. ... *true hearts lie withered... fond ones are flown.*
When friendships decay...

SIXTEEN

Cara entered Cillian's room in the dark, the glow of the candle not stretching far. She set it down on the bedside table. She could have used the torch on her phone, but with the electricity gone, she needed to save every last bit of battery life.

She was exhausted. Too tired now to even be sad. Or scared. She was spent. She kicked off her shoes and took off her leggings, but otherwise touched nothing and climbed into bed. She looked at the door and considered getting out of bed again, pulling the chair over from the desk and jamming it under the handle. But given the state of the furniture in this house, the chair would probably crack with the slightest shove. And was she just absorbing too much of Sorcha's panic anyway? Surely they weren't at risk? Cara decided to stay in bed and not bother. She hadn't bothered closing the curtains either. What point was there when there was no light to keep out or let in?

They'd all quietly gone off to bed. Daithí had decided to risk trekking back to his pub. With its own generator, it had stayed open. He didn't want to leave Courtney in charge any longer, he felt he'd already asked too much of her.

Cara blew out the candle and rested her head on the pillow.

The tendrils of acrid smoke lingering as her eyes adjusted to the darkness. She stared in the direction of the window. On a clear night it would be beautiful, the stars in the night sky sparkling all the brighter out here, on the island. Tonight instead, there was just muddy darkness, malevolent shapes of clouds half visible. She couldn't make out a single feature on the landscape, this was the darkness of an ancient past. In the room, what little light existed revealed a censored topography. The desk under the window, the shelves on the wall. The slatted wardrobe doors. All just about visible in the near pitch black.

Cara's eyes quickly grew heavy and her last thoughts as she fell asleep were a plea to her subconscious for no dreams.

Cara took a moment to come back to the land of the living. Sleep had come quickly and now, as consciousness once more gained ascendancy, no disturbing dreams came with it. But it wasn't morning. The lack of dreams seemed more a symptom of the shortness of her time asleep, no time to enter that cycle of circadian rhythm, not a favour granted by a sympathetic subconscious. Cara reached out for her phone, knowing she'd placed it on the bedside locker. Her fingers fumbled, then found it. She pressed the home button and it came alive, like a flash grenade in the pitch black. The nanosecond before its brightness reduced Cara's already limited vision to just the phone screen, she'd seen something.

Her sleepy subconscious translated it.

In the window. There'd been something.

No. *Someone.*

Two eyes. Staring in at her. Even with the non-existent light, she knew what she'd seen.

Cara leapt out of bed. She rushed to the window, bashing her leg on the desk in the dark.

'Dammit,' she hissed, rubbing her shin. She looked left, then flicked her head right. Searching. But there was nothing. Nothing now, anyway.

Cara started to shiver and her heart was pounding. She'd told everyone to lock the door, but had they in the end? Whoever had been at her window, were they now rounding the building to come in the back door? Cara grabbed her leggings. Pulled them on, nearly toppling in her haste. She dragged her hoodie over her head and picked up the candle from the bedside. She lit it, then opened her bedroom door and put an ear to the hallway first. No sounds, not even snoring from Ferdia and Sorcha's room tonight. She crept out. Like last night, the sound of her feet on the ground felt cacophonous, her breathing deafening.

She reached the front door. Tried the handle. It was locked. That was something. Cara continued to the kitchen. Pushed the door slowly open. The fire was still glowing a soft orange, casting a small amount of light into the room. Cara looked around, nothing out of place. No one sitting in either armchair tonight, ready to scare her. She looked into the kitchen.

The back door was open.

Only a little bit, but it was definitely open.

Cara spun around, checking the room again, the candle flame flickered with the rush of air. She stopped. There was definitely nobody here. She moved closer to the back door, the cold breeze raising goosebumps on her legs, even through her leggings.

She heard a voice, and then another.

Muffled, rushed and urgent, an angry conversation in Irish. She strained to hear the voices. Who was out there? What was happening? Then three words even the youngest Irish student recognised: '*le do thoil*'. Please. And a second time. Please. Louder this time. Was someone pleading for their life? Cara rushed for the door. But it swung open before she got there and she fell back to avoid being hit by it. The sudden gust of cold air extinguishing her candle, she felt hot wax splash on her hands as the icy gust slapped her cheeks.

'JESUS!' a male voice roared, inches from her, nearly running her over. Cara stumbled backwards, banging into the counter. A torch suddenly shone in her face. She raised her hand, shielding her blinded eyes.

'Stop creeping around in the dark, Cara!' Seamus's voice bawled at her. He pushed past her, and Cara made out a faint outline as he barrelled out of the kitchen, slamming the door behind him. Cara's heart, already racing, pounded, thumping in her chest, trying to escape. She leant over, hands on her knees, willing her breathing to slow. Taking a deep breath, she straightened up and forced herself to the door. Pulled on a pair of boots left there.

She looked out.

Who was outside?

A red glow, a pinprick of light in the darkness, showed her where someone was standing, smoking. Like a beacon on the buoys which rocked violently in the harbour right now, it fixed their location. The fiery end of the cigarette lighting up, flaring, at each intake of breath. The smell of marijuana hung in the freezing air. Cara stepped outside, barely noticing any temperature difference.

'Who's there?' she said, annoyed at the tremble in her voice.

The figure moved.

'Cara, hey. What are you doing up?'

Ferdia.

Cara felt every cell in her body unclench. It was just Ferdia.

'I'm awake because someone was staring in at me from my window.'

'What, seriously?'

'Was it you or Seamus?'

'No, definitely not. We just stepped out here so I could smoke this.'

Ferdia put out the joint.

'And argue, it seems. I'm going to be asking you about that later, but right now, I need to search for whoever might still be on the property.' Cara turned to the corner of the house.

'Hang on, Cara, I'll come with you. I haven't the energy for anyone else getting murdered.'

Ferdia pulled out his phone and switched on its torch. He shone it on the path in front of him. The joint certainly improved his mood, thought Cara as she looked left and right, scouring the area for signs of life. She wasn't sure how she felt about that. His good humour seemed vulgar, disrespectful. At least morose Ferdia was acting appropriately. Not even the argument with Seamus seemed to be upsetting him.

They headed to the front of the house, trudging through the snow. Once around the corner, the wind hit them, and Cara pulled her hood up, tightened its drawstrings. Ferdia huddled close in beside her.

'What was that argument with Seamus all about?' asked Cara as they went.

'What argument?' he replied, his teeth chattering.

'Don't mess with me, Ferdia. You were arguing out here, I heard you both.'

'It's a long story.'

'I bet it is.'

'And it's between him and me. It was nothing.'

'Nothing?'

'Maybe focus on finding the killer on the loose outside your bedroom right now, Cara.'

Ferdia's voice had gained an edge. Cara dropped it. For now.

They passed the front door and walked down the drive, both of them looking, searching for something in the black night.

'Cara, I'm sorry, this is impossible,' cried Ferdia. 'We might as well be blind.'

'I know,' she called back. They walked back up to the front door.

'Maybe you imagined it. Your brain just playing tricks on you. Thinking you see the monster under the bed.'

'Maybe,' Cara replied, doubt in her tone, still searching the darkness for something. She shivered.

'You've had a pretty shitty day and you're exhausted.'

Cara looked at Ferdia. Listened to his words. Maybe she hadn't seen anything and it had been a figment of her exhausted mind. Perhaps the sounds of Ferdia and Seamus arguing drifted round to her and that's what disturbed her?

'Come on, it's freezing, let's get back inside,' Ferdia said.

Cara looked down the front of the house, towards her window. Instead of following Ferdia, she headed for it.

'Ah, Cara,' whined Ferdia, but he stopped and followed her instead. Cara got to her room, turned to Ferdia.

'Shine your phone down there, would you?' She pointed to the ground at the foot of her window. He did as he was told. They both looked down. And there, unmistakable, deep, crisp and fresh, two footprints sunk into the small drift.

SEVENTEEN

'Did you manage to get back to sleep last night?' asked Ferdia, standing at the counter, pale and red-eyed as if sleep had eluded him.

'Eventually,' said Cara, as she pulled her coat on.

Sorcha, kneeling on the ground in front of the fire, buttering some bread she'd toasted, put down her knife and looked up.

'Did something happen?' she asked, eyes darting from one to the other.

'There was someone outside Cara's window last night,' he said matter-of-factly. Cara could hear the note of anxiety in there somewhere, though. She shook her head, irritated at Ferdia for not taking more care to not alarm Sorcha.

'Somebody was creeping around outside, last night?' Sorcha's voice rose a few pitches. 'Seriously?'

'I might have been wrong...' fudged Cara.

'I don't think the footprints outside your bedroom window just magically appeared,' said Ferdia.

'Oh God,' gasped Sorcha.

'Ferdia!' snapped Cara, which only elicited a shrug from him. Sorcha stood up. She looked from Ferdia to Cara and back.

'We have to leave,' she said, words tumbling over each other. 'I'm getting my things, we're going, going home, getting away from this place. We should never have come back.'

'There's no way off the island, dear,' Ferdia sneered.

'There must be! Cara, there must be an emergency helicopter, something? We can't just stay here waiting to be murdered in our beds!'

'Christ, calm down,' said Ferdia.

Cara shook her head.

'I'm sorry, Sorcha, the weather's too wild, it's too dangerous for boats or planes.'

'But if you tell them, that someone is out there, trying to kill us—'

'Would you stop being such a bloody hysterical cliché, woman. No one is trying to kill us,' said Ferdia.

'I'm not being hysterical, Ferdia, I'm being appropriately terrified! And how do you know they're not trying to kill us? Who was at the window? Were they looking for a way in? To pick off the next of us?'

'For goodness' sake. I'm sorry they didn't succeed with you!'

'Ferdia!' snapped Cara. 'You really aren't helping.' She turned. 'Sorcha, I'm afraid we're on the island until the storm breaks, but that will be soon.'

'When is soon?' asked Ferdia. Despite his dismissal of his wife's fears, he was doing a poor job of fully hiding his own.

'Late tomorrow evening. New Year's Eve. That's the official forecast.' Cara looked out the window at the snow and wind. It seemed hard to imagine it changing by then.

'That's too long! Ferdy, I want to go home now.' Sorcha looked at her husband, tears welling up. He just shook his head. She looked back at Cara. 'Maybe one of the fishermen would risk it? I could ask them...'

'You'll get yourself, and any fool who decides to take you up on that, killed. And I think that's what you're trying to avoid?

Just stay here, keep the doors locked and don't go anywhere on your own. That's the best we can do right now.'

'It doesn't sound like much,' sniffled Sorcha.

The kitchen door opened, making Sorcha jump and Ferdia roll his eyes. Seamus appeared. Like the rest of them, he looked aged in the morning light. Pale despite his Californian tan, with dark circles under his eyes, he looked like he'd added little to the total of hours slept in the house last night.

'Did you know about the killer too?' asked Sorcha.

'What?' asked a confused, barely awake Seamus.

'He was at Cara's window! Last night!'

'Sorry, what now?' Seamus looked at Cara.

'Someone – no idea if it was the killer or not, Sorcha – was outside, last night. I saw them looking in on me, and there were footprints in the snow outside my window.'

'Bloody hell,' said Seamus, running a hand through his hair, completely awake now. 'Really?'

'Yeah, I'm afraid so.'

'Is everybody all right?' Seamus looked around the room at everyone. Cara noticed that he and Ferdia didn't quite make eye contact. Last night's argument, whatever it had been about, still lingering, if overshadowed by the more alarming developments.

'No, I'm not alright,' wailed Sorcha, 'I just want to go home!' Seamus walked over to Sorcha and gathered her into a hug. Gently stroked her hair.

'It'll be okay,' he said softly. 'It'll be okay.'

Still holding the upset Sorcha, he looked over at Cara.

'Why have you your coat on?'

'I'm going out. Retrace Maura's steps and go see Patrick Kelly, ask him about his odd behaviour.'

'You can't go out there on your own, especially if you're going to talk to that guy.'

'I'll be fine.'

'You had someone staring in your window last night, and

one of our friends was murdered less than forty-eight hours ago. Saying you'll be fine isn't something you can guarantee. Let me grab something for breakfast and I'll come with you.'

'There's no need, Seamus.'

'I beg to differ.'

'Can you take her highness as well?' said Ferdia, nodding at Sorcha. 'I'm walking into Kilronan. I need to make a few phone calls for work and I need the Wi-Fi in Derrane's. So I'm not going to be here to stop the island slasher from killing her. Sadly.'

'Oh God, no, don't leave me here on my own.' Sorcha looked pleadingly at Cara.

'Okay, fine, fine, you can both come with me.'

'So, what are we doing then?' asked Seamus, clapping his gloved hands together for warmth. 'And remind me again why we're walking?'

The blizzard was taking a break but they still faced wading through deep snow. The wind whipped up any loose powdery flakes, making them dance in the air. Cara pulled down the edges of her red woolly hat. The roads, undriven by the island's scant car population, and untouched by any modern convenience such as a snow plough – Cara laughed at the mental image – remained a sea of snow, knee deep. In some places where the wind had found a path, the snow was skewed to one side, slanted drifts forming mini ski slopes. At spots along the road where memorials, small stone pillars with simple crosses on the top, stood behind walls, only the top half could now be seen. Hedgerow briars peeked thorny arms out of the top of some of the drifts, a hint to where the field boundaries were hidden.

'We're going to retrace her steps... or at least what I think were probably her steps. And no car 'cause I want to really look along the route, okay?'

Seamus and Sorcha nodded.

'Daithí saw her at around 10.30 a.m., when she cycled by the pub,' said Cara, her feet sinking deep with every step. 'She stopped at my house and spoke to Mamó around 11 a.m. Daithí and I went by her house yesterday and her bike is there, so that suggests she made it home. I think her killer might have caught up with her there.'

Cara turned to the waist-high drift beside her. She poked a hole in the snow and looked over at Seamus and Sorcha.

'Derrane's,' she said, then drew a line in the snow until she poked another hole. 'My house.' Cara continued the map, drawing the line until she poked a last hole. 'Maura's. It's a pretty straight line. I wanted to walk it, see if anything jumps out at me along the way. Knock into any houses on the route, see if they saw her. That kind of thing. Anything that might provide some insight.'

Cara then poked a hole some distance from the last.

'Where's that?' asked Sorcha.

'Patrick Kelly's home,' said Cara as she began to walk again, trudging through the snow. The other two followed.

'Patrick Kelly? Not that awful Paddy Kelly man, from the cottage not far from me?' said Seamus.

Cara sometimes forgot how long Seamus had been away from the island. He was so intrinsic to her DNA of what Inis Mór was she forgot that he'd left and it had moved on without him. The addled Patrick Kelly from the middle of the road yesterday would have been a child of eleven or so when Seamus had left for the US.

Cara nodded. 'He's Paddy Kelly's kid.'

'Oh, that poor lad whose mother fecked off on him?' said Sorcha, catching up with her. 'The strange, quiet one?'

'Yes, that's him. Not so little now.'

'Still strange?'

'I guess a bit, yes.'

'Why do you want to talk to him?' asked Seamus, walking just behind the other two, snow to either side of the road narrowing it.

Cara recounted the sighting on the cliff edge and the encounter in the middle of the road later. Seamus stopped walking. Cara looked back at him.

'Why are you only telling me this now? He sounds incredibly suspicious, no?'

Sorcha looked at her too.

'He does, I agree with Seamus.'

Cara started walking again.

'No?' pressed Seamus, catching up with her.

'I'm keeping an open mind.'

'And closed doors I hope! The Kelly place isn't that far down the road from us.'

Cara said nothing. She wasn't in the habit of making assumptions or jumping to conclusions. And just because someone was a little strange didn't get them a VIP spot on the suspect list.

'We'll see how dangerous he seems after a few questions. Come on, let's not dawdle or we'll freeze to death.'

EIGHTEEN

They took Cottage Road out of the village, up through the centre of the island. All the time, Cara was imagining which way Maura would have gone, what she would have looked at, any clues she might have left. But this island was so barren, so featureless beyond the ruins that were scattered about the place. Otherwise just limestone wall after limestone wall. But even if Maura had left something behind, the snow was keeping her secrets.

They came to a row of houses clustered together.

'I'm going to knock in here, see if anyone saw anything.'

'I'll wait by the gate if you don't mind,' said Sorcha. 'This is Mrs Joyce's house and I've never been a fan.'

'No worries, I won't be a minute.'

Cara walked up the path and knocked. Seamus followed halfway, casting glances back at Sorcha.

The door opened a suspicious crack.

'Hi there, Mrs Joyce, sorry to disturb you,' began Cara. The door didn't open any further. The snout of a tiny, frantic dog yapped and snarled at her through the small gap. Its claws clacked and scraped on the hall floor tiles as it fought to get at her. 'I'm just looking for a little help on a matter.' Cara raised her voice over the noise of the animal.

'It's far too cold, Sergeant. Come back when the weather's better.'

The door started closing over.

'Hello, Mrs Joyce.' Seamus's voice carried over Cara's shoulder. He trotted up behind her.

The face reappeared. Seamus looked around Cara and smiled at the woman.

'Hi there, Mrs Joyce, how are you? I'm here with Sergeant Folan, we're just talking to a few people.'

'Seamie Flaherty! Is that you?' The door opened all the way. Mrs Joyce bent and scooped up her apoplectic dog. With her free hand, she smoothed down the moss-green tweed of her skirt. Fingers then brushed back stray grey hairs from her forehead. A little colour came to her pale cheeks. She beamed at Seamus as the dog fought furiously to get out of her arms.

Seamus risked a pet of the animal.

'It is indeed me, Mrs Joyce.' The little dog snapped at a finger.

'Ah, how are you? I didn't know you were back! How is Hollywood?'

'Not a patch on Inis Mór.'

'Oh I can't believe that, and all the big film stars you must see! It must be so exciting.' Mrs Joyce emitted a girlish giggle.

'Could I ask you—' Cara tried again. But all she got was an irritated side-eye.

'Mrs Joyce,' said Seamus, catching Cara's eye, 'can I ask you, did you happen to see Maura Conneely passing by here, on her bike, on Wednesday morning? The snow started that evening.'

'Hmm,' said Mrs Joyce, pursing her lips and looking up. 'Let me have a think.'

Cara rolled her eyes, and folded her arms, turning half away from the woman.

'No... no, I'm sorry. I don't think I saw her.'

'Did you see anything usual that morning? Anyone you didn't recognise pass by?'

Mrs Joyce shook her head.

'I'm afraid not.'

'No worries, Mrs Joyce,' said Seamus. 'Tell Proinsias we say hello.'

'I will.' She beamed at him. 'Was lovely to see you.'

Seamus and Cara waved and walked back down the drive.

The three of them moved on to the next house. Sorcha waited again by the gate and this time Seamus didn't loiter halfway but came all the way to the door. A variation on the Mrs Joyce encounter played out. And the same again at the next door they knocked on.

Outside Cáit Óg O'Riordan's, Cara knocked on the door.

'Sergeant Flaherty,' she said, 'I'll let you handle this.'

'It's just the fame, Cara. I'm the local boy done good, you know that's all it is.'

'Seamus, don't patronise me. If it was just me, the doors would just be closed. They'd open them for you, celeb or not. Don't worry, I'm used to it.'

'I'm sorry to hear you are. You shouldn't have to be.'

Cara shrugged.

The door opened.

'Hi, Ms O'Riordan, I'm just conducting a few house-to-house inquiries. I need to ask you a couple of things.'

The door stayed open, much to Cara's surprise.

'I was wondering if you saw Maura Conneely pass by here, Wednesday morning? She'd likely have been on her bike.'

'I did see her,' said Cáit Óg, holding on to the door, not opening it fully. 'She went by on that bike of hers. Too fast as ever.'

'Is there anything you can tell me about the sighting?'

'Like what? I was cleaning the good room as I usually do on

a Wednesday and I happened to look out and she cycled by. I'd see her often go by on her bike. It was nothing strange.'

'Did you notice anybody else about?'

'The storm was kicking off, no one was out,' she said, her tone letting Cara know how stupid she thought this question was. 'Why are you asking? Has something happened to her?'

'I'm not at liberty to say right now.'

'Is that right? Not at liberty, I see.' 'Liberty' was enunciated reluctantly, as if it was the foulest swear word. She noticed Seamus for the first time.

'Is that actually Seamus Flaherty?' She looked at him, searching under the hat and scarf for confirmation.

'Hiya, Cáit, it is.' He rolled out his most megawatt smile.

'Right well, that house of yours is in a right state. Now you're back, are you planning on doing anything about it? Eyesore so it is.'

'Ah. Yes. Sorry about that. Yes, I'll be sorting it out...'

'Okay, thanks, Mrs O'Riordan,' said Cara with a bit of a grin at Seamus. 'If you remember anythin—' The door was shut in her face before she'd finished her sentence.

Shaking her head and shaking it off as she always did, Cara led Seamus back down the path. The trio continued north, walking in the centre of the road where the camber meant the snow was ever so slightly less deep.

'I'm sorry that's what you've to put up with,' Seamus said again, shoulders hunched against the cold. Cara watched the vapour of his breath dissipate into the air.

'Was everyone being horrible to Cara?' asked Sorcha.

'A bit,' said Seamus.

'As I said,' said Cara. 'I'm used to it.'

'Which isn't right.'

'I know... I think sometimes that it's not so much that I'm an outsider, but that I'm an outsider who married Cillian and took him away. First to Galway and then... You think you're popular? People *adored* your brother.'

'But how can they blame you for what happened?' said Sorcha. 'That makes no sense.'

'Yeah,' said Seamus. 'If they want to blame someone it should be me. I was the one there that night.'

'Don't try and bring logic into it.'

They walked on until the delighted shouts and squeals of children reached their ears. They turned the corner where the road passed by Cara's front garden. Dressed head to toe in hats, gloves, scarves and what looked like more hats, gloves and scarves, Saoirse and Cathal were out in the garden building a snowman. Under the watchful eye of Mamó.

Cathal spotted her first.

'Mam!' He waved a snow-encrusted glove at her.

'Hi, sweetheart. Hi, Saoirse!' Cara walked over to Mamó who stood by the edge of the garden, watching the children play. Cara gave her a hug. She turned to Seamus and Sorcha, beckoned them over.

'Mamó, look who I have here.'

Sorcha smiled at Mamó and gave her a little wave. Seamus stepped forward and proffered his hand. 'Áine, it's been too long.'

Mamó took his hand and shook it. 'I think we last saw you about a week after the funeral. Other than on the telly, that is.'

She turned to Sorcha and opened her arms.

'Sorcha McDonough, it's lovely to see you dear. You look as lovely as you ever did.'

'Aw, thank you, Mamó.'

'You shouldn't stay away so long.'

'I know, I know.'

'So, how is life treating both of you?'

'I can't complain,' said Sorcha.

'Me neither,' said Seamus.

'Terrible business with poor Maura.' Mamó frowned and shook her head. 'You wouldn't have seen her in a long time?'

Seamus was quiet a moment. 'No, I hadn't. It's still awful, she and I were so close once.'

'True,' said Mamó.

'Seamus,' said Cara, 'come meet the kids, you'll notice they've changed a bit. Sorcha, why don't you come too?'

Cara brought the pair over and made the introductions. As Cathal and Saoirse roped them into snowman-building, Cara returned to Mamó. She stood for a moment, watching Seamus, Sorcha and the kids laughing and joking.

'How are things down at Flaherty's?' asked Mamó.

'A bit emotional.'

'I can imagine. And how are you holding up?' Mamó reached up and gently brushed a stray auburn hair off Cara's rosy cheek and tucked it behind her ear. She then pulled the edge of Cara's red woolly hat down to cover her ears more. Cara smiled at her grandmother.

'I'm doing okay, not much choice. Investigating.'

'Be careful.'

'I will, don't worry.'

Cara watched as Saoirse jammed a carrot into the snowman's head, pointy end first. Heard Cathal laugh and good-humouredly object to his sister's unconventional approach to adding a snowman nose. Seamus laughed and tightened the scarf around the snowman's neck. Madra, the cat, sat safely inside in the living room window watching them all. Sorcha smiled back at Cara. She pointed to Saoirse and mouthed 'mini-me!' Cara grinned and nodded, giving Sorcha a thumbs up.

'Did you manage okay with the power gone?' asked Cara.

'We were absolutely fine. Sure, once upon a time there wasn't electricity on this island at all.'

'Did you keep the doors locked?'

'Yes, and there was nothing strange, don't worry. We had

Maurice and Conor in with us too. They'll stay with us as long as we need them. And I might be seventy-eight but I'm an island woman, I'm made of different stuff. I'm a tough old broad, I think that's what that Courtney girl would say.'

'That, and you are.'

'Stay down there at Flaherty's as long as you need to. I'll look after things here.'

'I don't know. There's someone out there who has done something pretty awful. I don't like the idea of you and the kids, even with Maurice and Conor, on your own here.'

'Conor's a big lad, a strong fisherman, I'm happy with him about, don't worry.'

'Sorry, Mamó, I just worry.'

'Loveen, I understand entirely.'

'We should probably keep going.'

'Okay. Best of luck, I really hope you work it out.'

Cara waved to the kids, ducking to avoid a snowball launched by a giggling Cathal.

'Come on, Seamus, Sorcha,' she called over to the smiling and red-cheeked pair.

Running over to her, waving at his niece and nephew, Seamus joined Cara as she waited at the end of the drive. Sorcha detoured to hug Mamó goodbye and caught up with them. They resumed their journey. Headed back to following the road through the middle of the island. It was about 11 a.m. now and it was getting colder, not warmer, as they got closer to midday. As they reached Maura's house, the clouds began to sag under the weight of impending fresh falls.

Sorcha stopped and stared at the quiet house. Her eyes filled. Seamus put his arm around her shoulder, pulled her in.

'Oh, it's just so... so...' Sorcha couldn't finish the sentence. Cara looked at them.

'I know. And that's why I'm going to find out who did this. I'm doing it for her.'

Sorcha nodded and sniffled. She rubbed her eyes.

'Wait here, you don't need to come any closer, I'm just going to do a quick look around. Daithí and I were here yesterday, I just want to make sure we didn't miss anything.'

Cara circled the building. Checking the doors and windows. She moved around to the back. Looked more closely at the bike which still sat propped up against the wall. Snow had fallen since she'd been here yesterday but Cara could still see that there was nothing in the basket. And nothing else out of the ordinary about it. She turned to the back door, took a few steps forward, and stopped.

Walking briskly to the front of the house, she summoned the others.

'What's wrong?' asked Seamus.

Cara beckoned him round. She pointed at the back door. It was open.

'Someone's been here.'

NINETEEN

'Stay close. Okay?'

'What's going on?' said Seamus.

'I don't know but someone has jimmied the lock since I was here yesterday. Stay here where I can see you both.'

Cara used her elbow and pushed the door open. Her pulse thumped in her chest. Seamus grabbed her arm. Cara swung around.

'What are you doing?' he asked, eyes wide.

'I'm looking to see what's going on.' She looked at his hand which was still grasping her arm.

'Sorry,' he said and let go. 'You just gave me a fright. But look, don't go in, there could be someone dangerous inside, no?'

'We won't know if we don't look.' She stepped in but like yesterday only went as far as the doormat inside the door.

'What can you see?' Sorcha asked.

Cara surveyed the whole living area from this spot. Someone had definitely been here. The place hadn't been trashed exactly, but Cara could see what had changed. The books weren't flush on the bookshelf. The cushions were lying awkwardly on the sofa. She could see further down the hall and the bedroom door was open. It had been closed yesterday.

'Someone's been searching the place.'

'Any sign they're still here?' Seamus tried to look around her into the house.

'I don't know.' Cara looked back at him. 'Why don't you do a quick run around the building, look in the windows, see if you see anyone. Sorcha and I will wait here.'

'Okay.' He turned and started a tour of the outside of the building, getting up close to the windows, holding his hands over his eyes and staring right in.

Cara looked to her left. There on the window sill, the snow globe still sat on the newspaper and letters pile. Her gloves were wet so she didn't touch it. She looked at the figures of the two friends, laughing and smiling, relieved nothing had happened to it. She stared at it. Again, she felt sure Maura had been trying to tell her something. Had left the message she couldn't send by text. But still, she had no idea what it was.

Seamus came trotting back around the house.

'Nothing. Seems empty.'

'Whomever it was is gone, then.'

'What were they doing?'

'Looking for the package, I suspect.'

'What package?' asked Sorcha.

'I think you were asleep for that,' said Seamus.

'Maura showed Mamó a mysterious package, something she was worried about,' Cara explained.

'You think that's what they were after?' said Seamus.

'Yes. I suspect so. Like, *I'm* looking for it. I want to know what it is. Maura thought it was something I needed to see. So it wouldn't surprise me if it's something someone thinks I *shouldn't* see.'

'Maybe they have it now.' Seamus looked around the room over Cara's shoulder.

'I think they might have left empty-handed.'

'What makes you say that?'

Cara pointed at a smashed plant pot a few feet away from her, a plant displaced and earth spilled out over the floor around it, mingling with the shards of bright orange ceramic. It usually sat on the ground. No way to fall and be smashed by accident. Had it fallen victim to a frustrated foot lashing out as they left?

'I might be wrong, but that looks like someone left here in an irritated state. I think the package is still out there.'

They set off again from Maura's, quieter than before. Her ghost following them as they left her little cottage behind. Fists shoved into his pockets, and head down against the chill, Seamus eventually spoke.

'Who did it, Cara? Do you have any idea?'

Cara shook her head.

'I haven't a clue. If you want to talk statistics, most women are murdered by their partners.'

'So who was her mystery man then? Surely you need to find that out?'

'It would help, yes. I'm not sure he was from the island though – she seemed to head to the mainland a lot.'

'Why didn't she ever tell you who it was?' asked Sorcha, eyes narrowed. 'You two were so close and all.'

Cara held Sorcha's gaze. The undertone, the resentment about Maura was still there.

'Sorcha, can we not do this again?'

Sorcha held her gloved hands up.

'I'm not trying to make a point. Honestly. I'm just curious. She told you everything. Why keep this guy a secret?'

'I think there must have been something about him that I would have disapproved of. That's all I can imagine. I didn't mention this the other night, but she'd told me she was looking to end it. She didn't like some things she'd learnt about him.'

'She was going to end it?' asked Sorcha.

'That's what she said to me last week. She didn't think it was going to work out. But I don't know, maybe she changed her mind.'

'I wonder what she learnt about him?' said Seamus. 'Maybe he wasn't a nice guy. Which would fit with her coming to harm.'

'That's true.'

They stopped a moment, and Cara looked out over the fields. She could see Patrick Kelly's dilapidated little caravan in the distance. Seamus followed her gaze.

'I suppose there's this fruit loop as well. Off his face on something, maybe he did it?'

'Don't call him that, okay? He's a vulnerable person,' replied Cara.

'Fine. But if he hurt Maura I don't care if he's supposedly vulnerable or not.'

Cara said nothing and started trudging through the snow again. They followed the road as it sloped gently downwards, the grey angry sea to the left of them. The Flaherty house just about visible not too far on from Kelly's.

They stopped outside the Kelly house. Ivy was growing through the cracked glass panes of the house windows. Moss peeked through the snow on what was left of the roof. A few escaped sheep from the neighbouring field were sheltering in what had once been the kitchen. No one had lived in the shell of a family home with the collapsed roof for a long time. It was just Patrick left and he had long preferred the small green and white dilapidated caravan that sat at the end of the garden. A tree, bent, blasted and stunted by the ubiquitous storms, hung over the caravan, its bare winter branches like a bony possessive clawing hand.

'Do you guys want to head back to the house? We're close and it's so cold. You both look freezing.'

'I don't want to leave you to talk to this guy on your own, he might be dangerous. He might have been the one who broke into her house.'

'Ah, I can't see it, Seamus. I'm not that worried about him, I just think he might have seen something.'

Seamus looked at Sorcha.

'I think we'll stay, okay, Sorcha? I don't want to leave Cara on her own, despite what she says.'

'Just nobody leave me on my own,' said Sorcha. 'That's all.'

'Fine,' said Cara. 'Just stay behind me and try not to spook him. I think he'll find a delegation a bit intimidating.'

'We'll be quiet as mice, won't we, Sorcha?'

'Totally,' she whispered.

'Right, okay. This way then.'

Cara led them past the gable end of the house, where its cream render was cracked and chipped, exposing some of the breeze blocks beneath. They followed a path worn in the snow to the caravan door.

Cara leant forward and knocked. Seamus and Sorcha kept their distance.

A face paused at the small, grimy caravan window, tattered and discoloured lace twitched aside momentarily.

Cara knocked again. The door opened a crack.

'Morning, Patrick. It's me, Sergeant Folan, I'd like to have a little chat with you about yesterday.'

'Yesterday?' A small voice emerged from behind the door.

'When I nearly ran you over? Remember?'

The door opened a fraction more. Cara could see the young man's pale face. He looked confused.

'You were in the middle of the road, I screeched to a halt... any of this ringing a bell? Can you open the door a bit more please?' He did as he was told. Though inside, he had his coat on, a long black wool number which had seen better days. Cara wouldn't have been surprised if it had been his father's. His dark hair was lank and looked like he'd cut it himself. From the limited view Cara was getting of the interior of his home, it was messy and the smell that was drifting out wasn't promising.

'He probably doesn't remember because he was stoned,' muttered Seamus, just loud enough that Cara could hear him. Loud enough that at the sound of his voice, Patrick threw the door fully open. He stuck his head out of the small, curved door frame. Spotting Seamus, he glowered at him, an intensity on his face that unsettled Cara. Seamus took a step back. Snatched a glance at Cara.

Sorcha moved behind Seamus. Shot Cara a nervous look.

'Cara?' she said. Cara shook her head.

Patrick stepped out of the caravan and sidestepped Cara, walking right up to Seamus. Sorcha scrambled away, dashing to Cara's side. Patrick paid her no attention. He had eyes only for Seamus. A head taller than him, and even though his scrawny build was no match for Seamus's Californian gym physique, the energy that vibrated from Patrick had a power of its own. Cara could see Seamus visibly shrink.

'I saw you,' Patrick said, eyes never leaving Seamus, his voice getting louder with each word, stepping in. Spittle flying. Patrick Kelly's body shook, an anger starting in his toes, coursing through him, Cara could feel the waves of it wash over him and radiate outwards, a blast radius of fury. He jabbed a finger at Seamus's chest.

'I saw you, I know what you did!' He jabbed again. Seamus stepped back once more.

'What are you talking about?' Seamus darted a look at Cara and Sorcha and then back at his accuser. He held his hands up in defence. 'I've done nothing.'

'I saw you!' Patrick spat. 'How could you do it to her? How could you do that to Miss Conneely?'

TWENTY

'Hey, buddy, back off!' said Seamus, stepping back, his chest puffing out, fists balling, ready for a counter-attack. 'I don't know what you're going on about.'

'Patrick, step back,' snapped Cara, putting herself in between the two angry men. Patrick pushed her aside. Threw himself at Seamus.

Wrong-footed, Seamus went down easily, Patrick following him, fists flailing. Sorcha cried out in fright.

'I saw you, I saw you, you bastard,' yelled Patrick as they rolled, limbs tangled, Patrick attempting to make contact and Seamus attempting to stop him.

'Stop it!' yelled Cara. She leapt on Patrick's back. Grabbed an arm and pulled it back. A screech of pain from the lad, and Seamus pushed him off, sending Patrick and Cara tumbling to one side, Cara now holding tight to both Patrick's arms. Seamus jumped to his feet, panting, out of breath. Woolly hat dislodged, and his hair wet from his contact with the ground, a scared Sorcha grabbed his arm and pulled him back. He shook snow off himself, patting down his coat and trousers, but keeping a wary eye on his assailant. Patrick went to buck Cara off, but she held firm.

'CALM DOWN! You can calm down,' she roared at Patrick. 'I'm not letting go until you do.'

'He's a crazy man!' breathed Seamus, cheeks red from effort as well as cold. 'He's raving! I had nothing to do with it!'

Patrick gave another attempt to dislodge Cara and when it was unsuccessful Cara felt his limbs go slack. But she could see the anger still burning in his eyes.

'If you promise not to attack Mr Flaherty again, I will let you get up.'

Patrick said nothing.

'Or I can take you down to the station, and book you for assault. Would you prefer that?'

'No,' he muttered.

'I'm letting go now, no funny stuff.' Cara released his arms, disentangled herself and stood. She felt the freezing wet snow seeping into her clothes. Goosebumped flesh prickling underneath. Patrick stood, rubbed his shoulder. Seamus took another step back.

'What's going on, Patrick, what do you think you saw?' asked Cara. Seamus shot her a furious look.

'What?' Seamus spluttered. 'You're taking him seriously?'

'Give me a moment, Seamus, please.' Cara held up her palm at him, her attention never leaving the angry young man. 'Patrick, go on...'

'I saw this guy,' Patrick repeated his mantra. 'With a woman in the village.'

Cara and Seamus turned to each other, brows furrowed. Sorcha sidled over to Cara, an identical confused expression on her face.

'What's he going on about?' she whispered in Cara's ear.

'What?' Cara asked Patrick.

Patrick looked at her, irritated.

'A woman who wasn't Miss Conneely.' Patrick repeated slowly as if they were fools. 'I saw them kissing.' He looked at Seamus. 'Miss Conneely mightn't know but I'm going to tell her when I find her.'

Cara put her hand on his arm, reminding him to control himself.

'I'm going to tell her! You can't stop me!'

'Patrick,' Cara spoke slowly and calmly, 'what Seamus does in his private life is none of Miss Conneely's business.'

'I have no private life!' said Seamus. 'I haven't been kissing anyone in the village, what are you talking about? I told you he was addled, Cara.'

'Liar,' spat Patrick.

Cara looked at the assembled group. Patrick doing his best to not launch himself at Seamus again. Seamus, glowering at the lad, rubbed a sore arm. Sorcha gently stroked Seamus's back.

'What did you see, Patrick?'

'Seriously, Cara?' Seamus was furious. 'Don't entertain this nutjob!' Cara held her hand up to Seamus again and looked at Patrick.

'Go on, Patrick,' she said.

'I saw this guy,' he said pointing at Seamus, 'in Derrane's, with a girl, and there was a gang of them, and they were very cosy. I saw them kissing. Right there, in the pub!'

'Was there a guy with a beard and baseball cap with them?'

Patrick looked at her, surprised.

'Yeah.'

'And did the girl have red hair like me? But a tan, like Seamus? Was she very slim, very pretty?'

'Yes,' Patrick replied, his voice quieter.

Cara turned to Seamus. 'I think I know what's going on here. I think it was Aiden, your actor double. I noticed him and Lexi holding hands when we met. I didn't think much about it at the time. But he looks so much like you. It'd be an easy mistake.'

'Aah!' said Seamus. 'Of course!' His shoulders sagged, the tension leaving his body. Cara turned to Patrick.

'I think what's happened is that you saw an actor who looks very, very like Seamus with his girlfriend. Seamus has a crew in town, filming his book. This must be who you saw.'

'An actor?'

'Yes, and he really is Seamus's double. I can understand anyone making that mistake.'

'But why did you think Maura and I were together?' asked Seamus, looking at the lad. 'Why'd you think I was, what, cheating on her?'

Patrick said nothing, just stared back at him.

Cara walked over to Seamus and Sorcha. Walked them out of Patrick's earshot.

'Look, why don't you continue back to the house? I'm going to get him back inside and have a sit down with him. Have a chat. He's obviously anxious and stressed out. And I still need to talk to him about yesterday, it's the whole reason we came here in the first place.'

'I don't like the idea of leaving you on your own with him,' said Seamus.

'I appreciate that, but I don't think he's going to talk to me with you around. I might have convinced him that he was mistaken but he's still quite worked up.'

Seamus pondered the situation.

'We'll wait for you, down by the road. Is that compromise enough?'

Cara looked at the snow-capped pillars at the end of the path.

'You'll freeze.'

'We'll be fine, won't we, Sorcha?'

'Yeah, sure.' She didn't look convinced. She sighed, 'Fine.'

·   ·   ·

Patrick stepped into the caravan, leaving the door open behind him.

Cara followed.

The interior was small and compact, a bed at one end, and tight benches and a screwed-down table at the other. Every surface was covered. Rubbish. Clothes, books, paper, food. Detritus of every kind. The smell was mitigated only a little by the door that remained open. Despite the cold, Cara didn't move to shut it.

Patrick sat down on the unmade bed. Looked at Cara with wary eyes.

Cara turned and considered the bench seating. Its fabric was stained and ripped. She sat reluctantly and rested her elbow on the table, but even through her thick coat she could feel the stickiness of the surface. She removed it. Kept her elbows close to her body and arms rested on her lap.

'Are you doing okay, Patrick?' she asked softly. 'Is anyone looking after you?'

'I'm looking after myself. I'm not a child.'

'I'm sorry, I know you're not. You're just out here, alone. That's all I mean.'

He said nothing.

'You seem to care a lot about Miss Conneely's feelings.'

'Miss Conneely is a good person, she doesn't deserve to be treated badly.'

Cara took a deep breath.

'She is.' The present tense hurt. 'She's wonderful. She's my best friend.'

'She's the only one who ever...' Patrick stopped talking, eyed up Cara, irritated that she'd nearly coaxed something out of him.

'She's the only one who what, Patrick?'

He just glared at her.

'Does it feel like Maura is the only one who ever cared about you?' Cara reckoned this was how that sentence had been going to end.

Patrick gave a sad little nod.

'She spoke about you to me. When I arrested you for the trouble you got into before. She asked me to go easy. She said you'd had it tough and deserved a break.'

Cara looked around the squalid caravan. She recognised a green jumper lying at the end of Patrick's bed. It was a jumper Cara had given Maura last year for her birthday. It had gone missing and Cara had been a bit irritated that Maura hadn't taken greater care of it. Cara also recognised a small stone owl ornament that should have been in Maura's front garden. It looked like Maura's kindness had been appreciated a bit too much.

'She's so good.' He rocked, small movements, gentle, comforting, like a mother nursing in a rocking chair, a grandmother by the fire. 'She doesn't get cross at me. She makes time for me. She's the only person on the island who's nice to me.'

'She is wonderful like that. I think you and I know her well. Know how kind, generous and lovely she is.'

Patrick smiled for the first time. Just a small one. But Cara could see a difference in the young lad. She looked out the window at his childhood home. Uncared for and neglected just like he had been as a child. She'd heard the stories. Seen Paddy Kelly, his father, about the island before he died. Heard about his wife who'd fled the island, gone to London, never to be seen on the island again. Leaving a bitter drinker of a husband and a heartbroken child behind. That had been before her time on the island. When she'd moved here full time after the accident, she had called to the house a few times. Patrick had been eleven or twelve by then. A silent child paraded in front of her with reluctant nods when questions were asked. She'd made referrals at Maura's instigation. But sometimes nothing happens, nothing changes, despite the best will in the world. She'd been young herself too, learning. She'd been a grieving widow just trying to keep herself and her babies afloat. And she wasn't the only one who had tried and failed. Maura and Dr De Barra had too. There were a lot of happy families on this island, a lot of strong bonds and happy times. But there were a few where those ties and times had not been so strong nor happy. Seamus and Cillian had lived that alternative experience. Patrick Kelly had too.

At least he'd had Maura looking out for him. She felt a tug at her heart that this protection was gone. She realised that she and Patrick had more in common than she'd have thought possible. The recipients of Maura's care and kindness when no one else was interested. And outsiders in their own communities, outsiders in their own homes.

'Maura looked after me too, Patrick.'

His expression changed a little at this. He didn't look away quite as quickly.

'But I don't think she'd be too happy with you going after Seamus Flaherty.'

'Is that his name?'

'Yes. He used to live on the island, when you were a kid.'

Patrick nodded, his fingers gathered up a bunch of the bedsheet, pulling and twisting it.

'He asked a good question,' said Cara. 'Why did you think Maura would be concerned with who Seamus was dating? They're not a couple. Not now, anyway, they haven't been for a very long time.'

'That's not true.'

'I think it is, Patrick.'

'But I saw him and Miss Conneely together.'

'I don't think so.'

'It was at that house, down the way from here. The place that's usually empty.'

Patrick stood up, agitated again, his head not far from touching the roof of the caravan. Filling the space. He paced by the bed. Cara could feel the caravan floor vibrate. He repeated, 'I saw him, I saw him,' to himself in a quiet little whisper.

'That's Seamus's house.'

'There, see, that was him then! I'm right!'

Cara shook her head.

'I really don't think so. Everyone's just home for my husband's anniversary, they're all staying there. That's why you might have seen her.'

'I'm not stupid and I understand what I saw.'

'But, Patrick, how can they be together? Seamus has lived in America for nearly ten years now. And Maura has always been here. They haven't seen each other in all that time.'

'She leaves the island a lot. She could have been seeing him then.'

He was right about that, thought Cara. Maura did leave the island a lot, particularly since the mystery man had appeared in her life. She doubted it could have been to see Seamus though... All the way from California for a weekend hook-up? That seemed a bit much. Cara assumed she'd been meeting up with the mystery guy in Dublin or Galway, not because that's where the major airports were, but rather just to keep away from prying eyes. Whatever the reason, it hadn't gone unnoticed by this set of prying eyes.

'Patrick, have you been keeping track of Maura?' Cara looked at Maura's jumper at the end of the bed. How far did his interest in her go?

Patrick looked at Cara quickly and away again. A look of guilty admission on his face.

'You can't be doing that, Patrick.'

'I'm just making sure she's okay.'

Cara shook her head.

'You'll get in trouble for that kind of behaviour.'

'I'm just making sure she's safe from him. I don't like *him*.'

Cara sighed. She was losing patience with Patrick.

'You've nothing to worry about with Seamus, and anyway, as I said, they aren't even in a relationship.'

'Then I know more than you. I saw them. Together.'

Cara shook her head.

'I did! Just two days ago. It was early in the morning. She was leaving his house. Her clothes – they were the clothes she was wearing in Derrane's the night before. I'm not stupid, Sergeant! I know what that means.'

Cara said nothing.

This sounded like the same sighting that Mamó had mentioned. And the same implication Mamó had taken from what she saw.

The incident Seamus had insisted had never happened.

Cara looked out the grimy window at Seamus, standing at the gate pillar, stamping his feet to keep warm.

He'd lied to her.

TWENTY-ONE

'It's okay, calm down, Patrick. I'm sorry.'

He glared at her.

'I believe you,' she said. She meant it. She did believe him. It was Seamus who was the liar. He'd flat out denied this had happened. She looked out the window at him again. Watched him chat to Sorcha with their hands stuffed in their pockets, jogging on the spot to keep out the cold. Why lie about that? People would have been happy to know he and Maura were together again. It's not as if either of them were married or had partners they were cheating on. Well, Maura wasn't cheating on Seamus if he was the mystery man, that is. Cara felt an unwelcome stab of anger at her friend. Why all these secrets, Maura? Why have you left me and left this puzzle behind? Did you not trust me?

Patrick sat down again.

Cara looked over at him. This poor lad had fixated on the one person in his life who had shown him kindness. She knew she should be wary, with Maura's possessions in his caravan, his stalking – he knew what Maura was wearing and that she'd been at Derrane's the night before. But it was hard not to see him also as a lost duckling who had imprinted on the first kind face he'd seen. Followed her about, taking what comfort his life had from her things. And perhaps he would be able to repay her kindness by providing Cara with the information she needed. This nugget about Seamus told Cara more than the fact that Seamus was telling lies. It told her that Patrick had followed her two days ago. What might he have seen? What else did this kid know?

Cara sat forward.

'Patrick, can I ask you something?'

He looked at her, but was silent.

'I think you've been paying a lot of attention to Miss Conneely. Kept an eye on her around the island.' Keeping an eye on her sounded a lot better than stalking her.

'Sometimes.'

'And you were keeping an eye on her that morning?'

'I was going to. But I was going to go to her house. I'd seen her go home after Derrane's the night before, and I didn't think she was at that house. I was only passing it because it's just down the road from here. I guess she must have come back later after I'd gone home.'

That would fit with them keeping it a secret, thought Cara. There'd have been nothing stopping her heading back to Flaherty's with the gang after leaving the pub. And that had been a bit weird too, when Daithí had told her Maura had headed home. Now it made more sense.

'I got a surprise,' said Patrick, 'when I saw her. And I dropped behind a wall when I saw them there, at the door. I don't think she'd like it if she saw me there, even though I just do it to make sure she's okay.'

'Of course you do. Did you go after her once she left Flaherty's?'

'Just for a bit. She was on her bike, and she was too quick for me.'

'You don't know where she went then?' Cara wondered if this was when she'd set out to see her.

'No, I don't. On her bike I can't keep up. I just went off and... did something else.'

Cara had a feeling she knew what he might have been doing when not following his beloved Maura. Drugs.

'Were you getting high, Patrick? I thought that was something in the past for you. You certainly haven't come to my attention in recent years.'

Patrick released a long, emotional sigh.

'When I nearly ran into you yesterday, you didn't seem yourself. You seemed under the influence. Were you?'

'Don't tell Miss Conneely, please.' He looked anguished. Cara hung her head. Her heart was already in tiny pieces, it felt ground down finer, into dust. She had thought telling the gang that Maura was gone had been bad. This simple lad, a pest really, a stalker, telling him would be worse. It looked like Maura was the only one left in the world who had been looking out for him. But she wouldn't tell him now. And in this poor creature's place, a few more days without the news would be the only kindness she'd be able to offer.

'Please don't tell her. I just... It wasn't my fault. I didn't mean to take them.'

'Patrick, I'm not so interested right now in whose fault it is. I'm more interested in something you said, when I stopped the car and got out. Do you remember?'

The lad shook his head. His fingers reached for the bed sheet again, gathering it together in his hand. He shook his head again.

'You said, "it hisses", do you remember that?' His hand stopped gathering the cloth. His face was blank. Then once more his head shook in denial.

'There's been an accident on the island, Patrick. Someone ended up in the Serpent's Lair. They died there. It's that serious. I don't know what happened, and I need to know. I saw someone up on the cliff yesterday morning. Someone who might know something about how the person died. I think you would understand if I thought that person on the cliffside could be you? What do you say to that?'

The winds were picking up again outside. The little caravan rocked suddenly with its renewed force. It whistled a minor key through the cracks in the caravan. Cara was back on the clifftop, rocked by the wind, looking down on the body of her friend, luxuriating in a blissful state of ignorance. Innocence soon to be lost forever. Had Patrick Kelly been the figure on the cliffside? Watching. He was a watcher, that was now well established.

'Was it you on the cliffside, Patrick?'

'Mmm,' he said. The rocking motion began again, his fingers tapping the bed now. His forefinger rapid-fire tapped a morse code of panic.

'It wasn't me. It wasn't me... it wasn't!'

'It wasn't you on the cliffside, Patrick, honestly?'

'No. Not that. I didn't do it.'

Cara went cold.

She spoke slowly. Clearly.

'What didn't you do?'

He gasped for a deep breath, but only managed short, shallow gulps.

'I didn't throw them in... I just saw the person do it.' He started to cry. 'I just saw them... it wasn't me.'

Cara stood up. Had Patrick witnessed Maura's body being thrown into the Serpent's Lair? Had been at the scene? An eyewitness.

She took the steps across the shaking caravan, shaking like its inhabitant. She crouched, touched his knee. Looked up into his anguished face.

'Who did you see, Patrick?'

'I don't know. I don't know. I had taken some p-p-pills, I didn't even know it was real until later. I-I-I woke up... I was behind the rocks. I went back, I thought it was the pills. And I saw, I looked down... it was hard to see, there was so much snow and the wind I was scared it would blow me off. But I snatched a quick look. And in the waves I saw a leg, I knew the thing I'd seen was real and the thing they'd thrown must have been a person...' Sobs ate up half the words he managed after that.

Cara sat beside him on the dirty bed. Put her arm around him. Shushed him as she looked at Maura's crumpled jumper at the end of the bed. He didn't realise the full extent of what he'd seen... who he'd seen. Perhaps somewhere at the back of his mind, the pieces of this horror jigsaw puzzle were waiting to be put together, but if so, right now they were holding back, protecting him.

'Patrick,' she said gently, 'this is really important. Can you tell me anything about who did it? Who you saw?'

He shook his head.

'Can you say if it was a man or a woman?'

'It was too dark. I'm sorry.'

'How many? Could you tell me that?'

'Just one. I saw the outline of just one person.'

'Thank you, Patrick. That helps me.'

He dragged his sleeve across his face, wiping snot from his nose. Still shuddering from sobs.

'I called you though, I didn't leave them there.' Red-eyed, he looked at Cara.

'You called?'

'I rang 999. I said, I told them that there was a body there. I hung up then. I didn't tell them it was me because no one would believe me if it was me. And then no one would come. I stayed until you came. I hid. Kept hiding to make sure you came.'

'And when you saw we'd gotten there, you left?'

He nodded vigorously.

'I didn't want you to see me there. You'd think I'd done it. No one would believe that I was helping. I went to Miss Conneely's house, I knocked on the door. I never knock on the door, I know she wouldn't like it. But I thought this was different. This was serious. But she wasn't there. There was no one to tell. No one who'd listen. I came back here.'

'You must have gone out again? When I nearly ran into you.'

'I don't remember.'

'Did you take more drugs? Is that why?'

He nodded. Closed his eyes.

'I didn't want to see it. I didn't want to hear it. The dragging. The crack when it hit the water. In my head. I wanted it to go.'

TWENTY-TWO

Cara walked down the path. Passed the cracked rendered wall. Seamus looked up.

'Oh, thank God you're back. We're nearly frozen solid.'

'I said you could go on home.' Cara failed to keep an edge out of her voice. She was feeling unsettled. It seemed so unnecessary for Seamus and Maura to lie to them. She felt a little unmoored when parts of what she felt were steadfast turned out to be a lot less firm than she'd thought.

Seamus looked at Sorcha with raised eyebrows. Cara turned out of the drive and started walking. They fell into step beside her.

'No need for the snark,' said Sorcha. 'We stayed 'cause we were worried about leaving you alone with that oddball.'

Cara threw them a quick side glance.

'Sorry,' she said. 'Sorry, guys. It's all just... Patrick saw whoever it was dump the body. Heard Maura's body hit the water.'

'What?' Seamus's eyes were wide. 'He was there?'

'Yeah, stoned.'

'Christ,' said Seamus. 'He was there... What did he say that he saw? Did he see who did it?'

'No, sadly, he was too out of it.'

'That sounds like an excuse to me,' said Sorcha. 'He must have done it, Cars! Surely?'

'I don't think so, honestly. He's just... he's a lost soul. He just doesn't seem capable.'

'He could be lying? Why would he tell you, the Guard, the truth? Think about it.'

'He can't keep his caravan clean, Sorcha. I don't see how he'd manage to do what the murderer did.'

'You haven't told us those details,' said Seamus.

Cara looked at him.

'I can't. Not now.'

'I understand.' Seamus nodded solemnly. 'What else did he tell you though? Did he have anything useful for you?'

Cara shook her head.

'He was barely aware of his surroundings, by the sounds of things. Seemingly he saw what happened, but didn't think it was real. He came back a little while later when he was sobering up, to check if what he saw actually happened. That's when he spotted Maura. And he called us.'

'He made the anonymous call?' said Seamus.

'That's what he said.'

'I still think he's suspicious,' said Sorcha. 'He just did those things to cover up. To make it look like he was innocent. And it's working, you don't think it's him.'

'I don't know, Sorcha.'

'Who else could it have been?' Sorcha's pitch rose, anxiety not far from its edges. 'Someone did it. Someone killed her. And you've a disturbed kid right there, just sitting in front of you. What's the problem?'

'The problem is I don't make assumptions! I deal in hard evidence.' Cara's lips drew a firm line.

Sorcha scowled but said no more.

They trudged on in silence, all lost in their thoughts. In the distance, the waves crashed. They heard and felt the wind rushing across the island like a banshee. Cara turned up the collar on her coat, regretting now taking this grim pilgrimage on foot. She snatched a glimpse at the sky. Fresh snow looked imminent.

'Come on, let's get back to the house,' said Seamus, putting an arm around Cara. 'Don't forget you're not alone, you've always got us.'

'Thanks, Seamus,' said Cara, leaning into him. It was hard to resist. This was Seamus, Cillian's little brother whom she'd known since he was a kid. He was her brother-in-law. Family. Whatever he was keeping from her, well, he was still him. He must have his reasons. He was still someone she loved.

Sorcha reached out and squeezed her hand. A shy smile played on her lips.

'You've always got us,' she repeated.

Sorcha pushed open the back door. The trio entered the cold, empty kitchen. The mottled marble-effect countertop was frigid under Cara's hand.

'Come on, let's get the fire lit. This bloody house is such a disaster.'

Seamus kicked off his boots and crossed the room, rubbing and clapping his hands together. He started prepping the fire. Cara and Sorcha took off their coats and hats, neither sure that was the best move. Every exhale of breath released little clouds of vapour into the air. Cara looked at the useless kettle. What she wouldn't give for a hot cup of tea right now. She flicked the button on and off, hoping that maybe the electricity had come back. But no, it was still out. Daithí had said something about bringing a gas stove from Derrane's with him whenever he came back. She hoped it would be soon. She shivered.

Sorcha made her way to the sofa and pulled one of the throws around her. She settled into an armchair and looked back at Cara.

'So, we didn't learn too much, did we? Weirdo Kelly sorta saw what happened but couldn't tell you anything useful about it. And no one else saw a damn thing. We're cold and miserable and none the wiser. Let's all just sit here until the psycho comes for us! At least we won't be freezing any more.'

'Hang in there, Sorcha,' said Cara joining her, also grabbing a throw and settling down on the sofa. Seamus, on his knees in front of the fire, turned to look at them.

'It's a bit of a worry, Cara. An island this small, and we've no idea who did such a thing? You'd have thought it'd be obvious.'

Cara shrugged.

'There aren't even that many people on Inis Mór,' said Sorcha, sitting up in her chair as an idea took hold of her. 'Couldn't you like, interview them all? Surely it'll be obvious who did it? Couldn't you do that? We could help!'

'If it comes to it. But I'm not even meant to be investigating, I was told to wait. And they had a point. Whoever did this isn't getting off the island. They're just as stuck as we are. The troops will arrive the moment the storm breaks...'

'So we just have to not get murdered until then, is that it?' Sorcha said. 'Great plan.' Seamus reached out and stroked her arm.

'It's okay, Sorcha, don't fret, we're all here.'

'And so was the killer, staring in windows last night, watching us. Jesus, Seamus. What if he decides to strike again? It's not as if Ferdia will be bothered to try and save me!'

'Deep breaths, Sorcha, come on, deep breaths. No one is

coming for you, no one is going to attack you. We're all here, even if Ferdia doesn't step up, we will. Right, Cara?'

'Absolutely.'

The back door opened. Seamus, Sorcha and Cara whipped their heads around at the noise. Daithí and Ferdia, laden with flasks and foil-covered trays, bustled in. The smell of bacon and sausages filled the room. A fine Parisian perfume wouldn't have lifted the mood so well.

'We're back,' called out Daithí. 'We come bearing gifts from the kitchen of Derrane's.'

'Perfect timing, guys,' Cara said. 'Come on, Sorcha, you're cold and hungry. It can't be helping how you're feeling.'

Cara grabbed some plates and mugs and Daithí grabbed cutlery. Everyone sat down at the table. Daithí peeled back the foil, releasing a burst of the fried food aroma. Cara could feel a drop in tension from everyone around the table. They all filled their plates and fell on the food like starving people.

Cara took a bite of a plump, hot sausage and felt all the pleasure centres in her brain ping. She instantly felt less awful.

'Thanks for bringing all this, Daithí, we needed it,' she said, lifting her mug of steaming tea to her lips. And even though it was still too hot, she gratefully took a deep slug.

'Happy to. And I dug out the countertop hob, and a few decent torches too,' said Daithí.

'Great,' said Cara. 'We can look after ourselves again then. Thanks. Though I'll be sorry not to get this every day.'

'You'd be spoilt.' He grinned at her.

'God forbid!'

'So, Ferdia told me about the nocturnal visitor last night.' Daithí's grin slipped away. 'I don't like the sound of that.'

'Yeah,' said Cara, sausage halfway to her mouth. 'I'm not happy about it. We need to make sure to keep the doors locked and no one should be left on their own. And everyone stays alert. I'm not sure what else we can do right now.'

'How'd your morning go? Ferdia said you went out investigating.'

'Yeah, find anything out?' Ferdia asked.

'We didn't learn much, I'm afraid.'

'That's not strictly true, Cara,' Sorcha replied. 'We learnt the Patrick Kelly kid was there!'

'What?' asked Daithí, stopping eating.

'Yeah, he happened upon the scene when Maura's body was being thrown into the Serpent's Lair,' said Cara.

'Christ,' said Daithí.

'I know. But he was high, so he doesn't really know what happened.'

'Cara doesn't think he's a suspect. But he attacked Seamus. I think he is suspect number one,' said Sorcha.

'He attacked Seamus?' asked Ferdia, with a hint of amusement in his eye. 'What happened?'

'Bizarrely he'd some notion that not only was I involved with Maura, but that I was also cheating on her too.' Seamus shook his head. 'So he decided to defend her honour by attacking me.'

'Seriously?' said Ferdia, the twinkle lessening. 'That's weird. Where'd he get that idea? Were you?'

'What?' replied Seamus, confused. 'Was I what?'

'Were you seeing, cheating on Maura...?'

Seamus paused with a piece of toast halfway to his mouth.

'What a weird question, Ferdia. Obviously not.'

'He spotted Aiden with Lexi,' said Cara. 'That seems to have been the root of the problem.' She left out the little nugget about the doorstep encounter.

Ferdia looked at Cara, and then back at Seamus. The twinkle was back.

'That's hilarious,' he laughed.

'No it's not,' said Seamus, drinking back a gulp of coffee. 'He took a swing at me.'

Cara grabbed the flask and poured herself another mug of the hot, steaming tea. She added a dollop of milk from the open carton on the table. Her fingers were coming back to life, the warmth of the mug in her hands causing a thaw. She blew on the steam. All her limbs were beginning to defrost, throbbing and tingling as the ice left her bones.

'Anyway, you were never in danger, Seamus. He's just a sad, confused young man, and Maura – typical Maura – was the only one looking out for him.'

Sorcha stood up.

'My socks are damp. I'm going to go change them. Be back in a mo.' She left the table and trotted out to the hall, the door swinging shut behind her.

She appeared back a few moments later.

'That was quick,' said Seamus, looking up from his food.

Cara looked over at her too. Noticed her pale face. The look of terror on her face. She was holding something in her hands.

'What are those?' asked Ferdia.

'I... I don't know,' she said, eyes wide. 'But there's one for each of us.'

Seamus stood up.

'What? What are they?'

'Letters,' said Sorcha. 'I found them on the mat, under the letter box.' Cara watched the envelopes shake in Sorcha's trembling hands. She stood up and went to her.

'Let me see.' Cara took them from Sorcha without any protest. Indeed, there were five envelopes. A name on each one. Their names.

Everyone at the table put down their cutlery and mugs.

'What'll we do?' asked Sorcha.

'Read them?' suggested Ferdia. He stood and took the envelope with *FERDIA* carefully written on it.

'Perhaps you shouldn't,' said Cara.

'Seriously?' said Ferdia. 'I'm opening mine. Do what you want.'

Cara put the remaining letters down on the table. Slowly everyone took theirs. They looked back at Cara. Ferdia turned his over. Slipped his finger under the edge, ripped the top. He pulled out a single, folded piece of paper.

He frowned in puzzlement. Unfolded it.

'Oh,' he said, surprise writ large across his face.

'What is it? What does it say, Ferdy?' whispered Sorcha.

Ferdia turned it around, for everyone to see.

In large, bold, capital letters, one sentence.

GIVE IT BACK.

TWENTY-THREE

Seamus, Daithí and Sorcha took their letters, slipped their thumbs under the sealed edge and ripped. Sorcha stole a quick anxious glance at Cara, then looked back down at her letter. Cara studied the others, watched as nervous hands each took a letter out of the envelope and unfolded them. Cara held her breath. She didn't blink. After a moment's consideration, like judges in a competition, they turned the letters to show everyone else.

GIVE IT BACK.

The same sentence in each one. The same writing. The same sense of threat.

They put them down in the centre of the table, a malevolent pile. Plates of food, so recently attacked with gusto, were pushed aside, forgotten about. Each of the friends stared wordlessly at the sinister collection. Seamus got up and went to the window, looked out, even though whomever had dropped these letters would be long gone. Who knew how long they'd even been lying there on the mat?

Slowly Cara opened hers. Took out the sheet within. She unfolded it and stared.

GIVE IT BACK.

The same sentence again.

She threw her letter on the pile. Seamus came back from the window and sat. Everyone looked at her.

Daithí was the first to speak.

'What on earth are these all about?'

Cara looked over at him. Looked back at the letters.

'A message from our killer, it looks like.'

'Oh boy,' said Seamus, wide-eyed.

'I thought you said he wouldn't be interested in us, Cara,' said Sorcha. 'You said he was just interested in Maura!'

'I was wrong then, I guess.'

'What is "it"?' asked Daithí, picking up a letter and staring at it.

'I suspect "it" is the package. It's at the centre of all this. Someone wants it badly and I think it's what got Maura killed, whatever it is. And whomever hurt her didn't seem to get their hands on it then, or later when they searched her home. I think this is their latest attempt to find it.'

'Jesus,' said Sorcha.

'Why do they think one of us has it?' asked Daithí.

'I don't have anything!' cried Sorcha, jumping up from the table. She hugged her arms around herself and started to pace. 'Why did they send me a letter? I've nothing to do with any of this.'

'Shut up, Sorcha, you're giving everyone a headache,' said Ferdia, shaking his head. 'Though, for the record, I don't have any mystery packages either.'

'Me neither,' said Seamus.

'And, Daithí, I'm going to presume you don't?' said Cara.

'You presume correctly,' he said, looking down at the letter, his finger tracing the words.

'Well, that's a full house because I certainly don't have it. I wish I did though. It's obviously the key to whatever the hell is going on.'

'Cara,' said Daithí, turning the letter over and back.

'Yeah?'

'How?'

'How, what?'

'How are we meant to give it back? Like, if one of us had it – I know, we're all denying that – but how are we supposed to give it back? There are no instructions.'

'Hmm,' said Cara. She sat back down at the table. Looked at the pale and shocked faces around her. She lifted each of the pages and inspected them. All were handwritten, but looked nearly identical. She turned them over and back, but there was nothing else. She held each one up to the light from the window but saw no hidden messages.

'I think the only implication then,' said Cara, the words coming slowly, her stomach as tight as a fist, 'is that whoever has it, will *know* how to give it back?'

That settled and sank in around the table. Like a polaroid slowly developing, the full picture gradually becoming clear.

'Does that mean one of us... *knows* the killer?' Sorcha near whispered, paler still.

'Well, perhaps,' said Cara. 'It certainly suggests that having the package means you'd know enough to get it back into their hands.'

'So someone around this table,' said Ferdia, 'knows more than they are letting on? Is that it? And these,' he pointed at the letters, 'mean that person is hiding something?'

'And the killer doesn't know which of us that is,' said Seamus. 'Jesus. We're all at risk.'

An already subdued table got quieter. There were snatched

glances at each other and averted eyes. Uncomfortable shuffling in their chairs.

'It could be mind games, Cara,' said Daithí. 'An attempt to unnerve us. Look at everyone now, we can't look each other in the eye. It's been two minutes and we're already acting differently.'

'Yeah, that's a possibility,' said Cara, looking at each of them, holding each gaze, an act of defiance, rebellion against the insidious force who'd entered the house unasked. 'But why would they want to unnerve us? Why would the killer do that? What do they have to gain?'

'What did they have to gain by killing Maura?' Daithí asked.

'True. The answer is in that package. Whatever the hell it is.'

'Could this be a prank?' asked Seamus. 'Someone with a sick sense of humour?'

Cara shook her head.

'I don't think anyone else on the island knows what's going on. Even if there are half-rumours out there. No one but the killer, and us, knows enough to do this.'

'First the eyes last night, now this. Did he leave them here last night? Is that why he was here, oh God,' Sorcha babbled, all the while shooting glances at the others across the table.

'We'd have noticed them this morning, love,' said Seamus in a calm tone. 'Come on, Sorcha, sit down again. Get that food into you. We need to keep our strength up, it won't help anything if we let ourselves get sick.' Seamus stood and put his hand out to Sorcha.

She reared back.

'Don't touch me! I'll stand if I want to!'

'Oh for crying out loud, Sorcha, calm down,' sighed Ferdia.

'Don't! Don't you! Just don't, Ferdia Hennessy. Don't paint me as the crazy one! One of you knows something, don't you!

And you, Ferdy, you keep disappearing to make "phone calls" for work. What's that all about? Huh? You're on holiday, it's Christmas, you're not that important that your gigs and bands need you. Maybe you're up to something?'

Ferdia stood. Glared at his wife with his dark, black hole eyes.

'Like what?' he said in a low, slow, menacing growl.

Daithí looked at him.

'Sit down, Ferdia. She's obviously just anxious. We're all upset.'

Ferdia turned to Daithí. Made him the recipient of the death glare.

'So you'll be happy if I accuse you of murder? Yeah?'

Daithí stood up. Returned Ferdia's glare across the table.

'Sit down. All of you,' Cara said quietly, but with a firmness borne of fifteen years as a guard and twelve years a parent. Everyone complied.

'Right. Well, I guess I have to ask,' Cara looked around at her friends, took a deep breath. She couldn't believe she was saying this. 'Is there anything anyone here wants to tell me?'

'No,' Sorcha snapped.

'No,' said Ferdia.

'No,' said Seamus.

Daithí shook his head.

'It's a no from me as well,' said Cara.

TWENTY-FOUR

The sound of a car pulling up in the driveway outside drew everyone's attention away from their thoughts. Cara stood with her mug in her hand and walked to the window. The heat from the tea steamed up the glass and Cara wiped it clear with her hand. It was only 2 p.m. but the light outside was already beginning to fade. The car door slammed.

A hooded figure got out and approached the front door. The snow had started again. Her squad car would once more soon be indistinguishable from the hedges and walls. A little flurry of snow danced around the visitor's feet.

'Who is it?' asked Sorcha, alarm in her eyes.

The doorbell rang.

'I don't know,' said Cara, turning to look at her friend. 'But murderers don't tend to ring the doorbell.'

'I'll get it,' said Daithí and he stood up. Ferdia half stood out of his chair. Daithí stopped and looked back at him.

'I don't need a chaperone. I won't murder anyone or be murdered on the way to the door.' He left the room and Ferdia sat back down. Sorcha, despite Cara's reassurance, looked anxiously at the door. Bit the skin on the edge of her finger.

Cara came back to the table and scooped up the letters.

'I'll just put these away somewhere.' She went into the kitchen and placed them in a drawer.

They all heard the muffled sound of voices at the front door, and Daithí came back into the room with the driver of the car. Everyone stared. The atmosphere of tension was tangible. Like the snow outside it seemed to cover everything. The visitor took down his hood and Cara realised it was Maura's boss, the school principal, Cormac Mullen.

White-haired and balding, he was a man in his early sixties. He looked about the room, initially with a smile on his face, but it slipped away as he took in his tense audience.

'Sorry,' he said, looking at them all, 'have I interrupted something?'

Seamus recovered first.

'No, no, not at all, Máistir,' said Seamus standing. Old school habits instinctively returning, Master Mullen. He'd been teaching in the village school for nearly forty years. He'd taught both Saoirse and Cathal at some point. He'd also taught Daithí, Seamus, Sorcha and Ferdia – before Ferdia had gone back to Dublin for secondary school – back in the day. Maura had always said he was a wonderful boss.

'It's Cormac, Seamie, and you can sit down and relax, you're not in school any more.'

'Old habits.' Seamus smiled, doing as he was told and sitting back down.

'Hello there, Sorcha McDonough, Ferdia Hennessy. It's been a while since we've seen the pair of you home.'

Ferdia grunted and started poking at his lukewarm fry.

'Mr Mullen,' Sorcha said. 'Are you here because of Maura?'

Cara shot her a warning look. She didn't notice.

'Ms Conneely? No, why? It's the holidays, Ms Conneely is on her own time.' He smiled, a little puzzled.

'How can we help you, then?' asked Seamus.

He looked at Cara. 'I'm here for the sergeant.'

'Really?' said Cara. 'What's up?' She came round the counter, out of the kitchen. Maybe this was about Maura after all.

'It seems we had a break-in at the school.'

'A break-in, oh dear. Tell me more.' Cara relaxed a bit. She probably only had days, maybe even hours, before Maura's death became common knowledge. And the storm outside would pale into comparison with the storm it would unleash among the islanders.

'We got an alert from our alarm service yesterday. They should have called us the day before, because it seems that's when the problem occurred. But between the storm and the electricity being out and it being Christmas time there was a delay and they only got through to me late yesterday.'

'Was anything taken?'

'No, not as far as I can tell. Which is a bit weird. Everything seems fine,' said Cormac. 'Nothing disturbed other than the door. I'm presuming it was some bored teenagers but I felt I should let you know all the same.'

'You were right to. I'll check it out.'

In the squad car, Cara followed the school principal's fifteen-year-old battered Ford into the village. She was happy to get away from the tense atmosphere at the house. They pulled up outside the three-roomed primary school. White, with a slated, pitched roof and windows as big as doors, the school looked uncharacteristically dull and empty today. Dull like the darkening sky. Normally such a hive of activity, the storm and holidays had taken the life out of it. The wind, which unlike the snow never took a break, was whipping at the Green School flags in the yard. There was a constant rhythmic snap and hollow clang as the rope fought and struggled with the flagpole.

Hoods up, Cormac led Cara around to the back of the building. They stopped in front of a single, half-glazed door. The door that let the children out to the yard at break times. A concrete overhang above the doorway protected them slightly from the increasing snow.

Cara examined the door. Looked at the crude indents on the damaged lock. The offending implement – a rock – lay abandoned on the step.

'Shall we go in?' Cormac asked. 'Have you seen enough there?'

'Yes, let's get inside.'

He led them through the door into the dim back corridor. Without the lights – and the kids, thought Cara – the school was unnaturally lifeless and murky.

'And you're sure nothing was taken?' said Cara, her voice echoing about the empty hallway.

'I checked the iPads, and the laptops and the petty cash. All present and accounted for. There's nothing else here that would be worth anything. So unless someone was after paper and crayons, then nothing is missing. That's why I assume it was bored teens.'

'Yes, that does make sense,' agreed Cara. 'I can have a look around, see if anything jumps out at me. But I suspect you're right. Shame there's no need for CCTV on Inis Mór.'

'Well. Funny you say that. There happens to be a motion-activated camera on the alarm sensors. It's no security camera – it doesn't have a particularly wide angle of vision and it only grabs a few seconds – but it might have captured something.'

'That could be useful.'

'I've asked the alarm company to send me whatever footage they have.'

'When do you expect to get that?'

'Soon, hopefully.'

'Send it on to me when you get it. Right now, do you mind if I have a look about the school?'

'No problem.'

Cara looked left and right at the three rooms. She knew the first classroom was Maura's. She taught the youngest kids, little four-year-olds up to six and seven.

'Can we look in Maura's room first?' she asked, forcing out the words 'Maura's room'. Knowing Maura would never be back here. This would be someone else's room in the future. She looked at her feet, hiding her face from the principal.

'Of course,' said Cormac, leading the way. He opened the door and they stepped into a room with twelve small desks. The walls were festooned with Christmas art. Cotton wool snowmen and red pom-pom-nosed reindeer. Paper snowflake bunting strung across the room. Colourful books sat on book-shelves. Mugs full of crayons and multicoloured lollipop sticks, pipe-cleaners and all the sundries of make-and-do. This room was the most perfect manifestation of the joy Maura brought. Cara had to force herself over the threshold. The wrench was awful.

Cormac crossed to the interactive whiteboard.

'So this bit of kit here – it's the most expensive thing in the room. And it doesn't look like it was touched. She's left her laptop here, on the desk – I don't know how many times I've asked her not to do that – but anyway, it's still there. Nothing is out of place around the room.'

'Do you mind if I have a look around?'

'Sure,' said Cormac. 'But I'm not sure if it'll be particularly enlightening.'

Cara had begun to wonder about something. Those letters had started her thinking. The killer wanted that package. Obvi-ously didn't have it. And they were getting annoyed, annoyed enough to risk sending those letters. Maura must have hidden it somewhere on the island. If nothing had been taken from the school... What if then, instead, something had been *left* here? The timing of the break-in was similar to when Maura had been moving around the island, looking for her. When she had the package and was looking for Cara. Cara hadn't thought she'd been in the area of the school... but perhaps she had? And maybe she'd passed the school and decided to hide the package here? If she hadn't had her keys with her that would explain the need to break in.

Cara looked about the room, trying to see through the decorations, and consider where Maura would have put it, if that's what had happened. She checked the bookshelves under the windows. She opened the presses at the back of the room. As Cormac had said, everything looked as it should.

'I can't help but notice,' said Cormac, who had observed Cara's search, 'that you look rather like someone who might be looking for something specific?'

Cara glanced at him. Pondered what was best to say. The truth probably.

'I have a theory about something,' she said.

'Ah.'

Cara zeroed in on Maura's desk. She crossed the room to it, and sat down in Maura's chair. A quick scan of the desktop revealed nothing suspicious.

'Can I ask what the theory might be?' asked Cormac, joining Cara at the desk. Cara looked up at him.

'There are some things going on on the island right now, Cormac. Things I can't talk about. But what I can say is, I'm wondering if someone left something here, rather than stealing something.'

'I see, interesting,' he said. He thought about that and then opened his mouth as if to say something else, then stopped. Cara waited.

'Can I ask you something?' he said after a moment, reconsidering.

'Sure.'

'I'm not one for gossip. But you know what island life is like, nothing happens and you don't hear about it.'

'I know.'

'I heard a rumour, yesterday. I heard that a body was found on the island.'

Cara looked at his open, curious face. She wasn't entirely surprised he'd heard something. Nothing happened here without someone knowing, despite the best will in the world. She'd just like the news to remain a little contained until they weren't cut off. She didn't need panic sweeping the island while everyone was stuck here.

'I'm not sure I can comment on that, Cormac.' Cara couldn't hold his gaze. If he only knew it was one of his own. And this wouldn't just affect him on a personal level. This wasn't some large urban school where the loss of one teacher would be a tragedy, but remote for many. The island primary school had only around fifty pupils. Three classrooms. Three teachers, of which Cormac Mullen was one. Cara didn't want to think about what his job would be like in the school, coping with this when the time came to reveal the awful news.

'I'm sorry,' she said, sorry for so many things.

'That's okay. I just wanted to ask, it just felt a little less baseless than some of the things one hears. And what you just said there, about things going on on the island...'

Cara nodded. She then looked back down at the desk. She wanted to get away from this conversation. Far away. She slid open the top desk drawer. She and Cormac peered in. Pens, Post-it notes, rulers and toys, sweets, general detritus of teaching. She opened the second, deeper drawer. Pulled out folders and books. Flicked through them all. Nothing that matched what Mamó had described.

'All the usuals I would expect in there,' said Cormac.

Cara opened the last drawer. The deepest, bottom drawer.

More books, more folders with reports. But unlike the drawer above it, this pile wasn't lying flat. A bit like the princess and the pea, there was something at the very bottom, underneath everything, causing a bump. Cara pulled the contents out. Piled the books on the desktop. She found herself looking at a tin box. Decorated with a cartoon dog with swirls for eyes and a pattern of cannabis leaves and peace signs. This certainly didn't look like what Mamó had described. And it felt wrong. Wildly inappropriate to be stored here in a classroom for small children. Cara felt very anxious. She pulled on her new leather gloves. Picked the tin up.

'Is this what you were looking for, Sergeant?' asked Cormac, leaning over her, very curious about this small, suspicious, tin.

'No,' said Cara, frowning. 'Not at all.'

She carefully prised open the lid.

And nearly dropped it.

Inside were a dozen, maybe more, multicoloured little pills. Smiling faces stamped on all of them. And just in case there was any doubt about what they were, alongside them was a trio of joints with their twisted, tapered ends.

TWENTY-FIVE

'This isn't hers,' blurted Cara.

'I certainly hope not because that's an instant suspension, disciplinary action, you name it.'

Cara fixed Cormac a look.

'I'd appreciate it very much if you keep this information to yourself right now.'

'To be honest, Sergeant, there's only so much I can do before I'd end up putting myself in the way of disciplinary action. Keeping illegal drugs in her school desk. This is a serious breach. Covering it up? No, no, no.'

'Trust me on this, Cormac, it isn't going to be an issue. Take it from me that you won't get in any trouble, just keep this to yourself right now. If needs be, I will back you up one hundred per cent.'

'What's going on?'

'I can't say, but these aren't hers. Believe me. Would the Maura you know do this? Leave these here, so vulnerable?'

'No, she wouldn't.'

'Exactly, Maura would never be so careless. Her pupils mean the world to her. Hold on to that and consider her reputation.' Drugs that looked like sweets in an unlocked drawer in a classroom full of small children. Her memory would be in tatters if this got out. So, the break-in hadn't been her. Hadn't been where she'd hidden the package. It was just more of the same, another layer in the attempt to destroy her. Her reputation, her life; someone so intent on punishing her. Why, though? What was with this campaign against her friend?

Cara grabbed a fresh tissue from the box on Maura's desk, and wrapped the tin in it. Then wrapped it again and slipped it into her inner jacket pocket.

'Give me a few days, then you'll be able to make a decision, okay?'

'Just a few.'

'That's all that'll be needed. Well, that and the video footage from the alarm. Please, the minute you get that footage, no matter what the quality, please send it on to me. I know it's hard, with the electricity gone, to manage electronic communications, but it's vitally important I see it.'

'Of course. I'll let you know the moment it's in.'

'I might be in Seamus Flaherty's place, and there's no reception or Wi-Fi there. But if you leave a message at Derrane's, it'll get to me.'

'I'll do that.'

'Thanks, Cormac.'

'What are you going to do?'

'Go see someone who might know where those drugs came from.'

Cara parked her car. Turned off the engine. As the wipers stopped, snowflakes landed on the windscreen, first a few, then more, each swathe of new flakes filling in the gaps. Cara sat in the car as the snow covered the full windscreen, the light taking on an eerie glow. She couldn't understand what was going on on her island. Ten years she'd been here, ten years of slow and steady. Now, murder? Break-ins and planting of evidence? Sinister letters? Sure, she didn't have proof that the drugs had been put there by someone other than Maura, but it was the only thing that made any sense. She needed to find out the source on the island. That might tell her something. She looked out the passenger-side window. Looked up the path to the little green and white caravan. She got out of the car.

Cara pulled up her hood. Even in the walk from the car to the door of Patrick Kelly's little caravan, the snow had gotten heavier. The branches of the claw-like tree that stretched over the caravan were collecting snow, smaller branches bowing under the weight. Cara reached out a hand and knocked. The tinny plastic sound reverberated. She heard a noise from within, but the door didn't open.

'Patrick, it's me, Sergeant Folan. Sorry to bother you again.'

Still nothing.

'I'm only back for a moment, there's nothing to worry about. I just have a question I need to ask.' She knocked on the door again. And again.

'I'm not going away until you open up.' The caravan was so old and flimsy Cara reckoned it wouldn't take too much to get in there if she needed to.

She knocked again.

Finally, more sounds from within.

'Please, Patrick.'

The door opened a crack. Cara could see those two familiar eyes staring out at her.

'What do you want?'

'Let me in, please. I won't keep you long.'

The door swung open and Patrick headed back in without a word. Cara stepped in, glad to be out of the snow. She couldn't help herself and quickly scanned the caravan for writing materials, or anything that suggested he was the origin of the letters.

There was nothing and she shook off the moment of doubt. Focused on why she was here. Patrick had retreated to the bed, rumpled blankets suggesting he'd been keeping warm there. She really needed to do something about his accommodation. The second this whole mess was sorted out, she'd look into getting him help. And this time she'd make sure he got it.

'I need to ask you a question. And if you give me the truth, I promise there won't be any consequences. You'll be helping me and so we'll strike a deal. How does that sound?'

He looked at her from the bed, his face a mosaic of distrust and suspicion.

'Depends.'

'I need to know where you got your drugs. You haven't been in trouble with the law in a long time, I don't think you've been using in a long time. What's changed? Where did the drugs you've been taking come from?'

He looked away. Out the end window. There was a sudden thud from the roof. They both looked up. Snow from some of the branches had fallen. Patrick stayed silent.

Cara sighed.

'Am I right that you've only just started again?'

He nodded.

She reached into her inside pocket and drew out the tin from Maura's room. Using the tissue it was wrapped in, she opened it. She moved closer to Patrick, and showed him the contents.

'These type look familiar?'

Another nod.

She wrapped it up again and placed it back in her inner pocket. That was very useful. Suggested the same source for Patrick's drugs and these. He could tell her who had given them to him.

'I just wanted to not remember,' Patrick finally spoke.

'I know, Patrick. I promise you that you won't get in trouble if you tell me who gave them to you. It'll be helping me.'

'I went to him, and he gave me some more pills and I took them.' Shoulders slumped, Patrick hung his head. He took in a juddering breath. 'I'm sorry.'

'It's okay, I understand.' Cara sat at the end of the bed. 'Who is "he"? Who gave you the drugs?'

'I don't know... I don't think he'd like it if I said who...'

'Patrick, you don't need to be afraid of him. I'm on your side...'

'I don't know his name.'

'Can you describe him?'

Patrick, fear now a fellow traveller on his face, companion to misery.

He couldn't look at Cara. He dropped his gaze to the ripped lino on the floor by the bed.

'Your friend,' he muttered.

'What?' Cara replied, confused. 'My friend?'

'Uh-huh.'

'Are you sure?'

He nodded.

Cara had very few friends. And Maura it hadn't been. Daithí? Never.

'Which one, Patrick?'

'The posh one.'

Ferdia.

TWENTY-SIX

Cara pulled the car into the Flaherty house drive. Despite the wind and snow, and freezing temperature, Noah was out the front with a few of the actors. He was standing beside one of the cameramen, who was circling the group with a handheld camera, strapped to him with some contraption. A crew member was holding a boom above their heads. Noah, the crew member and the cameraman were lost in layers of woolly hats and coats and scarves. The actors were less lucky, testing their dedication to their craft with far lighter layers.

Cara got out and slammed the door. Noah turned around at the noise and called 'Cut!' with more than a little irritation in his voice.

'Sorry to ruin the shot,' said Cara, failing to sound any note of contrition in her voice. While they were playing pretend with her life and the life of her friends, she was living the real thing. And she couldn't yell 'cut' when it went wrong.

She walked through the cast, and rounded the house to the back door. She stepped into the kitchen to find Seamus, Ferdia and Daithí still at the kitchen table, now a bottle of whiskey open in front of them. They were staring out the window at the filming. A liar, and a dealer. And Daithí. Her friends.

Daithí looked over at her.

'What was going on at the school?'

'Bored teens, it looks like. Mr Mullen was right.' She kept her eye on Ferdia, looking for any reaction. Nothing. He kept staring out the window at the actors outside.

'That's something,' said Daithí. 'You didn't need any more on your plate. Speaking of plates, your food is beside you there, under the foil. Afraid it's probably stone cold by now.'

Cara lifted the aluminium foil off the plate. Fat had congealed around the once-appetising bacon and sausages. She wrinkled her nose and pushed it away.

'Heya,' said Seamus, looking over his shoulder at her. He lifted his glass. 'Join us?'

Cara looked at her phone. It was ten past three in the afternoon.

'Bit early, no?'

'It's eight o'clock somewhere in the world,' said Ferdia without turning around.

'We needed a bit of something to steady our nerves,' explained Seamus.

'*Et tu*, Daithí,' said Cara, surprised at him.

'When in Rome...'

She sat with them at the table but refused the offer of refreshment.

'Sorry,' said Daithí. 'That was flippant. We're all just feeling a bit shook.'

'We're stuck here, a psycho is out there somewhere...' said Seamus.

'Maybe he's right out there,' suggested Ferdia, pointing with his glass at the crew outside.

Daithí shook his head.

'I don't think so. They were all at Derrane's during the time she went missing. Either sleeping off jet lag or drinking in the pub.'

'Not impossible, though,' said Ferdia.

'True, not impossible.'

All eyes rebounded back to outside, transfixed by the filming. The actors, near blue with the cold, were returning to their marks, beginning again the scene that Cara had ruined.

'I wish my guy was more handsome,' said Ferdia. He turned his head to look at Seamus. 'Was that deliberate? I bet it was.'

Seamus sighed.

'No, Ferdia, it wasn't.'

Cara watched the pair of them, faces in profile. Their attention glued to their avatars outside. Glasses raised to their lips, sips taken.

It had seemed quite simple when they'd got back in touch. A hint of sun and the scent of carefree days from the past had wafted in with their communications. The promise of simpler happy times. When they'd been young and nothing bad had happened yet. When Ferdia was just an obnoxious, entitled brat. Not a purveyor of poison. Cara still couldn't understand what was going on there. Sure, she'd talked to him the other night as he enjoyed a joint. But if she arrested everyone who indulged in that habit, she'd do nothing else. Much like the whiskey in front of them now, in the right hands, it wasn't a problem. But drugs didn't always make it into the right hands. Look at poor Patrick.

'How's the investigation going?' asked Daithí. 'We were trying to think of suspects. Who might have sent the letters and what the package might be.'

'Did you come up with anything?'

Daithí shook his head.

'No, we're still drawing a blank.'

'Seamus had some wild ideas,' said Ferdia.

'No I didn't, I was just making suggestions.'

'I'm surprised your movies make any money at all the way your mind works. His best theory was some randomer came to the island for kicks. And swam off again, something wacky like that.'

'I wasn't saying that's how it happened, I was just throwing out ideas!'

'Nah, you were serious.' Ferdia grinned.

'I was not, you idiot!'

Ferdia pushed his chair back and turned fully to Seamus.

'Who are you calling an idiot? Me? Really?' There was no humour in his voice now.

Seamus went red in the face but was silent. His body fizzed with restrained anger. But he did nothing.

'Good boy. Stay. Sit.' Ferdia gently slapped Seamus's cheek, and turned back to looking outside at the crew. Sipped his whiskey.

'Guys. Can you cut it out,' said Daithí. 'I know those letters have us unsettled but we can't take it out on each other.'

Ferdia ignored Daithí's plea. Seamus, blushing from the humiliation, just scowled.

'What are you doing next?' asked Daithí of Cara. Ignoring the others.

Good question, thought Cara. She stole a quick glance in Ferdia's direction.

'I will need to pop back to the station. Do a few things there.' Do a background check on Ferdia.

'Are you looking into that crazy kid? That was my favourite theory. I know you said you didn't think he could fight his way out of a paper bag, but I'm inclined to disagree... I'll have the bruises in the morning to prove it,' asked Seamus.

'I'm keeping an eye on him.'

'Good.'

'I don't think he's much of a letter writer, though.'

'Looks can be deceiving, Cara.'

'It's strange watching our doppelgängers,' said Ferdia, still staring outside at the filming, seemingly unconcerned with the mood or conversation around him. 'Watching our lives happen again. Doesn't that normally happen when you die? It flashes before your eyes.'

'They're not doppelgängers,' said Seamus with a sneer.

'Doubles, lookalikes, you know what I mean. Don't be such a bloody writer. Think you're smarter than the rest of us.'

'Doppelgängers are evil. Evil versions of yourself. Not just a twin. People get that mixed up.'

Ferdia took a sip of his whiskey. Watched the camera move outside. 'The Sorcha actress is cute,' he said.

'Where *is* Sorcha?' Cara asked, looking around the room as if Sorcha had been there and she just hadn't noticed her.

'Took another pill. Went back to bed,' said Ferdia.

'Another pill? I don't think she's handling this okay.'

Ferdia shrugged.

'I don't think anyone is,' said Daithí, raising his glass.

'Nope,' said Seamus, raising his and clinking Daithí's glass.

A faint cry of '...and action!' floated in to them from outside, through the pathetic single glazing.

'Have either of you checked on her recently?' asked Cara.

'I'm sure she's fine,' said Ferdia.

'I might go and check on her.'

'If you want.'

Cara stepped into the hall. She went to the front door and locked it. Behind her, the kitchen door opened. Daithí came out, pulling the door gently behind him.

'What's up?' asked Cara.

Daithí ran his hand through his hair. Then rubbed his face, letting out a sigh.

'Is there any progress?' he said in a quiet voice. 'Any better idea what's going on?' Cara walked over to him.

'I'm afraid nothing much yet. Are you okay?' She reached out her hand and rubbed his arm. 'You're feeling the strain.'

'I think everyone is. Those two inside have been at each other since you left, since those weird letters arrived. I wanted to head up to Maura's, to fix the broken lock on her back door, but I didn't want to leave them. Whoever wrote those letters has done a good job of getting under everyone's skin.'

'Yeah,' said Cara. 'If they've managed to get to you they definitely have.'

'Do you really think one of us is hiding something about the package?' asked Daithí.

'The killer seems to think so.' Those two in the kitchen were hiding other things, she knew that for certain. Assignations with Maura. Illegal dealing. Cara looked into Daithí's open, tired face. She was tempted for a moment to share what she'd learnt about them. But she stopped herself. It wouldn't help him, knowing. And friend or not, he wasn't a Garda.

'Go now, while I'm here, go up to Maura's. Those two will be fine. Especially if Noah and his lot are still here. I think you could do with a bit of a break from this house.'

'Maybe you're right.'

'It'll be dark soon, you don't want to leave that door much later. I don't like the idea of you being up there when the light is gone. Maybe you could take Seamus or Ferdia with you? That gives you backup, and gives them a break from each other.'

'That's a good idea. Ferdia was talking about heading to the pub for the Wi-Fi yet again, so it could all fit.'

'Perfect. And thanks, Daithí.'

'For what?'

'For being you, you know.'

'Really? Things must be bad if you're grateful for that.' He smiled down at her. Cara leaned in and gave him a hug. She forgot sometimes that just because he was the strongest, steadiest person she knew, under that stoic exterior he mightn't have it all together.

Daithí headed back into the kitchen.

Cara continued down the corridor. She slipped her shoes off at the door to Ferdia and Sorcha's bedroom. Quietly, she turned the handle and slipped in. Half-closed curtains and fading light had left the room murky. Under ancient blankets Sorcha's sleeping form lay quietly, soft breaths advancing and retreating at a steady rhythm. Cara looked at her. Blonde hair still pulled into a messy bun, getting messier the longer she stayed in bed. Of them all, Sorcha seemed to be coping the worst. But Cara had a feeling her stress had its origins as much in London as Inis Mór. For a moment, Cara sat on the end of the bed, looking at her old friend. Her words about Maura had hurt. And she still didn't agree with her that Maura had been anything but the best of friend to her. But Sorcha was obviously hurting, vulnerable. Cara could see that and it upset her. She hoped that the Stace and Lucy she'd mentioned yesterday were good friends. Because it was obvious she was getting very little from Ferdia right now. Cara pulled the edge of the blanket back over Sorcha's feet, where she'd kicked it off. Pulled another blanket up over her. It was so cold in here.

Cara got up again. She looked around. On either side of the bed were two white laminated chipboard bedside tables. Across the room the four white wardrobe doors matched them. The peach and cream curtains had probably once been the height of fashion. Cara walked over and looked out the window, ran her hand down the curtain edge, drawing it back. The white expanse of the island lay beyond. The muffled words of the actors floated down to this end of the house, indistinct.

Cara crossed to the wardrobes. Eyes on Sorcha, she carefully opened the first cupboard. Moving untouched in decades' clothes, the wire hangers on the rail were rusty, speckled with tiny auburn flecks, the colour of her hair. Sorcha

didn't move. Cara turned her back on her and stared into the
darkness of the wardrobe. Patted down the clothes. Looked
among the deflated shoes on the bottom. Nothing out of place.
She checked the shelf above. A moth-eaten purple straw hat.
She lifted it down, bringing a rainfall of dust with it. She
coughed, Sorcha stirred. Cara froze. Waited. The gentle
breaths returned. Cara let out her own held breath. She placed
the hat back on the shelf.

Cara moved to the next wardrobe. This time populated
with men's clothes. She knew Ferdia had been through this one,
borrowing ridiculous warmer clothes. But there was nothing
amiss here either. She closed it quietly. Watched Sorcha again.
Checking she was still deep under.

Under.

Cara's eyes glanced to under the bed. The corners of suitcases caught her eye. New ones, nothing historic about them. As
Cara kneeled down she reckoned Mr and Mrs Flaherty probably hadn't owned suitcases of their own, had never spent much
time off the island. She drew the first case out. Opened it as she
stayed kneeling on the floor. Sorcha's clothes. Inappropriately
light and impractical. As if Sorcha had forgotten what her first
twenty-four years of life had been like. Cara closed the case and
carefully moved it back into place. A second case, Ferdia's
presumably. She eased it out and opened it. More practical,
though just as fashionable gear. Unmistakably Ferdia's. But just
his clothes. Nothing else. Cara closed it, sat back on her heels.
Perhaps she was wrong. Her intuition confused. She gazed
about the room but even in the descending gloom Cara could
make out that there weren't many other places to look. She
pushed Ferdia's case back under. Felt resistance. She pulled it
back out, lay down on her belly and stared under the bed.
Another bag. Smaller. She reached to get it. Wrinkling her nose
at the dust and debris she dislodged. Tried not to gag. Her
fingers felt the fabric of the bag, managed to grasp it and pull.

Kept mouse-quiet, careful not to disturb the sleeping beauty above her.

Emerging from beneath, Cara sat up, looked at the small, black bag in her hands. She unzipped it, the sound of each tooth releasing like a lion's roar. She peered inside. An Aladdin's cave of narcotics greeted her.

Enough to subdue the population of the island many times over.

And pills just like those she'd found in Maura's desk.

TWENTY-SEVEN

Cara pushed the bigger cases back under. Sorcha tossed in the bed. Groaned. Well you might, thought Cara. She pushed the bag of drugs back too. Back where it'd been. She slipped out of the room and returned to the kitchen.

Only Seamus sat at the table now.

'Daithí and Ferdia gone to Maura's?'

'Yep, said they'll be back later,' said Seamus. 'How's Sorcha?'

'Asleep.'

Cara sat down at the table.

'How much do you know about what Ferdia does in London?'

'Not a huge amount,' said Seamus. 'Only what I said to you the other night. Gigs, music, bands, that kind of thing. Why do you ask?'

Cara shrugged.

'Just something someone said... Do you think he's up to anything else, other than the bands and stuff?'

'Like what?' asked Seamus, eyes narrowing.

Cara pondered what to say. *I believe Ferdia is a drug dealer?*

'Anything illegal?'

'Really?'

'Honestly, it's probably nothing, I just have to follow everything up, you know.'

'I haven't heard anything, if that's any help.'

'No problem.' Cara stood. 'Okay, I have to pop down to the station. I'll be back as soon as I can. Can you keep an eye on Sorcha? And I know it's hard with that lot outside, but try and keep the doors locked.'

'Are you okay going to the station on your own?'

'We don't have much choice, there isn't an even number of us to pair up. And I'd much prefer someone was here to mind the sleeping Sorcha. Anyway, I'll be fine. This is my job, after all.'

'True, but still. Be careful, Cars, don't take any risks. I'll keep an eye on Sorcha.'

'Thanks, Seamus, and don't worry, I'll be fine. Right, I'm going. Sooner I'm gone, the sooner I can get back.'

Cara rounded the counter, zipping up her coat as she went. The snow attacked her the moment she stepped outside. The filming still continued though, regardless. Not that Cara gave a damn, it seemed so frivolous right now. She stalked through the actors without a word. Noah Jackson yelled, 'Cut,' and shot Cara a daggers look, but kept his mouth shut. Cara passed Lexi and caught the eye of the actress version of herself. Lexi was grasping a cup of coffee, fighting off the chill.

'Spoiler,' Cara muttered, 'it doesn't end well.'

The computer screen flickered that very particular backlit glare into the gloomy Garda station. The sun was nearly set and the station closed in around Cara. The backup generator had done its job and kicked into life. But Cara had left the lights off. She didn't want to advertise her presence in the station any more than necessary. She needed to focus without interruption.

Cara was relieved to be able to plug in her phone and get it back up to full charge. And, with the sudden reconnection to Wi-Fi, it lit up like a pinball machine with notifications and news alerts. 'Storm Susan causing chaos around the country' multiple news alerts informed her. She snorted a bitter little laugh at that. Really? I hadn't noticed. The forecast said they had another twenty-four hours of it. That late tomorrow, late on New Year's Eve, it would break. As she contemplated the storm, she wondered what would happen then. What would she be left with on New Year's Day? She wouldn't need to look at herself in a mirror, see a red-headed woman first thing, to know she would have a tough year ahead.

Cara plugged Ferdia's name into the system, and slowly read through the results it returned. A not inconsequential rap sheet. Six months in Mountjoy, when he was twenty years old, for possession with intent. That six months he claimed he was abroad, six months in France for his degree. They'd all been so jealous. If they'd only known. And it didn't look like Ferdia had learnt his lesson. At regular intervals, the additions to his file. The seriousness that increased. And there were violent incidents. Cautions and one conviction for assault. More time behind bars they'd never known about. Hidden during the non-summer months spent in Dublin. Cara shook her head. Sarcastic, arrogant Ferdia had always been an acquired taste. But she never would have thought he was capable of violence. She'd never have been afraid of him. Yesterday, when he'd come back to the cottage after storming off, when they heard him lose his cool with Sorcha, that had been a glimpse. A look behind his carefully cultivated curtain. Cara wondered if she checked in with her colleagues in London, what the last ten years in London might have to say.

There was a knock at the station door. Cara stood up. Her

lights-out routine didn't seem to have done the job. The station door opened and a familiar face appeared around it. Daithí. With a smile of relief, Cara sat down again.

'Hey there. Can I come in?'

Cara nodded.

'Grab a seat,' she said.

Daithí took a chair from a desk opposite and sat down across from her. He placed something down on the desk. A key.

'I've fixed the lock, it was a quick job. I thought you might want this.'

'Ah, perfect. Thanks for doing that.' Cara took the key and put it in her pocket. 'How was it up there? No one else disturbed the place since earlier, I hope.'

'It seemed just as you described, so hopefully not.'

'Good.'

'What are you doing here?' Daithí nodded at the computer screen. 'If you don't mind me asking.'

Cara's resolve to keep this to herself weakened a little.

'It seems our old friend Ferdia has dabbled a bit in some drug dealing over the years.'

'Drugs?' said Daithí. 'Really? Ha. I'm surprised.'

'I know, me too. I'm beginning to wonder if Sorcha was right,' she said. 'Perhaps it's been too long. What do they say, "Never go back"? Maybe we should have just remembered the good times, and left them there.'

'Yeah, I don't know. Things are different, I have to agree with you.'

'Don't mention this, about Ferdia, to anyone. I probably shouldn't have said it to you.'

'I won't, don't worry.' Daithí mimed pulling a zip across his mouth. He stood. 'I'm going to go now. I left the drug lord making his work calls in the pub, which makes me wonder now, I can't lie. I said I'd walk back with him to Flaherty's. Will we see you there later?'

'Yep. I'm just going to finish this here and I'll come back.'

'Great. See you soon. And be careful.'

'I will.'

Daithí left the station with a wave. Cara looked back at the computer screen, pondered her next move. What was she going to do with this information? And the stash under the bed? Her phone pinged in the middle of the pensive silence. It was a text from Cormac Mullen, the principal. The footage was in.

She launched her email app. Watched a bunch of emails ping into her mailbox. Eventually, the last one, *Mullen, Cormac* with an attachment.

Cara clicked the icon at the bottom of the email. Impatiently she clicked it a couple more times. Kilobyte after slow kilobyte the file downloaded. Cara's phone rang, but she ignored it. Eyes only on the computer screen.

A video file appeared. Cara pressed play. She leant in closer to the computer screen. Her pulse, unlike the download speed, was galloping. A tight angle of the school back door appeared. A black blur that revealed nothing, then an individual stepping back, the video just catching them in profile. A two to three second loop.

Not of Ferdia.

And not Maura as Cara had initially speculated.

The quality was poor, but there was no one else it could be. And in their back jeans pocket? A bulge of familiar proportions. About the size of a small tin. A tin that could fit some spliffs and pills.

Finger to her lips, biting the skin at the edge of her nails.

Messy blonde bun.

Sorcha.

TWENTY-EIGHT

Cara stared at the screen. Sorcha? What the hell?

Cara's mobile, which had stopped ringing, began again. Without looking she reached for it, her eyes still transfixed by the image of Sorcha on-screen. What on earth was Sorcha playing at? Cara had so many questions she didn't know where to start. The phone's insistent vibrations tingling against her palm dragged her eyes down to look at who was calling.

Mamó's name was flashing on screen.

Cara jabbed the answer button.

'Hey, Mamó.'

'Cara,' Mamó's voice whispered from the other end of the line. 'Oh, thank God I got through to you.'

'What's wrong, Mamó?' said Cara, standing up. 'Why are you whispering?'

'I think there's someone in the house.'

'What?' Cara's heart leapt as if shocked by the paddles of a defibrillator.

'The kids are at Bríd's, don't worry. It's just me here. I'm in the TV room, hiding. I've got the sofa against the door. I'm too scared to make a break for it.'

'Mamó, I'm coming!' Cara scrambled around the desk, throwing her coat on as she ran. She pulled the station door shut behind her, fumbling to lock it with a key that seemed to have grown in size and wouldn't fit. Slowing a moment she got it locked and ran for her car. Her house was no more than five minutes away, but right now that felt like five hours. She slammed the car into reverse. She hit the road with a spin of the tyres and threw her car headlights on high beams, lighting up the road ahead of her, darker in the early evening half-light due to the blackout.

She tore by Derrane's, her peripheral vision taking in Daithí and Ferdia standing by the front door. She put her foot down, the sweep of her headlights illuminating a maze of all-white roads. The car skidded and slipped in the slush and fresh falls. Cara grew terrified she might wreck the car. That she might crash and not get to Mamó. That she wouldn't save her. Yelling in frustration, she slowed down.

Cara turned the last corner, gliding too close to the stone wall as she went. She pulled up outside the house, getting out of the car. Grabbed the door as she nearly fell, her feet hitting an icy patch of drive. The snowman from this morning, with his too-tight scarf and wrong-way carrot nose, sat out front. The shadows of near total darkness cast malevolent shapes, transforming the jovial, rotund snowman into a shadow-dwelling ghoul.

She left the car door open, no slamming to alert the intruder. She wanted them out of her house, away from her grandmother. But she wanted to see who it was first.

She opened the boot of the car as quietly but as quickly as she could. Took out a large, brick-like torch.

She approached the front door. Slipped her key in gently. Thankful the wind had died down a little. She crept in. Battery-powered camping lamps with bright white LED bulbs lit areas of the hall. Casting a little pool of light within the complete darkness. Cara paused and listened. She had stopped in front of the hall mirror. A softer light on the hall table cast an upward orange glow on her. Grotesquely lighting up her neck and chin. She looked as they had as teens when telling ghost stories, shining a torch from below. Only this was no story.

She stayed still and listened, casting a quick glance in the direction of the TV room where she knew Mamó was hiding. Cara pleaded with her heart to stop hammering, the rapid pulse in her ears deafening her. She counted her breaths in, held them, then out again. Slowed her heart rate. Listened again.

Nothing.

She moved a step into the corridor that led to the back of the house.

Nothing.

Another step.

Then she heard it.

From her room. The sound of her wardrobe being opened. Quietly. Whoever was in there was hoping not to be detected. Her room was at the back of the house and she'd approached in the car from the village road, so they probably hadn't heard her arrive.

She took a couple more steps down the corridor, sidestepping the floor where it creaked, years of avoiding waking babies providing an instinctive map. She heard more sounds from her room. There was only the beam of light from her torch down here, no camping lamps. She swept the beam across the end of the hall by her door. The sliver of light catching on the ground a demonic grin, blood dripping teeth, crazy eyes. Cara screamed. Then her brain caught up with what she'd seen. Just the evil clown toy Cathal had insisted on getting for Christmas. Left lying around.

'Jesus,' whimpered Cara. And now silence from her bedroom. There was no way she hadn't alerted the intruder.

She heard Mamó open the door down the hall and call a terrified, 'Cara? Oh my God, Cara!'

'I'm okay, Mamó! Don't worry! Get back in!'

Then a scrabble from inside. The sound of her window being opened.

Cara rushed her door. But the blast of freezing air as she burst in, the curtains flying, were enough to tell her they'd fled. She ran to the window. Hurled herself out. Into the darkness. Tumbling onto the snowy bank beneath her window. She rolled and then scrambled to her feet, still grasping the torch. She waved it left then right, an arc of desperation, so close to the answer, to the knowledge of who was doing this. Who was behind this nightmare. But they were gone. She ran to the garden wall, tripping over unseen obstacles. Stumbling then regaining her footing. The torch beam illuminated nauseously, shaking as she ran. Its beam picking up nothing.

In the dark, Cara ran out into the road. Panting, her frozen breath steaming from her, snapping each way, she looked, searched. In the early evening gloom – not quite the blind pitch black of later – but dark enough that the world was just ideas and memories, no longer concrete or real. There could have been an army of the worst the world had to offer, hiding behind the low walls and she couldn't know. She couldn't see.

Cara roared into the emptiness. Screamed her rage and sadness and frustration. Bellowed so the creature, the demon who had done this, would hear her pain, wherever they'd escaped to. Whatever bit of hell they'd crawled back to. Know that she was there, know she had been close. And was coming for them. One way or the other.

TWENTY-NINE

Cara looked around her bedroom. And though it was quite dark – there was only so much light a battery-powered lantern could cast – she could still see that it was like a tornado, a very isolated tornado, had swept through the space.

'And nowhere else?' She turned and looked at Mamó.

'No, I've checked the whole house. Nowhere else seems to have been touched. It's dark, and maybe in the morning light something will become obvious, but I don't think so.'

Cara nodded.

'And are you feeling okay? It must have been terrifying.'

'I'm not the better for the last half hour, no. But I'll be fine. I'll be fine.'

'I hope so. If I'd thought this might happen...'

'Stop it, you couldn't have anticipated it at all. I'm only sorry I was hiding behind the sofa the entire time and I can't tell you anything useful about whoever it was.'

'Stop it yourself now, Mamó. Thank God you stayed safe. I'll get whoever it was, don't worry.' Cara hugged her grandmother again. Neither of them were better for the experience.

'Can you go back to Bríd's, for the night? Does she have a

spare room? I don't like the idea of you guys here, on your own. Even with Maurice and Conor. I still need to be coming and going as I need to keep investigating, especially as this has gotten even more personal. I don't think I could focus if I thought you were still here.'

'I suspect that whoever it was won't be back, but I agree, I'm not happy taking the chance. I'm sure Bríd would be happy to have us and I know the kids would be delighted to stay there.'

'Okay, maybe you ring Bríd while I'll pack a few things for the kids?'

'I'll do that.'

Mamó headed for the kitchen and the landline which mercifully worked independent of electricity and Wi-Fi. Cara didn't want to think what might have happened if Mamó hadn't been able to stretch the long handset cord into the TV room and call her. Though the rest of the house was untouched, and her room had been the epicentre of interest, Cara shivered at the thought of what the intruder would have done when they came up empty-handed. Because it was obvious what they were looking for. The elusive package. They'd have started to search the rest of the house and would have found the cowering Mamó in the TV room. Maura had been murdered. This person wasn't messing about. Despite their efforts this morning with the letters, they weren't sitting back and waiting for the package to be delivered to them. And they must know that Cara was unlikely to give it back, even if she had it. Cara listened to her grandmother's muffled voice from the kitchen and felt a massive urge to sob. To release this awful dread and terror. Instead she screwed up her eyes and took a breath so deep she felt it in the soles of her feet. She had to keep going, to keep pushing. She couldn't stop and weep. Not yet.

Cara went into the kids' rooms and packed some pyjamas and a change of clothes for them. And here the wave of guilt found her. She wished she could pack it up too. She thought having Maurice and Conor stay was enough. But she'd left her grandmother vulnerable. Only luck had prevented something bad happening. She couldn't shake the weight of this. What if the kids had been here too? What if Mamó hadn't been able to grab the landline? What if Cara hadn't been at the station which had working Wi-Fi, meaning her phone had reception? So many what ifs. She didn't want the safety of her family to hang on what ifs.

She heard a car pull up outside. Cara went to the window and drew back the curtain. Bríd and Maurice in their ancient car. The light was on inside it and she could see Saoirse and Cathal in the back.

She met Mamó in the hall, each with a small backpack in hand.

'The kids are in the car,' said Cara.

'Yes, Bríd said they wanted to see you for themselves, they overheard our conversation on the phone.'

'Ah, no.'

'They've only worked out there's been a break-in, nothing more than that.'

'Okay. Well, I'll come out with you and talk to them.'

Cara put the front door lock on the latch, and the two of them made a break for it, buffeted by the wind and chased by the cold. At the car, Mamó gave Cara a quick hug. She kissed Cara on the cheek. *'Bí cúramach,'* she whispered in her ear. A phrase Cara had heard her say to the kids so many times. When too close to the fire, when little fingers pulled a door behind them, when dangling wool in front of a giddy cat – *be careful*.

'I will,' whispered Cara in return.

Mamó rounded the car and hopped in on the far side. Cathal wound down the window.

'Mammy, are you okay?' he asked. Saoirse, big blue eyes doubtful, leaned around Cathal, looking at her, her stare asking the same question.

Cara bent down, resting on the window frame, and reached an arm inside. She squeezed the pair of them together in a silly squished hug. She inhaled their innocent, comforting scent. It was nearly too much.

'I'm fine, sweetheart.' She looked first into his eyes, then his sister's. 'Everything is fine.'

'Are you sure?' asked Saoirse.

'Absolutely. It's more than fine. And even if it wasn't, I'm the best Garda on Inis Mór, so you've nothing to worry about.'

'Mammy,' piped up Cathal, 'aren't you the *only* Garda on Inis Mór?'

'You got me there, kiddo!' She pinched his cheek and grinned at him. She was rewarded with a wide grin in return.

'Now, go on, I promise things will be a bit more normal around here once the storm passes. Go with Mamó, be good and enjoy Bríd's house. I'll see you guys in the morning.'

'Okay, Mammy,' they chimed, her good humour reassuring them.

Cara thanked Bríd and Maurice and waved the car off. She turned back to the house, went in and shut the door. Locked it. She grabbed two of the battery-powered lights from the hall and headed back down the corridor to her bedroom. Picking up the terrifying clown toy and popping it in Cathal's quiet, empty room as she went.

Cara stood in her bedroom and looked about it. She placed one of the lights on top of the chest of drawers, the other on the bedside table. It would have looked cosy, romantic even, if it wasn't for the clothes and boxes pulled out of her wardrobe, the books strewn across the floor and each drawer in the chest of drawers upended. No corner had been left un-ransacked. It looked like a bombsite, not a boudoir.

She began to tidy and investigate. Look for anything missing. But Cara knew she wouldn't find anything gone. Whomever had done this had done it for the package. They knew enough to know Maura might have brought it here and given it to Cara to hide.

When they'd left through the window, into the darkness, they'd have left disappointed.

She folded and placed clothes back into the drawers. Reshelved the books. She gathered the boxes of summer clothes that had been pulled down from the top shelf in her wardrobe. Tidied them, and put them back. She stopped in the gloomy half-light for a while over one box. Sat down on the carpet. Old photo albums. From those summers. Cara crossed her legs and opened the first one. It was too dark to make out the faces. History stared back at her. Those fresh faces. Innocent faces in the shadows. She could have picked up her phone and shone the torch on it. But it would waste her precious battery. That's what she told herself. Not that she couldn't bear to really look. And what would she see anyway, if she did? Shadows of people she once knew. Who were they now? Ferdia and Sorcha, mixed up with drugs. Seamus and Maura nurturing secrets. It was hard not to feel alone. The world she thought had been made up of people she knew and loved now felt full of strangers.

She packed up the photo albums. It wasn't helping her mood nor the investigation. She picked up the nick-nacks, the memorabilia of youth she'd kept in the same box, which had scattered about the floor. She realised that this was where her snow globe, the pair of Maura's, should be. She didn't have the whimsy to keep it out on display like Maura had. But she certainly would never get rid of it. She grabbed her torch and shone it around the room. She couldn't see it. She turned and looked at the bed. Got down on her hands and knees and shone the beam under the bed. The light bounced off a reflective glass globe. For the second time that day, Cara lay down on her tummy and retrieved something from under a bed. This was a happier find though. It must have rolled in an awkward pattern across the floor and under the bed. Cara sat back up and shook the globe. Even in the semi-darkness, its snowflakes swirled and glittered. Two friends, two happy friends. Cara upturned it, watched the flakes swirl and settle again. She kept repeating the action. Watching the fake snow. She knew Maura had meant something by leaving hers where she had. If only she could work out what it was.

A trill echoed down the hall. The phone was ringing. Cara got up and grabbed one of the lamps. Made her way down to the kitchen. The outline of the Christmas tree in the window, just visible in the last hint of light, looked like a tentacled monster. The echo of the ringing phone in the dark empty room, its alien cry. Cara crossed to the phone. Realised she still had the snow globe in her hand. She placed it down and picked up the phone.

'Hello?' she said, feeling weird not knowing who was on the other end of the line.

'Cara, it's Daithí. Is everything alright?' His voice sounded strained. 'Ferdia and I saw you fly by in the car and you're not back at Flaherty's.'

'Everything's okay now – but I got a call from Mamó. We've had a break-in. Someone was trashing my room while Mamó was here.'

'Oh, Cara, that's awful. Is she okay?'

'She's upset, but otherwise unharmed, thank goodness.'

'It's all connected, right?'

'Absolutely. They were looking for the package, they have to be. Which obviously isn't here.'

'What the hell was this package? It's so strange.'

'I know, Daithí. The killer isn't the only person who wishes they could get their hands on it. I wish I could work out where she hid it. I've retraced her route, stopped into every house on the way. Nobody saw anything or knows anything. No clues. I haven't been able to search her house, but it looks like that's been done for me and nothing. They wouldn't have come looking here if they'd found it already. I've quizzed her stalker and he lost her after a sighting first thing that morning. So no help there. And I think she left me a clue, but I just can't work out what she meant by it.' Cara looked at the snow globe. She'd placed it down on a little pile of bits and pieces that had gathered by the phone. A little pile that every house but the most efficiently neat had. Just like in Maura's, that pile of letters and newspapers inside the door. On top of which she'd sat her snow globe.

'What's the clue?' asked Daithí. 'Maybe I can help?'

Cara stared at the snow globe. Felt a heat rise through her body. An idea forming.

'You know, no need,' she said, her heart rate picking up again. 'I think I might have just figured it out. I gotta go.'

Cara hung up, grabbed her car keys and ran out of the kitchen. The little glass orb stayed there, resting on the kitchen counter, on top of the bills and flyers. The camping lamp beside it casting a low glow of light through it, illuminating a last few synthetic flakes softly falling, gently, around two tiny friends.

THIRTY

Cara jumped in her car, and tore out of the driveway. The back of the car swung on the ice, the screech of metal telling Cara she'd made contact with the pillar at the end of the drive. She slowed down, again frustrated at the hold-up. It had come to her, standing there in the kitchen, looking at the globe as she spoke to Daithí. Sitting on the letter pile. That was it. It wasn't the globe itself. But what was under it. It had to be. That must be what Maura wanted to tell her. She knew that Cara would notice the globe. And know that it was out of place.

Even taking it easy, Cara was at Maura's house in three minutes. She grabbed the bulky torch from the passenger seat and rushed to the back door. Through the path she'd made in the snow earlier. Its whiteness like runway guiding lights reflecting back the torchlight. She fished around in her pocket for the key Daithí had given her. Even in her new leather gloves, her fingers were cold, the tips numb. The part of her face left exposed above her scarf and beneath the line of her hood took the brunt of the minus temperatures air. It wasn't yet 6 p.m., but Cara needed the torch to get the new key in the lock. She flashed the beam up, through the window into the back of the house, lighting up the snow globe, still in place inside the door, on top of its pile. What secrets did it contain? Cara opened the door and stepped. She shone the torch about the house and was relieved to see that everything was as it had been this morning, no further disturbances.

With gloved hands, Cara carefully lifted the snow globe and put it to one side. She pointed the torch at the pile beneath it. Letters, newspapers. As she'd noted before. She rested the torch on the sill, angling it so that she could check through the pile in its beam of light. She flipped through them quickly, looking for a note. There wasn't any. She then examined each item from the pile. Two letters. An electricity bill and a bank statement. Cara looked back and front at the letters and envelopes, looking to see if there was a message to be seen. Nothing. There was also the parish newsletter, and Cara flipped through the pages. Nothing but the local news. Next she checked the newspaper, turned it over and back. It was folded open on the crossword, which Maura had started, one answer filled in, but nothing else. Cara unfolded it and checked each page. Nothing yet again. She folded it back the way she found it, increasingly frustrated, decreasingly confident that her flash of inspiration had been correct.

She picked up the pile – maybe she needed to be in better light. That something was there, she just couldn't see it. She grabbed the torch and backed out of the house. Locked the door behind her. Turning away, the torch slipped from her fingers, dropping with a dull crack on the ground. Cara could hear rather than see the batteries roll away. Keeping the paper aloft with one hand, Cara crouched in the darkness, trying to find the missing pieces. But her fingers just touched cool mounds of snow, disappearing into them like sandcastles. She didn't want to risk getting the letters wet, if there was anything there, it would be destroyed. She'd put them in the car and then come back for the torch.

With care, one foot in front of another, guided by what little light there was bouncing off the white snow, she made it to the car. She placed the letters on the passenger seat and closed the car again. The slam of the door seemed to reverberate for miles, echoing off into the lonely distance. Cara looked up at the outline of the little house. The roof line darkly visible against the last hints of light in the sky. A bird, she thought, sat huddled in by the chimney breast, sheltering from the wind. She felt a shiver not caused by the cold.

She retraced her steps, back to behind the house. Slow and steady again, watching her step. To get her fallen torch. She rounded the house, darker still back here. She crouched down, fingers outstretched, feeling for the batteries, the pieces of the torch. She reached a snow-wet gloved hand to her face, brushed back a loose strand of hair, leaving a damp trail across her cheek. She found one battery. Then two.

Cara heard a sound. Not of wind through the low stone walls. Not of heavy snow falling from burdened roofs. Not an animal cry. Something else. Cara turned left and right. Her ears trying to narrow down where it had come from. She stood slowly, the torch not fully retrieved. She took a few careful steps around to the side of the building where she could at least see a few feet in front of her. She stopped. Stood statue still.

To her left.

She turned. The shed.

An outline emerged from behind it. Features impossible to make out.

'Who's there!' yelled Cara.

Nothing came back to her.

Cara stood her ground.

'Who are you?' she shouted once again.

In the darkness she heard someone begin to cry.

Stunned, she went in the direction of the pathetic sound, all fear dissolved by the tears. A face came into view.

'Patrick,' she said, seeing the anguished face of Patrick Kelly.

'I haven't seen her in days,' he gulped. 'Normally... normally if I lose her I can find her again. Where is she? Where is Miss Conneely?'

'Come here.' Cara reached out for him, felt his hand, its chill so deep she was nearly repelled. 'Patrick, you're frozen. How long have you been out here? You're freezing.'

'I've just been waiting... for her.' His sobs began again. Cara gently took his arm, guided him down the driveway, to her car. She opened the passenger-side door, lifted up the paper and post she'd put there a minute ago, placed the pile carefully on the dash, and guided Patrick in to sit. She closed the door after him, went to the boot of the car and pulled out an old blanket she kept in there. She returned to him and told him to put it around him. She then got into the car herself.

Cara put the key in the ignition and started the car. Turned the heating up to full blast and switched the tiny car light on. The poor lad was white as a sheet.

'You can't be out in this cold, Patrick. You'll make yourself sick.'

He sniffled but said nothing.

'Can I take you home?' she asked. He shook his head. And she wasn't sure that that was even the best idea. That tiny caravan hadn't appeared to have good heating installed. Cara decided to stay put for now, keep him in the car and at least warm him up a bit.

'Can you pass me those?' she asked, pointing to the pile she'd brought out from Maura's. She'd have a look at them again, now, in the inverted V spread of light in the car. It would also give Patrick some time to warm up and not feel under pressure to talk to her, to have to do anything other than thaw.

He handed her the pile. Cara left the newspaper resting against the gear stick and went through the letters again. Clearer now. But still, nothing odd or additional about them. Cara checked the insides of the envelopes, in case something had been written within. But nothing there either. She sat for a moment, looking out at the dark, her eyes searching for recognisable forms in the indistinct shroud of night and snow.

She was probably wrong. She'd jumped to a conclusion in her excitement. She put the letters down in front of the paper by the gear stick.

'Don't,' said Patrick. Cara turned and looked at him.

'Sorry, what?'

Patrick reached out a frozen hand and picked up the newspaper that Cara had just obscured with the letters.

'It's her handwriting.' He pointed to the one filled-in clue.

'It is, you're right,' said Cara.

'She likes puzzles,' he said while staring at the crossword.

'She does,' agreed Cara. Maura had indeed loved puzzles. Finished the whole crossword puzzle in double-quick time, the knack she had for them. But this one had only one clue filled in.

Cara took the newspaper from Patrick, looking more closely at the crossword. The sole answer, written in the boxes for ten down, was *THE HUSBAND RESTS*.

Cara looked at the clue for ten down: *The President of Ireland*.

This answer really didn't match. And it wasn't as if this was the tough cryptic crossword where the answers seemed as strange as the questions. This was the bog-standard crossword that anyone could work out. Simple questions with simple answers. This made no sense.

Except, perhaps it did. She hadn't been answering a clue. She'd been leaving one.

This is what Maura wanted her to see when she'd placed the snow globe on that pile.

THE HUSBAND RESTS.

But now there was a new puzzle. What the hell did it mean?

THIRTY-ONE

Cara turned on the full headlights of the car. Small eyes reflected back at her from hedge corners. She turned the steering wheel, and began to ease the car out. She started driving, following the road, but had no particular destination in mind. Those three words kept going around her head. *THE HUSBAND RESTS*. What did it mean? Maura wanted her to look somewhere, that felt certain. This package was the key to everything. And it was clear from the lengths she had gone to that she didn't want it to fall into anyone else's hands but hers.

Patrick sniffled beside her in the car. Cara grabbed a quick glance over at him, huddled in the thin blanket. She'd have to get him sorted or she wouldn't be able to focus and work out what Maura wanted to tell her. Cara could see just a handful of dots of light over in the direction of Kilronan, the few buildings with their own generators. It wasn't ideal but she decided she'd head to Patrick's home, make sure he had some working heating, that he'd stay warm there. When the storm was over she could get him some real help. It's what Maura would have wanted. But in the meantime she needed to be free to investigate. She couldn't babysit him, not now.

'Do you have a heater in your caravan?' she asked.

'There's a small one.'

'Is it working?'

'Yes. But it costs a lot.'

'Keep it on. Don't worry about the money. I'll look after that.'

Silence fell in the car again. Cara kept running the words over and over. *THE HUSBAND RESTS*. She must have been talking about Cillian. Did she mean Cillian's bedroom? Could it be hidden in the room she'd just spent two nights in? Was that possible?

'Where is she?' Patrick's voice crept into the distracted silence.

Cara sighed. This wasn't the time to break the news to Patrick. He'd need support around him when he learnt the truth.

'I usually see her every day. I know where she goes on the island and I haven't seen her anywhere.'

Cara slowed the car. Subterfuge and distraction seemed the only option right now.

'She's around, Patrick. And you can't be following people like that.'

'I'm just keeping an eye on her. It's a good thing.'

'I don't know, Patrick.'

'Where is she?'

'You saw her yourself with Seamus Flaherty, at his door, the other day.'

'That was two days ago, I haven't seen her since. I went all round the island. I even went back there, to the empty house, the guy's house, to check in case she was there. I looked in all the windows but she wasn't.'

'You looked in all the windows? When was that?'

'Yesterday.'

'Patrick, did you do that in the middle of the night?'

Patrick said nothing but Cara saw a nod in her peripheral vision.

'That was you? At my window last night? You scared me half to death!'

'I'm sorry, I was looking for her.'

That had been Patrick at her window. Not the eyes of a killer come for the next member of the group. Cara wasn't sure what to do with this information. Before the arrival of the letters, those eyes had given this person, whoever they were, corporeal form. Made them real. But it had just been Patrick, and despite what the others felt, Cara just couldn't see him as the killer. Whoever was responsible for this felt further out of reach to Cara now, even more of a mystery.

'I was looking for her,' he repeated, barely above a whisper.

'She's around, you've just been missing her.' Cara could hear the anxiety building up again in his voice. She slowed the car to a stop and pulled in, turning to look at Patrick.

'She means a lot to you, doesn't she?'

'She, she is... is always so kind.' Patrick's voice was a mix of sadness and hope. 'Everyone said I was stupid. When I was growing up. Even my dad. The other kids in school were mean to me, they made jokes about my mam leaving, called me bad names. But Miss Conneely, she was different. She was always kind. She worked out it was the letters that got all jumbled, that my brain couldn't work it out and I wasn't stupid. It wasn't my fault.'

'You have dyslexia?'

'Yes, yes, that's the word. She said it was why doing my spellings was so hard too. But she helped me all the time and I got much better. Even when I wasn't in her class any more. I'm still bad at it though.' He shook his head. 'I used to get so mad. I used to hit the other kids sometimes, when they wouldn't stop. She didn't even get cross at me then. She said she knew someone who got angry like me so she knew it wasn't really my fault. She said I reminded her of him. He used to get mad. But she knew he was good, in his heart.'

'Really?' said Cara, wondering if this individual was real or had Maura invented them to help the poor young kid.

'That's what she said. She told me he was her boyfriend when she was growing up. His dad had hit him, just like my dad hit me. He got angry like me. That's what reminded her of him. But she said she knew I was good too.'

That was no invention. That sounded like Seamus. His awful father, and he'd been the only boy she'd dated. Cara had seen him frustrated, angry, when they were young. Maura had always been such a calming influence on him.

Patrick's voice got quiet, wobbled with emotion, nearly whispering the next bit. 'I hit her once, by accident. She didn't even get mad then. I didn't mean to hit her, she was just stopping me hit Sean McDonough in the yard at playtime... she, she... said I couldn't do that. Even by accident. She said that boyfriend, he'd hit her and she'd had to tell him they couldn't be friends any more, and it'd be the same with me if I didn't learn to control my temper better.'

Cara went cold.

She kept staring out of the window. Didn't look at the lad.

'Is that true, Patrick, did she say all that to you?'

'I swear she did. I swear it's the truth.'

Had Maura told poor, sad, abused Patrick Kelly that Seamus had hit her?

Oh, Maura.

Oh, Seamus. She couldn't believe it.

'And are you sure that's what she said? That he hit her? You're not misremembering 'cause you were a kid and it was a long time ago?'

Patrick nodded vigorously in the seat beside her. 'Definitely. It made me sad when she told me. I didn't mean to hit her, it was an accident. But her boyfriend. I don't agree with her. I don't think he was good in his heart at all.'

Cara couldn't say anything. A great sadness moved from her heart outwards, a dark, creeping inkblot, moving slowly, but steadily to her extremities. This might be the worst secret she'd learnt so far. Seamus had hit Maura. They'd seemed so in love. Like Cillian and herself. Sure they were Heathcliff and Cathy, but they had been violently in love, not damningly, physically so. And had it just been the once? Like she told Patrick? Cara was a guard and she knew it was rarely a one-off. Why hadn't Maura told her? Instead confiding in the poor simple boy she looked after? Maybe it had been easier that way.

'Have I said something wrong?' said Patrick. Cara turned and looked at him, she shook her head.

'No.' It was all she could manage to say.

'Where is she?' Patrick asked again. Repeating his plaintive mantra. Cara just shook her head. 'Was it her?' he then asked. His voice different.

Cara looked at him, but said nothing. She understood the question he was asking. Like a child who asked if Santa existed, they weren't looking for the truth, that no, he didn't. They were looking for the lie to be made real. When he repeated 'Where is she?', he wanted reassurance that she was somewhere. Reassurance that she still existed. This new question. It was the answer. The one he didn't want.

'Was it her at the Serpent's Lair? Is that who it was? Is that why I can't find her?' His voice cracked.

'Patrick—' Cara grappled with her next words.

'If I hadn't been high, I could have saved her. If I hadn't been weak.'

'No, Patrick, that's not what happened.'

'I could have saved her.'

'No, that's not how—'

'NO!' he roared. Filling the car with a pain that a whole planet couldn't contain. A boy who had lost and lost and lost. The force of it opening the door. Patrick jumped out. Ran. Cara leaped out her side and ran around to the other side of the car, searching for his shape in the darkness. Already lost to the black starless night.

'No, Patrick, you couldn't have saved her,' said Cara to the emptiness. 'She was already dead.'

THIRTY-TWO

Cara knew it was pointless. She'd never find him in the dark. She'd circled the island twice at this point. Even when the electricity wasn't out and a storm wasn't blowing, she'd have had a hard time finding him at night on the island.

She slowed down as she went by his house. In the dark she could just make out the clawing tree as it shook in the wind, like the hand of a desperate crone, cleaving Patrick's caravan to her. Cara parked the car. Her torch was still in pieces on the back seat, damaged beyond repair. But her phone had gotten a recharge at the station earlier so she used it to guide her up the path to Patrick's home. She peered in the dark windows, shone the light in. No one was home. The tree above her creaked and sighed as it was abused by the gusts. Snow fell, thumping onto the caravan roof.

Cara retraced her steps back to the car. Moved off. She approached Flaherty's soon enough. Slowing down, she switched off the lights and engine, coasting to a stop. She pulled the handbrake and sat there, watching them, hidden by the dark. Seamus, Sorcha and Ferdia were gathered in the living room, lit by candlelight, half obscured by shadows. Like

MacBeth's three witches summoning evil from their cauldron. Mixing a poisonous brew of secrets. Cara wasn't close enough to see their expressions. But their body language told a story. No one seemed relaxed. When one of them got up, they were followed by another. Suspicion sown by those letters. Instead of eye of newt and toe of frog they were supping from a concoction borne of pernicious suspicion and malignant doubt.

Cara took off the handbrake. Let the car roll again. She didn't trust herself right now. Every fibre of her being wanted to burst in there and arrest them all. Haul them all off to the station and lock them up. These so-called friends. As she went, she looked back, felt she could make out the outline of Cillian's bedroom window. She wanted to get in there. Search it. She would wait though, till it was later, even darker. She'd creep in without them knowing she was there. She could keep secrets too. A few metres from the house, she switched on the car and drove off.

The road twisted around and Cara stopped searching the dark expanse outside her car. It was hopeless looking for Patrick. Slowing down, she noticed she was outside the grave-yard. She stopped and got out. She was getting used to the plummeting temperatures and barely flinched when hit by the freezing air. Using her phone torch, she guided her way through the graveyard pathways. The headstones loomed around her, the light from her phone providing a slim arc of protection. Her feet crunched through the listening silence, feeling the company of the graveyard residents.

Cara headed to the top left-hand corner of the sloping site. She stopped at the last grave in the corner. With a gloved hand, she brushed snow off the front of the granite memorial. She shone her phone on it. The quartz in the granite sparkled. Like snowflakes forever suspended.

Cillian Flaherty 1988–2012

Beloved husband, father and son
'In ár gcroíthe go deo'

In our hearts forever. Simple, but true. Cara crouched down and wiped off the snow from the edge of the border that surrounded the grave. She sat.

'Hi, love,' she whispered, her quiet words a confusion of tenderness and anguish. 'I miss you. I miss Maura already. Things here are a mess. An almighty mess. But it's been a mess since you died.' Cara hugged her arms around her. Felt the skin on her cheeks tighten in the cold. She scuffed her foot on some loose stones. 'It'll be ten years tomorrow. I can't believe it's been so long. Do you remember our last evening together? We'd sat down in front of the telly, after eating the last of the Christmas turkey. Do you remember? The babies were in bed, finally. And we had a glass of wine. Just you and me on the sofa watching some stupid rom-com. You told me you were thinking of going out on the trawler with Seamus for New Year's Eve. That you could make a lot of money providing fresh catch for the restaurants around Galway for New Year's Day. That it would help us pay for Christmas, all those toys we got Saoirse and Cathal. You asked was that okay with me? I said, "Of course, love." You worked so hard for our little family. When you left me that next evening, you kissed me and said, "I love you." The last words you said to me. If I'd only known you wouldn't be back I'd have chained myself to you. I'd have made you stay or sunk to the bottom of the sea with you.'

One of the wild goats in a field beyond cried out its strangled cry, a plaintive call that always sounded to Cara like they were in pain. A second goat replied, the screeches meeting somewhere in the distance behind Cara. She was shivering. It was decision time. Go on foot to search for Patrick, make sure he was okay. Or double back and search Cillian's room.

She wanted to search for the package. She wanted to get to

the bottom of this. Make it stop. But she was worried about Patrick. What must he be feeling right now? As she sat here on Cillian's gravestone, pondering the greatest loss she'd ever had, she knew he was experiencing the same, his greatest loss. But unlike her, he had no one else. No one to pick up the pieces. She was it. She feared the worst for him. She couldn't abandon him now.

But so close to the last, vital clue, could she afford to waste goodness knows how long on what could be a fruitless search for someone who likely didn't want to be found? For all she knew the killer was set to strike again. Did that not take precedence?

'Dammit!' yelled Cara into the night. The word echoing out into the emptiness. This was an impossible choice. There had to be another option? She needed help. There was only one person she could ask. Daithí. She could ask him to look for Patrick. He would do it.

Cara hurried back to her car. Hopped in and turned for Kilronan. Following the quiet beacon of light from Derrane's, guiding her to the village. She pulled up outside the pub, unsurprised at the number of cars already there. Locals, sick of being without electricity, had made a choice to go out and, like moths to a flame, had gathered where there was power. Warm light glowed gently from the windows. Cara walked up and peered in. She could see the regular suspects inside. And others, as she'd reckoned. She couldn't face any of them right now. If Cormac Mullen had heard talk, then there were rumours out there. There wouldn't be silence this time she entered the pub. There would be questions. Many of them. She wasn't in the humour. But she didn't have much choice if she wanted to find Daithí. Not that she could see him. No one appeared to be behind the bar right now. He was probably in the back, changing a keg, or something. Cara watched the drinkers a little longer. Watched the fire dance in the grate. Feeling like Tiny

Tim, or the Little Match Girl, some banished urchin outside to the cold. She touched the glass, it wasn't freezing. Her fingers didn't stick.

Cara took a deep breath and pushed on the door.

Her first feeling was one of relief. The heat of the pub was like a warm blanket. But pretty quickly the comforting feeling slipped away. Eyes turned on her.

'Oh, look who it is,' she heard a voice from the corner.

'Is it true?' asked an old man on a stool at the bar.

Angry, frightened faces stared at her from every table and stool and corner of the pub. Pent-up fear and resentment released like a genie, flexing its bitter muscles. Cara walked up to the bar without answering. She recognised some friendly faces at a table closest to the counter. Noah and some of his crew. Aiden and Lexi. Noah whispered to her, 'They've heard rumours about a body.'

'Who is it?' the old man asked her. Mrs Powell, the supermarket owner's mother, came up to him, and looked at Cara. Her face wasn't unkind, but her words were laced with worry.

'Someone told me there was a report of a body found on the island,' she said. 'Is it true?'

'I heard that too,' chimed her friend from a nearby table. 'Who's dead, Sergeant? Tell us, we want the truth.'

The noise level exploded, everyone talking at once.

Cara cleared her throat.

'You all need to calm down. Rumour and speculation, especially at a time like this, will only upset matters.'

'You're a Garda not a politician, answer the bloody question,' came another voice from the crowd.

Cara decided that maybe a bit of limited information might help.

'Okay, yes, there has been an accident. But as islanders you know this happens. It's a harsh life we lead out here. Accidents happen.'

'Don't lecture us on the hard life out here, we've been living it all our days,' said Mrs Powell.

'And who are these guys, these strangers?' asked one of the crowd. Tomás, the walker from the first night of the storm, looking at Noah and his table. Tomás didn't look any friendlier today.

Cara saw concern in Noah's eyes.

'Tomás, these guys are just visitors to the island, tourists.'

'They don't look like tourists to me! And someone dead on the island too. Are we meant to believe it's just some strange coincidence? You take us for fools, Sergeant.'

'You're right, they aren't the usual tourists – this is film director Noah Jackson,' she pointed to the director, 'and his film crew. They're here with Seamus Flaherty, whom you all know very well. There's nothing to worry about.'

'I heard about the body too,' said a voice from the back.

'Is it Maura Conneely?' asked Cáit Óg from the middle of the crowd. 'Is that why you were coming asking questions about her this morning? Is Maura dead?'

'She asked me questions about Maura too,' piped up a neighbour of Cáit Óg's. 'Is it Maura Conneely?'

'I've said what I can say, for now.'

Cara turned to go. She didn't have time for this. She headed to the end of the bar where a section lifted up, to find Daithí. Torches and pitchforks and angry villagers be damned.

'Hey, come back!' a voice called out.

'We deserve some answers, Cara Folan!' another angry voice demanded.

Cara let the side of the bar drop. The almighty bang shut everyone up.

'It's *Sergeant* Folan,' she said to the stunned silence. 'And you'll get more information when I think the time is right. Now. Goodnight.' Cara pushed open the door behind the bar and let it swing closed behind her. She'd pay for that later. But right now she didn't care.

'Daithí?' she called out.

Cara checked the storerooms. No sign of him. She followed the corridor down to the back of the building to the living quarters.

'Daithí? It's Cara, I need a favour.'

She put her head into the tiny kitchen. The lights were on, but no one was there. There were plates and glasses by the sink and the smell of a recent dinner hung in the air. Cara's stomach grumbled and she wondered when she last ate. The sound of the wind outside rattled and howled through the window at the end of the room. She backed out, turned. Headed across the corridor to the sitting room.

'Daithí?' she called out again. She knocked on the door and entered. 'Daithí? Are you in here?'

He was. And so was Courtney, in Daithí's arms. The pair of them turned and stared at Cara, like teenagers caught by the parish priest. Cheeks red, flushed with a cocktail of their private moment and this public sharing of it.

'Oh,' said Cara, rooted to the spot like the pair of them. She recovered first, and turned. Got out of the room quickly. She hurried back down the corridor, and out a side door, avoiding the disgruntled crowd out front. On the street she heard Daithí behind her. A faint cry of 'Cara!' She kept going. Daithí and Courtney. That hadn't looked like something new. More secrets. She'd thought Daithí was different.

She stood in the middle of the road. The windows from Derrane's cast a small radius of light about the place. The trees, where her cap had flown the other day, stood sentinel. She couldn't be bothered to look up and see if it was still there.

'Cara.'

Daithí was outside now. Standing on the path. Looking at her.

He was holding something out to her. She stepped closer.

Her phone. She must have dropped it in her rush to get out.

'Oh. Thanks,' she said flatly. She had no other words. She took it.

'It was on the floor in the hall.'

'Uh-huh.'

Daithí stood there and said nothing. Cara looked at the phone in her hand.

'Is that it?' she managed eventually.

'Is what it?'

'Don't act dumb.'

'Am I seeing Courtney, is that what you're at?'

'Of course it is.'

'Do you care?'

Cara couldn't answer the question.

'I was done waiting, Cara. I couldn't do it any more.'

'Do what?'

'You know what. Live in Cillian's shadow. Not be as good as him. Not be enough.'

'I don't—'

'You don't have to say anything. It's not your fault. Cillian was pretty perfect, it's why I loved him as a brother. But I can't wait any longer for you to love me as anything *other* than a brother. Life, sadly, moves on.'

'I never meant to...' Cara felt the dial point to empty. The warning light had been flashing red but here, now, she rolled to a stop. She looked at Daithí and then walked to her car. Opened the door.

'Cara, wait.' Daithí walked towards the car. 'Don't go. Please.' She looked back at him. Caught a glimpse of Courtney by the door. She got in the car, turned the key in the ignition and drove.

THIRTY-THREE

Cara drove along the dark island roads. She'd no reason to be angry at Daithí but she was all the same. He could have trusted her to tell her about Courtney. Or to talk to her about his feelings. It had been there for a long time, between the pair of them. Neither willing to take that next step. Or at least that's what Cara thought had been happening. It seemed Daithí hadn't seen she'd felt the same way. And now he was with Courtney. And though it was a different league, he, too, was keeping secrets. Daithí too had lied to her. Lies of omission counted.

Cara drove. Found the car pointing in the direction of Flaherty's. Also the direction of Patrick Kelly's empty house. She'd run away shocked from Daithí so quickly she'd entirely forgotten why she'd gone there. So she was back where she'd started. Having to make a choice. Look for the young lad who might be a danger to himself, or search for what might be the smoking gun in this crime.

She'd have to do both.

She'd look for the package first. Then she wouldn't have anything distracting her as she searched for Patrick. And with any luck he might even have gone home by the time she'd had a look. Cara knew she was rationalising what she wanted to do first. But, in the end, she argued with herself, both tasks were vital; it was an impossible choice. A little voice told her to go back and talk to Daithí and get him onboard. But she ignored it. She didn't want to talk to him. Not right now.

Cara drove past Flaherty's and then Kelly's. Candlelight radiated from Flaherty's, still nothing from Kelly's. She parked the car, got out. She'd do this bit on foot. No car noise in the night to alert them.

She checked once more at the caravan as she went. There was a chance that Patrick had no candles or torches and was inside in the dark. She banged on the door, peered in the windows. Nothing. She continued on to Flaherty's.

On through the dark, just about seeing one foot in front of the other. Not using her torch just in case. She slipped and slid, nearly losing her footing a few times. She reached Seamus's. She stood still, knowing she didn't need a tree or a wall or anything to hide behind. The night was enough right now. Cara walked as lightly as she could up the drive. Praying the feeble single-glazed windows wouldn't betray her and let the sound of her approach in. Alert those inside. She could see them clearly now. Seamus, eyes drooping, head nodding, trying to stop himself falling asleep on the sofa. Sorcha was curled up on one of the armchairs, drink in one hand, a book in the other. Cara recognised it as *Is Mise An tOileán*, Seamus's memoir. Ferdia was in the other armchair, sipping on a whiskey and staring into the fire. She felt like Patrick now, the Peeping Tom, watching them all illicitly. Cara saw Ferdia steal glances at Seamus, as Seamus's heavy eyelids fluttered and struggled. She caught Sorcha's quick glimpses over the top of the book at the other two when she thought they weren't looking. A finespun Mexican standoff.

She realised she had a problem. How was she getting into the house? The back door led into the kitchen, where everyone was. And she didn't want them to know she was there. She looked left, down the front of the house, on the side of the bedrooms. Perhaps she could jimmy one of the windows and get in that way. Cillian's room would be ideal. But she stopped. Looked at the front door. Something inside her told her to try it. She reached out a hand and, without rushing, and as quietly as she could, she depressed the handle. It gave. The latch clicked and it opened. Unlocked. How many times had she reminded them? And even if she hadn't, wasn't fear enough of a motivator? They were the only house that knew the truth, that there was a murderer on the loose, after all.

Cara stepped into the house. Thankful for the carpet that soaked the sound of her footsteps. An LED camping lamp the only light in the hall. She closed the door behind her with two hands, slow and careful.

Cara looked right towards the kitchen. Weak orange light a line under the door. It was shut firmly. Keeping the heat in. It was still icy in this part of the house. She was thankful now for the first time – it would hopefully keep everyone out of this side of the building. Give her time to search.

She turned for Cillian's room.

She opened the door and stepped in. She looked at the bed first. This seemed the most logical place to start. She dropped to her knees. Bent and shone her phone torch under the bed. Nothing. Forced her hands in under the mattress, spreading them out like she was swimming, fingers feeling for anything. Again they came out empty-handed. Perhaps Maura had just meant the bedroom, not literally his bed. She stood. Shone the torch on the bookshelf. Nothing out of place. Nothing strange or unusual.

Cara stopped. Turned and looked towards the bedroom door.

Was that a sound? A door opening?

She listened, strained to hear. Footsteps. Definitely footsteps.

Someone was coming. And she couldn't be sure they weren't coming in here. She spun on the spot. Where to hide? She had moments to decide. Under the bed, or in the wardrobe? The bed. That was the clue, it would keep her safe. She dropped and rolled. Tucked herself up tight against the wall.

Just in time. The door opened.

THIRTY-FOUR

Whoever it was didn't have a torch. The faint hint of light suggested a candle at most. The room was in darkness, a sucking black hole. All Cara could see as she held her breath were faint outlines, muddy shadows. She heard them move around the room. Take the books off the shelf. And then place them back again. The drawer on the desk opened and shut with more force than was necessary. Then the doors of the wardrobe. Searching, searching. Repeating so much of what Cara had just done.

How long till they looked under the bed?

Cara's heart was pounding so hard she was surprised the floor wasn't vibrating.

Then the feet were back at the bed. She could tell by how close the sound was and the barest of outlines where candlelight fell.

Thump. They were down on their knees. Cara felt the mini-earthquake of the mattress above her being upset as they searched. They'd find nothing, like she had. And then they'd look under. Even the weak light of a candle wouldn't be enough to protect her.

The bed had been a mistake. At least in the wardrobe she'd have been on her feet. Able to run or fight.

Here, she was trapped. A dead end. No way out.

The mattress settled. No more searching. They'd looked everywhere she hadn't. There was only one place left.

Cara braced herself. This was it. She was about to be discovered. The only relief would be in knowing, finally, who was the searcher.

The murky outline of two hands now, on the carpet. Ready to bend at the elbow, to dip down. And look.

Then a sound, from down the hall. A voice.

'Ferdia?' Sorcha's voice from the kitchen, calling her husband. Out of her sight for too long, suspicious, she'd come looking for him.

Ferdia.

'Shit.' His voice came from a foot away from her. As he knelt by the bed.

A shuffle and the hands made the bed springs creak as they helped push him up.

As Ferdia left the room. Empty-handed.

Ferdia was the one searching for the package. Cara lay there, paralysed. Rendered immobile by the implications. Ferdia was the searcher. Did that mean he was the letter writer too? And did that mean he was...

Cara unfroze. A cascade of adrenaline propelled her out from under the bed. She had to get out of here. She couldn't be found. She'd had a reprieve but how long until he came back? Pausing at the bedroom door, she peered out. Ferdia was gone. The kitchen door was shut. She made a dash for the front door. Heart hammering. She slowed down and opened the door gently, as if she had all the time in the world. Pulled it shut behind her just as she heard the kitchen door open again. She threw herself flat against the front of the house. Surrendering to the darkness.

Ferdia. He'd been searching for the package. Repeating everything she'd just been doing. Just like her he'd obviously been waiting to choose his moment. Seamus asleep, Sorcha seemingly engrossed in the memoir, Cara nowhere to be seen. Had it been him up at Maura's, breaking the lock and tossing the place? Was that why he had turned up that first morning in the stupid garb at her house, not looking for Maura, but the package? And had it been him up at her house, terrifying Mamó and trashing her room? A lot less careful with her things than Maura's? She felt a rage build up. How dare he put her grandmother through that. She wanted to rip the front door open and go in there and batter him. Forget about arresting him. That wasn't enough now.

She stepped back from the house, looked around. Saw only Sorcha and the sleeping Seamus in the kitchen. Ferdia was gone again. Cara moved as quickly as she could without falling to the window of Cillian's room. She didn't care if they heard her. But there was no glow from a candle. The room was empty. She followed the wall around. No one in the end room, Ferdia and Sorcha's bedroom. Cara kept going. She was at the back of the house. The tell-tale shimmer of light from the next window down – Seamus's room – told her where Ferdia was now.

She shimmied along the wall, and peered in, keeping as far back and in the dark as she could while still watching him. Ferdia was going through Seamus's things. Repeating what he'd done in Cillian's room. Looking through the wardrobe, in the desk. Going through Seamus's bags.

Still searching.

So Cara had been wrong – the package hadn't been in Cillian's room, neither she nor Ferdia had found it. That hadn't been what Maura was trying to tell her. Cara felt a stab of despair. The confusion was excruciating. She wanted to cry out in the night, rent the air with her frustration. But she kept her silence. Stayed clothed in the dark, watching Ferdia. Let the freezing night numb her pain.

Something else began to dawn on Cara.

Ferdia couldn't have been the one who broke into her house. He was back in Kilronan, she'd driven by him and Daithí on her way to help Mamó.

What did that mean? The more she discovered, the less she understood.

Were *two* people searching for the package?

THIRTY-FIVE

In the darkness, she watched the shadowy Ferdia methodically go through Seamus's room. He wasn't finding anything. Cara watched his level of frustration rise. He stopped being as careful when putting things back in place. He slammed the wardrobe door shut. Through the thin glazing she could hear muffled swears.

Cara moved back from the house and placed herself against the wall of the turf shed. She could see the entirety of Seamus's room from here and she knew she was invisible in the shadows. She felt like an audience of one at a horror show.

She saw it before Ferdia did. If she'd been at the pantomime the audience would have yelled, 'He's behind you!'

The door opened.

A bleary-eyed Seamus stepped into the room, candle in hand. In the dim, dual candlelight it took him a moment to realise what was happening, that someone was there. To recognise Ferdia.

He was now wide awake.

Immediately, Cara could hear their raised voices. Seamus yelling at Ferdia. With the raised volume Cara caught some of the words – they were all in Irish. Without her there they'd slipped into their native tongue.

Seamus raged on but Ferdia just stared at him, silent. Then he said something that Cara couldn't hear. She watched Seamus shake his head. Ferdia stepped forward. Closing the space between the men. Nose to nose, fists tight and like peacocks, the pair of them increasing the physical space they inhabited. Chests puffed out. Legs planted firmly, spread apart. The threat of violence, ready to erupt.

Cara heard that phrase everyone knew – 'le do thoil'. Please. Like the last argument they had, outside the back door yesterday evening. And like last night, this 'please' didn't sound that humble, that pleading. It sounded angry and mad. Perhaps she was wrong? Maybe it wasn't 'le do thoil' that she was hearing, maybe it was a different word that just sounded like 'please'?

A movement. Cara looked behind them. The door opened again. Seamus turned.

It was Sorcha.

Like marionettes whose strings are suddenly cut, the pair of them slumped back. Ferdia half turned away. She watched Seamus turn to Sorcha, reach out to her. If she could see his face, she knew there'd be a smile planted there. Charming as ever. Sorcha didn't look so sure. She glanced over at Ferdia and back at Seamus. Cara wondered what lies he was telling her. How he was explaining away the raised voices. Ferdia wasn't bothering to help. He walked to the window. Cara stepped back, further into the shadows, though she knew he couldn't see her. Ferdia stared out into the night. Looking right in her direction. Cara had to force herself not to move. Not to give in to the instinct to hide, that he must see her. Only further movement would give away her position out here.

Holding her breath, clinging to the wall of the shed for support, Cara didn't move a muscle. She watched as Sorcha left the room. Seamus followed her but waited in the doorway, not going a step further, until Ferdia turned and joined him. And then they were gone.

Cara took a moment. Breathed out and slumped too, just as Ferdia and Seamus had.

What had she just witnessed? What had she just been a part of?

Her idea about the clue had been wrong but she'd figure it out, she was confident of that. Yet that paled into insignificance next to what she had discovered.

Ferdia was searching for the package.

If she hadn't realised that the person who trashed her room at home couldn't have been him, would she'd be arresting him for murder right now? The thought took her breath away. Was he who the letters had been aimed at? And just because there was another searcher, it didn't absolve him either. It just muddied the murky waters further.

Cara started back around the house, down and around the bedroom half of the house, slipping away, further from the inhabitants' eyes. The more she learnt the less she understood. She was no closer really to understanding what had happened to Maura. All she had seemed to have achieved was to replace the firm, solid foundations of her world with tectonic plates that shifted and crashed against each other causing earthquakes at every turn.

Cara threw one look back at the house. The trio were back where they'd started, in the armchairs and sofa around the fire. A wary, watchful and suspicious truce settling on them. Cara walked down the drive, careful to remain as quiet as she'd been when she'd arrived. She turned out onto the road. It was time to go look for Patrick. She'd put it off in favour of a lead. A lead that she'd gotten wrong. An outcome she hadn't even considered in her confidence that she'd cracked the clue. She'd find Patrick now, even if it took her all night. She'd take him back to her home, get him warmed up and put him in the spare room. Sit with him. She'd had two days head start with her grief. Had Mamó and Daithí and the others to support her. And it was still terrible. Still fresh and excruciating as if someone had stabbed her in the belly. That poor confused boy could only be feeling worse. Her thoughts fuelled her feet. She picked up the pace. Started to shake off the self-pity that had been building. If she felt alone, how much more alone must Patrick feel? She had Mamó and the kids. That perfect unit that nothing could sully. But Patrick didn't even have that.

Cara found her feet more confident in the total darkness now. She was getting used to it, her other senses were compensating. Her ear was understanding the information the echo of her feet sent back to her. Creating confidence to step further into the unknown. Her sense of smell picking up notes of the gorse and briar at the edge of the stone walls under the snow, helping her keep straight.

Cara stopped. Smelt the air. Took a deeper breath. The musky scent of the hedgerows filled her lungs. She walked on. Heading for her car just beyond Patrick's. She might check his caravan one more time. Third time lucky, perhaps.

She stopped by the dark end wall of the crumbling family house. Looked up the path to his home. Too far to make out its outline at the end of the field yet. And though she felt it safe to shine her phone torch now – she was far enough away from Flaherty's not to be noticed – it was the sound that alerted her first.

The creak of the tree branch struggling. Struggling under a heavy weight.

Cara broke into a run. She got a couple of feet before an obstruction, hiding under fresh falls of snow, tripped her, took her down. Cara went down. Her head slammed against the ground, her hands too slow to save her. A burst of bright light flashed before her eyes. She groaned. But crawled to her knees.

Got to her feet and ran again. Head pounding. Feet pounding the path.

Cara stopped. Midway up the path. Shone her torch above the caravan. Spotlighting the branches of the gnarled tree that stretched over it. The grasping crone had succeeded. Gathered her possession to her. Cara saw him. Swinging. Silhouetted. Saw it was too late.

Patrick was dead.

THIRTY-SIX

'Can you look after her? She shouldn't be alone tonight after that bang on the head.'

Cara could hear Dr De Barra's voice, but it seemed to be coming from far away. Daithí was nodding, his arm around her shoulders, where a blanket had been draped, though she didn't remember it being put there. She didn't even think she needed it. She couldn't feel the cold. She couldn't feel anything. She was numb.

Help had come quickly. Cara running to the nearest neighbour, and then back to the Kelly place. The island's volunteer firemen came, helped get the body down. When they'd arrived, they pulled Cara back, stopping her as she repeatedly tried to reach Patrick. It was clear he was gone, but Cara had been desperate to get to him. Then Dr De Barra had arrived. Cara wasn't sure when. One minute she wasn't there, the next she was examining Patrick's body which the men had laid out at the bottom of the path. De Barra had shaken her head. Sighed as she examined him. Then she'd come over to Cara and taken a look at the bash on her forehead. Next Daithí was with her, his arm around her shoulder, talking to the GP.

'Yes, we'll keep an eye on her. Thanks for coming out, Doctor.'

'Don't worry, this is the job.'

Daithí looked down at Cara.

'Come on, I'll take you back to Flaherty's. We can all look after you.' Despite everything Cara had seen, everything she knew about her friends, she didn't object. She didn't tell Daithí to leave her alone or to take her somewhere else. She walked with him back down the road, docile as a child. Back to the house she'd been sneaking around less than an hour earlier. She didn't mention what she'd seen with him earlier still. Him and Courtney. Because all her mind had space for right now was one thought – 'Patrick is dead because of me.' Cara's focus on finding Maura's killer had led her to choose to search for the clue instead of Patrick. Chances are he'd been in his caravan all that time, just hiding from her. If she hadn't made that decision, driven by her need to find out who had done this to her best friend, then maybe she'd have found Patrick in time. One of the firefighters handed her a note he'd found in Patrick's coat pocket. It was addressed to her – Sergeant Folan. Scrawled in a tentative hand, on a scrap of paper.

Im to sad witout Mis Conneely. She was the ownle one who cared for me. Im sorre I didnt cee who did it. Im sorre I cudnt help.

He was right about one thing. That Maura was the only one who really cared about him. Even Cara, with her ideas that she was a good person, and her notions to help Patrick, hadn't been there for him. When he'd needed it most. And as Daithí led her up the drive to Seamus's house, as she saw the trio through the window on the sofas as they rounded the building to the back door, she didn't feel as high and mighty as she had. She felt as bad as them. She couldn't kid herself.

'Come on, it'll be okay.' Daithí gave her a squeeze and turned the handle of the back door. They stepped into the kitchen and the others looked up. Surprised to see them.

'Hey, guys...' Seamus stood. 'Did you see anything going on? We thought we saw the fire tr—' He stopped talking at the sight of Cara. He rushed across the room. 'Cara, are you okay? What happened? Your head...?' He looked from her to Daithí. Daithí led her to the sofa.

'What's happening?' Seamus asked. Ferdia and Sorcha looked on, concerned.

'Patrick Kelly killed himself,' Daithí explained. 'And Cara took a tumble. She's okay, Dr De Barra looked her over.'

'Oh God,' said Sorcha. She stood, taking Cara's hand and sitting her down. She turned to Ferdia. 'Get her a whiskey, Ferdy.'

'Of course.' Ferdia stood and grabbed a glass for Cara and poured her a large measure. Cara took a sip and felt the liquid burn her throat as it went down. But even its fiery flames didn't move her. Seamus sat down in an armchair, his face a picture of concern. Daithí and Sorcha sat either side of Cara. Sorcha stroked her cold hand.

'What happened?' asked Seamus.

Cara turned her head to him and spoke slowly.

'He... he found out that Maura was dead.' She shook her head. Took a deep breath. 'Maura was the only person who cared for him, which would have made the news hard enough. But, also, he'd been there. Heard whoever killed Maura throw her over. The guilt that he was too high to understand what was happening... to save her. I tried to tell him that she was dead already... I should have tried harder to find him, made sure he knew that.'

'Cara, don't torture yourself,' said Seamus. 'He was a troubled lad. You know that.'

'Seamus is right,' said Sorcha. 'The damage was done a long

time ago by his shitty parents. Even if you'd found him, and told him, that wouldn't have fixed his problems.'

'They're right, Cara,' said Ferdia. Cara looked at him. Felt a nauseous wave at Ferdia's casual dismissal of poor Patrick. As the man who had supplied those drugs to him. And whatever else he was up to. She couldn't look Seamus in the eye either. Patrick's awful story about the young Seamus and Maura would haunt her. Whyever had Maura forgiven him? Cara was disgusted. Disappointed. Heartbroken. But at this moment, she felt like she'd tumbled from the higher moral ground. Fallen to the bottom, and could no longer stand in judgement with an unblemished record. She hung her head. Shrugged.

'Cara. You're a fine person,' said Daithí. 'And even the best people in the world don't get it right all the time. You can't judge yourself by some one-hundred-per-cent-right-one-hundred-per-cent-of-the-time criteria. That way leads to madness. It can't be done. Sometimes bad things happen.'

Cara could feel the tears well up. These past couple of days had been horrific. Nothing in the world could have prepared her for this wretched whirling chaos. She had thought that losing Cillian all those years ago was the worst thing that could possibly happen. And in lots of ways it would always be. But how Maura died. Patrick. The truths she'd learned about these people, these people who had been so dear to her. It felt like she was part of an experiment, or a sick reality TV show. Nothing was real. Nothing was as it seemed. If she travelled far enough she'd be able to knock down the façade of the illusion around her. If they'd wanted to make her feel even more alone – and she wouldn't have thought it possible – this did the trick. She felt that if she were to scream, right here, right now, no one would hear her. Instead she sat, rooted to the sofa, staring at the fire. Lost.

Seamus stood and topped up everyone's glass. Cara watched him move from friend to friend. Sorcha held up her glass with a sad smile. The three who Cara had seen through the windows were slightly glassy-eyed and slower moving, the alcohol they'd been consuming over the evening showing. She remembered Seamus's words from earlier, about the doppelgängers. When Ferdia had called the actors that and Seamus had corrected him. That the word doppelgänger implied evil. Ferdia had actually been right, just not about which group was the doppelgängers. It was them. Each of them were bad.

Cara watched Daithí get up and go lock the back door. Slip out to the hall and do the same with the front. Maybe Daithí didn't deserve the designation of doppelgänger, that was probably unfair. He hadn't lied to her really. She still felt hurt though. And worse still, she felt that she didn't know him quite as well as she'd thought. That cut the deepest.

'Guys, can we keep an eye on the doors?' he said when he was back in the room. 'I know it's not usually necessary around here, but let's keep them locked, please?'

'But it's okay now, isn't it?' said Sorcha looking over at Daithí while snatching a quick glance at Cara.

'What now?' replied Daithí.

'He did it, didn't he? He must have?' Sorcha said, looking to each of the other inhabitants, looking for support. 'So we don't need to worry any more?'

'Yes, surely,' said Seamus. 'He was obsessed, didn't you say that, Cara? And I saw his temper myself.'

'He's only just dead, guys, and I don't think that he—' started Cara.

'You're not a detective, Cara,' said Ferdia, quietly.

'Maybe not. But I'm not stupid either.' Cara glowered at Ferdia.

'I don't think Ferdia was suggesting you were,' Seamus replied. 'I think he's just saying, you're not trained, you might have missed things. This kid, I'm sure he had a good side, and it might not have been his fault, but sometimes if it walks like a duck and quacks like a duck...'

'Do you have to be so flippant, Seamus?'

'I'm sorry, Cars, I didn't mean to be disrespectful.'

'Who else could it have been? And why?' said Ferdia, again, with little emotion. No smart-arse comments or smirk on his face. 'It was someone who had a reason to kill Maura. And that is nobody except for him. This kid had a reason. I don't see you with any long list of possibilities.'

'I don't know...' she said.

'Come on, Cara,' said Seamus, 'look at the facts. He was an odd young man who was obsessed with Maura' – he started ticking off the facts on his fingers – 'followed her around, admitted to being at the location as her body was thrown over, *and* was high at the time. And then he kills himself over guilt and loss. I for one will sleep better tonight.'

'What about the letters?' said Cara. 'You met him the other day. Do you think he was capable of that? And anyway, the kid was badly dyslexic. Do you want to see his suicide note?'

'The letters were hardly *War and Peace*, Cara! And he wrote a suicide note. He liked to communicate by letter. I'm all the more convinced.'

Cara stared at him.

Sorcha piped up.

'I'm convinced too, Cara. It's the only thing that makes sense.'

Cara said nothing. Because she couldn't argue against that point. It did make sense. On paper. If you hadn't spent time with the kid. Hadn't seen his anguish. His innocence. But who was she to say he hadn't been playing her? Or it hadn't been some awful accident? She didn't know that. And without the full backup from Galway, she couldn't say either way. Her gut instinct about Patrick Kelly was worthless. Gut instinct would be laughed out of court. It was being bounced out of this kangaroo court anyway.

'Why don't we just focus on tomorrow, for now,' said Daithí.

'Tomorrow?' said Sorcha. Cara, Ferdia and Seamus all looked at him in confusion.

'Tomorrow. Cillian's anniversary, New Year's Eve. Remember? Anyone?' he replied. 'The whole reason you're here.'

THIRTY-SEVEN

Cara washed the breakfast dishes in lukewarm water boiled on the camping rings Daithí had lent them. The light through the frosted back door had a different quality to it this morning. Brighter. Less grey. Ferdia, uncharacteristically helpful, was drying.

'God. My head,' he said. 'Why did we drink so much whiskey last night?'

'I think that was mostly you,' said Cara, passing him a wet dish. 'My head is hurting for other reasons.'

Sorcha came in the back door, a burst of freezing air coming in with her. She stamped her feet to knock the snow off her boots. Placed a bucket of turf down on the mat as she took them off. 'How *is* your head, Cara? And I mean the bump, you barely touched a drop last night, unlike the rest of us. Well, bar you as well, I guess, Daithí.' She looked over at Daithí who was finishing his coffee at the breakfast table. He raised his mug in greeting.

'I promised Dr De Barra I'd keep an eye on her.'

Sorcha stepped up to Cara and with cold fingers gently

moved her hair back from her face. On her right temple there was a nasty bump and a dark purple bruise.

'Ouch,' said Sorcha with a wince at the sight of it.

'It's not too bad. And the headache is easing.'

Seamus looked up from the fireplace where he was laying down the fire for the day. He was pale. He smiled over at Cara, but didn't say anything. Cara finished the last dish and pulled the plug in the sink. Dried her hands on a towel.

She grabbed the bucket of turf.

'I'll bring this over,' she said with a smile to Sorcha.

She crossed the room and placed them next to the hearth. 'Here you go.'

'Thanks.'

'You doing okay?' Cara asked. 'The day that's in it, and everything.'

Seamus picked up a few of the pieces of turf and put them on the pile. Laying a large fire, ready for when they got back from the cemetery. He nodded, but didn't look up at her.

'It's always a hard day,' he said, still fussing around the fire. 'I know this is the first time we've spent it together... I'm sure it's been the same for you all these years.'

'It's never easy, no.' She sighed and looked over at the photo on the wall of Cillian.

'Will you take the kids to the grave?'

'We usually go tomorrow. On New Year's Day. To make it a positive experience for them, well, as much as it can be. I take them down, and we all chat with Cillian about our hopes and dreams for the coming year.'

Seamus looked up at her.

'That's lovely.'

'Yeah, it's helped make it more of a celebration.'

'Well, we'll try our best to do that today, have a celebration for him.'

'We will.'

'Right,' said Sorcha, from in the middle of the room. 'Can we all get ourselves organised, and we head then? Go say our hellos to the man himself?'

Daithí pushed back his chair and stood.

'Yep, let's get ready.'

Ferdia put away the last dish and folded the tea towel. Seamus got up from the fireplace. Rubbed his hands together, brushing off the dust. He circled the sofa and joined Sorcha by the kitchen door.

Cara looked at them all. Those hands of Seamus that just brushed off dust after building a fire, had they once beaten her friend? How many vulnerable young people had Ferdia supplied with drugs? How easily Sorcha had shown concern when gently checking her wound a few moments ago. Where was that milk of human kindness when she went to plant drugs in her friend's workplace? But Cara felt flat. She couldn't feel rage or sorrow as she regarded this rogue's gallery. The ground beneath her feet felt temporary. The walls around her optional. She was a battery that had been let to run down. No amount of turning the key could kick her back into life. Other than the quiet Seamus – understandably so on his brother's anniversary, the accident that he'd been there for – she sensed a difference to the rest of them. Everyone was lighter. Was it their belief that Patrick had been responsible? And now he was gone, the threat was too? Or was it that the forecast said the storm would begin lifting this evening? Boats would start again soon, planes too. Little Inis Mór would be rejoining the rest of the world. Maybe it was both that gave this morning its incongruous, nearly inappropriate air of lightness.

They reassembled at the door of the house twenty minutes later. Each wrapped up against the cold. Cara had Seamus's old violin. Sorcha some dried flowers she'd brought from London to put on the grave. At the sight of them Cara remembered the small white petals she'd found in Maura's pockets, the shepherd's purse. She shook it off. She didn't want to think about that, not now. Ferdia came out of the kitchen with a box of biscuits in his hands.

'What are they, Ferdia?' asked Sorcha.

'Jaffa Cakes,' he replied.

'I can see they're Jaffa Cakes, just why do you have them? You can't wait to snack later?'

'They're for Cillian.'

'Sorry?'

'They were his favourite.'

'It's true,' smiled Cara. She reached out and touched Ferdia's hand. 'He loved them.'

'I just thought... you know,' Ferdia half smiled, 'that he might like them.'

Cara smiled back at him, and felt the tears touch the corners of her eyes. She took a deep breath.

'Okay, come on, let's go.'

Daithí opened the front door and they all trooped out. The light felt a little less gloomy this morning. There still wasn't a patch of blue to be seen, but the total cloud cover was letting more light through, was thinner, less dense. Signs the storm was giving up the fight. The wind was also less harassing. They walked down the drive and could choose the path they took, not having to negotiate with the gusts to get from A to B. They had decided to go on foot. Just like they'd roamed the island as kids. To take the time and walk there. Remembering Cillian as they went.

'Oh my goodness, here come the Seven Churches...' giggled Sorcha, walking with her arm linked through Cara's, as they approached the ruins of a group of ancient churches. Only two houses of worship stood there, roofless, among other centuries-old remains of dwellings. At the moment everything was hidden under the snow. Underneath its white cloak the grounds were a tight maze of nameless graves and stone steps. Celtic crosses and domed headstones crooked and askew. The perfect place to be on a sunny summer evening if you were looking for some privacy. 'Are you blushing, Cara Folan? 'Cause you should be! First kiss alert!'

'Oh my God!' Cara laughed. 'I can't believe you remember that!'

'How could anyone forget?' Ferdia joined in. 'You two had been mooning over each other for months! How do you think you got left behind, at dusk, here among the shadowy – and private – ruins? Hmm?'

'What, no, you didn't!'

Seamus stopped by the entrance to the churches. Beamed at Cara.

'Oh yes we did.'

'Aw, goodness...' Cara was overcome. Those days from so long ago. She could feel Cillian close to her now. The two of them, fifteen years old. The sun warming their skin. Love warming the rest of them. Cara could feel Cillian's tanned arm resting next to hers as they sat with their backs against a wall older than time. And it had felt timeless. Just the two of them. The sound of the birds. The butterflies that chased and swooped after each other. A single cloud that had moved lazily across the sky, in no hurry. And Cillian's hand that had taken its time, reached slowly out for hers. And she'd let him take it. It felt like they'd captured some of the sun's rays there, in their clasped palms, the warmth enough to sustain the life of a planet in their hands.

THIRTY-EIGHT

Seamus bent over and rubbed away snow like Cara had done last night. And it had just been last night. Already that felt so long ago.

Cillian Flaherty 1988–2012
Beloved husband, father and son
'In ár gcroíthe go deo'

Cara read the words again. Beloved. So beloved.

'We should have added brother too, Seamus. I'm sorry. Husband, father, son and brother.'

'Cara, no, don't apologise to me about anything like that.' He waved away her concern, shook his head with a wistful smile.

Sorcha placed the dried flowers at the bottom of the head-stone. Its muted pinks and oranges, its golden foliage, seemed fitting. Cillian was that now to them, beautiful, but a memory.

'Eh, I feel a bit stupid now,' said Ferdia with the biscuits in his hands.

'Why don't we eat them?' suggested Daithí.

'Eat them for Cillian,' smiled Seamus.

'That's a fine idea.'

Ferdia ripped open the cardboard box, took the cellophane-wrapped chocolate and orange biscuits out. Handed them around. They all stood around the grave, biscuit in hand.

'All we need now is a cup of tea,' said Cara. 'He loved a cup of tea and a biccie.'

'Next time,' said Seamus. 'Tuck in, everyone!' He demolished the biscuit in two bites. Smacked his lips afterwards. 'I'd forgotten how wonderful Jaffa Cakes are. They don't have them in California! Cill, you were right to have them as your favourite.' There were mumbles of agreement around the grave as everyone demolished the treats.

Ferdia handed the packet to Seamus.

'Here, have another, mate.'

Cara opened her fiddle case. Cillian's grave was the last in its row at the very back of the cemetery. It sat where the two low walls met at the corner. She brushed the snow off the top of the wall that ran parallel to the grave and then perched back against it. She placed the fiddle case on the wall behind. Slowly Cara drew the bow along the strings, a low, clear note vibrated into the crisp silence. She looked up at everyone, and then pulled the bow back, a big smile on her face as she danced the bow across the strings playing 'Always Look on the Bright Side of Life'. It took everyone a moment, but they laughed. Sorcha started singing and the others joined in, Ferdia with a mouth half full of the remaining biscuits.

'Oh my God, close your mouth, Ferdy!' Sorcha laughed. He smirked and did as he was told.

Cara finished her tune and the gang gave her a round of applause. Seamus cleared his throat. All eyes turned to him.

'I guess I just want to say a few words.' Seamus ran his hands through his hair and was quiet for a moment, collecting his thoughts. 'This day never gets easier. But it's been wonderful, just now, laughing, singing, snacking! I think my big brother is laughing with us wherever he is. I miss him. I know you all do too, so much. And this week… well, I don't think there are any words, are there? Our darling Maura—' His voice caught, he looked at his feet and shook his head. Ferdia stepped forward and embraced him. His own chest heaving with emotion. A truce. The strange enchantment that seemed to have them in its grip this morning, allowing this.

Cara though, instead of feeling the warmth of the reconciliation, began to feel the tendrils of the spell loosen. She felt the dead battery of her courage, of her conviction, looking for a spark. These two who'd been at each other's throats last night. Now, embracing. What should have been heart-warming, redemptive, instead felt wrong. She watched them, feeling her resentment building, as if she was waking from a dream. But she kept the sad smile she was wearing on her face. Didn't move a muscle.

Daithí came over to her and put his arm around her shoulder. He hugged her. Kissed the top of her head.

'I'm sorry,' he whispered.

'Oh, Daithí, no,' she whispered back. 'You're the one who doesn't have to apologise.'

Seamus, Ferdia and Sorcha looked at the pair of them. Cara looked at each of them in return. The snow-topped graves around them, she stared at Seamus's handsome boy-next-door face. Ferdia's angular, dark gorgeousness, Sorcha's dirty-blonde beauty. All looking at her. Through masks. All hiding, not one of them sorry. For anything.

'Maybe we should head now? This has been really lovely,' said Seamus. 'It's the happiest New Year's Eve morning I've had since we lost Cillian. Thanks, everyone. This has been an awful week, but I'm glad we came. Let's do what we planned to do all along, cook a big-ass meal, drink a barrel load of wine and talk about Cillian all day long. We can celebrate Maura too.'

'Yes, let's do it,' agreed Sorcha. Ferdia nodded.

'I think it would do us all good,' said Daithí.

Seamus turned to look properly at the grave.

'Cillian. I won't leave it so long again to come back here, to see you. Rest easy, brother, I love you.'

Ferdia stepped forward and touched the top of the headstone.

'Rest easy, friend,' he echoed.

Daithí and Sorcha took a quiet moment and then stepped away from the grave. Everyone, bar Cara, started to walk away. Seamus looked back at her.

'You coming, Cara? Are you okay?'

Cara nodded.

'Yes, it's okay, I'm good. I think I just want a couple of minutes with him. Just on my own. Is that okay?'

Seamus came back and drew Cara into a hug. She had to force her muscles not to tense up.

'Of course, you don't have to ask that.'

Cara nodded.

'Catch us up at the supermarket,' said Sorcha. 'We're going to get all the goodies in.'

'Yeah, I'll see you there.'

The gang smiled and waved and headed out of the grave-yard. Cara listened to their happy voices as they moved off in the direction of Kilronan. She stood there a long time until she couldn't hear them any longer. Then she turned back to Cillian.

'I think I have it right this time, Cillian.' Cara stepped closer to the grave. Touched the headstone where Ferdia had touched it. 'Did you hear what they said to you? "Rest easy. Rest."'

THE HUSBAND RESTS.

THIRTY-NINE

Cara looked at the grave. Where was it? Where had Maura hidden it? It. The package. The elusive, precious, much sought after package. It hadn't started snowing yet when she'd passed here. Passed here on the way back from Cara's house and on her way home. When she'd had the good sense to hide it. Or maybe it hadn't been good sense. If she'd let her killer have it, she'd still be with them today. Cara knew she would. So whatever this bloody package was, Maura had felt it was worth the risk.

Cara was close. She could feel it. She paced back and forth in front of the grave. Stamped her feet on the path as the cold replaced her friends for company.

Right. So, it hadn't been snowing, but it had been wet. And windy. The storm just hadn't cooled down enough yet. So where would Maura have put it? Kept it safe, but hidden? There weren't many options. For a moment Cara doubted herself. She'd gotten it wrong again.

No. No. No. It was here. Cara was sure of it.

She looked at the slope of the grave. Did she have to dig? Could that be possible?

No. That didn't feel right. She looked up and around. The

fiddle case on the wall behind the grave caught the corner of her eye.

With a quick glance over her shoulder – making sure she was still alone – Cara hurried to the top of the grave. Leaning on the headstone, she looked behind it, at the space between it and the wall. There was only a little snow here, in the narrow space. And some of it looked like the snow she and Seamus had brushed off the headstone. This was a sheltered little spot. But nothing immediately jumped out at her. It was just scraggy grass and weeds.

Actually it wasn't just grass and weeds. It was grass and a familiar weed. A familiar wildflower.

Growing here, behind Cillian's grave, was a bunch of shepherd's purse. The flower she had found in Maura's jeans pocket. The only thing that had been there. The wildflower with the tiny seedpods in the shapes of hearts. Cara had gotten it right this time. This was where Maura wanted her to be.

But there was nothing here. Cara twisted around the headstone, dived her hand into the grass, and felt around its damp interior. Nothing. She got down on her knees, heedless of the snow on the ground, her trousers instantly soaked, her skin wet and freezing. She leant one hand on the wall, bracing herself as she searched deeper behind the grave. Still nothing. The stone in the wall moved, unsteady in its unmortared state, and Cara cursed as she grazed her hand on its roughness.

She sat back on her heels and blew on her cold, sore hand.

Stared at the wall. With an explosion in her belly, she sat back up.

She poked the rock. It moved again. She started pulling now, not pushing. Her heart began to race. It slid out.

And there, wedged down, in the centre of the wall, was something wrapped in a grey and pink silk scarf that Cara recognised had belonged to Maura. She reached her hand in, no longer feeling the scrapes and grazes, and carefully pulled it out. The dimensions looked like Mamó's estimations. Cara started to unwrap the scarf, her fingers fumbling with its knots. As its corners released, she saw the battered brown paper wrapping Mamó had also described.

This was it.

The cause of all this awfulness. This horror. A shot of adrenaline electrified her.

Cara turned around and looked out over the graveyard. The sea of grey granite and limestone headstones, to the walls protecting them, to the island beyond. Checking for people. There was no one here. She was completely alone. She strained to hear, listening for voices, just in case anyone was coming. But no. It was safe.

She sat down on the low edge of the grave. Stretched her legs out. She lay the package on her lap. Began to unwrap it.

She stared down at the contents.

A notebook.

An old notebook with a black cover. Battered, dog-eared. Cara turned it over and back. This was it?

She opened the front cover, and looked at the handwritten inscription.

Is Mise An tOileán – Seamus Flaherty

Seamus's memoir? What on earth?

She flicked through a few pages. It was handwritten, all in Irish. This looked like an original handwritten draft. Was that possible? Could it be the very first? The one that had really started life as a diary, according to Seamus?

Why on earth was this worth killing for?

Then she noticed it.

A hint of green peeking above the page. From towards the back of the notebook. Cara opened the marked page. A sprig of the shepherd's purse. Ah, Maura, clever to the end. At every turn she'd used the friendship they'd shared to guide Cara. To help her. To get her here.

Cara scanned the page. What had she wanted Cara to know? What was she telling her? The whole lot was in Irish. But she didn't need to be able to read Irish to recognise one word in particular. A word that was all over this page. Except it wasn't a word, but a name. Cillian.

In every paragraph of the page Maura had marked.

Cara stared at the words written here. Traced her fingers over the lines, lingered on Cillian's name. Then she shut it. Snapped it shut. On autopilot she wrapped it up again in its paper and in Maura's silk scarf. She stood. Slipped it in the pocket at the front of the fiddle case, behind the sheet music. She stole a last glance around to make sure she was alone. She zipped up the case. Took it in her hand. Knew what she had to do.

FORTY

Cara stood outside the Garda station. Patted her jacket, checking for the radios secreted in her inside pocket. She knew they were there, she'd put them there only a few moments ago while inside, but her head was buzzing, thoughts and realisations tumbling over one another, rushing to the fore, each bringing with it a new nugget of clarity. She looked over the horizon, out to sea. Taking in the calming waves, the lighter clouds. And while she couldn't be one hundred per cent sure, she thought she might see a tiny patch of blue, far off in the distance. Coming this way.

Cara started walking towards the supermarket. Noah and a couple of the actors passed her by. Noah stopped.

'Hey, Cara!' He beamed at her. 'I just saw Seamus, thanks for the invite! We'll see you later.'

'Yeah, thanks,' said Aiden. 'Nice to get to party a little.'

'See you later,' smiled Lexi. She waved and the trio moved off.

'Great,' said Cara, waving back. That sounded like Seamus had invited them over for the New Year's celebration later. Cara did a quick pass over the idea that was forming in her head. Did it still work if they were there? She'd make it work. She rounded the corner and headed for the supermarket entrance. Shoppers coming out spotted her and put more space than usual between them. Cara saw Sorcha at the checkout and headed towards her. Another person sidestepped her by a country mile. Sorcha watched it happen.

'What was that all about?'

'I presume the *piseog*,' Cara replied.

'But it's only 2 p.m.! If it was 11.55 p.m., fair enough...'

'Fair enough?'

'Well, no, obviously, but you know what I mean.'

Cara nodded.

'Hey there, you found us.' Seamus joined them with two carrier bags laden with food and bottles of wine. Ferdia and Daithí arrived behind him with more shopping bags.

'You invited Noah and his crew?' asked Cara.

'Yeah, we bumped into them, felt rude not to. Sorry if that's a problem?'

'Ah, no.'

'And,' said Seamus grinning, 'it'll mean you will finally get a New Year's Eve party where everyone doesn't run away scared from you and your red hair at midnight. Won't that be a treat?'

'I suspect people will find a reason to run away from me at midnight regardless.'

A local passed the gang, giving them a very wide clearance. All eyes watched them go.

'See!' she said.

'I agree, Cara.' Ferdia put his arm around her shoulder. 'The *piseog* is stupid. The natives have got it all wrong about you being bad luck on New Year's Day.'

'Thank you, Ferdia.'

'You're bad luck all year round!' he laughed. Sorcha dug an elbow in his side.

'Stop it,' she hissed.

'Come on,' said Daithí, coming around to lead the pack. 'These shopping bags aren't getting any lighter, let's get home.'

'Yes, sir,' said Seamus.

On the road back to the house, the lighter mood from breakfast seemed to grow and intensify. Everyone was giddy. Unfamiliar sounds of animated conversation and laughter echoed through the small roads as they walked. It was so like the old days. Though with the obvious absences. But for some reason, right now, the missing pair just felt like they'd stepped out for a while. That they'd be back later. And maybe, thought Cara, they are here, in spirit. Keeping an eye on things.

Sorcha, walking ahead, looked back at Cara as she walked with Daithí.

'The storm's stopping, isn't it?' she said, eyes shining, hope dancing across her eyes.

'It's definitely calming,' agreed Cara.

Seamus, leading the pack, looked over his shoulder.

'Forecast to break by dinner time.'

'Oh, fantastic! I hope there'll be boats tomorrow. What do you think, Cara? Will they be running tomorrow?'

'Maybe,' said Cara, 'I'm not sure.' And no, she thought to herself, it's okay, I'm not offended by your eagerness to get away. Nothing personal, I'm sure.

'There'll be a boat,' said Ferdia. Sorcha looked at him.

'You sure?'

'Yep.'

'I wouldn't be quite so confident, Ferdia,' said Daithí. 'Firstly, it might be forecast to break by dinner time, but there's meant to be a sting in its tail and it's going to get rough again this evening. Also, I wouldn't be so confident of the boats running on New Year's Day.'

'We'll see,' said Ferdia.

'You heading too, Seamus, if the boats are on?' asked Sorcha.

'Noah and I and the crew still have filming to do, so we'll be around for a while yet.'

Cara placed her hand on Daithí's arm, and with a side glance, slowed him down. They gradually fell back, putting a little distance between them and the others. The chatter about filming, and the storm, and the getting off the island floating back to them, indistinct.

'You okay?' he asked.

'I am.'

'I guess we probably should talk about things.'

'You're right, we should. But not now. That's not why I slowed you down.'

'It isn't?'

'No... look...' Cara paused and looked at the other three walking ahead of them. Waited a moment as she listened to how much she could make out of their conversation. She adjusted the volume of her voice accordingly.

'I need you to do something for me,' she said in a low voice.

'Sure,' he replied, looking at her, puzzled. Cara reached into her inner pocket and took out one of the radios and slipped it quickly into his coat pocket.

'That's a police radio,' she whispered. 'I've one here too.' She patted her jacket.

'What the—' His confusion deepened.

'Just listen to me... later I'm going to give you a nod. And I'll need you to make an excuse, like, you've just remembered that you said you'd change the kegs at Derrane's, but had forgotten in all the chaos. Something like that. That you have to go there immediately, the night that's in it, et cetera.'

'Okay...'

'But I want you to go down to the harbour instead. And find a spot where you can't be seen, but you can see what's going on.

I think if you put yourself around the steps of the Harbour Guesthouse, that might be a good spot. And I'm sorry to ask you to go there in these freezing conditions but I really need you to do this for me.'

'Cara, what's this all about?'

'I'll explain later, I promise.'

'So, what am I meant to do when I'm down there?'

'Keep watch and contact me on the radio, okay?'

'What am I watching for, Cara?'

'Someone making a break for it.'

FORTY-ONE

'Shut the door, Ferdia! You'll freeze us out of it!' called Seamus over the chatter of the crowd at the dinner table. He did as he was told, and closed the back door.

'What are you doing, anyway?' Seamus asked.

'Nothing.' Ferdia grabbed a bottle of wine and brought it back with him to the table. He topped up his glass and then put the bottle down.

Noah pushed his plate aside. He took the bottle and filled up the glasses around him. He said something to Seamus and they both laughed. Cara didn't catch what was so funny, the chatter and laughter drowning them out. She watched him pass the bottle to Seamus, who then sent it down the long table to the others. They'd dried off an old garden table and brought it inside to create enough places for everyone. With a tablecloth over it, you could hardly tell, except for the slight damp smell that hung around. Sorcha and herself had rounded up as many candles and camping lamps as they could find to light the room. The warm glow from the candles – clusters of them on top of bookshelves, by the fire, in every safe nook and cranny they could find – gave the room a cosy basement restaurant feel. It was around 9 p.m. but felt like 2 a.m. in the huddled half-light of the many flickering flames. Daithí was at the other end of the table, across from Lexi. He caught Cara's eye. He raised his eyebrows questioningly. She shook her head. Not yet, she thought. A barely perceptible nod from Daithí and he turned back to Lexi and continued chatting. Cara turned to the crew member who was sitting to her left – Alex, was it? He was the sound guy, she remembered that much about him. He was talking about something to do with his job, but Cara had tuned out a good few minutes ago. He hadn't noticed, or cared. Ferdia's foot was tapping incessantly beside her to her right. And he was fidgeting with his cutlery. It was getting very annoying. She looked over at Sorcha. Leaning over her empty plate, chin resting in her hand, her eyes sparkling, and Cara reckoned she could hear her say, 'Oh, fascinating,' over and over. The actor who was playing Ferdia in the movie was the recipient of her coquettish attentions. But Cara didn't miss the quick side glances at the real Ferdia. To check if he was watching. Cara was disappointed to see Sorcha's carry-on. She and Ferdia had seemed to be getting on better today.

'Can I take your plate?' Cara smiled and reached for the finished dinner plate in front of Alex, the sound guy. The knife and fork clattering as she lifted it.

'Thank you, that was all delicious,' he smiled.

'Hey,' called Seamus across the table, 'don't be doing that, you and Sorcha cooked, we men can clear up.' He turned and picked up the plates around him.

'Daithí, Ferdia, a little help?'

'I can help too!' said Noah, standing up and grabbing and stacking nearby plates. 'Thank you so much for the lovely dinner and thanks so much for including us. This has been really special, to be included in tonight's celebrations and to be ringing in the new year with you lovely people.' Noah put down the plates and grabbed his glass instead. The wine within nearly spilling as he raised it without caution, with a hand that had already liberally partaken of its contents. 'Everyone, to your very good health!'

A cheer went up and the music of clinking glasses and laughter filled the air. Seamus stood up, his glass in hand also. Noah sat. Seamus looked around the table.

'I just want to say, this has been a tough anniversary and a tough week. I am raising my glass to absent friends.' He paused and a hush fell over the group. 'And I also raise my glass to new friends. A traditional Irish toast for you all... *Go raibh do ghloine lán go deo. Go raibh láidir go breá an dion thar do cheann. Go raibh tú i Neamh leathúair roimh a bhfuil fhios ag an Diabhal go bhfuair tú bás.*'

'Oh, that's beautiful,' said Alex, turning to Cara. 'What does it mean?'

'Don't ask her,' said Ferdia. 'She's a disgrace and doesn't speak the lingo. It's why the locals don't like her.'

'I thought that was the red hair?' said Noah.

'No, that's just for New Year's Eve. The rest of the time is because she's an annoying outsider.'

'Er, shut up, Ferdia, thanks,' said Cara, elbowing him in the side. 'Seamus, perhaps you'd like to translate for us?'

'Absolutely, *mo stór*. It means, May your glass be ever full. May the roof over your head be always strong. And,' he smiled, his glass raised even higher, 'may you be in heaven a half hour before the devil knows you're dead!'

Another cheer went up, fists banging the table in appreciation, glasses clinked again. A 'hell yeah!' came from someone at the other end of the table.

'I gotta learn that,' said Alex.

'So does she,' chimed in Ferdia.

'Christ, Ferdia, enough of the digs. Give it a rest.'

'*Gabh mo leithscéal!*' Excuse me, that's what that meant. Cara had once heard Maura talk about the phrase. Its literal translation was 'Take my half-story'. A translation that amused people. Half-truths offered to get off the hook. Cara looked around the table. There were a lot of half-stories, half-truths around here right now. Excuses. Lies. Murder.

Cara took a deep breath. She looked down the table to Daithí and met his eye. She nodded ever so slightly. Daithí stood up, his chair scraping back across the floor. The group hushed and looked up, expecting another toast.

'Oh, dear.' He pulled at his cuff, as if he had a watch obscured beneath it. 'Has anyone the time?'

Seamus looked over at him. 'I think it's about nine fifteen? What's up?'

'I forgot the kegs – I promised Courtney I'd change them. It's going to be mental down there tonight. I hope she hasn't run out already.' Daithí stepped away from the table, headed for the back door.

'Ah, Daithí, you can't go.' Sorcha looked upset.

'I'll be back. I promise,' he said. 'Save me some dessert.'

'It's tiramisu again, too.'

'Definitely save me some then. Apologies everyone.' And Daithí slipped out the back door and was gone.

'Is it nine fifteen already?' asked Ferdia. He stood. But then sat down again.

'Come on, give us a hand,' said Seamus as he and Noah started clearing off the plates. Sorcha tore herself away from fake Ferdia and began gathering the necessary for dessert. She and Cara had made double quantities of it for the extra guests.

'Maybe you'll play for the guys later, Cara?'

Seamus's voice dragged Cara's attention back to the table.

'What's that?'

'Seamus was telling me that you play the fiddle beautifully,' said Noah.

'Oh, he's too kind. I'm mostly self-taught.'

'Don't let her fool you, Noah. When I left here a decade ago it sounded like she was killing small animals! But she's brilliant now!'

'Stop it, Seamus, you'll make me blush. All it really is, as Ferdia so kindly pointed out, is that I'm not the most popular person on the island. I have plenty of time on my hands to practise. YouTube has been very instructive.'

'You must play for us then,' he said.

'We'll see, I might later.' Cara smiled at his eager face. She looked around the table, at the happy faces. Sorcha, standing at the head of the extended table was passing out bowls of dessert, greedy hands happy to take some. 'I gave you extra,' she heard her say when handing the bowl to the object of her attentions. Ferdia must have heard it too. He shook his head and muttered 'embarrassing' to himself.

'She's doing that for you, you know,' Cara said.

Ferdia turned and looked at Cara.

'You noticed?'

'Hard not to.'

'Well, she can keep doing that all she wants, I don't give a damn.'

Cara looked at him. But said nothing. She looked back at Sorcha.

'Sorcha,' she called out to her.

'Yes, hon?'

'I just thought you might like to know that Ferdia says he doesn't give a damn about your flirting. So, you can probably give it a rest now.'

Conversation around the table faltered. Lexi laughed nervously.

'What the hell, Cara?' whispered Seamus through a clenched jaw. 'Why are you embarrassing Sorcha like that?'

Ferdia stared at Cara, his expression blank.

'She's embarrassing herself enough, I don't think I'm doing much to make it worse?'

Sorcha stared at Cara, her mouth slightly opened, her eyes already tear-lined around the edges. She dropped the serving spoon with a clatter, cream and sponge splattering everyone close.

'Don't be horrible, Cara.'

'I'm sorry, Sorcha. That was a bit low of me. Was Maura like that, Sorcha? Was that how she was mean to you as a kid?'

'Eh... well.' Sorcha spoke slowly, Cara's strange attack throwing her off.

'In truth,' said Cara, 'I don't think she was awful to you when we were kids. I would have noticed. Someone would have noticed.' Cara turned to Seamus. 'Ever see Maura be mean to Sorcha, ever?'

Seamus, as stunned by Cara's behaviour as everyone else, stared at her, uneasy.

'Well, did you?' Cara pressed.

'Eh. No. No, can't say I did.'

'You, Ferdia? You ever see it?'

'No,' said Ferdia, still watching her closely.

'But I do think she hurt you, Sorcha. I think that much is true. But it was a lot more recent than you suggested. What could someone you hadn't seen in ten years have done to you that made you so mad that you'd try and destroy her career?'

'I never—'

'I have the video footage of you breaking into the school to plant the drugs in Maura's classroom, don't waste your time denying it.'

'What?' Seamus gasped. He turned and looked at the end of the table. All eyes at the table did the same.

'Yeah, she planted a tin containing drugs in Maura's classroom. It wasn't bored teenagers who broke into the school. Sorry to have lied to you all about that. I presume, Sorcha, that there'd have been an anonymous tip-off to the principal when the time was right? Don't bother answering...'

'I never...' began Sorcha, but her pale face and scared eyes told the truth.

'YOU DID WHAT?' roared Ferdia, bursting out of his mask of calm. He stood. His chair toppling backwards. Alex, the sound guy, and Noah across the table, reared back, startled.

Cara reached out a hand, placed it on Ferdia's.

She looked up at him, at his face contorted with rage. He looked down at her, but barely seemed to see her.

'I don't think you can claim the high moral ground, Ferdia. And she only did it because of you anyway. Just like her efforts to make you jealous with Daithí and her carry-on here tonight. Trying anything to make you as jealous and upset as you made her. Yeah?'

Ferdia glared down at Cara, the ball of fire he'd been about to unleash on his wife, stalled.

Cara stood. Pushed back her chair.

'How long were you and Maura having an affair?'

FORTY-TWO

'Actually, don't answer that. I think I know how long. About eighteen months? That sounds about right. That's when you came back to Inis Mór to scatter your mother's ashes, wasn't it?'

'I... didn't... We, no...' Ferdia spluttered. The anger from moments ago extinguished.

'Don't bother coming up with any stories or lies, Ferdia. Don't waste your energy.' Cara took a few steps away from the table. Like planets orbiting their sun, everyone – Ferdia included – turned with her. 'It looked like her secret man was Seamus. Because that made sense. Our own star-crossed lovers. Weren't they always destined to be together? But why would she have kept that a secret? We'd all have been delighted if the pair of them got back together. And was he really jetting back and forth from California to see her? In all honesty it was too unlikely... It just felt possible because all the best misdirects rely on that. Our lazy assumption, our desires for things to be a certain way.'

'You thought we were back together?' said Seamus. 'No, not at all.'

'It made sense, briefly,' said Cara, looking at Seamus. 'Don't worry, I know the truth now.'

Cara took another step away from the table. Ferdia, like a ballroom dancing partner, did the same, mirroring her. Cara felt all eyes on her. Various mouths were suspended open, she might have seen one of the film crew with a phone, videoing them. But she didn't care. She was focused only on what she had to do.

'I asked myself a question. Why do people keep secrets? Because they *need* to keep info from people. They've something to lose. Maura would have known we'd have disapproved of her seeing a married man. And not just any married man, but the husband of a friend. She'd have been risking our friendship. She obviously bought whatever bullshit you were peddling – marriage on the rocks? Whatever lies you told her. I can't see her getting involved with you otherwise. She still should have known better.'

Cara turned to Sorcha who looked frozen to the spot, as if it was she who was the focus of the revelations.

'Sorcha, I want to apologise to you. You were right. I always thought Maura was perfect, I would have defended her to the very end. But she shouldn't have done that to you, even if Ferdia lied to her, and I do think he must have. Maura was a good person. But she made a mistake. She's not here to say sorry to you, but I think if she could, if she saw how upset you are, she would have.'

'Thank you, Cara,' Sorcha mumbled.

'How did you find out?' Cara asked gently.

Sorcha was silent for a moment. One of the cameramen snickered, elbowing the guy beside him, dipping his hand into an imaginary bag of popcorn. Cara shot him a withering look.

Sorcha glanced at Ferdia. Looked down at the table, at the mess of the tiramisu.

'Checked his phone. He'd been acting like he was cheating again.'

'So Maura wasn't the first, then?'

Sorcha shook her head.

'I loved Maura!' blurted Ferdia, self-righteous anger blazing in his black eyes.

'You were meant to love your wife,' snapped Cara.

Ferdia snarled at Cara. 'Sanctimonious bitch.' He kicked his chair, sending it clattering across the floor. Seamus and Noah stood. Cara turned to them and motioned with her hand for them to sit back down.

'It seems your lie became the truth, Ferdia. The affair quite obviously has put your marriage on the rocks. You two have been at each other the entire time you've been here. Made me wonder why you bothered coming. You,' she turned to Sorcha again, 'made it clear your friends were in London, not on Inis Mór. You came back for revenge, right? And Ferdia? I think you came back to convince Maura not to leave you. She told me she wasn't happy with her mystery guy. That she was worried there was something dodgy about him. And I don't think she was just talking about your marriage.'

Ferdia's eyes narrowed.

'What are you going on about?'

'I think it was related to the massive stash of drugs you hid under the bed in your room.'

'I do not have drugs hidden anywhere!' Ferdia threw his hands up and rolled his eyes.

'Well, true, you don't have any any more. I retrieved them earlier and they're secured in the squad car outside. Documented and photographed for when my reinforcements arrive tomorrow.'

'What? But I need—'

'Which is it, Ferdia? No drugs or a stash you need? That's

one little mystery I haven't worked out yet. Why do you need enough narcotics to kill every man, woman and child on this island?'

Ferdia stood there, glowering at Cara, but remained silent.

'What isn't a mystery is how Maura was beginning to feel about you. She might have originally been weak and let herself be convinced things were done between you and Sorcha. But a sniff of anything illegal... no. She would have walked away. Run. She was ending things between you, wasn't she? That was the thing about Maura. She might have made a mistake, but once she realised she had, she corrected it. Like when she ended things with Seamus because he hit her. Isn't that right, Seamus?'

The colour drained from his face.

'I never, I didn't...'

Cara shook her head.

'Seamus, don't bother. She never told me, I suspect she didn't want to make a big thing of it. But she ended it with you, didn't hang on in there. She didn't forgive you. Another reason why, when I found that out, that it seemed far more likely that you weren't her mystery guy. You two weren't really our Romeo and Juliet after all. Maura made mistakes, but unlike the rest of us, she learnt from them. If she ended it with you, Ferdia, she wouldn't have been changing her mind.

'Did that make you angry, Ferdia? Sorcha told me how you'd liked Maura all those years ago, when we were kids. That Sorcha felt like she was your second choice... were you angry that you'd messed it up after finally getting your chance after all these years? So many reasons to be angry...

'And we've all seen you worked up. The cool, laid-back Ferdia can really lose his cool, who knew? When you came back the other night, after you learnt Maura was dead, you could barely contain yourself. I asked Sorcha if she felt safe with you in the house, you were that angry. And I've seen your police record. I was at the station earlier yesterday and looked you up on the database. A couple of convictions for assault. As well as all those drugs convictions. You've got form, Ferdia Hennessy. Which leaves me with one question.

'Did you get so angry with her, Ferdia, that you killed her?'

FORTY-THREE

'Oh, Ferdia, you didn't,' Sorcha gasped.

'Of course I didn't!' Ferdia snarled, his nostrils flaring. 'This is ridiculous! I didn't do anything to Maura.'

'So you weren't enraged when she ended things?' said Cara.

'You're wrong, she didn't end things. In fact, I was going to end it myself. It was getting too awkward to get to Dublin and Galway all the time. It was getting expensive. Anyway, why would I bother getting cross over her? She didn't mean that much to me. She was a diversion. An unresolved conquest from long ago.'

'A moment ago you were in love with her!'

'I was going for the sympathy vote,' bit Ferdia.

'I see,' said Cara.

This time Ferdia led in the dance, taking a step closer to the kitchen, and Cara followed. Quick, quick, slow.

'Anyway, even if we were in love, or broken up, or whatever, that doesn't mean a damn thing, Sergeant. It's a big leap from a break-up to murder.'

'Where were you on the morning she disappeared?' Cara kept her face a mask of calm.

'What?'

'Simple question.'

'I was asleep, here.'

'Can anyone confirm that?'

'Sorcha can. She hadn't taken a pill that night.'

'Sorcha can't. She was off planting evidence in the school at that time. She wasn't in the bed beside you. A fact you'd know if you, yourself, had been there.'

'I was asleep, I didn't know that.'

'I knocked at the door that morning, at that time, and no one answered. Still claiming to be asleep?'

'Yes! What about Seamus, he was asleep at the time too, why does he get a pass?'

'Leave me out of it!' yelled Seamus. 'I really did love her, you creep.'

'So much you hit her? Huh! Some show of love.'

'We were kids, it was a stupid misunderstanding and you know that!'

'Do I?' spat Ferdia. 'I know a lot of stuff, Seamus Flaherty, so you can sit down and shut up. I know that the good sergeant said a few days ago that they look at the victim's partner as a suspect. Especially violent ones. That's why she's pointing her bloody finger at me!' Ferdia, sparking with furious energy, turned to Cara and jabbed his finger in Seamus's direction. 'I want to ask you, Cara, why aren't you looking at this chump? He fits that profile just as much as me.'

'Because he hadn't been recently dumped by the murder victim, wasn't hiding massive quantity of drugs about the place, he doesn't have a record as long as his arm...' Cara counted the reasons on her right hand, touching each digit with each devastating fact.

'That all means nothing.'

'And it wasn't him who was searching Cillian's room, and his own room last night. I presume for the elusive package.'

Ferdia was silent. His aggression took a step back. The quick blinking of his eyes told Cara she'd surprised him. He was scrambling for an answer. She got in there first.

'Yeah, I was under the bed. You nearly caught me.'

Ferdia's eyes widened at this bit of news.

Cara continued, 'Those letters told us the killer wanted the package, and you, Ferdia, you wanted the package too.'

'Oh no. No, no. It's not what it seems. You're twisting stuff.'

'Explain it to me then.'

Ferdia took another step back. Looked over his shoulder at the back door. Looked back at Cara. Looked across at Sorcha and then Seamus.

There was a noise from Ferdia's pocket.

He dipped his hand in quickly and produced a pager.

'It's the nineties again,' muttered Aiden at the table. Cara shot him a look. He shut up.

'You got a message?' asked Cara.

'That'll be from his people,' said Sorcha.

'His people?' asked Cara.

'Uh-huh. The drugs guys. He's actually scared of them.'

'Shut up, you bitch!' Ferdia snapped. He jammed the pager back in his pocket. Another glance over his shoulder. 'It wasn't me,' he said. 'I didn't kill Maura.'

'Prove it,' said Cara. 'Show me how I'm twisting stuff.'

'I will.' Another step back. 'I just have to do something first.'

A crackle and screech. The radio, hidden in her pocket, screamed into life.

'*Cara, Cara, come in.*' Daithí's robotic voice crackled from the handset. Ferdia grabbed the distraction. Dashed towards the back door. Was gone. Cara threw herself after him but stopped. Daithí's voice again.

'*Cara, can you hear me? There's something very strange going on down here.*'

FORTY-FOUR

'What is it, Daithí?' Cara called into the radio as she ran out the back door, all stunned eyes at the table watching her go.

'There's people, so many people. Just get down here. As quick as you can.'

Cara ran around the house, coming to a halt at her car. Ferdia already swallowed up by the blackness of the night. She looked at the boot of the car. It was open. A rock lying on the ground. Ferdia had retrieved his goods.

'Dammit,' yelled Cara, kicking the back tyre in frustration. At least she had taken multiple photographs of the stash and fully logged it. It was better than nothing. She pushed the rock aside and quickly fixed the boot shut as well as she could. She jumped in and sped down the drive, skidding on the ice.

Going at least double the island speed limit, the car only half under her control, she flew in the direction of Kilronan. But as she approached the village, she had to slow down. Like a herd of sheep clogging up the country roads, hordes of young people filled the streets. Young people in party mode. The streets were black with them. Actually, thought Cara, it wasn't black with them, it was *glowing* with them.

Because everyone one of them was illuminated not just with torches, but also a cacophony of incandescent fluorescent accessories – neon sticks, headbands, bracelets, some were even in head-to-toe luminescent outfits. They looked like radiant aliens.

Cara stopped the car and stood out.

'Who the hell are you people?' she yelled at those nearest to her. One girl, fluorescent glowing tubes snaked through her plaited hair and jewels dotted around her technicolor make-up, looked at her with mellow eyes. Despite the freezing temperatures she was wearing short sleeves and a short skirt.

'We're here for the party. It's New Year's, you should join us. Everyone is welcome.' She beamed at Cara.

'Bloody hell,' replied Cara, hopping back in her car. Revving the engine and slamming her palm on the car horn, she forced her way through the crowd. And it was a crowd. As she drove she tried to estimate how many people she was passing. Hundreds, it felt like. All of them young and excited.

She got to the harbour.

She leapt out of the car and raised the radio to her lips.

'Where are you, Daithí? And what the hell is going on?'

'*I'm at the pier-side. Try and find me in the melee. Look for the blue ferry.*'

Cara stretched her neck and pushed through the crowd.

'Out of the way, out of my way.' Her commands made very little impact as she tried to make her way against the flow. Eventually the crowd thinned enough that she spotted Daithí. Standing next to a man who had all the appearance of a captain of a boat. She ran over.

'Daithí, what the hell?'

As she spoke a faint, far-off rhythm sounded. Daithí looked up over her shoulder. Cara turned. It was coming from Dun Aengus, the cliffside fort ruins, on the highest point of the island. The faint thump, thump, thump kept coming. And then there were lights. Strobing, flashing, beaming onto the clouds and out to sea.

'I'm sorry, Cara, it seems there's a New Year's Eve rave happening. Caitlín in the Harbour Guesthouse told me some lads landed a couple of hours ago, when the storm calmed down. She assumed all the gear they brought on was for Seamus's film. But this is what they were at.'

A rave in Dun Aengus. The ruins looked out over the Atlantic. And had a sheer 300 foot drop into the ocean. Originally a circle, half the fort had fallen into the sea over the centuries. Cara couldn't think of a more spectacular – or dangerous – spot for an illegal rave. Daithí turned to the boat captain.

'Captain Smyth here can tell you the rest.'

'I just go where I'm told,' the man said.

'You were chartered, that's what you said.'

The man nodded.

'By whom?' Cara asked. 'Did a Ferdia Hennessy have anything to do with it?'

'Yep, he was one of them.'

Now she knew what the massive stash of drugs was for. And no wonder he was so sure earlier that there would be boats off the island tomorrow. He'd chartered them. Right. Well, it meant one thing. She'd know where to find him now. Up there, in the ruins, on the edge of the world.

FORTY-FIVE

'Can you stay here, Daithí? I need you to keep doing what you were doing, make sure no one goes anywhere. Not even these guys.'

'We're scheduled to go at 6 a.m. tomorrow,' said the captain.

'You'll go when I say you can go. And you do anything else I'll have you up on charges and your licence revoked.'

The captain held his hands up.

'Relax. That's fine. No need to pull out the big guns. You'll be the one having to deal with two hundred hung-over, crashing kids stuck on your island. I don't care.'

Daithí took Cara's arm and guided her away from the captain. The last of the partygoers had left the pier and were streaming up through the island toward the lights and sounds. The wind was picking up, just as Daithí said earlier it had been forecast to. The smaller dinghies in the bay were beginning to bob and sway violently again. Cara's hair began to dance to the wind's beat. She pulled it back behind her ears and held it there. She looked at Daithí's earnest face.

'Cara, what's going on?'

'I can't explain right now. I have to go get Ferdia. It can't wait.' She looked off in the direction of Dun Aengus.

'I'll do my best here, I promise,' said Daithí, 'but... look, keep in touch.'

Cara reached out and squeezed his arm.

'I will. Just keep everyone on this island, okay?'

Daithí nodded. 'I'll do my very best.'

Cara turned and began to run. Careful of her footing in the dark, she was aided by the first clear night sky in days. The moon, a stranger to them, was back, and its crisp rays shone a reflection on the snow and stones. The island sparkled in the darkness.

As she left the village, she caught up with the stragglers of the crowd. Laughing and drinking, they smoked and ambled towards Dun Aengus. Cara wove her way through them. No one was too concerned about her presence. There were offers of tokes, and more exotic fare. Cara felt hemmed in, so many of them taking up the narrow island roads, shoulder to shoulder, pushing through the crowd. She'd spent the last four days seeing barely more than the four faces of her friends and the wide open spaces of a silent island. This sudden volte-face, this alternative universe she seemed to have woken up in, was disorientating. The thump-thump of the bass beat was getting louder. She felt dizzy.

The fort ruins were up a winding, stony path that gradually got steeper and steeper the closer to the top you got. The kids, in their garish colours, with their lights bobbing and weaving like multicolour fireflies in the darkness, tackled the terrain like wild goats, only the most intoxicated slipping or stumbling. Each was caught by laughing friends and righted. The wind was stronger on the higher ground, and Cara, even with the windbreaker of the crowd for shelter, felt its power.

She stopped midway up the path. Let the ravers move around her like a river flowing uphill. She turned and looked out over the coastline. The sea, though not as wild as before, was choppy and churning. Alive and angry. The frantic rhythm of the music seemed powered by it. Her eye was drawn down the outline of the island. To the indent she knew hid the Serpent's Lair at its foot. Where this awfulness had begun. When Maura's story had ended. Well, tonight would be her epilogue. Cara would close the covers.

She turned back to the path and continued to climb. The stragglers had overtaken her and had reached the top of the path. They were passing through the gap in the outer grey stone wall into the first semicircle of the fort. Electronic music was booming. Occupied the space all around Cara as if it had corporeal form. Beams of white lights from inside the fort itself flashed and criss-crossed the sky. She could feel vibrations under her feet with every step. She got to the top of the path and passed through. In front of her, those who couldn't fit in the fortress itself danced. Consumed by the bass, the ravers moved like a sea on land powered by the driving beat and the command of the wind. Dotted flashing spotlights at the base of the two-metre-high walls of the fort lit up the scene. Through the one rectangular entrance in the fortress's inner wall, Cara could see an even denser crowd inside, moving as one, a lattice of strobing light leaking out over the walls. Once a fortress for protection, tonight it hosted instead a spectacular party. The only discordant note was the smell of diesel from the generators when the wind whipped inland. Not that anyone seemed to care.

Cara hurried on. Searching out here for Ferdia. Looking at each blissed out face for him. The vibrations jarred her bones now from feet to chest to her skull. The music was so loud her thoughts had to yell to be heard.

She passed through the opening into the innermost part of the fort. The walls curved around her, enclosing them all. The only way out other than the opening she'd come through was over the edge of the cliff and its sheer 300-foot drop to the ocean below.

It was a crucible of noise, smoke and lights, an assault on the senses. Ravers were all turned to the DJ who was raised on a natural stone platform that interrupted the cliff edge line, his backdrop the ocean. A perfect, naturally formed stage. The waves behind him seemed part of the show, programmed like the lights to crash in frenzied time to his beats. A temporary rig framed the DJ, the whirling dervish of the spots and strobes disorientating Cara even more. She felt no need for chemical enhancement, the environment was mind-altering on its own. The heat of the crowd and lights had cleared the dance floor of snow, the walls wore what snow remained like an ermine collar.

She scanned the crowd as best she could. Searching through the dancers, searching for the familiar in this wildly unfamiliar situation. The tempo to the music was building. The dial turning. The crowd roared their appreciation. Cara felt her heart rate increase. They danced on. Steam rising from many of them. Body heat meeting the frigid air. The icy wind whipping in off the ocean. The moon competing with the light show to be the most spectacular. The tempo ratcheted up a few more notches. Cara could feel its tensions in her cells, begging for the bass to drop and give them release from this pressure. The crowd cried out its tortured ecstasy.

And wham, a gasp after a syringe of adrenaline plunged into the crowds' collective chest, the DJ dropped the beat, a female vocal sang out, and the lights strobed. The vision in front of Cara was like a movie with every second frame cut out. Everyone moved jerkily. Here then there, with no in-between.

She spotted Ferdia. To the left of the DJ's platform. In dark silhouette against the sea. His movements jerky, robotic in the strobing light. Appearing and disappearing in alternate flashes. She started in his direction. Weaving through the transfixed and mesmerised crowd. The hypnotic light show making each step a twitching nightmare.

Near him, a figure stepped out from the shadow of the fort walls.

And like everyone they moved in spasms as the lights flashed.

Seamus.

Ferdia spotted him too. Cara moved quicker. Pushing dancers out of the way, frantic. She was closer. Could see Ferdia and Seamus now nose to nose.

And so close to the edge.

To three hundred feet of oblivion.

And even though the booming music meant she couldn't hear them, the expressions, the fists, the energy between them spoke loud enough. Screamed anger. Rage.

She pushed through the last of the crowd. Saw Ferdia swing a punch.

It connected. Seamus fell backwards. Into the crowd.

'Stop!' screamed Cara, the sound swallowed up instantly. Her heart pounding. Seamus was on his feet again. Dancing an entirely different kind of dance, circling Ferdia.

Tumbling out, Cara was disgorged from the crowd, behind the line of speakers and the DJ. Staring at her friends.

'Stop!' she screamed again. Behind the speaker line it was slightly quieter, they could hear her this time. Both turned. Surprise from both at her sudden appearance. Then a different look in Seamus's eye. Cara understood it. He'd seen an opportunity in the distraction she'd caused. He swung. His punch connecting with an unprepared Ferdia. Propelling him backwards.

Towards the edge.

Ferdia's arms flailed. His feet stumbled on icy ground. His eyes wide, as horrible understanding dawned. Knowing what was about to happen. Cara threw herself at him. Stretching out, trying to reach him in time. Their fingers so close. A hair's breadth separating them.

And then he went over.

Consumed by gravity, like a demon dragging him to hell, he plummeted.

Cara teetered on the edge. She hadn't thought about her own momentum. It pulled her, beckoning her also to the verge. Arching over, helping her see Ferdia as he got smaller and smaller.

Calling her to be gravity's second victim.

Three hundred feet screaming for her.

FORTY-SIX

Cara was jerked backwards, her arm nearly torn from its socket. Pulled back from the brink. Her momentum reversed, now she was tumbling backwards towards the crowd, tumbling onto the recoiling Seamus, her saviour, his hands still steel-gripped to her arm. Both of them hitting the firm, cold ground. Staying on the cliffside. Living. Not falling. Not dying.

They lay there, in a panting, horrified heap. Cara gasping, Seamus sobbing. The ground vibrating.

'I didn't mean to, I didn't mean to. Oh God, Ferdia, my friend. My friend. Oh, what have I done?' Seamus's cries, so close to Cara's ears, she heard each plaintive wail. She rolled over and put her arms around him, drawing him to her.

'I was just so angry, he killed my Maura, my Maura, I still loved her, Cara. I always loved her,' he gulped and gasped, his body shaking in her arms. 'I didn't mean him to go over, believe me, believe me. Oh, Cara.'

'I believe you, Seamus. I believe you,' she whispered, her words swallowed up by the music that hadn't stopped. Cara held him tight and stared heavenward. She gazed at the bright Atlantic moon in the darkest of navy skies. Beams from the spotlights shot across above them. Cara could feel the crowd moving as one behind her. Unaware of what had just happened. Cara watched the stars, remembering a New Year's Eve just like this ten years ago. A night when the sea was also as rough. Another night when she and Seamus had lost someone dear to them. She felt her own tears come. She held Seamus a little tighter, and he pulled her closer too. Both of them lay there, sobbing once more under the careless gaze of an indifferent, heartless moon.

FORTY-SEVEN

They walked hand in hand down the steep incline from Dun Aengus. Past the partying young people, lost to the beat and altered states. Neither spoke until they reached the road and had turned towards the house. Seamus began, in a quiet voice.

'I followed him. After you left. I didn't want him to get away. He might have got off the island and then maybe he'd never have paid for what he'd done. I couldn't bear that.'

'It's okay, Seamus, I understand.'

'I didn't mean for him to go over... I just...' Seamus shook his head. 'Oh God... what's going to happen?' He gulped in some air. And ran his arm across his face.

'We'll go back to the house now. Don't worry. I'll look after everything.'

'Thank you, Cara. I'm so sorry this has all happened. And today, too.'

Cara squeezed his hand.

'I can't believe he did that to Maura.' Seamus's breath juddered, emotion still the better of him.

Cara shook her head.

'Me neither. I assume he didn't mean to. That it was unintentional. That he was overcome with rage.'

Seamus's chest began to heave again. Cara understood. The mental images of Maura, stricken, helpless. It was awful. Unthinkable. She pulled Seamus closer.

They walked on in silence for another few minutes. Cara spoke again.

'Did you leave Sorcha back at the house? We'll have to tell her.'

Seamus stopped. Turned and looked at Cara. His face was pale.

'She ran.'

'She what?'

'You and... Ferdia... left. Noah and his lot went right after. Couldn't get away quick enough. Sorcha then rushed to her room. Stuffed her case full of her things and ran. That's when I decided to go and find Ferdia. I got scared that they were all going to get away.'

'Shit.' Cara reached into her pocket. Took out the radio. She pressed the button and it screeched into life.

'Daithí, it's me.'

'Is everything okay?' his voice crackled back.

'No, I'm afraid not. I need a couple of things from you. Firstly, can you contact your fellow RNLI volunteers, tell them there's a body in the water. Went in from the cliff at Dun Aengus. Tell them it's a recovery operation only.'

'Do I know who they're looking for?'

Cara paused. Took a breath.

'It's Ferdia,' she replied into the handset. There was nothing for some time. Then it came back to life.

'You sure?'

'Yes. I'll tell you everything back at the house.'

'Christ. Okay.'

'I need something else from you. I need you to look out for

Sorcha. If she's not there already, she'll be in your vicinity soon. She'll be trying to hitch a ride out of here. I'd like you to bring her back to the house.'

'*What if she doesn't want to come?*'

'You have my permission to make her.'

'*I'll have to trust you on this, Cara. But force is not my style.*'

'Don't worry, Daithí. I think when we get to talk, you won't feel so bad.'

'*And if I find her, are you sure you want me to come back to the house? There'll be no one watching the harbour then.*'

'It's okay, that's not a concern any more.'

The house was in total darkness when they returned. Cara had been worried that, abandoned with lit candles dotted all over the living room, there'd be a danger of fire. But the house was still standing. They went in the back door. The moon shone in through the windows by the fire, casting an eerie glow around the room. The fire in the grate was glowing but was near to going out. Wax had dripped down the side of the bookcase where a group of candles had melted completely. The aromas from a good meal still lingered in the air. It felt again like a room caught in a moment of time. Cara looked around. Only recently it had been full of people. Alive with chatter, laughter, good food and wine. Now it was deserted. The plates with half-eaten desserts left there on the table. Glasses of wine abandoned. It was like when Seamus had compared the house to the mysteriously abandoned ship, the *Mary Celeste*, that first evening here. Cara looked around the room, shivered. She heard the voices of her friends. From when they were teens. Laughing and innocent. And their voices now. Grown, twisted, rotten. She hadn't been happy to come back to this house. So many painful memories. She'd convinced herself that today, Cillian's tenth anniversary, had been the right time to lay those ghosts to rest. All that had happened was they'd made more. She didn't want to come back here ever again. It was time to lock this place up and never return.

Seamus crossed the room and threw a few logs on the fire. Added some turf as the flames caught. Cara grabbed candles from the kitchen and lit them. Put a few on the kitchen table among the abandoned dinner dishes, and added some around the hearth. A fraction of the cosy warm light from earlier returned.

Cara went back to the table and picked up the glasses she and Seamus had been using, grabbed the half-full bottle of red wine. Walking over to the fire, she filled up the glasses. Handed one to Seamus who was sitting in an armchair, watching the flames grow. Staring, unseeing. He took the glass and knocked back half. Cara grabbed her fiddle case from against the wall, rounded the sofa, and placed it on the coffee table as she sat.

'It'll be okay,' she said, taking a sip from her glass, hearing the lack of conviction in her voice. Of course it wouldn't be okay. It would never be okay again. She placed her glass on the coffee table and gently opened the fiddle case. She took the instrument out. Took the bow out. Lifted them to her shoulder. But then, with a long sigh, she placed them down again, unplayed. Back into the case. There wasn't a lament sad enough to carry her heavy heart. 'It'll be okay,' she repeated again. With even less conviction.

'I don't know,' said Seamus in a half whisper. 'I've lost my oldest friends. I'm cancelling the movie, I can't stay here any more. Even if I could, I don't want to watch that movie. No Maura, no Fer—' He couldn't complete the name and just shook his head. Tears started to fall again. He drained the rest of his glass as he wiped them away.

'Perhaps not,' Cara agreed. Seamus topped up his wine glass. Offered Cara more. She shook her head. 'Go easy there on that. For an AA attendee you've been hitting it pretty hard this week.'

'I told you that was just for the contacts.'

'You also said you didn't drink that much either. I'm just worried about you. You're probably in shock.'

He placed the glass on the coffee table. Sat back. Looked over at her.

'How much trouble am I in, Cara? Can I leave tomorrow? I really don't want to stay here any more.'

'I don't know. My bosses will be arriving in the morning and it'll be in their hands. I'll talk to them for you and maybe something can be worked out...'

'Thank you.'

'I'll probably like to join you.'

'It'll be okay for you here, Cara. Don't worry.'

'Our beloved Maura is dead. Ferdia – not so beloved, but my friend, a pretty damning recommendation, was responsible. Life is going to be pretty hard.'

'I'm sorry.'

Cara shrugged. 'Don't be. It's not your fault.'

Seamus looked out the window at the moon. In the distance a faint thump, thump, thump could be heard as the rave continued, oblivious. Seamus looked at his watch.

'It's getting late.'

'What time is it?'

'Eleven twenty-five.'

'I don't think we'll need to wait till 12.01 and my presence to know it's going to be a pretty awful new year.'

'Cara, don't be sad.' Seamus's hang-dog eyes looked at her.

The back door opening made them both turn. A sour-faced Sorcha came in, jerking her case behind her. Daithí followed behind. The burst of cold air from the open door rushed the room and put out the candles on the table. The flames of those by the fire flickered but stayed lit.

'So what is it? Huh?' Sorcha snapped. 'I was nearly off this godforsaken rock, I actually found someone who'd take me. I was nearly gone and you've dragged me back. Do you hate me too, Cara? Is that it?'

'Cut it out, Sorcha,' said Daithí in a quiet voice. Quiet but firm. Loaded with unspoken words.

'Do you want to sit down?' Cara pointed to the empty armchair on the other side of the fire.

'That sounds more like an instruction, not a question.'

'Sorcha, please, drop the attitude. We've something we need to tell you.'

Sorcha opened her mouth to speak, but changed her mind. She sat down, in the instructed chair. Daithí handed her a glass of wine. She looked up at him, surprised at this. She took the glass without a question. She glanced quickly at Seamus, and then back at Cara. Daithí sat down next to Cara on the sofa.

'What is it? What's wrong?' Sorcha looked from one of them to the next. Then raised her glass to her lips and took a drink, her face resigned. 'What *more* is wrong, I should say. A murdering husband is nearly as bad as it gets, don't you think? I can't imagine you've anything worse.'

Cara took a deep breath.

'I know things were complicated between you two... but even still... Look, Sorcha, there's no easy way to tell you this. Ferdia is dead.'

'What?'

'There was an accident,' said Seamus.

Sorcha stared at them, open-mouthed.

'I... I don't believe it,' she finally managed, staring at Cara.

'You should. And don't act so surprised. This was your plan all along, wasn't it?'

FORTY-EIGHT

Sorcha's tear-filled eyes stretched wide. Her mouth opened and shut, waiting for her brain to catch up.

'Plan? What do you mean? I didn't want him dead,' she gasped. She whipped around, looked at Daithí then Seamus and back to Cara. 'How could you say that?'

Seamus and Daithí reflected a similar shock on their faces.

'Okay,' said Cara, holding her hands up as she sat back into the sofa. 'You're right, this wasn't your exact plan. I think this whole horrible debacle can be characterised like that. No one thought their plan would end this way. You didn't want Ferdia dead. Nor Maura. But that's what's happened. And I think you'll find they'd still be alive if you hadn't hatched your little revenge scheme.'

'What on earth, Cara?' Daithí found his voice.

Cara shook her head. 'I have this, Daithí. Don't worry.'

Sorcha stood up. Eyed the back door.

'This isn't all my fault. What the hell!'

'I can explain, if you want to sit down again? Don't bother making a break for it. You won't get far.'

Sorcha sat back down. Her shoulders slumped.

'As I mentioned at dinner, you planted the drugs to get Maura in trouble. But that was only part one. You needed to ruin Ferdia as well.'

Sorcha looked around the room, at Daithí and Seamus and Cara. She hesitated, then sighed.

'Yes, I wanted revenge. After what they did to me, Cara, you would have wanted it too.'

'I don't know about that.'

'Ha! That's because you had it perfect.' Sorcha threw her hands up. 'Perfect husband, perfect kids, perfect BFF. What did I have? Nothing. All I wanted was to marry Ferdia, settle down. It wasn't much to ask for.' She sank back into the armchair, her face half shadowed in the firelight. 'From day one he cheated on me, wouldn't settle down and get a proper job. He fell in with that drugs crowd and got into debt with them. He thought he was smarter than them and could make a few bob without them copping it. Stupid Ferdia. Of course they worked it out. They beat him up and made him work more for them. He could never repay them. The debt just got bigger and bigger. It was awful. The last ten years have been horrendous. But I hung in there. Never strayed, never gave up on him. And what did I get in reward? He comes back here last year and hooks up with Maura. Perfect, first choice, Maura.'

'I'm genuinely sorry about all that, Sorcha.'

Sorcha sniffed and turned her head away. Now fully hidden from the light.

'Whatever you think I did,' she said in a quiet voice, 'I didn't kill them.'

'No, not directly. But you lit a fuse.'

Sorcha looked back at her.

'I just don't see how. Really, Cara, this sounds ridiculous.'

'Sadly, it isn't. It was the part of your plan to punish Ferdia that did it. You were going to expose his illegal activities. Am I right? To get him into trouble about his dealing.'

Sorcha said nothing, but there was no denial.

Cara continued, 'I suspect you also wanted to destroy their relationship. That's why you didn't come directly to me and tell me what he was up to. Instead, you decided to kill two birds with one stone. You'd open Maura's eyes to his wicked ways, break them up *and* get him in trouble with the law... You knew she'd come straight to me. That she'd be disgusted and disillusioned with him. You might claim she was a bad person, but you knew she wasn't really. You knew she'd absolutely do the right thing. Feel free to correct me if I'm wrong?'

Sorcha kept her silence.

'Are you sure about this, Cara?' asked Daithí.

'Oh, yes. You see,' Cara sat forward and looked at Daithí, 'all along I thought it was odd that the night in Derrane's ended early. Daithí, you told me how it all wrapped up at 11.30 p.m. and that Maura went home then. You walked her there yourself.'

Cara got up and grabbed a fresh lump of turf and put it on the fire. She stoked the fire with a poker, and continued talking as she stared into the flames.

'The first time you've all seen each other in ten years and you call it a night so early?' Cara shook her head and shrugged. 'It just didn't sound like us at all. Especially as you hadn't seen each other in so long. I thought later, when I learnt a few things, that perhaps it was all part of a plan to throw us all off the scent, about Maura and Seamus. The truth being that Maura snuck back here, so we wouldn't know about them. Wasn't she spotted by two people on the doorstep, the next morning, wearing the outfit she'd been in the night before? The old walk of shame. It all seemed to fit. The only thing I couldn't find a reason for was why Maura was keeping the relationship with Seamus quiet. We'd have all been delighted.

'But once I realised it was actually Ferdia who was the mystery man, then there had to be a different reason for the night ending early. Remember when you and Ferdia paid a visit to Maura the afternoon you arrived on the island – when she told you about the neighbour's cat destroying her Wi-Fi router? – I think that Ferdia had something with him then. Something he didn't want to risk leaving here. And he knew Maura would keep it safe. Later, in the pub, you had a word with Maura. Told her you knew all about her and Ferdia. Told her a few home truths about him. Told her that that package she'd so innocently agreed to mind was drugs, and she was risking her career, her freedom, everything, by having it in her house. Of course Maura had to go immediately. Get rid of it. She'd have freaked out. You knew she'd do that and then be on to me as soon as possible. And that all hell would rain down on Ferdia. That's how you'd hoped it would happen, am I right?'

Sorcha glowered at her. She lifted her glass and took a sip. Her eyes never leaving Cara. She lowered it again, her lips stained blood red from the wine.

'I don't hear anything,' said Sorcha slowly, 'in any of that, where I was responsible for their deaths.'

'That's because, despite your careful planning – you made a mistake.'

FORTY-NINE

Cara paced in front of the fire.

'A mistake? What mistake?' asked Sorcha.

'The package.' Cara stopped and looked over at Sorcha. 'It wasn't drugs.'

'What? It wasn't?'

'Nope.'

'What was it then?' asked Daithí.

'Yeah, what was it?' asked Seamus, his face tight.

Cara paused, turned to face the coffee table and knelt. In the low light, she reached out and unzipped the sheet music pocket of the fiddle case. She drew out the package. Sorcha, Daithí and Seamus all leaned in. Cara sat back on her heels and began to carefully unwrap the parcel. First she untied the scarf. She let it fall across her lap, displaying the next layer of old crinkled brown paper. She peeled back the paper, revealing the tired, battered notebook, displayed in all its unremarkable glory.

'Oh my goodness,' Seamus exclaimed, recognising it, even in the dimness. 'Cara, where did you find this? I've been looking for it for years.' He reached out for the notebook. But Cara moved it away from him.

'What is it?' Sorcha looked at Seamus and then Cara.

'It's Seamus's memoir,' Cara replied. She looked at Seamus. 'The original, isn't it? The first handwritten in Irish version?'

'It certainly looks like it.' Seamus shifted forward to the very edge of his seat. His hands and arms jittery, he looked like he was barely keeping himself from snatching it off her. 'I couldn't say unless I had a proper look... May I?' He reached out his hand again.

Cara ignored him. She stood up and began flicking through its pages.

'I thought it was a diary initially. But I think you said that it began life as one, so that makes sense.'

'Yeah, it did. A private diary,' he said, pointedly.

'I'm so confused,' said Daithí. 'The package you've been looking for. This mysterious item that a killer – that Ferdia – wanted so desperately that he killed Maura... was Seamus's memoir? Why on earth?'

'I'll explain.'

Cara turned and looked directly at the antsy Seamus.

'And the first little detail I'll clear up is that Ferdia didn't actually kill Maura. Did he, Seamus?'

FIFTY

'I don't know why you're asking me! You're the one with all the answers, apparently.' Seamus sat back in his armchair, crossed his legs, and folded his arms. He pivoted a few degrees away from the fire, and from Cara.

'Not all the answers. Enough of them though. Perhaps I'll share more?'

'Do whatever you want,' said Seamus.

'Okay. I'll go back... start at the beginning. That night in the pub,' Cara turned and looked at Sorcha, 'when you kicked off your revenge plan. You had your quiet, meddling word with Maura, sent her rushing off to confirm that she had drugs in her house. This,' Cara slapped her hand with the notebook, 'is what she found instead. This is what she stayed up reading all night. Not taking a break to even change out of her clothes. She was a smart woman, she was going to wonder what was so important about this notebook that Ferdia had her keeping it safe and you thought it was drugs. She sat down and started to read. And she read something in here that shocked her.

'She confronted you, Seamus, about it. That's when Mamó and Patrick saw her on your doorstep here. She wasn't emerging after secretly spending the night. No, she came here after reading this.' Cara held the memoir close. Her fingers played with the shepherd's purse that still peeked out the top of it. 'But she underestimated you, didn't she? Despite that incident in your past Maura saw the good in everyone, always. She didn't think she'd be putting herself in the way of danger coming here. But she must have seen something in your reaction. Seen she'd misjudged the situation terribly. She retreated and came looking for me. She talked to Mamó, but I wasn't there. I'm sure she tried to ring me but we all know what this island is like for coverage. I was out and about on the island, no call would have connected. She didn't want to leave the package with Mamó and put her at risk. But she also knew taking it back to her house was the obvious thing to do and you'd work that out. She needed somewhere to stash it 'cause she had no doubt that you were coming after her. Her route home took her past the graveyard. And that's where it's been since she hid it there.'

'It was at the graveyard?' said Daithí. 'That's why you stayed back?'

'Yep. It was there all along. Good old Cillian, reliable even in death, minding it for her. For me. I don't know if she went straight home then, or if she tried looking for me again. Whatever happened, by the time she got back to her house she was in a hurry. She didn't take the time to put her bike away, she just abandoned it against the wall and rushed into the house. There she knew she had to find a way to get a clue to me. A clue you wouldn't notice but I would. That's why she chose the snow globe.'

'Snow globe?' Seamus looked blankly at her.

'See, you don't know what I'm even talking about. Clever Maura. It guided me to a pile of papers where I found a second clue, hidden again, this time in a crossword puzzle, just in case you came across it by accident. She couldn't just write "I've hidden it in the graveyard." Feel free to jump in here, Seamus, anytime you think I might have got any detail wrong?'

Cara waited, giving him a chance to say something. He remained tight-lipped.

'Okay, so I'm going to take from your silence that I'm right on track then. You arrived at her house. I expect you tried to use your charm on her initially. But she wouldn't have been swayed. Wouldn't tell you where the memoir was. I wonder how fast it escalated? How soon did you lose your temper? What was the final straw, Seamus; what finally made you lash out?'

Seamus stood up. Pointed a finger at Cara.

'Don't be ridiculous! I'm the writer here, not you. This is all nonsense. I killed Maura? Seriously? You've lost it completely. A few hours ago it was Ferdia. Then it was Sorcha's fault. Now it's me? Will it be Daithí next? To collect the full set? Hey, maybe Maura killed herself? Huh? Tied herself up and threw herself into the Serpent's Lair?'

'I should probably clarify, I never actually thought it was Ferdia. I asked him if he was angry enough to kill her. I never actually accused him. If he hadn't surprised us all by running off like that to sell his drugs and do his drug gang's bidding – and you hadn't decided to make sure he couldn't issue any further denials – then I would have said as much.'

'Why accuse him in the first place then? What are you trying to achieve, Cara? I know this has been an awful few days, but I think you've lost it.' Seamus shook his head. He turned to the others, eyebrows and hands raised, looking for support.

'What was I trying to achieve?' said Cara, her focus never wavering from Seamus. 'I wanted you to think I'd got it wrong, that's what. I wanted you to be confident that you were about to get away with it. I hoped this confidence would make you drop your guard. Slip up.'

'What?' Seamus looked defiant, taking a step closer to her. 'I've done nothing so there was nothing to slip up about.'

'I beg to differ. In fact, you did it just now.'

'What?'

'Just now, you mentioned Maura had been tied up. I never told you guys that.'

'Yes, you did.'

'Nope. Daithí knew because he was there with me. But I didn't share it with any of you because that would have been unprofessional.'

'But...'

'Daithí, have you mentioned it to anyone?'

'Not a soul.'

'I really don't think Dr De Barra let you know – the only other person who knew was whoever tied her up. Which nicely brings me to what happened after you killed her...'

'Oh, for God's sake!'

'Let her finish,' said Sorcha, moving to the edge of her seat, her brow furrowed.

'Yeah, I want to hear this too,' said Daithí. 'And sit back down.' Seamus stared at the bigger man for a moment, then complied. He sat down, but perched on the edge of the seat.

'Thanks, guys. Okay... where were we? Oh yeah, you'd lost your temper with Maura and now you've killed her. You've got to cover up the results of your lost temper. So you put your little writer's brain to work and came up with a story. You needed to tell us a story that would point the focus away from you. You knew a crime of passion would put you in the frame – especially if Maura or Cillian ever told me about your past violence to her. They hadn't, in case you're interested. They kept your secret so I wouldn't hate you. Such good people. So misguided in their kindness. So, what did you come up with? A violent burglary gone wrong? Was that to be the story? You tied her up and gagged her to make it look like anything but a spontaneous crime of passion. You must have been raging when you learnt about her little stalker later. Patrick would have made a perfect patsy. That would have been a nice, neat little ending for Maura.

'You changed your mind though. Abandoned that plan. That really confused me for a while. Tied up after she died? Thrown in dead to the Serpent's Lair? What was going on? Then I remembered what you said about writing the end of movies, that the end was the hardest part. I wonder how quickly you realised your staged burglary was a stupid idea. Was it when you had to force open her jaw that was locked shut by rigor mortis? Was it then? Or as you tied her stiff arms together? Did you realise you were trying to write the end of a movie, but this was real life? When you stopped panicking for a moment you knew the cops would scour that house for forensics and your fake violent burglar façade would fall apart like a house of straw. You decided instead to keep it simple. Throw her into the sea and hope she was washed out. Hope she'd be sucked out those underground channels, never to be seen again. Sadly, for you, the sea was a poor accomplice. It had other ideas. No one was leaving this island, not even Maura.

'So, how am I doing? Have I missed anything yet? Shall I wrap it all up now?'

'Knock yourself out,' Seamus sneered, his lips twisted into a mocking smile.

'Thank you, I will... That night, the night I was here first, after I got back from Galway. You acted completely normally, as if nothing was wrong. And Maura was lying somewhere in her house, hidden, flat on her back, waiting for you to come back and set up your little story. Did you think about it over dinner, come up with the idea as you regaled us with stories about Hollywood? Telling us you weren't drinking much because you were in AA when all along you were just trying to keep your wits about you for the task you had ahead, later, when we were all in bed asleep? You've been drinking plenty ever since, that mask dropped once you didn't need it any more.

'When I found you in that armchair, at 6 a.m... I hugged you and you were so very very cold. I felt so sorry for you. Hugged you as you cried. But you were freezing because you'd just got back from throwing her over into the Serpent's Lair, hadn't you? That is why you were crying. For yourself and for another mess you'd managed to create.'

FIFTY-ONE

'Christ, Cara,' said Daithí, 'are you sure?'

Cara nodded. 'I'm afraid so.'

'Complete fantasy,' muttered Seamus.

'Why is the memoir at the centre of all this?' asked Daithí. 'You haven't explained that.'

'Yeah, what's so fatal about Seamus's stupid memoir?' said Sorcha. 'Why'd he get so cross with Maura for reading it?'

'I didn't get "so cross"! Cara is making all this up! She's desperate. Her bosses are arriving tomorrow and she wants to have something to show them. You're not going to make me your scapegoat, Cara Folan,' said Seamus, standing up. He made a lunge for the notebook. Cara reared back.

Daithí leapt up and took a step towards Seamus. Seamus backed away.

With a half glance at him, Cara flicked through the pages of the notebook.

'So, what's so special about this tatty old notebook? I know, that was my first question too. Then I spotted this page. Marked with the shepherd's purse. Like the snow globe, Maura was guiding me with things that meant a lot to us. When I opened it on this page, I saw a word I recognised. Well, not a word, but a name, *Cillian*. My darling Cillian's name.'

'Give it to me,' snapped Seamus. 'I'll read you whatever page she's marked – 'cause you can't – and I'll show you there's nothing sinister in this at all, it's just my bloody memoir!'

'Okay then, please, read it.' Cara offered him the book. With a side-look at Daithí, Seamus stepped forward and took it.

He scanned the page and looked up at Cara.

'Go on...' she said.

Seamus sat down and began to read.

'*December 31st 2012. We're on the sea again. It's New Year's Eve. Cillian wanted to come out. To fish. He knows all the restaurants in Galway. They'll pay a premium for our catch – for all those New Year's Day lunches. For families that are normal, not like ours. Families who go out together, eat together. We never went out to fancy restaurants on New Year's Day. Or any day. We always sat at that same wooden table. In the kitchen with yellow cabinets. We tried not to look each other in the eye. We tried not to cry. Mealtime after excruciating mealtime. We hoped not to provoke him. Not to get a punch...*'

Seamus paused and looked up at Cara.

'It's okay, go on,' she said.

Seamus looked back down.

'*Cillian wants to fish and not party this New Year. He's got kids of his own now. But he hasn't been poisoned like me. The punches bruised him but didn't scar. He understands how to love his children. The rage I feel is always there, somewhere, no matter how hard I try to hide it. He seems to have found a way to make it go away.*

'*Over the water I can see Kilronan glistening. I wish I was at the pub there with Ferdy and Sorcha. With Maura especially. But I'm out here. With my brother whom I love. Who loves me. The sea is rough though, I don't like it. I tell Cillian that and he just laughs. He tells me to go to the cabin, check the dials. I do as*

I am told. As I always do. Because Cillian knows best. Has always known best. When our father was raging, he knew where it was best to hide. When it was best to come out. I go back into the cabin and I check the dials. I am nearly knocked off my feet as a wave hits the side of the boat. Then I come out. And I am alone. I grab the rail as the boat is hit by another swell and it rocks. I search but it is a small boat on a vast open sea. There is only one explanation. I scream his name. Cillian! I run to the stern. Look over. Scream his name again. Cillian! Cillian! But the night and sea are black and quiet.'

'Cara, please, I don't want to read any more.'

'Okay, you can stop.'

Seamus sighed and closed the notebook.

Cara, standing close to him, suddenly dipped and snatched it back.

'Hey!' said Seamus, caught off-guard. 'That's mine, give it back!'

Ignoring him, Cara opened the marked page again.

'The funny thing is, Seamus, I don't think you translated that bit very well. I really don't. I think you're getting rusty, talking English all this time in California. I think it says something very, very different.'

FIFTY-TWO

'How would you know?'

'Good point, how would I know?' Cara looked at the page and looked back at Seamus. 'It's all gobbledygook to me, right?'

She glanced down at him in his chair then at the fiddle on the coffee table. She bent a moment and ran her fingers over the rosin-dusted strings. From the corner of her eye, she caught the pale, stunned faces of Daithí and Sorcha. She touched the fiddle strings again. Listened to them vibrate, releasing the building blocks of music into the air.

'You've been impressed with how much I'd learnt, Seamus, on the fiddle, haven't you?'

'What? Now you've really lost it.'

'But you have, haven't you?'

'Yes,' he said slowly, wary.

'I told you it was because I've had so much time on my hands. Lots of time to practise.'

'Why are you wittering on about this?'

'Why? Because it wasn't just the fiddle I was teaching myself.' Cara started pacing again. Notebook still in hand. She touched the wildflower bookmark. Looked at Seamus once more. Opened it on that page again. The page where Seamus talked about how Cillian went overboard. Drowned in a storm. A tragic accident that had robbed her of the love of her life and the most perfect father to her children. 'In the evening, once I packed my fiddle away. Once my music practice was done. I took out my books and my apps. I taught myself something else. I finally took Daithí and Maura's advice. I realised they had a point. Maybe my stubbornness was part of the problem on this island. Maybe I needed to meet the islanders halfway. I was going to surprise everyone...You see, I taught myself Irish. To speak it. To understand it. And, you know what else? To read it.'

Seamus sprang from his chair. Lunged at Cara, grabbing for the notebook. Cara dived left, dodging him, but fell back, nearly ending up in the fire. Sorcha screamed. Daithí was standing seconds after Seamus. Careering through the coffee table, cracking it, demolishing the fiddle, grabbing Seamus. He pulled him back.

'Give it back!' Seamus yelled, struggling as Daithí restrained him. 'Give it back to me! You've no right to look at that! No right!'

'Rights or wrongs, shall we read that passage again and see how well I'm doing? What do you think?'

Cara looked down at the page.

'December 31st 2012.' Cara looked up at them. 'We'll skip past the bad family bit... right, here: ...*right now we're out on the water. I can see Kilronan glistening in the distance. I wish I was at the pub there with Ferdy and Sorcha. With Maura especially. But she's not talking to me. She is saying she won't forgive me. And I'm out here. With my brother whom I love. Who loves me. But he's angry at me. I've never seen Cillian angry. It's me who is the hothead. Who has the temper. He knows what I did to Maura. He saw me hit her. He's so angry with me. Says I'm not to turn out like our father.*

'*The sea is rough though, I don't like it. I tell Cillian that and* he ignores me. I tell him not to compare me to our father. I'm nothing like him. He asks me how I'm different. How was my smacking Maura across the face any different from Dad doing that to Mam. I yell at Cillian, that it's different, because I didn't mean to do it. I said sorry. Because I won't do it again. And he laughs. You idiot, he says, you don't think Dad said those things to Mam in the beginning? Of course he did. And unlike Maura, Mam gave him a chance. See where that got her. Cillian tells me he admires Maura. For dumping me. For not forgiving me. And I can feel it surge. I can feel the demon energy surge through my body and it's in my fists and my head and I run at Cillian. I hit him. Just like Dad. I hit him and he tries to stop me. I land a punch and he's stunned. He stumbles backwards and the treacherous boat sways and he stumbles more. He is bleeding. His eye is bloody. He raises his hands and says we don't have to do it like this, we don't have to be like Dad. And I don't hear him. I can't hear him. And I hit him again. One big punch with all the hate I have for the world. And I turn my back and walk back into the cabin. In there my chest heaves as I check the dials. I shake and my breath begins to go back to normal in the cabin and I check the dials once more. I'm nearly knocked off my feet as a wave hits the side of the boat. I realise what I've done. How terribly stupid I've been. I have to fix it. I come out. And I am alone. I can't see Cillian. I grab the rail as the boat is hit by another swell and it rocks. I am alone. I search but it is a small boat and a wide open sea. There is blood on the winch. There is blood on the edge of the stern. There is blood on the steel boom, at head height. He must have ricocheted off it with my last punch. He must have gone over. Dazed and bleeding. Unable to save himself. I run to the stern. Look over. Scream his name again. Cillian! Cillian! But the night and sea are black.'

Cara looked at Seamus, who had gone quiet.

'Oh, Seamus, how could you?' said Sorcha, her hand over her mouth.

'You're a fine one to talk,' he bit.

'Oh, I'm not finished yet,' said Cara.

'There's more?' asked Daithí.

'I'm afraid so,' said Cara. She looked Seamus directly in the eye. And then started reading again. '*He is injured. I have injured him. It is my fault he has gone overboard, with a head injury in the black of night. If I call the coastguard now, and they find him alive I'll be charged. He'll tell them what I did. How will I not go to prison? And surely they can't find him alive? It is freezing and he is injured. We Aran Island men don't learn to swim, superstitions stop us – to learn to swim would rob us of our fear, our caution of the dangerous sea. If I wait, just wait a little bit before I call the coastguard, then there will be no doubt...*'

Everyone stared at Seamus.

'You left Cillian. To die,' said Cara, her voice as calm as the sea was wild. Calm because this is what Cillian needed her to be right now. She had to see this to the end.

Daithí loosened his grip on Seamus, as if he was suddenly too hot to touch. He stared at him as if some spell had been broken and his true, hideous face was finally visible.

'You waited to call the coastguard?' Daithí could hardly get the words out. 'Your own brother was injured, and in the water, and you waited? Because you might get into trouble? Jesus, Seamus, what kind of messed up thinking is that? You call the coastguard, you jump in the water! You do something! He was my best friend...' Daithí's voice cracked. And he began to cry.

Seamus grabbed Daithí's hand.

'But he wouldn't have stood a chance,' he said, pleading. 'He wouldn't have made it either way, if I'd called them, or if I hadn't.'

'You let him die,' Daithí said very slowly, his voice quivering as he tried to control it. 'You stood by...'

Seamus dropped Daithí's hand. Turned to Cara.

'You must understand, Cara? You know I loved him. He wouldn't have wanted my life ruined...'

'I also don't think he would have wanted that punch that you threw. That led him to end up in the water. He wouldn't have died if you hadn't attacked him,' said Cara.

Seamus was silent.

'You killed Cillian. You killed your brother. My husband. And what's worse, you didn't even learn from it. You lost your temper, again. Didn't you? Ended up doing it again. When you killed Maura.'

FIFTY-THREE

Seamus snatched a glance at the dark, kitchen end of the room. Daithí took a step closer to him. In the weak candlelight Cara could see the framed pictures of him and Cillian as children behind him on the wall. Innocent, smiling, clean slates unprepared for everything life was going to throw at them. And life hadn't held back. Freckled and smiling, young Seamus, side by side with this corrupt, flawed Seamus. It broke her heart.

With a sudden burst, Seamus lashed out. Kicked the broken coffee table at Cara. She jumped out of the way. Seamus made a break for the back door. Dashed into the darkness.

'Stop!' Cara yelled, darting after him.

Daithí jumped over the sofa. Launched himself after Seamus. Silhouetted by the moonlight in the frosted glass of the back door, he tackled him as he reached the kitchen counter. They crashed to the floor. Cara heard an umph from Daithí as he went down and a groan of pain from Seamus under him.

Sorcha wailed.

Cara turned.

'Shut up, Sorcha, please can you—' Cara stared behind her.

At the curtains. And the candle on the ground under them. Knocked there by the coffee table Seamus had kicked.

'Fire!' Cara yelled.

Daithí and Seamus scrambled up. Sorcha turned.

'Oh God!'

And suddenly the dark room was lit up. The peeling wallpaper, the dusty shelves, the dated pattern on the ancient sofa all floodlit by flames. And then the flames began to speak. A crackle and roar as synthetic fibres of the curtains provided no resistance and started to melt and drip, sending flaming raindrops falling. A burning relay taken up by the carpet with gusto. Barely thirty seconds since Seamus had knocked the candle over, the corner of the room was entirely ablaze.

'Out! Out!' screamed Cara.

Daithí, grabbing hold of Seamus's collar, dragged him the rest of the way to the back door. Cara dashed back and grabbed the hand of a transfixed Sorcha.

'Come on, Sorcha, come on, we need to get out!' Smoke was beginning to fill the air. Cara coughed. Sorcha turned and stared at her wild-eyed.

'I only wanted to hurt them like they hurt me. I didn't want them to die.'

'This is not the time!' Cara grabbed her wrist and dragged her. As they rounded the counter the sofa caught with a lusty hunger and Cara's last sight of the room was of the photos of Cillian and Seamus as the flames closed in on them.

FIFTY-FOUR

Locked in the squad car, Seamus stared straight ahead, ignoring the inferno outside. Rabid flames reflected on the car windows. Cara, Sorcha and Daithí stood, watching the house engulfed. Feeling the heat of the flames and the cold of the evening breeze.

'We need to get to a neighbour, alert the fire brigade,' said Daithí.

'Let it burn,' Cara said, her face lit up by the orange glow.

'Cara, you'll be sorry. I'm sure that's how you feel right now, but I don't think you really want that.'

Cara looked up at Daithí.

'Don't I?'

He shook his head. They all turned. Sirens. They saw the flashing blue lights of the island's small fire engine. The flames against the night sky on a blacked-out island raising the alarm quicker than any technology.

'Come on,' she said. 'Let's get out of their way.' They got into the car, Sorcha squeezing in the front with Daithí and Cara. They reversed out of the drive. Cara parked a few metres up the road.

They watched the soaring flames.

If it was razed to the ground, Cara thought, she'd have no complaint. A house of bad luck. A house of bad memories. A house where the only good thing to come out of it – Cillian – was so long gone.

'Will they be able to save it?' asked Seamus from the back in a small voice.

'I doubt it,' said Cara. She wondered if she was imagining it, but it looked like Seamus relaxed a little in the rear-view mirror. 'I doubt they'll save it, or anything from it. I'm only thankful I never let go of this.'

Cara lifted the memoir up so Seamus in the back could see it. This time, there was no mistaking his reaction. He slumped down in the seat. Whatever last bit of hope that he would get away with this, gone.

'I wouldn't be that stupid, Seamus. This, the key to everything. And it's not just the truth in here that was a problem but what Ferdia decided to do with it. You said inside that you'd been looking for this for years. That's not quite right, is it? I think you've known *exactly* where it's been. You've been looking to get it *back* for years, might be more accurate.

'The last piece of this awful puzzle... Ferdia was black-mailing you. I thought when you two were arguing that you were saying please – *le do thoil*. But that didn't make sense. Turns out that there's a word that sounds awfully like *le do thoil*. *Dúmhál. Do thoil. Dúmhál.* I'm still a learner, my ear still struggles. But you three will all know what that word means – black-mail. He must have known what was in the memoir. Did you tell him? You two were so close back then. But relationships change. I don't think you were as close as you thought you were. He turned on you.

'So when you attacked Maura, three days ago, trying to get the memoir back, you didn't just want to save your reputation and your liberty. Getting it back also meant you could stop Ferdia blackmailing you. That's also why it was you who wrote the letters, to try and work out where it was when you couldn't find it. You wanted to get to it before Ferdia did. Behind our backs you two were racing to retrieve it. Both of you with the high stakes – you looking to keep your crime a secret and get out from Ferdia's control. And Ferdia needing to pay off his drugs gang – 'cause he knew you wouldn't give him a dime if you got your hands on the memoir first. Not after how he'd treated you.'

Seamus hung his head. Ran his hands through his hair.

'It's time to admit it, Seamus.'

'Maybe it is,' he began, sighing quietly. 'Maybe it is.'

He turned and looked out at his burning home. The volunteer firefighters racing around the building, the first arcs of water, like a lion tamer's whip, unleashed, attempting to quell the enraged beast. The blue light on the engine blinked and flashed like the strobed light at the rave.

'Not long after it happened... after Cillian died... I thought about turning myself in. The guilt was awful. I asked Ferdia what he thought I should do. He was my best friend. I let him read the memoir in all its awful cowardly glory. And he thought it was funny. He told me to just move on and forget about it. I listened to him and I tried to. I rewrote the memoir, with that sanitised ending. As if that would make it true. And to everyone's surprise it took off. I realised I should destroy the original. But by then Ferdia needed money and saw its potential. He stole it before I had a chance to burn it. And then began a decade of torment. He demanded cash, lots of it. Do you really think he could afford the rent on that London apartment, Sorcha? Really, were you not suspicious?'

'I presumed it was the drugs money.'

'He wasn't that big a player. He bled me dry. I churned out those awful film scripts, not an ounce of integrity in them, just to keep money coming in, to keep him quiet. He even said he was the good guy, that the papers would give him lots of money for it, but he was letting me pay him instead and saving my reputation and liberty. He loved tormenting me. It all changed this year though. He got more desperate. The gang was really pushing him to repay his debt. He was actually afraid. The famously feckless Ferdia Hennessy was finally cowed. He wanted to get out of the situation. He also wanted to come back here and be with Maura. Leave that life behind. Sorry, Sorcha.' Seamus looked at Sorcha and shook his head.

'Don't worry. It was all fucked up,' Sorcha said sadly, tears beginning to fall.

'Anyway, that all led up to a conversation we had, a few months ago,' Seamus continued in a sad voice. 'I saw an opportunity. I told him I'd pay it all off, his entire debt. But in return he had to give me back the memoir. He was that desperate he agreed. We said we'd do it here, this week. He had Sorcha email you about celebrating the anniversary. I rang a few weeks later... it was all organised.'

'What?' Cara's face fell. 'This week, this coming back to remember Cillian... the pair of you engineered that, so you could conduct your grubby little deal? Oh, how much lower can you sink?'

'We wanted to do the exchange on neutral ground. Somewhere it wasn't easy to get away from quickly. We didn't trust each other not to try and scam the other. It's pathetic, Cara, I know. I was desperate... so lost without Cillian... it was never meant to go like this... I just wanted Maura to tell me where she hid it. If she would have just done that we'd have gone back to how we'd been for the last ten years. Maura wouldn't listen to reason. She said I needed to tell the truth. I got mad. She just wouldn't listen...'

Seamus began to sob. Cara heard some distant church bells

ring. A discordant duet with Seamus's tears. She looked at the clock on the car dashboard. It was midnight.

'Happy New Year, everyone. Well, Seamus, looks like the superstition is true. In your case, anyway. This red-headed woman has a very unlucky new year in store for you.'

EPILOGUE

Cara turned her face to the winter sun. Closed her eyes and felt its caress on her face. She then felt the warmth of an arm around her shoulder. She turned to her left and opened her eyes. Daithí beamed down at her. Kissed the top of her head.

'You okay?' he asked.

'Ah, not really. But I will be. It's what they both would have wanted.'

They looked down at the fresh new grave at their feet. A small wooden cross with a brass plaque marked it.

Maura Conneely 1988–2022
I ngrásta an ghrá go deo

In the grace of love forever.

Cara sighed. She threw a glance to the top corner of the graveyard, at Cillian's resting place. Happy to see green among the granite now, no more blankets of white. The sun had given the island back to them. They could see the roads and the walls and the ruins again. The familiar places, the landmarks, the places they loved. The people came out of their homes again.

Walked the roads, greeted each other. Began again the normal things they always did. The sea was remorseful, calm in its contrition. Embarrassed at its excesses during the storm.

Cara opened her bag. Rooted around its inner pockets. She drew something out. Held it up to the sun, watched the glitter within sink and settle.

'Why do you have that with you?' asked Daithí.

'A reminder.'

He looked puzzled.

'A reminder of our good times, of what we meant to each other, to the fact that even after she was gone she helped me.' Cara knelt down beside the grave. Placed the little snow globe among the week-old flowers, nestled it carefully at the foot of the headstone. She watched the flakes slowly float to the feet of the two little friends held forever within. Love you too, chick, thought Cara, remembering Maura's last words to her. In the video message. Last words of love. Like Cillian too. His last words had been words of love. How lucky had she been to have such beautiful people in her life. Gone too soon. She would honour them by living a life full of love. Not hate.

She took Daithí's hand, raised it to her lips and kissed it. He smiled at her. Raised their entwined fingers to his lips and kissed her hand. They began to walk towards the gates of the graveyard.

'Are you sure Courtney doesn't hate me?' asked Cara.

Daithí laughed.

'No, and if she were to hate anyone it should be me. Turns out she had a boyfriend back in New York. She thought she'd have a bit of a fling before she headed back. She told me she knew I was unavailable, no matter how much I protested. She knew there was no risk I would fall in love with her. So fling I was.'

'That's terrible! Do you feel used?' Cara laughed.

'Yes, poor me.' Daithí's deep laugh rumbled.

They reached the gates. Cara spotted a local passing. A stern look on his face. Disapproving of them laughing in the graveyard? He came closer. It was Tomás, her biggest detractor. Cara braced herself.

'Is that you, Sergeant Folan?' Tomás squinted in her direction. The scowl was due to the sun in his eyes, not disapproval. Cara was surprised at the novelty.

'Provisional *Inspector* Folan,' said Daithí to Tomás.

'Ah, *Inspector*,' said Tomás. A nod of acknowledgement. He coughed and cleared his throat.

'I just wanted to say... that whole Flaherty mess. Rotten just like his father. Had us all fooled. An islander.' Tomás shook his head. Tutted. 'We've all learnt something from the sorry story.' Tomás stepped back, turned to go on his way. 'Thank you, Inspector.'

'Just doing my job,' said Cara. 'But you're welcome. *Slán*, Tomás.'

He looked at her for a moment. Daithí squeezed her hand.

'*Slán*, Cara.'

A LETTER FROM TRÍONA

Dear Reader,

I want to say a huge thank you for choosing to read *The Snowstorm*. It really means so much to me that you did. If you enjoyed it, and want to keep up to date with all my latest releases, just sign up at the following link. Your email address will never be shared and you can unsubscribe at any time.

www.bookouture.com/triona-walsh

I loved writing this book. It was a joy to write about the fascinating Inis Mór and its amazing landscape and mystical past. All the locations are real places – from the stunning natural pool of the Serpent's Lair (*Pol na bPéist*) to the dramatic cliff edge fort of Dun Aengus. I have laid down on my belly and peered over that edge, looking all 300 feet down to the Atlantic below. Terrifying and breathtaking in equal measure! It is a truly stunning island on the edge of the world. It was also a joy to write about Cara. The storm that rages around her is matched only by the storm that rages within her as everything she's trusted and believed in is whipped away from her. I think we've all had those times in our lives where what we thought was true turned out not to be the reality. Hopefully less dramatic times than Cara, though. And even though she loses so much, at least we leave her on a hopeful note, rebuilding her life with the wonderful Daithí. I think they will be very happy together.

I hope you loved *The Snowstorm*, and if you did I would be very grateful if you could write a review. I'd love to hear what you think, and it makes such a difference helping new readers to discover one of my books for the first time.

I love hearing from my readers – you can get in touch on my Facebook page, through Twitter, Goodreads or my website.

Thanks,

Tríona

www.trionawalsh.com

 facebook.com/TrionaWalshAuthor

 twitter.com/thetrionawalsh

 instagram.com/trionawalsh

ACKNOWLEDGEMENTS

No acknowledgements could begin without a massive thank you to my editor Christina. She took a chance on me and believed in this book from its very inception. It's hard as a writer to keep self-doubt and creative angst from the door, so Christina's unflagging enthusiasm, support and knowledge have been utterly invaluable.

And to the whole Bookouture team, it is a privilege to work with you all.

Thanks to Eileen Casey, such an inspiring writing teacher, I wouldn't be here now if I hadn't ended up in your class. Louise Phillips for showing that the dream was possible, and to all the original Saturday morning Lucan Library writers' gang. Especially Joan who I know would have loved this moment. Still missed dearly.

Cait, Joe, Niamh and Siobhan. For the thousands of words you've read for me. For the pints and coffees shared. The had-hads and POVs. For the encouragement and shared joy at success and the support with disappointment too. Thank you!

To my first and continued writing partner, Kevin. We've been at this a long time. I think we're getting there! And to all the Second Mondays writers' group. Such a great bunch of writers, thank you for all your feedback and encouragement.

Lisa and Ruth – I could take up an entire acknowledgement section just for you two. I think it's fair to say I wouldn't be here if you two hadn't been on the same journey. Two truly amazing women.

Thank you to John Walsh and the extended Doire Press family.

Kate Dempsey and Maeve O'Sullivan, two Divas who I have had the most fun with traipsing all over the country in our feather boas. You've always been unfailingly supportive and such inspiring writers yourselves.

To my parents, Tom and Pat. Words won't do you justice! Brilliant on every front, you are also my most invaluable first readers. Thank you for putting up with all the anxious emails! My brothers, Ciarán, Dara and Garry, always so interested and encouraging. And Betty, your support over breakfast in The Square has always meant so much.

Thanks to the wider Walsh family whose support I've always appreciated.

Remembering my mother-in-law, Anne, who was a great lover of books. I would have loved to have shared this time with her. Thank you to Owen and the O'Malley and Cassidy families. Thanks to Deirdre for the help with the *cúpla focail* in these pages. (Any errors left, though, are entirely my fault!)

Lea Boyne, who has read my work and encouraged and supported me, your enthusiasm has meant a lot! Kathy M and the Codys, Elaine Fortune, Orlaith McGlade, Lisa Burke, Bernardine Waters, Sheila Spillane, Sara Nolan, Sinead Murrell, Blathnaid Nolan, The Crop Tarts, and everyone who has helped and encouraged me along the way.

Thank you to the Irish Writers Centre, who twice chose me for the IWC Novel Fair, this belief in me kept me going when the going got tough.

For the real Inis Mór islanders who are genuinely welcoming and lovely. Their island is one of the most beautiful and remarkable places in Ireland.

And to my husband, Dan, and kids, Harry, Charlie, Ruby and Lily. There would be no book without you. You've collectively put up with enforced plot discussions, been repeatedly cornered for writing opinions, and have coped with living with a very distracted wife and mother. Thank you doesn't do justice to how brilliant you all are!

And lastly to my cats Bob, Maggie and Zuzu, whose constant demands for the front door to be opened and for food in their bowls kept me from spending too much time sitting down as I wrote.

Made in the USA
Coppell, TX
22 February 2023

13272101R00198